A REFUGE
IN THE PANDEMONIUM

— WORLD OF PAERRIES SERIES | BOOK 2 —

A NOVEL
BY DAN SLONE

FOR MY WIFE:

Martha Barnes Slone

A Refuge in the Pandemonium
By Daniel K. Slone

WorldOfPaerries.com
Follow the author through
Facebook at Daniel K. Slone.

Book design by SparkFire Branding, LLC
Cover illustration by Curtis Newman curtisnewmanartist.com

Published Richmond, Virginia
Printed in the United States of America.

ISBN 978-1-7326518-2-1 paperback
Library of Congress Control Number:
2020900018 Paper Edition

"The Human definition of the natural world is always going to be too small, because the world's more diverse and complex than we can ever know. We're not going to comprehend it; it comprehends us."

— Wendell Berry (Digging In)

"The world is full of magic things, patiently waiting for our senses to grow sharper."

— W.B. Yeats

Pandemonium: a wild uproar; chaos; the capital of Hell in Milton's Paradise Lost; a flock of parrots

CHARACTERS

SILTH

<small>CALLED PAERRIES BY THE TROW AND, SOMETIMES, THEMSELVES</small>

ARAN
Storyteller who became a
shaman, also called *Heartless*

CASIUS
Aran's brother, high priest of
New Faerie

SHRA
Aran's lover, deceased

TELLICK
Chair of the World Silth
Council

STORNG
Shaman, also called
Storm Rider

TEMKAA
Chief of the Congo Silth

NADARA
Leader of Tiki Crew

RANGI
Leader of the New Zealand Silth

DON, MARINA, VIC, KIRSTN, NICK, LOANA
Tiki Crew members

NESTOR
Rangi's lieutenant

KRACKLE
Silth shaman in Brazilian
Refuge

MERIT
Battle leader, also called
Dawn Defender

CHARACTERS

SILTH

CALLED PAERRIES BY THE TROW AND, SOMETIMES, THEMSELVES

JULES
Leader of the Steamer Crew

AERITAL
A young shaman

SLATT, JEETER, TARA (3 OF 5), ABNEY (4 OF 5), BLAY (5 OF 5), ADA, VANDER, VALENTE
Steamer Crew—a group of mercenaries

JABTAR
Head of the shaman council

TAI'MON
Silth general

TRANDAN
Aran's assistant

CHARACTERS

HUMANS

JOCELYN (JOSS)
Human manager
for the refuges

KATE
Joss's friend, manager
of Costa Rica Refuge

**DR. BRANDON STRIDEMAN
(TINY)**
Volcanologist

ALEXANDRA PRUNA
Major, Ecuadorian air force

ALONGI MAFAULA
African guide

DIMBA TSAGO
Congo Ranger

HASSAN GARGAF
Poacher

REVEREND JERAMIAH TOBIAS:
International televangelist

JOAO LUIZ SOUSA
Brazilian ambassador to U.S.

CATHERINE PERCROW
President of the United States

DR. IRVIN PENFIELD, JR.
U.S. Assistant Secretary of State

MARIA LUIS
Caretaker in Brazilian Refuge

TONHO
Caretaker in Brazilian Refuge

GENERAL JOHN COGBILL
U.N. General

CHARACTERS

TROW

CALLED FAERIES BY THE HUMANS AND THE SILTH

FAELEN
Former general of Trow army,
son of Xafar

LORNIX
Sohi nurse

TEGRAT
Implementer of the Sohi will

THEST
Current general of Trow army

CAPTAIN ZERCOM
Trow captain

XAFAR
King of the Trow

OTHERS

SHADOW
Tiny's dog

MACHO
Joss's dog

KIMPER
Aran's flower fairy

STALBON
Merit's harpy eagle

GLOSSARY

Coati
A raccoon-like mammal native to Costa Rica.

Colony
A place where larger numbers of Silth live. Typically surrounded by villages, each of which is centered on an extended family.

Glamour
As a verb, the act of disguising the true appearance of a Silth or a Trow. As a noun, the particular appearance projected by a being.

Harvest
The annual process of Silth gathering Human products for their own use.

The Land
The home world of Trow. Also referred to as Faerie by some Humans and Silth.

Hather
The hair-like feathers of a Silth.

Silth
The progeny of Trow and parrots. About the size of a large parrot. Humanoid, with the arms, legs, torso, and sharp features of a Trow, but with wings and the coloration of a parrot. The Trow call them Paerries as a derogatory term, but when they apply it to themselves it is meant as a show of defiance.

Trow
A race of inter-dimensional beings who have visited the Earth since mankind's early days. Some Silth call them Faeries because of their place in the Silth mythology, but the Trow hate the name and use it to refer to their lesser animals.

Sohi
A band of Trow that have styled their society on the ancient Human Sohi.

CHAPTER 1

1

ARAN (SILTH)

History would be divided into the years before today and the years after. Aran just didn't know how many more years there would be for Silth ... or Humans. As he perched on the pile of books at the edge of the heavy teak table, stacked so his wings and tail could extend comfortably behind him, he wondered if their history would be lost or someday sifted from beneath the layers of volcanic ash growing higher each day. He looked out the window at the rain forest surrounding them and wondered who would study that history—Human, Silth, or Trow.

Joss's big common room shimmered with the sweat, pheromones, and tension of the twenty or so Humans and Silth gathered in Costa Rica watching the big screen television livestreaming the United Nations Council meeting convened to discuss the Earth's fate. The screen, occupying half the wall, was mounted high making it easy to see.

Aran flinched when a young man leaned in close to speak with him, overwhelming him with the smell of meat on his breath and the competing fragrances of aftershave, body wash, and antiperspirant. From his harvesting experience he knew these products' labels described themselves as the smells of nature but to him they, and the perfumes, shampoos, conditioners, and mascara that Humans wore, had harsh, chemical odors.

"Silth hearing is so acute I can hear a jaguar step even in a chorus of jungle bird calls," he said, leaning back and signaling for the Human to back up. "If you stand too close it hurts my ears." If the Human noticed the ruse to spare his feelings, he didn't show it. Even with their more acute hearing the room's Silth talked and hooted louder than the Humans, their speech laced with nervous squawks and whistles. Most of the Humans read the captions scrolling on the bottom of the screen.

Aran listened to the generator outside, cleaned only an hour earlier but again laboring to pull air through its ash-clogged filter, wheezing like a tapir chased by a cougar. The hather on the back of his neck stood up as the room's static electricity rose. He leaned forward, hoping the televised event would begin soon. Joss was biting her nails impatiently, and Kate kept jumping up and refilling half-empty glasses. She silently placed a thimble full of papaya juice next to him, sat down and whipped through the pages of a beautiful people magazine. Aran thanked her and drank, trying to wash the near constant taste of ash from his mouth.

The video feed showed a split screen, one view toward the podium and the other a speaker's-eye view across the assembly's almost two hundred seats. A gold-leafed wall, with a prominent U.N. emblem flanked by enormous video screens, rose behind the massive lectern and six throne-like chairs in the center of the stage. Men and women standing on each side of the stage wore suits tight over bulging upper arms, with the taser rifles across their chests removing any doubt about their role.

It was eight in the morning in Costa Rica, and most of the room's occupants had been up all night. In New York it was an hour later. The Australian Prime Minister had just finished speaking. The caption indicated the next speaker was the President of the United States, who was making her way toward the stage.

Storng appeared three feet above the lectern. He made no sound, hovering there, and several moments passed before the room noticed him. The U.S. President was backing away from the stage bumping into people in the aisle. Arms were raised and mouths agape as Storng landed on the flat surface of the podium, wings still spread, and advanced to the microphone. He flapped his wings—Aran thought more for theatrics than anything else—making the blue, black, and yellow front colors alternate like a signal flag. As he folded his wings and gripped the microphone, the camera view moved closer but was still far enough away so all that was visible was a human-like figure with wings and bright colors. Storng had chosen the shaman's formal attire of long white robe and white cloak. When the camera moved closer still his milk white tattooed face filled the left side of the screen and his eyes, one black and one white, stared directly at the camera. The Costa Rican room was completely silent but the noise level in New York grew and the captioning changed to read loud crowd noise.

So that was how the old world ended, Aran thought, *with loud crowd noise.*

The speaker's eye camera showed sudden movement as two guards broke free from their shock-induced immobility and rushed the dais, weapons forward. Quickly releasing the mike, Storng shot a pair of blue bolts from his hands, knocking the guards to lie twitching at the base of the steps leading up to his perch.

The room erupted in screams and the scraping of chairs as delegates rushed for the open doors at the back of the assembly hall. Before they could reach them, a line of armor-wearing Silth appeared, hovering at eye level. When the doors slammed shut and vanished, Aran grinned—the use of the door glamour had been his idea.

Storng's deep, gravelly voice filled the room. "Please calm down. We mean you no harm. You will be all right." He waited for the room to quiet a little. "Please calm down. We mean you no harm. Shhh ... please take your seats. I just need to speak to you for one moment and then we'll leave." Warily the delegates quieted and returned to their seats, never taking their eyes off him. The stunned guards struggled to their feet.

As the audience muttered their way back into position, Aran focused on the Silth assembled in front of the glamoured doors. They flapped their wings just enough to hover, heads swiveling, faces taut. One of Aran's biggest fears had been that they'd injure someone in the first moments of chaos. So far, Merit's discipline held, even though these Silth were violating the almost religious instruction given them since they were babies—*never show yourselves to Humans.*

"Good morning. My name is Storng." As he spoke, the assembly hall went silent. "I apologize for startling you, but as you might imagine, there was no good way to begin this conversation."

He smiled and paused, as the noise suddenly increased again, and Aran assumed the delegates had just realized they were hearing Storng in their own languages. The camera operator backed off enough so delegates could still read Storng's face on the big screens but could also register that all foot-and-a-half of him stood on top of the lectern. *This camera operator must have seen it all in order to stay so cool.*

"I am Silth. That's what our species is called—*Silth*. On another day I'll tell you our history, but today you should know we've shared this Earth with you for centuries. Some say we were here before you. We were once a very large civilization, but as the wild habitats dwindled and your population swelled, ours was diminished. Because you became hostile to every species, including your own, we've remained hidden, believing little was to be gained from contact with you. But things have changed."

Storng spoke slowly as though lecturing beginning Silth students.

Aran wondered how Storng had learned to speak on camera—knowing him, he'd read about it. As Aran glanced around the room, he knew that most of the Silth in this room read books, having learned how to just a few months earlier. Unfortunately, the Silth were developing two classes, those who could both read and talk to Humans and those who could do neither. Some other day's challenge, not today's.

"Another race of beings sometimes occupies this Earth. They were definitely here before you and before us, and you may be surprised to learn that you've seen them periodically or even had contact with them. While you refer to them as fairies, they call themselves *Trow*, and they come from a place they call the *Land*. They've visited the Earth, where they have magical powers, for hundreds of thousands of years.

"As Humans emerged, there was little conflict with the Trow until you began to develop electricity-using technology. Something about your use of it, or perhaps simply how much of it there is now, drives the Trow insane if they stay on Earth too long. This has made them angry enough that they've decided to eradicate Humans.

They don't care about the consequences to the other species, which they believe will recover over time. The Trow live a very long time, thousands of years. They put their plan in motion about six months ago, when they caused the volcanoes to erupt. You've told yourselves this was done by Humans, but the Trow actually did it. Humans were involved, fooled into participating. The U.S.'s *Homeland Security* has a video of the Trow involvement with the volcano in what you call *Yellowstone*. It also shows that we, the Silth, helped stop this action. However, the Trow ignited several other volcanoes, left Earth, and plan to return in roughly four and a half years.

"The Earth will be very different by then. What creatures the volcanoes don't kill, you Humans will have eaten or burned for fuel in your desperation to survive the long winter we all face. They'll finish what they started, meaning that Humans will be no more. Their weapons are superior to yours. It's likely that the Silth and most other Earth species won't survive."

Storng paused, his white eye squinted and his black eye scanned across the crowd, daring them to deny his statement. Toward the back of the room Aran could see a Human guard casually edging closer to the line of hovering Silth. Suddenly one of the Silth warriors swooped over, hovered at eye level in front of the guard, tilted her head, and gestured for him to back away. Three or four times her size, the guard hesitated briefly, and then rejoined the others. The Silth warrior resumed her place as well.

"One volcano in *Ecuador* simmers," Storng went on. "The Trow tried to ignite it, but they seem to have only irritated it. I believe you understand, as do we, that if this volcano erupts, it will likely stimulate the eruption of surrounding volcanoes. This will assure that few animals survive the conditions over the next several years. Bugs and jellyfish will rule Earth. Humans will disappear quickly. So will the Silth."

"At 3 p.m. by your time here, the Seven Nations of Silth will quiet this volcano, calming it so there's no threat of explosion. While this will eliminate the most immediate threat to us all, it won't change the pressure you're under. We know Humans are starving in parts of the world. Your armies are at one another's borders trying to stop the large numbers of refugees searching for food. Everything with protein is being eaten, the land stripped of life in desperation. We sympathize. But we don't accept the proposition other species must be sacrificed for Humans." The noise of voices rose in the assembly hall as Storng paused and took a drink from the flask he pulled from his robe.

Anticipating Storng's next words, Aran leaned toward the big screen. All movement in the room ceased. The gasping generator worried him, but thankfully electricity continued to flow.

"The Seven Nations of Silth will establish animal sanctuaries in the areas around our villages and in a few other key biological zones. This is our price for fixing the volcano and saving you, and it's our right and that of other species to survive. That's not just a Human right, it is a world right. Humans won't be allowed to hunt within these areas. The Silth will work with Humans to protect and expand the animal populations around the world. We'll create conditions on the edge of these sanctuaries conducive to Human farms. Ten percent of the yield from these farms will go to the sanctuary, and the farm operators may keep the rest to do with as they want. Please understand we have no wish to quarrel with you, but we will repel any effort to occupy or harvest from these sanctuaries. Humans living in these areas may continue to do so provided they follow our rules. If unable to obey the rules, they'll be relocated."

Storng spoke over the rising background noise. "We will provide an ambassador to the United Nations. At least initially, this will be me." He gave a shallow bow. "We must discuss how to prepare for the return of the Trow and how to deal with the remaining volcanoes. Each of the refuges will have a representative to deal with the Human governments surrounding them. Let me show you where these refuges will be."

Storng pulled a tightly folded map from a pocket in his cloak. He unfolded it and held it facing the assembled group. He frowned and muttered something causing the map to project in the air in front of him, magnified twenty-fold. "The green areas are where the refuges will be." The map showed nine large green zones, each the size of a country in and of itself and three more large blue zones in the oceans. "I'll leave you this and other documents containing more details about the Yellowstone events, as well as about the Silth and Trow." He placed the map on the podium and pulled additional papers from a rowling bag beside him.

In Costa Rica Joss clapped her hands. "My map! Ha!"

Back in the assembly hall, the delegates seemed to be realizing the size of the refuges, and Aran knew it was sinking in for some that large portions of their countries would be occupied by the new group. Angry shouts, like flaming arrows, sailed toward the podium.

"We will save the Human race this afternoon," Storng shouted, causing the room to settle down again. "We will save all of your countries, at least for now. This will be our price. I'm sorry to say there will be no chance for negotiation. Once we've completed our task, I'll return here and we can begin planning." Slowly flapping his wings, he rose about three feet in the air.

"How do we know you didn't start the volcanoes?" came a shouted question.

Storng hovered and eyed the questioner. "You'll see in the Homeland Security's record that we fought to stop what we thought was the only target—Yellowstone. And why would we set off the volcanoes when we too face destruction as a result?"

"What if you can't stop the volcano in Ecuador?"

"Then we'll all die," Storng said almost cheerily.

Careful, Storng, Aran thought, *don't show your humor.* Humans might not realize that after an endless review of scenarios, the course laid out by Storng was the only one that made the survival of Humans, Silth, and the Earth's other creatures even possible. Nor did they know that Storng wasn't only exhausted but also skeptical that this course assured survival.

"Do you speak for all Silth?"

Storng paused for a moment. "I speak for the World Silth Council, which is authorized to speak for all of the Silth nations. But can I say all Silth believe we should help Humans at all? No."

Over the increased chatter came another shout. "What makes you think a tiny species like yourselves can stop a volcano that we can't? And that you can impose your will on all of the nations required to accept your *refuges?*"

The room went quiet. Storng's eyes flashed as he said, "We have magic!" He flew toward the ceiling, flickered and disappeared.

The line of Silth in the back of the room vanished simultaneously and the doors reappeared. The assembly hall erupted into chaos as some delegates shouted to the Secretary General and at each other. Cell phones were alight everywhere as many presumably downloaded their recordings to others.

The screen in Costa Rica went dark as someone decided to stop the video feed. Aran, Joss, and the others spent the next couple of hours watching the various news channels and discussing what had happened. The smell of microwaved popcorn filled the air. Joss defended popcorn as a breakfast food. "You eat cornflakes, right? That's the same thing." Like all Silth, Aran had a weakness for the stuff, the more salt and butter the better.

Watching the video stream was like watching someone wake up. The first commentators were mostly established news anchors and reporters reciting the events in stunned, hushed tones. Then the waves of surprise, rage, hope, and questions rolled around the world. *Humans are not alone—either on Earth or in the universe. This is a hoax—there are no Silth or Trow. The Silth are real but they've made up the Trow to try to improve their position in a time of crisis. What has Homeland been covering up and why? How can they stop a volcano? We can't let them simply overrule all of the Human institutions and take large areas of countries for their own. Maybe this is good—Humans have destroyed the Earth and need the right leadership to heal it. Time to go—everybody on board the spaceships!* They frequently used the word *gobsmacked,* a term Aran didn't understand and asked Joss to explain.

When Aran flew into the kitchen for water, Joss cornered him and asked what he thought about the presentation. She'd been in the meetings where he questioned whether they should help the Humans. Not confident of Human gratitude, he was the one who advocated that they announce the refuges at the same time they promised to shut down the volcano.

"It's a start. But there's so much to do." He shook his head. "At least it's our plan now that's being implemented, not my plan." Just a few months ago he stood alone in challenging the Trow scheme to rid the world of Humans and take back control of the Earth.

"They'll help. Humans will help. After all other approaches fail, we'll do the right thing."

Aran squatted on the table's edge, his elbows on his knees. "Joss, of anyone in this place full of Silth and Humans, I trust you the most." She no longer winced at his damaged voice.

"You've saved my life. Kept our secrets. Shared your friends with us." He looked back through the door at the biologists, farmers and other Humans in the other room and lowered his voice to as close to a whisper as he could manage. "Do I trust Humans in general to do the right thing? Do you? And they don't have any reason to trust us yet. I'm not even sure I trust the Silth to do the right thing. So much at stake, and we seem to be distracted by religious debates."

He didn't tell her about his own doubts. He knew how much of their plan was based on untested hope. He was supposed to be the most powerful Silth in the world, gifted with Faerie powers as well as those of a shaman. Yet he felt that at any moment they would find out he was a scared fraud. He was really just a storyteller, and it was all a story. There were so many ways it could all go wrong, and only a few in which it could go right.

He stood, straightening his tunic and cloak. "We'll find out. Right now, I have to see if we really can stop a volcano."

2

TINY (HUMAN)

Tiny wrapped his bear-paw of a hand around the joystick and guided the drone closer to the volcano. Quilotoa was pissed. Steam poured from the cracks where its two-mile-wide lake once stood, and an angry red hole spit rock and lava over the edge of the crater the bomb had created. At 13,000 feet, the drone was being buffeted by the winds and the signal was spotty.

Still, Tiny could see enough to be concerned. The cracks were noticeably wider than yesterday, and the area around the crater showed much more debris had been ejected during the night. The visual confirmed what all the instruments told them—Quilotoa would blow soon, something it hadn't done in almost 800 years. That eruption had deposited ash across the northern Andes, its pyroclastic flows and lahars reaching the Pacific Ocean. But Tiny wasn't really worried about that. After the bomb went off, fortunately with much of its blast absorbed downward and within the crater, the region's villages and tourists had been evacuated within a 300-mile radius because of the radioactive fallout. Even here, fifty miles from the volcano, where Tiny sweated in a hooded clean-suit, a *bunny suit,* with a ventilator, the detectors still showed modest radiation. That would change when the volcano blew, radioactive debris was scattered across the mountains and valleys, and the seven-mile-high plume of radioactive ash joined the ash already in the atmosphere.

But Tiny wasn't really worried about that either.

He watched through the video monitor as the drone's camera showed the surrounding Andes. If Quilotoa erupted in a certain way, a way made more likely by the location of the bomb's explosion, it could likely set off Reventador and then Tungurahua, which meant *throat of fire* in the indigenous Quechua language. In a worst-case scenario, Pichincha, Cotopaxi, and Chimborazo could erupt as well, creating an enduring darkness that would end complex life on Earth. The fifteen volcanoes of the Galapagos and the twenty-eight Ecuadorian volcanoes located in what Humboldt had named the *Avenue of the Volcanoes* were the easternmost section of the *Pacific Ring of Fire. So many colorful names for instruments of death.*

"Dr. Strideman?" came a woman's voice from the doorway.

He didn't look up from his controls. "Tiny."

"Pardon? Are you Dr. Brandon Strideman?"

"Folks just call me Tiny."

"People call me *Major Pain* and on a good day don't specify where. I'm Major Alexandra Pruna, Ecuadorian Air Force. I understand you have the only working drone around here."

"Yeah, there was a military one here until a few days ago when it got overheated and fried. Hard to keep the filters working and deal with the altitude and heat when you get close."

"Well, you mind if we borrow yours for a little while?" Tiny thought it didn't really sound like a request.

He turned and looked at her for the first time. She wore the Ecuadorian military standard radiation bunny suit, a Velcro patch showing her rank on one shoulder. What he could see of her face inside the mask suggested she was relatively young. He looked back at the screen so he could keep managing the drone.

"Sure, Cuz. No problem. I'm just a government employee here anyway. Watch out, she's really twitching in these currents."

She took a step back as he suddenly towered over her, supporting the Bluetooth joystick with his right hand and operating it with his left. Still watching the screen, he handed her the controls and turned as if to leave.

"Please stay, if you would," she said as she settled into his chair. "I understand you *Macgyvered*—that's right, no? —this drone so it wouldn't have the problems that have grounded the others. In fact, to hear the other people here tell it, most of this equipment wouldn't be working if it wasn't for you. You're U.S. Geological Survey out of Hawaii?"

Tiny's spine popped as he stretched his arms above his head, his hands brushing the top of the field tent. Before responding, he eyed all the monitors, screens, and dials charting data being shipped out from the volcano and surrounding areas. Out of habit, he looked for Shadow before remembering that, with no doggy bunny suit, the black lab was at the base camp, about a hundred miles away. He watched the Major maneuvering the drone as she practiced getting a feel for it, plainly knowing what she was doing.

"The USGS doesn't get a lot of money," he said as he tweaked the seismic monitor. "So, we figure out ways to extend the equipment at Kilauea and Mauna Loa. Been studying them as possible energy sources and to mitigate the consequences of an eruption. USGS also loans me out to USAID Office of Foreign Disaster Assistance and the Volcano Disaster Assistance Program out of Cascades. I end up in the field a lot. Usually in jungles." Since she seemed less distant than some of the other military types there in the camp, he asked, "Why'd you want the drone? Another experiment? The last four haven't gone so well." He noticed she was now flying the drone in a circle, not just studying the volcano.

"You don't listen to much news up here do you? Must not talk to many people either."

He felt himself blush in the suit and said nothing. She was the first person he'd spoken to today, and his cell phone, which he could see behind the special clear plastic holder on his arm, showed it was 1:35 p.m. One of the perks of being a volcanologist was having his own customized heat, radioactivity, and re-breathing suits. He could use his phone to get news through the headset. But instead he listened to Hawaiian Reggie, Boo-Yaa T.R.I.B.E., and Nesian Mystik. On Sunday he listened to Samoan Methodist choral music. He might tune into an All Blacks rugby game, but that was the closest to news he got. He was suddenly conscious of the smell of sweat and stale breath in his suit. *That's irrational. We have these suits on.*

She laughed. "Sorry. Everyone else here seemed to know—I thought you were *pulling my leg.* That's the right expression, no? This morning a group of *beings* appeared at the United Nations and one claimed the volcanoes were started by another race. He then said they were going to shut down this volcano at 3 p.m. EST using magic." She told him about the interrupted Council meeting.

He touched an adjacent screen. Three o'clock in New York would be two 'clock here.

"If you want to stay up until after two, you're going to have to ride the thermals a little more to conserve the battery. Also let me show you something." He flicked a switch. Another video stream popped up on a second screen, showing a view from inside the volcano crater and looking across its base. A digital clock showed the date and the time in the screen's corner. "This is from a robot on treads I got up into the crater before it got stuck in the ash."

"Dr. Strideman, you don't seem all that surprised by what I just told you. I mean, two new races, stop the volcano. Magic. Seems to me a scientist would react at least a little."

Tiny adjusted the dials to brighten the picture. "I've looked at every way anyone has thought of to stop this volcano. None of them will work. I don't believe in magic, so I think that's nonsense. But you just convinced me I'm not crazy."

He replaced the live feed from the robot with another video, time-stamped from four days earlier. Ten parrots landed on the ash twenty feet from the camera. The Major gave an involuntary "huh" when they transformed into small humanoids. Each stood about a foot and a half tall, with parrot wings and tails, and brightly colored hair, very much like the beings she had described as showing up at the U.N. A bluish glow surrounded them, and it seemed to be protecting them from the heat and poisonous gases. Gathering around one of the beings, in a white robe and gray cloak, they appeared to converse animatedly for several minutes. Suddenly they flickered and disappeared.

Tiny restored the screen to the live feed from the robot. The other screen continued to show images from the drone. They sat for a moment surrounded by the beeps and clicks of the machines.

"Both of these are being recorded?" she finally asked, shaking her head. "You saw that and didn't say anything?"

"I planned to recheck it today. Thought maybe someone on the team hacked it and was playing a joke."

He checked the dials and confirmed the video was recording.

The digital clock said 1:55. Through the drone camera they saw a cluster of the little beings, *Silth* the Major had called them, appear in the sky. In the distance, it looked like similar groups circled the volcano spreading out to what Tiny estimated as about a thousand feet between the individuals. They disappeared in the gray distance. He did a quick calculation. If this was a circle and his estimate of how many of them were in the sky was right, the circle had a circumference of about a hundred miles, putting its edge out around sixteen miles from the volcano.

"Any idea of how many of them are up there?" the Major asked.

"Looks like about five hundred and thirty." The speed of his calculation drew a glance from her.

The Major flew the drone out toward the circle of Silth, trying to determine what they were doing. As the figures grew in the screen, they appeared to have their eyes tightly closed and were speaking in unison.

As the Major panned across the different individuals, Tiny recognized a pattern. "Look at their clothes."

Most seemed unremarkable in their attire, a mélange of homemade and factory-made, possibly doll clothes. "About one in thirty wears one of those long robes," Tiny pointed out. "Sometimes male and sometimes female. But always one hand raised toward the center of the volcano and … is that a lighter in the other hand?"

As the Major continued her pan, Tiny also noticed that spaced evenly among the figures were some kind of soldiers. The Major held the camera on one facing away from the volcano, wearing a leather uniform and carrying a bow in one hand. Tiny could see that the Silth had their fists clenched, faces drawn tight, and mouths open wide as they apparently shouted at the volcano. He regretted he couldn't hear what they were saying—*maybe they're chanting*—but the drone recorded only the noise of the winds across its mike. The ground beneath the tent started to shake, a low rumble rolled like thunder over them, and then there was silence. Tiny dashed over to a set of monitors. He touched some screens and checked the robot's streaming video, no longer showing steam rising from the former lake bed.

"Holy shit," he whispered. "They did it."

He could see what seemed to be confusion among the Silth regathered into small groups. The robed ones were being supported by others. Many looked distressed, not elated as Tiny would have expected. But before he could study them, the clusters began disappearing—just flickering and winking out. Tiny checked the clock—2:01p.m., just after 3:00 in New York. He collapsed onto a chair.

"Well, Dr. Strideman, it appears we go to sleep tonight in a world different than the one in which we awoke." She stood and walked toward the door. "The good news is Humans are no longer threatened with extinction from that particular volcano, though we still have to deal with the others. The bad news is igniting the volcanoes was apparently an act of war by magical inter-dimensional beings from which we have been saved by magical bird people who don't seem to have a lot of reason to like us."

"Holy shit," Tiny whispered again.

"Well, exactly," the Major tossed back over her shoulder as she left.

3

MERIT (SILTH)

Dried blood flecked his backpack and ringed the worn, wooden shaft of his spear. Merit watched as the mostly bald man with a gray stubble beard led the ten younger men along the jungle path. He wore dirty linen shorts and a faded t-shirt stamped with a happy wart-hog face proclaiming, *Hakuna Matata,* while the others were in camo-fatigues and carried large rifles. He seemed to be trying to walk quietly, looking down at the path and stopping periodically to get his bearings. The rest of the line talked and smoked cigarettes as they walked.

Merit wondered how this group of poachers ever got close to an animal, but she'd been told most of the animals were so used to the presence of tourists that they failed to realize these Humans meant them harm. In the darkness—the ash clouds obscured what moon there was—she was able to see their almost phosphorescent colors, but not well enough to read their faces.

"Mafaula!" shouted the short man following the old Human in line, the shout so unnecessarily loud it must have been for the benefit of the others, and he spoke. Merit turned to her translator, who repeated, "Mafaula, you've had us walking through this jungle most of the night. Are you taking us somewhere or just out for a stroll in the moonlight? Where are the elephants?" As the discussion continued, the translator whispered the translated version in Merit's ear.

"Not far now. The scat along this trail is very fresh."

"I don't think that is the only fresh scat around."

Merit knew it has been at least a day since the elephants had been through the area.

They moved toward the place on the path where six other Humans hid in the bushes. Merit and the band of local Silth she accompanied watched as these men hid, and the Silth told her they were *rangers*. The rangers took their positions, methodically cleaned their guns, and constantly monitored the area around them. Their heads swiveled without stopping. The slightest sound drew their attention. Merit watched one lift his head and smell the breeze moving through the jungle night. As the noisy group came down the path, the hidden men stilled.

The Silth were spread through the trees, getting their bows and spears ready. They too were alert and reacted to every sound the jungle made. Unlike the hidden men, however, who seemed relaxed in their attention to their surroundings, moving easily and confidently, the Silth's movements were jerky, their gaunt faces tense. Their clothing was a cleaner version of the old man's, worn to gossamer.

A hundred similar groups of Silth were spread throughout the jungle that night. They had been monitoring the Humans for the last two weeks, but this was the first night they would show themselves and assert control over the enormous Congo rain forest. Merit didn't think they were ready, but they were out of time. The local Silth knew the rangers and the old man, a guide for poachers, but the group he led was new to the area. Merit had seen the carcasses of the twenty elephants they'd gunned down a few nights ago. A century's worth of fury, contained only by the prohibition of contact with Humans, now threatened to boil over as the local Silth came out of hiding.

First, however, they would see if Humans could handle their

own. One of the rangers called out to the men walking toward them, "Alongi Mafaula, this is Ranger Dimba Tsago. What brings you into our preserve tonight?"

The men on the path froze in place, a few then slowly raising their weapons. Mafaula peered frantically into the darkness trying to locate the voice's source.

"Dimba, you know me. I'm just trying to feed my family. I have no quarrel with you. I'm putting my spear here on the path. Peace, my brother."

"Mafaula, I think that is Hassan Gargaf who walks with you. He's slaughtered many of God's creatures, killed many rangers. He sends money to bad people. We're here to arrest you all. Put down your weapons and no one'll get hurt."

The men on the trail started shooting into the darkness toward the voice and randomly in any direction. The rangers returned fire, and because they knew where their targets were, four of the men on the path went down immediately. But now the poachers could follow the muzzle flashes, and withering fire from automatic weapons rained upon the rangers. Two rangers dropped and the others retreated, trying to keep larger trees between them and the returning fire. Tsago spun and fell to his knees as a bullet struck his arm. But then the poachers screamed, twisting and writhing on the ground as if they were trying to slip out of their skins. One yanked out the dart sticking from his neck and studied it trying to comprehend what it was. As Mafaula crawled into the brush next to the path, Merit, projecting a blue shield, floated down the path toward Gargaf, the only poacher left standing.

"You have violated the rules of the Congo Refuge. You are being arrested by Silth for crimes against our brothers and sisters, the elephants, and for violation of the rules of this refuge." She'd memorized this line, because unlike Aran and Storng, she couldn't understand Human speech. Her translator was in a nearby bush if she needed help.

Gargaf fired his gun at her until it clicked empty, the bullets bouncing off her shield. Merit dropped it and knocked him to the ground with a stunning blue bolt. After allowing the rangers and poachers to bandage the wounded, the Silth herded them down the dark trail, leaving the dead where they'd fallen.

An hour's walk brought them to a clearing where burning tents lit up the night, and ivory, guns, machetes, and other objects blazed in a tall bonfire. A small refrigerator truck, which Merit assumed held the substantial volume of elephant meat the poachers had harvested, was still connected to a generator. A Silth with gray wings, dark skin marked by red tattoos, a crimson Mohawk and a solid black suit with a crimson tie and matching pocket square stood board straight on three stacked boxes. The procession, all marching with their fingers interlaced behind their heads, stopped in front of him. He conferred with Merit for a moment before he spoke. Again, Merit's translator stood beside her. Merit could understand when the Silth spoke even though the Humans could understand it as well. But when the Humans spoke, however, she couldn't tell what they were saying.

"I am Temkaa, the chief of the Silth council in charge of the Congo Refuge. I'm responsible for the disposition of those who break the rules within the refuge."

"What is this *refuge* you speak of?" Gargaf blurted out. "And what the hell are you tiny freaks?"

"The Congo Refuge is 1.5 million square miles now forbidden to you. If you are found within its borders again, you will be killed on sight. You'll have plenty of time to learn about its details and what we are."

When Temkaa raised his hand, Merit flew toward Gargaf, easily avoiding his swatting hands, and grabbed his shoulder. Just as she touched him, they both flickered and blinked out of sight. She reappeared almost instantly.

The other Humans were wide-eyed, some visibly shaking. Two tried to run, but sharp arrows pointed at their eyes by hovering Silth warriors brought them to a quick halt.

"Wha ... what did you do to Gargaf?" one Human asked Temkaa.

"Less than I wanted." Temkaa stared into the bonfire. "Too long have you Humans poured death upon our brothers and sisters. It would be bad enough if you simply killed for food. Then we might dislike you like our sister the leopard, but we couldn't deny your place among us. But you destroy whole herds of elephants to take their tusks. Sometimes their hides. They're almost gone and still you come to kill them, now for their meat." Temkaa's voice rose. "Our people have watched you and the hunters who come with their safaris, and we've done nothing. It's all we can do now to carry our shame as we think about the voices no longer in the jungle. If my colony was alone in passing judgment on you, you'd die now as we pulled the teeth from your head and flayed the skin from your bodies." He closed his eyes and blew out a breath as if to calm himself.

"Rangers, over here." He pointed to a space to his right. The rangers advanced, warily watching each of the nearby Silth.

"Who speaks for you?" When Tsago raised his uninjured arm, Temkaa nodded toward him. "We salute you. You've risked your lives, and many of your comrades have died to protect our brothers and sisters of the jungle. A small token of our thanks."

A Silth flew over and handed each of the gaping rangers a large diamond.

"When we finish with these men," Temkaa went on, "our shaman will tend your wounds. We hope you'll choose to work with us, help us guard this vast land. Whether you decide to or not, you have our thanks."

"What will happen to them?" Tsago waved his hand toward the six poachers still standing in front of Temkaa. "And what of Gargaf? Will he return?"

"Gargaf lives. Whether he returns will be up to the Chinese. It's our understanding he sent the ivory to them. So, a few moments ago he showed up on a street in Beijing. If he survives the night, then he'll deal with the Chinese authorities. When they finally figure out who he is, it'll be up to them to determine the consequences. They created him but have announced they're through with trading in ivory, so maybe he is an embarrassment. We were asked by the World Silth Council not to kill him so we can establish better relations with Humans. This time we complied. They have told us we can do whatever we want if he returns."

He turned toward the other poachers. All except Mafaula huddled together with their backs to one another. Mafaula stood apart, hanging his head.

Apparently emboldened by Temkaa's treatment of the rangers, Tsago pointed to Mafaula and said, "That one's different from the rest."

Temkaa stared at Mafaula for a moment. "We are the eyes of the jungle. We know what that one has done. But why do you think he's different?"

"You said you lived with the leopard. The others slaughter the elephants, and most of the money goes to fund the rebels or their cartel. Mafaula kills elephants to feed his family. Still a crime, but he is more like the leopard."

Mafaula said nothing, and his head stayed bowed. Temkaa stared at him for several moments before speaking.

"These are," he paused and looked again at the bonfire, "tricky times. Ivory is not likely to be valuable when people realize the world will not return to its old ways. Unfortunately, the animals of this jungle will be no better off. People will get very hungry as their cattle disappear when summer no longer returns and grass does not grow. Most will have no crops. This refuge will be under siege because it harbors many animals and plants. We will defend it. The WSC says it can create a hole in the constant clouds allowing sun to reach this refuge so it can thrive. Within the refuge and along its boundaries are farmlands that will benefit from our actions. They too will prosper. We'll work with the farmers to keep the jungle's residents from destroying the farms."

He rolled his eyes and looked at Merit. "Monkeys. But there will be rules for the farmers as well. They will not be allowed to kill the animals of the jungle. If a member of their family violates this rule, they all must leave. No matter what. They will not be allowed to use chemicals on the land. Or allowed to use more than minimal technology. Finally, they will contribute ten percent of what they grow to the refuge, but the rest is theirs to do with as they will—feed their family or sell. Mafaula, could you live like this? Could you live in peace with the other animals?"

Mafaula stared at him like his words were simply a continuation of the strange dream in which he found himself. The flames of the burning campsite crackled around them, and tiny embers swirled into the air.

Tsago prodded him. "Mafaula?"

Tears leaked down Mafaula's face. "This would be a dream come true. In such a place, from sunrise to sunset I, and every member of my family, would work to make it up to the spirits of the elephants for what I've done. There would be no better friend to the animals of the jungle than me."

"You have much to atone for, but you'll get this one chance. Don't waste it. If we ever find you hunting any of the children of the forest, we will remove you and yours from the refuge. If we find you hunting inside the refuge, we'll kill you. Go with the rangers, and the shaman will tell you how this will work."

"Thank you," he said to Temkaa. "Thank you," he said to Tsago pressing his hands together beneath his chin.

Temkaa turned his attention to the remaining men. His eyes narrowed. Having seen no one was dying, they appeared surer of themselves, no longer shaking. Merit moved slightly closer to the group to intervene if Temkaa lost his temper. He'd done better than she could have imagined so far, particularly as two weeks ago he believed they should isolate the refuge and kill any Human who approached.

"Kill them," he commanded, and when the surrounding Silth raised their bows, the poachers cried out and cowered.

Temkaa raised his hand. "Wait." He looked up into the canopy of trees, the intermittent firelight leaving his face first bright and then obscure. "What should I do with you? We are no longer willing to wait for Human justice to make you stop your marauding ways. I don't believe you'll reform. We have no prisons. When a leopard kills the goats of Humans, they hunt him down and kill him. But sometimes the wardens of the parks come and relocate him, put a tracking collar on him, and give him another chance. Hmmmm. What to do? What to do?"

When he glanced Merit, she thought he was going to ask her opinion, but he said nothing. She held her breath, ready to respond should he go rogue. She hoped he wouldn't. As she worked with him and the Silth of the region, she'd come to appreciate them and their struggle. They reminded her of the Silth of her own colony—proud with a default to action over discussion. But so disorganized. She didn't understand how they could stand so little predictability.

"Shaman Renk." A thin elderly Silth flew forward and landed next to Temkaa.

They conferred in whispers. The shaman shook his head, and Temkaa's face grew angry, the whispers more urgent. Finally, the shaman stepped away, calling for two other shamans. Each holding dirt in his left hand, the three faced the men and began to chant. The poachers grew more agitated as the chanting continued. Merit tried to catch Temkaa's eye, but he deliberately looked away. Finally, the chanting stopped. The three shamans slumped down, and other Silth flew over to help them away.

From the poachers' expressions, they were confused since nothing appeared to have happened to them. Temkaa stared at them. Then one screamed as he held up both hands, each missing the index and middle finger. The other poachers gasped and moaned as they held up their altered hands.

When Temkaa spoke, this time much louder, the poachers

moaned, arms crossed over their chests. "In our culture, when a wrong has been perpetrated, the punishment is banishment with clipped wings. You have no wings. But you had trigger fingers. We've clipped them, and your second finger in case you get creative. Without pain, because unlike you, we are not cruel. But now our people will know you. You are banished from these lands. Come within these borders again and you will die. When the rangers are finished, they'll escort you out. If they wish to apply Human justice to you as well, that's up to them. You have killed their brothers."

He lifted his arms high in the air. "I am Temkaa, and this is my word!" The Silth cheered and repeated his name.

As the rangers and poachers were led away, Merit flew to Temkaa. "Your words and actions were powerful … and restrained. Congratulations!"

Temkaa frowned. "So much slaughter for so long. This didn't feel like enough."

Merit paused to honor the statement before replying. "Aran told us a Human quotation. *Returning violence for violence multiplies violence, adding darkness to a night already devoid of stars.*"

"It's a beautiful statement, but hard to imagine such a statement would come from those men standing in front of me."

Merit nodded. "As we come back into the world, we, all of us, are trying to remember that the individuals we encounter, good or bad, are not the race. Anyway, you'll have your hands full dealing with Humans at this refuge. I'll finish training your soldiers, or at least set up their program. The other council representatives will help you set up the administration of the Human contacts through your shamans and create the sun umbrella for you. Once the Humans realize the extent and nature of this place, poachers will be the least of your problems. You'll have desperately hungry people at your edge. Armies who want to retake this land from you. Tribes inside the boundaries whom you will tell not to continue a way of life they've had for more generations than they can recall. Tonight was a minor warm up."

"Was that supposed to make me feel better? You might work on your inspirational talk."

Wind sent smoke swirling around them. "We'll need these people. They're part of the ecology, just as much as the antelope and the hyena."

As the morning sky shifted from black to gray, Merit stifled a yawn and tried to remember when she'd managed more than a couple hours of sleep. The morning was now full of jungle noise, yet she recalled the night as soundless except for voices and the snap and pop of the flames.

"If we survive the volcanoes and the Faeries, we'll need to work with the Humans to build a world we can share with all of the Earth's tribes." She found herself repeating this mantra frequently to the newly empowered but deeply angry Silth.

Repeat anything often enough and you will come to believe it.

CHAPTER 2

1

ARAN (SILTH)

Aran no longer dreamed. He missed Shra, and he didn't want to forget her, so sometimes he would summon her memory, imagining her embrace. But she no longer appeared in his dreams. Aran hadn't dreamed of anything for several moon cycles. He fell asleep and in what felt like seconds he awoke to find hours had passed.

He pulled on brown mid-calf pants with beadwork, a green tunic wrapped around the base of his wings and his shaman's cloak with its many pockets full of potions and paraphernalia. He slipped on the bracelet that had belonged to Shra and the locket from his mother. He could sometimes unlock magical energy stored in these. But access was unreliable and seemed to have something to do with his emotional state. Furthermore, storing energy didn't really seem to be their highest purpose. The helpfulness of these accessories was random because he didn't understand the mechanism. Whether useful or not, he still wore them.

As he tucked the open pen knife in his belt like a small sword, he looked out the window. The wind tossed the branches of the tree ferns surrounding the banyan fig that held their tree-house quarters on a limb twenty feet in the air. Other structures filled the branches making it look like a Human Christmas tree. The Australian rain forest was tight around him—familiar in its bird sound and insect thrum. The buttress trees, strangler figs, and heavy vines hanging from the tree canopy were familiar as well, but foreign in the strange shade of green eucalyptus trees blanketed by moss, the Antarctic beeches, and the ubiquitous tree ferns. The forest citizens were different as well, though in some cases that just meant a new set of creatures could kill Aran. The Australian Silth had told him about the rain forest dingoes, the crocodiles, the snakes, and the many types of poisonous spiders, including the redback and the funnel-web, the latter's bite able to kill a Silth in ten minutes.

He worked an oil into his blue hather beard and his head's green head hather. It kept the bugs away from his face and seemed to be one of the few oils the Silth used that smelled good to Silth and Human alike.

"Heartless, it's too early," Nadara mumbled from the big hammock.

She kicked off the covers but pulled the pillow over her face, her long blue hather with its blond tips fanning out around her head. Aran admired the blue tattoos and their orange highlights that covered her naked body. Her orange fingernail teased the small headhunter spear piercing the skin on her stomach.

"I can feel you looking at me, you know," she said through the pillow.

"Just checking to make sure no parts have fallen off," Aran said. "We've been to a lot of strange places lately."

Her pillow hit him as she headed to the balcony's shower, a bag full of holes connected to a bucket that caught rain from the roof. Her graceful movement was magic in itself.

Aran resumed his place by the window. The World Silth Council had been created in Costa Rica six months ago. They'd tried out their plan on the nation of colonies there, finishing in about one month. Then they rolled on through the other known nations—the one in Brazil, the one in western Africa, then southern Africa, India, and finally Indonesia. In each case Aran and the Tiki Crew went first and brought colony leaders up to speed. They helped the leaders reestablish lapsed central governments, negotiated their relationship with the WSC, and dealt with any local elements of New Faerie. They explained the volcanoes and their consequences, the coming war with the Faeries, and the plan to deal with the Humans by rescuing them from the impending eruption, but demanding the creation of zones for the protection of other species.

In return for teaching the Silth nations the Faeries' fighting magic, Aran required a bound commitment from them to defer to the WSC in dealing with Humans and Silth and to manage the sanctuaries close to them. Everything had gone pretty smoothly, and mostly he only had to tell stories and frame the negotiations. Another group followed him that finished all the official treaties, and Merit arrived after them, teaching and organizing their training as soldiers. In the meantime, Storng had been preparing to negotiate with the Humans. He and the shamans had worked on how to announce their presence, how to conduct negotiations, how to defend the borders of the refuges, what to do with the Humans in and around the refuges, and most importantly, what kind of world they were willing to share with the Humans. The last was the most controversial part of their plan, the part that sent the New Faerie adherents into a rage. It violated a principle every Silth had been taught every moment of their lives, but for the New Faerie religion it was damnation of the entire Silth race. If they broke that rule, they would never be allowed the powers of Faeries. The New Faerie members conveniently ignored the fact that Aran broke the rule and yet became the first Silth to receive such powers.

Aran hadn't seen Merit or, other than on the U.N. video feed, Storng in months. He missed them. Nadara and the Tiki Crew fanned out as they entered each nation, and they spread the word about what was going on to beat the rumors that normally rendered the truth unrecognizable. They also learned the power structures and identified the competent administrators so Aran knew how to help guide the very rapid reform of each nation's structure. But he felt lonely. He could have shared more of his fears with Nadara. While he knew she'd be glad to listen, he held back. And he had no idea why.

They'd been in Australia for three weeks. Unlike the other nations, all of which had been somewhat connected to at least one other Silth nation if only by some annual message, there had been no communication with the Australian Silth nation in more than a hundred years. No one had heard from them or encountered anyone from there.

Aran, Nadara, and the rest of the Tiki Crew arrived in Australia with no idea what they would find. It took a week to determine there was no governance structure left in the Australian Silth nation. There were still bands of Silth but no central organization with which to negotiate. There'd been a war between the Silth in Australia and those in New Zealand, and in the process, the Australian Silth colony had been broken and never recovered. The Tiki Crew pulled together as many Silth as they could locate during the last two weeks, and the WSC was arriving today to determine what to do.

Standing in the room, with the sound of the water from Nadara's shower in the background, Aran could barely breathe. He felt tension rising and ruining the morning's good mood. He sat down to try to meditate but within minutes was back on his feet and pacing.

Nadara was singing as she got dressed on the balcony, her voice joining the morning bird song in a joyous welcome to the day. Aran quietly flickered and blinked away—he refused to weigh her down with his concerns.

He appeared in the top of the canopy, looking out over the outback. The gray clouds hung low over his head as he squatted on a limb a few feet below the top. He wanted to just sit. Being on the very top of the tree would leave him too exposed to swamp harriers and wedge-tailed eagles. He wasn't sure where they lived, but the local Silth had warned him about them.

An hour later, he reappeared in the makeshift Council chamber. In this hall Aran had told the assembled Australian Silth about Yellowstone and the bravery of Faelen, the Trow warrior and only Faerie friend to the Silth. Because of the damage to his voice from his early mismanagement of magic, Aran couldn't sing Faelen's song, but he'd told the epic story of how Faelen had given his life to save the Silth. Today guards stood by the door in case the New Faerie followers—the *Newfies,* as the Silth called them—came back. Yesterday they attacked the chamber, and Nadara had been forced to stun four with a blue bolt. Today most of the central leadership of the World Silth Council was coming together, including Storng, representatives of each of the Silth nations, and perhaps Merit.

The members of the WSC began arriving, shuttled in by shamans. Only shamans and officers in the defense corps had been given the ability to use the Trow's method of transporting from one place to the next. The WSC had decided that while the shield and bolt magic could be widely disseminated, the general populace wasn't ready for this transport magic. Merit had expressed her concern that the ability to blip into battles would uproot centuries worth of tactics. Aran watched the newly appointed local officials greeting the Council members. He'd argued against his own membership on the WSC, as he would be too busy in the field. He didn't know or understand politics and he had no desire to gain such understanding.

The shamans had placed Storng on the Council as their representative. Although Storng pretended to be offended by this change in their view of him, Aran could tell he was pleased. The Council waived its age restrictions and Merit took her place as the representative of the warriors, not just in her own colony but throughout the Silth nations. That same waiver had allowed the Costa Rican nation to appoint Aran as their representative. When he met with Storng and Merit, he maintained none of them had time to sit in council meetings. Storng said they were *war chiefs,* something Aran was sure Storng read someplace. They would attend important sessions but spend most of their time in the field while the rest of the council managed day-to-day matters. Today's was one of those important meetings. Not because of the need to organize the governance of the Australian nation, or to figure out how to feed all the animals that would come into the refuges they established, or even how to maintain the eggs they had aggregated to create the climate *umbrellas* over the refuges. That was—what did Joss call it? —*administrivia.* There were more important issues.

Aran watched Nadara as she arrived and talked to the guards at the door. They straightened at her approach and so plainly basked in the glow of her attention that he had to smile. He was considering joining her when Storng blinked into the room, ferrying three more council members. He and Aran embraced and huddled to the side while the council gathered. A few moments later Merit showed up in the leather armor her colony's army wore and armed with weapons from head to foot. There were no public embraces with Merit, only the traditional greeting of the Silth—right arms grasped hand to wrist as she greeted everyone. Storng, Merit and Aran moved to a corner. No one attempted to approach them, deterred by the intensity of their conversation. Merit's harpy eagle, taller than any of the Silth stood guard outside the room, peering in the window periodically.

With the U.N. appearance only a few weeks behind him, Storng was still flush with excitement over the next phase. "I'm concerned, however, that both Humans and Silth are developing factions too quickly for them to reach an agreement. New Faerie insists the Silth not be contaminated by Human contact and simply prepare to welcome the Trow back into the world."

Merit glanced around before saying, "There are New Faerie adherents everywhere, including among the warriors and perhaps even in the WSC."

Storng added, "Even among the Silth who are not New Faerie, there is disagreement about working with the Humans. Some shamans think it would be best if the volcanoes or the Trow exterminate the Humans and for the Silth to protect only themselves and the other Earth species. In the long run, they argue, the Earth would be better off without the Humans. Then perhaps the Silth could make peace with the Trow."

Aran said, "We need to know more about the Silth enclave in

New Zealand. It was apparently led by a meat-eating, flightless Silth. No one knows if she's still around nor have any of the Australians had contact with the New Zealand Silth since their defeat. She never asserted her rule, but whenever they tried to reorganize, her spies would alert her, and she'd return and attack. I'm going looking for her."

Storng also talked about the need to accelerate the search for a solution to the remaining active volcanoes. He could only be successful in negotiating the kind of post-volcano world the Silth desired if they had the power to end their activity. That was their only negotiating chip since the Humans couldn't imagine they really needed the assistance of *little flying people* to fight a war with beings they'd never seen. But the first volcano had shown the Silth their power was exhausted by quieting just one semi-active volcano. It was hard for any of them to imagine how they would stop multiple eruptions. Aran told the others he had an idea he was working on to deal with the volcanoes, but he wasn't ready to share it yet. He needed to think about it some more.

They also discussed the challenge of world-wide communications. The *shaman calls* were a very inefficient means of communication. They were heard by every shaman, and could only be shared among themselves. They had begun using messengers who could blink from one point to another to pass along a message, but increased use of this approach risked proliferating the magic of that transport, something the WSC feared. Despite the risk of technological contamination, Storng advocated increased use of Human smart phones. He believed that with limited use and deactivation between uses, the risk was reasonable. He had read about how an African tribe of Humans, the Maasai, used smart phones as they tended their cattle and goats on the African savanna.

"The secret of war lies in the communications," said Storng. Since Storng had never fought a war, Aran assumed that he was quoting some Human general.

Finally, Aran shared what was perhaps uppermost on his mind "There are rumors of a Trow colony still on Earth. Fragments of stories of a secret enclave of Trow hidden in the Andes near Machu Picchu. I'm going to look for them right after this council meeting ends."

"Really?" Merit raised her red hather eyebrows. "So many things must be done, and you deem the most important ones to be checking on some has-been leader in New Zealand and chasing a rumor of Faeries?"

"No different than the tales of harpies," Storng grumbled. "Tales to scare small children."

"As to chasing the has-been, I've seen portents that she will be a factor in what is to come. Regarding the Trow, what will Silth fight for when they realize there will be no more Silth?" Aran asked. "Right now, they're focused on securing a future for their brothers and sisters of the Earth—safe from volcanoes, Humans, and Faeries. But will that sustain them in a war with the Faeries? Will they fight the only race that can secure their continued existence? I'm not so sure." He watched Merit shake her head at his reasoning, but she said nothing.

Their caucus broke when the chair called the council into its formal assembly, and everyone began taking their seats. As the morning passed, Aran got up and walked the room. When he sat back down, he watched the dim gray light's progress through the trees and the movement of the shadows. The most inconsequential bird held his attention. Even Merit seemed to tolerate the meeting better. The problem wasn't that the council ended up with the wrong conclusions, it took so long to get there. New to their authority, each member was compelled to say something on every point, even if it was to repeat someone's prior point.

Aran said little. Storng seemed to sense his mood and inserted points that Aran had made when they'd met with Merit. The group spent a great deal of time arguing about Humans. Some held them responsible for the condition of the world, the Faerie anger and the resulting volcanoes, and the coming war. Others believed the Humans were simply another species to be accounted for, no better nor worse than termites who didn't regulate their appetites by what was good for the forest. These council members said the Humans should be preserved like other species but in a way that would re-balance the Earth and undo their overwhelming influence on its ecosystems. But Storng argued they needed the Humans to fight the Trow. He maintained the Silth by themselves wouldn't win a war with the Faeries.

The council broke for lunch and Nadara joined Aran, Merit, and Storng as they sat outside downing nuts, berries, and an Australian bread with jam Aran believed might be the best food he'd ever eaten. When the others returned for the afternoon session, Aran flickered out of sight to reappear in an open meadow in the jungle. He filled his lungs with the moist earthy air. While the skies were overcast like everywhere else in the world, there wasn't as much ash at ground level. He listened to the breeze stir the branches and rile the insects into even louder song. He stretched out his wings. Between the ash-filled skies and his use of the Trow magical transport, he rarely flew the great distances he once covered. *I need to exercise more.*

He'd left a substantial cache of swag in the Land as he came to Australia. After experimenting with small amounts, he determined using the Trow magic transport didn't break his connection to materials in the Land even when he "crossed" water. He'd distribute some of his swag among the Australian Silth as a goodwill gesture before he searched for the Trow enclave. The Silth were now much more conscious of their use of the harvested materials. Aran laughed to himself as he imagined Humans negotiating with bees or sheep and trying to explain the honey on the table or the wool on their backs. Of course, the harder one to explain would be the lamb-chop on the table. At least the Silth didn't have that problem.

He went through the summoning ritual, chanting the words and holding some of the meadow's rich soil in his hand. Two large crates appeared in the clearing. As he approached the first to open it, he heard a furious tinkling nearby. At the corner of the crate, a small creature was struggling to remove its leg from beneath the crate, its movements creating the jingling sound. Aran bent over and as his shadow enveloped the tiny green form—vaguely humanoid, but more insect-like than Silth-like—it froze with head bowed, apparently hoping Aran wouldn't notice it. After a moment it began to tremble and slowly looked up, flinching as Aran reached out and dug gently below it. He quickly freed the trapped leg. The little wings on the creature's back flapped so fast they disappeared, and with a buzz of wings and a bell-like tinkle, it zoomed out from beneath the crate. When it circled the crate and disappeared into the trees, Aran was disappointed, but moments later it streaked back into the meadow and halted abruptly just three inches from his nose. Its hairless body was small, about the size of Aran's forearm, and its four arms were in constant motion. The eyes in the rounded face were black and unreadable. After peering at Aran a few moments, the creature zoomed up and landed on the top of the crate.

A flower fairy. That's what this is. Both Storng and Faelen had mentioned the small animals of the Land and how they magically transformed when they came to Earth.

The flower fairy watched as Aran opened the crates and sorted through their contents, deciding how to distribute them. The Australian Silth had agreed to create a *common house* where goods could be stored on behalf on the community and distributed as needed. By the time he finished, the sun was low behind the trees, the meadow was almost dark. Aran noted, without particular surprise, that the flower fairy glowed slightly in the dark. These creatures were the source of many Human stories and said to be sometimes mischievous or randomly helpful.

He filled a swag bag with the items he wanted to keep. Tonight, he'd direct the Australians to the crates.

Aran shut the last crate. "Goodbye, little one."

But as he flew down the path leading to the village, he heard tinkling following him through the forest. He breathed in a sweet burst of odor from the greenish-yellow flowers below, struggling to distill enough sunlight to survive.

He looked over at the glowing creature as it paralleled him in the trees. *Merit's familiar is a fierce harpy eagle. Mine is apparently a tinkling flower fairy, sure to inspire awe wherever I go.*

2

RANGI (SILTH)

Rangi stalked through the undergrowth beneath the tree ferns, pausing frequently to listen. Nestor flew through branches weighted down with green moss and lichens and watched. When she saw movement in the brush around Rangi, she imitated the call of the parrot whose glamour she wore with a descending, drawn-out *keaaa* ending in a quaver. Once meant the quarry was to the right. Twice, and it was to the left. It was a good system, as long as Nestor avoided being distracted by the barely detectable odor of sheep from the nearby farm.

Rangi could have someone besides Nestor spot for her, but she felt like killing something. Even though they tried to hide it, other Silth attendants were so disgusted when she ate her kill it took away the joy. Otherwise, Rangi loved to eat, and it showed in her unusual girth. More important at the moment, her rotundness made moving quietly through the underbrush difficult.

Keaaaaaa!

Rangi pushed quickly to her right.

One benefit of eating meat was it furnished her two-hundred-year-old body with more energy than Silth half her age. There. She spotted her prey hovering over a small mushroom. Unfortunately, it zoomed up about four feet to a bright yellow flower. For other Silth this would be no challenge, but Rangi's mother was a Kakapo—a flightless parrot once common throughout New Zealand—and Rangi could not fly. She settled in place but stayed tensed and alert, ready to spring.

These days the couple of hundred Kakapos left were only found on a few barrier islands where they'd been relocated to escape the dogs, cats, pigs, and goats accompanying Human expansion. Rangi had no love for Humans, but she knew Nestor, whose mother was a Kea, had a deep hatred for them. The parrot colony where she'd been born was later wiped out by sheep farmers. The farmers thought the Keas were sheep killers because they'd find them eating sheep carcasses. Rather than figuring out the Keas never killed sheep, the farmers simply eliminated them. While they occasionally ate already dead sheep, the Keas mostly consumed leaves, buds, roots, and seeds. They loved nectar, and the most harm they ever did to Humans was stealing wiper blades. Maybe I really do hate Humans.

Rangi's quarry zipped back down into the underbrush and she sprang, pinning the tiny blue flower fairy down. As the creature frantically wriggled beneath her hands, she tore off its head and chewed. She didn't know where these came from, but for the last two years more and more had appeared, and she found them much tastier than bush babies.

Nestor, now unglamoured, flapped down beside her, the orange and yellow under her wings a sharp contrast to her general olive brown hather and the drab Silth-made clothes. She squatted back on her heels without comment as Rangi tore apart the flower fairy and ate with enthusiasm, green blood splattering her clothing.

Rangi wiped her mouth with the hem of her tunic and picked up the conversation where they'd stopped before the hunt. "I think it's natural for one species to replace another when it's smarter. Humans have replaced m-m-m-many species around the world. Like the

Neanderthals, their cousins. We'll replace them, work with the Faeries to return the world to a place of beauty. Only two things I want out of this. One, to control New Zealand. When we fought with Australia, I thought I wanted to conquer the world, but I don't. I just want to m-m-make our home the way it should be. And to fly. That's the other thing. Not just do that Faerie transport thing, but to really fly. Faeries can fly without wings. I want that m-m-m-most of all."

Nestor said nothing, just smiled and nodded. The dullness of her eyes and her agreeable smile told Rangi she was chewing pitcheri, a habit maintained since their younger days. Diviners Sage, which she also used, would have made her manic and paranoid. Nestor resettled herself and continued to stare at Rangi.

"M-m-my spies say there are Silth in Australia who know the secret to the transport m-m-magic. But they guard it closely. We'll have to find something important enough they'll trade for it. We'll start today."

Rangi used the bone from the small arm of the flower fairy to pick stray pieces of meat from between her teeth.

3

Aran (Silth)

The Trow colony was rumored to be hidden in the Andes near Machu Picchu. Aran had listened to fragments of stories told by the Brazil shaman, and although the stories were too fantastic to believe, he knew there was almost always some grain of truth in a story.

According to legend these Trow were taller than normal, never spoke, and didn't fly. There were reports of them being seen in many places from Costa Rica to Peru, sometimes alone and sometimes in groups of two or three. They were always in long red robes, typically with a walking stick, and always hairless unlike normal Trow. Sightings were usually brief as the Trow usually spotted the Silth immediately, and their stares were so intimidating they frightened others away. But supposedly Silth had seen them walking high in the mountains and followed them from a distance until reaching an altitude so high and cold the Silth couldn't continue.

Aran had decided to search for them. He didn't know why. There were many legends and stories in the world, and he didn't follow up on others, but for some reason this one wouldn't let him go. Last night, after the WSC meeting, he'd started dreaming again, the same dream repeatedly through the night. He saw a mountain with red-robed Trow climbing three paths toward a cave near the top. In his dream he knew an answer lay inside that cave, but he was unable to find a way in. He tried to talk to the Trow as they slowly walked toward the entrance, but they refused to respond to his questions. When he tried flying toward the cave, he always awoke before he could enter.

In the Sacred Valley of the Incas, he'd tried to stop, planning to use magic in his quest for the hidden Trow. But the voices of the slaughtered Incas were too loud. They'd been cut down by the Spanish soldiers, their sacred sites destroyed by the Catholic Church, their civilization ground away by the clash of cultures. The Silth had been close to the Incas' forebearers. But when they were threatened by unrelenting floods, the Humans sacrificed hundreds of children and young llamas. The Human priests and the Silth shamans shared secrets and ideas about religion and nature as well as arts and crafts, but after the mass murder contact was infrequent and largely ceremonial.

The Silth watched the Incas rise as they crushed and assimilated other tribes to establish their great kingdom. The Incas were amazing engineers, and the Silth admired their ability to fashion the world around them. But the Inca practice of live sacrifice of animals and Humans continued to appall the Silth. For the Silth, all life was sacred, and while it might be taken, death could only occur as an act of defense or in the normal course of consumption in nature. Consequently, by the time the armor of the Spanish, together with their horses and lances, were ripping apart the world of the Incas, Silth had almost no contact with them. Still, the old contacts meant the restless voices called out to Aran when he came into the Sacred Valley.

He reflected on the success of the Spanish in quickly conquering the Incas. Stories of the Inca-Spanish clash were still told among the Silth. Aran knew most of them. Storng had also read about this time in history and told Aran the technology of the Spanish was superior to that of the Incas.

Aran worried that, in many ways, the Silth faced a similar

situation—the technology of the Trow was superior to that of the Silth and the Humans. While the Silth did have the shield and bolt created with Trow magic, these weren't the limit of Trow battle technology. It would be easier for the Trow to simply steal all the Humans' most awful weapons and use them against the Humans and the Silth. While the Trow had tried to create a situation where this was unnecessary, it didn't mean they wouldn't do it.

Faelen had said the Trow fought many wars among themselves, in their non-magical homeland, and that the bio-based weapons they'd developed were powerful. But they hadn't fought large scale battles on the Earth. So perhaps their magical weapons didn't give them that much of an advantage. Aran wondered if it was really technology that defeated the Incas. Storng had also told him about the civil war, fought between the brother Inca rulers, that undermined the Inca defenses and weakened them even as they tried to fend off the Spanish. There was no civil war among the Silth. Yet. All seven of the Silth nations had agreed to central leadership. But the Newfies were increasingly restless about the course Aran and the WSC charted for the Silth and Human alliance against the Trow. In a scary parallel, his brother Casius led New Faerie, but the two hadn't spoken since Casius fled to the old colony to organize the Newfies.

Storng also told him about the Comanche, a tribe of Humans in the old United States. While the Spanish continued their expansion north, crushing the advanced civilizations that had grown up in South and Central America, this tribe fought them to a standstill. At one time considered backward by the region's various tribes, the Comanches took a fundamental Spanish advantage, the use of horses, and in almost magical fashion they developed a relationship with and way of using them that the Spanish had never seen. Although their use of this skill halted the Spanish advance and briefly stopped the Americans, they were eventually bested by the latter's own technological advances.

While Aran needed to consider the lessons in that history, the moan of the ancients distracted and disheartened him. He flew off and joined the throng of tourists exploring Machu Picchu, the Incas' mountaintop retreat. Unlike the Sacred Valley, the Inca spirits were at peace here. The Spaniards had never found this city, so it was not sacked nor its stones carried off to use in building churches. When their civilization fell, the Incas hadn't finished its construction or occupied it fully. Aran had expected few tourists, given the difficulties for Humans traveling these days, but a swarm of tourists strained to deal with the altitude's thin air and the cardio workout demanded by its out-sized steps. Wild chinchilla hid among the ruins, and the few llamas who avoided being eaten walked through its paths, but no Trow hid there.

Aran relocated to the side of Huayna Picchu, the mountain overlooking the Inca city's ruins. During Incan times, it housed the Temple of the Moon, where the priest and his virgin acolytes kept vigil. The tourists continued to tackle this mountain as well, but only a few hundred were allowed on it each day, challenged by the steep steps and ladders and with little desire to explore anything off the path. Aran heard one tourist tell another it was called *the mountain you can fall off of.*

He located a small terrace which was mostly obscured from the tourists' sight by the brush of its edges but still allowed him to see the city far below. He watched the ant-like movements of the Humans, the Urubamba River wrapping around the city, and the Andes mountains framing the whole setting, heavy clouds flowing over their edges under the ash-gray sky. Although he was high in the mountains, the jungle managed to cover most of the slopes around him. He spotted snow on the even higher ones of the surrounding monoliths.

He gathered some brush and leaves and made himself a comfortable place to sit while he worked on finding the Trow hiding place, if it even existed. He knew he couldn't see it even if standing beside it as it would be cloaked in the same way Silth avoided Human observation. He suspected he wouldn't be able to locate it using the Trow techniques Faelen had taught him either, since there were ways to avoid these as well. A different kind of magic would be required.

He remained seated on soft leaves that gave the cool air a slight peppermint smell, and while unpacking his bag he ate a bar of pressed nuts and berries. He arranged the Silth-sized singing bowl—it produced a melodic ring when tested by running its pestle around the edge—sticks for the fire, a lighter, herbs to produce a thick smoke, and leaves and crushed roots he would consume over the next few hours. The sun was setting, the tourists' voices less frequent.

He lit the small fire and began to chant. He tossed the dried herbs and leaves on the fire and used a leaf rolled into a tube to inhale the smoke. Then he drank the first of the three teas he'd brewed with the roots. His chin dropped to his chest as the ash-filtered moonlight surrounded him in the quiet of the mountainside evening.

His pneuma expanded as a ghost-like physical presence, growing in fits and starts, but ever larger so he finally stood as tall as the mountain. He stepped over Machu Picchu and slowly worked his way through the Andes feeling loosely present in this mental giant. He left no footprint, and no plant bent beneath his step. He felt drawn in a particular direction, felt like he knew the way—a familiar path but one he had never traveled. He stepped over rivers and smaller mountains, though the larger ones were still twice his size. After walking for an hour, he came to an ellipse of volcano peaks, ringed in glowing clouds. An enormous cap of ice covered the area between them and spilled off the side. Earlier he'd studied maps and tried several other locations, including the Manu national park and the volcano Misti. Now he knelt, recognizing the old volcanoes as *Nevado Coropuna*. *This is the place.*

He leaned in close to the side of the volcano and looked at the bald, red-robed figure moving along its path. The deep crevasse toward which it was headed clearly led to a cave mouth that, because of the lay of the slope, could only be seen from above. He leaned closer to the figure to try to make out its features. *Definitely Trow.* As he stared, the Trow stopped short, looked straight up into Aran's eyes, and scowled. Aran recoiled and the sudden movement broke his trance, bringing him abruptly back to the mountainside of Huayna Picchu. But he had what he needed. He crumpled and lay prone on the ground waiting for his heartbeat and breath to calm.

He slept without moving until the black gave way to the dull gray morning and the birds, willing to welcome even this bleak start, began their chorus. He packed up his shaman paraphernalia and ate some more of the berry and nut bar, washing it down with cold water collected from a spring trickling out of the mountainside. Stretching his arms and his wings, he prepared himself mentally for what he was about to do. He had no idea what these Trow would be like. Why did they stay in the world when the rest had withdrawn? Were they outcasts like Faelen or an outpost for Thest? Should he be backed by an army or was his instinct he should come alone correct? They knew he was coming, so there would be no element of surprise. Was that good or bad? He stretched again, flickered and disappeared from the small plateau on Huayna Picchu and reappeared on the side of the mountain named Nevado Coropuna. This was an *Apu*, an Inca sacred mountain, made up of six summits.

Aran thought he would quickly recognize where the glacier met the opening in the mountain, but he searched for a week without luck. He found no tracks nor hint of where the entry could be. When he flew up and tried to identify it from the sky, the cold seeped through the Trow shield, and he was unable to stay aloft for long. Every few hours he left the glacier for the hidden spot above Machu Picchu so he could warm up again.

Finally, just as he was deciding he'd made a mistake even attempting this search, he noticed a swirl of snow that seemed to be sucked into the side of the mountain. He walked into the dark crevasse. After several moments of darkness, the walls started to glow with the bioluminescence of some sort of glow-worms hanging from the ceiling. The path angled downward, and a hot spring came out of the wall, feeding a steaming brook that ran alongside him and washed across the corridor. The light reflected off glassy brown rock interrupted periodically by bright quartz. Ahead the luminescence diminished and a doorway appeared framed by a deep brown root-like timber. Through it he could see ashen light.

He stepped out onto a southern-facing slope and into a woodland of gnarled evergreens with red, shaggy bark and small grayish-green leaves. Brightly colored parrots and toucans darted about, landing on the thick moss of tree branches and hurling through purple-flowered bushes. While the entrance to the passage had been thousands of feet above where vegetation, by then mostly grasslands and shrubs, had ended, here it was lush with a canopy of trees and a low carpet of wildflowers. As his eyes adjusted to the light, he realized he wasn't alone.

"The threshold of the door reads your thoughts and transmits them to me," said the red-robed figure standing a little to the side of the exit.

Aran's first thought was that the claim they didn't talk was wrong. Though he couldn't be certain, the Trow looked like the scowling figure from before. Seven feet tall, he was hairless, and the red robe flowed from shoulders to mid-calf. His sandals were made of some sort of hemp.

"And?"

"You are not welcome here, Aran Shaman. We would prefer none know of our existence, including you. However, you will not be harmed." He started down a path through the trees.

Well, they don't talk much. As Aran followed, he decided there must be heat vents from the nearby volcano. The sky was the same dull gray that covered the world, but when there had been sun, it would have shown warmly on these southern slopes. The trees gave way to a series of terraces built into the hillside with stone walls and openings through which water flowed, the steam suggesting its temperature. Crops planted on the terraces struggled in the pale light of the cloud-covered day just as they did elsewhere.

As Aran rounded the path's bend at the base of the terraces, a village rose back up the mountainside on the other side of an outcropping. Trow, all in red robes, walked the village streets or worked on various tasks while sitting on porches. An instant after Aran and his guide rounded the curve all movement stopped, and faces, devoid of expression, turned toward them. As Aran drew closer, he could see the single-story buildings of the village were carefully fitted stone for their first six feet or so and were topped by earthen blocks covered by thatched roofs. He struggled to keep up with his guide's long strides, forced to walk and fly, walk and fly to avoid having to stop and mount each wall of a step. No one spoke as they passed among the village occupants.

They stopped in front of a wooden door covered in moss and lichen. When the Trow extended his arm toward the door, Aran wondered how to open its latch handle. But the door swung open upon his approach, and he entered. Another Trow, holding the door open, motioned Aran further inside. He realized it was some kind of hospital room with several beds, all but one empty. Next to the occupied bed sat a Trow, red-robed and hairless like the others, but with more delicate features and smooth movements. Her voice was soft and feminine.

"You must eat," she said, some brown, mush-like substance flowing over the edge of the spoon as she hovered over a patient.

Although there was no verbal response, apparently some signal caused her to give up and lower the spoon back into the bowl on the short wooden bedside table. As he walked up Aran was too low to see the face of the bed's occupant. The Trow attendant turned to him as though he was expected.

"Aran Shaman, I am Lornix. If he does not eat, he will die soon." She hurried from the room.

Confused, Aran hesitated a moment before flying up to the edge of the bed. As he landed, the bed shifted slightly, causing the patient to twist his head in that direction. Aran found himself looking into Faelen's gaunt, scarecrow-like face. Neither spoke.

"I thought you were dead," Aran finally croaked, his voice thick.

"I *am* dead," Faelen said. "And I have been sent to the fourth realm for punishment."

4

ARAN (SILTH)

Faelen faced away, the rough-woven blanket tucked in tightly along his body. Aran sat cross-legged on the blanket, taking in the arrangement of the bed, the nearby bedpan, the lack of movement beneath the blankets. Besides the bowl, the table held various pouches of herbs and ground flowers which he assumed were being used for healing.

"Can you walk?"

Faelen gave an unamused guffaw. "No. Nothing works below my neck."

"The result of being shot by Thest?"

"The result of my own brilliant plan." His head twisted back toward Aran. "I knew Thest would not stop until he killed me. I practiced creating a shield contoured to my body—you would not notice it unless you were looking for it. Low enough its glow would not be obvious but strong enough to stop a Trow bolt." He took three deep gulps of air. "Two things went wrong. I underestimated the effect of a close-range bolt. It did not kill me but it was strong enough to immobilize me. And I did not think about the effect of dropping over a hundred feet from the canopy to the jungle floor while immobilized. I broke my back."

His eyes snapped shut and he took another gulp of air.

Aran thought about all the things he'd wished he had said to Faelen when he'd thought he was gone. He wondered if Faelen knew everything that had happened since he'd been hurt. Aran also had many questions about this Trow colony. But for a long moment he stared out of the window at the peaks of the volcanoes forming the bowl this slope faced.

"I'll have to change my story you know." He waited but got no response. "Right now, it ends with General Faelen, the hero of all Silth, the one who changed our lives by teaching us Faerie magic, the one who stopped the destruction of the Earth, dying at the hands of the evil Lord Thest. Silth all around the world have cried hearing that story. Of course, they cheer the earlier part where I rescue the doddering old Faerie from imminent death in the jaws of a crocodile..." Still getting no reaction, he tried a different tack.

"You saved us all. You saved me. Thank you."

He outlined the fight with Angel and how Faelen's hologram and count-down termination had ended the effort to ignite the Yosemite caldera. He caught him up on what had happened since then, including the recent interactions between Humans and Silth. In the half hour Aran spoke, Faelen never looked at him nor acknowledged anything he said, except once when he said, "Ahhh, that is why the skies are still gray." Aran could see enough of his face to know he hadn't fallen asleep.

Finally, Aran felt bold enough to ask him, "Will you be able to walk again? Can these Trow cure you?"

Faelen turned back to him, face twisted into a snarl. "These sheep do not practice magic. They believe technology only erodes their minds if they practice magic. You are surrounded by the Sohi, one hundred or so former Trow warriors who have now embraced a monastic life. They are refugees from my father's rise to power. They became pacifists and hid here in the mountains. They skulk throughout the region and had been watching the area in Costa Rica where Thest and his goons confronted me. After Thest left me for dead, they spirited me away to here."

"You're fortunate they were there."

"I was as cursed that day as I have been every day of my life. I lie here totally at the mercy of that torturer Lornix in a place devoid of liquor. I could forgive them their cowardly furtiveness, but I cannot abide teetotalers. I have been over half a year without a drink. Give me one."

Aran shook his head. "You know I have none." He petted the nap of the blanket. "You've passed the withdrawal period and could be sober now. Besides, I thought Trow were immune to addiction. You're not addicted to liquor."

"I never drank because I was addicted. I drank because without alcohol the days were long and boring. And filled with too many unwanted memories. Get me a drink or kill me. Or leave."

Lornix came back in. "You have not succeeded in getting him to eat. He will sleep now. Come."

Aran followed her down a path and into another building no more ornate than the first but beautifully covered in vines, mosses, and the occasional orchid. She pushed open the door to a room, spare as the other. An elder Trow, different only in that he wore a yellow robe, was seated at a large wooden table, on which several Human books were stacked.

Aran stepped past Lornix and stood in the doorway a moment, taking in the room before flying up to stand next to the books. He bowed. Lornix retreated and closed the door.

The old Trow said, "Sit, Aran Shaman." Once Aran had done so, the Trow went on. "I am Tegrat, and I represent the will of the Sohi. My line traces back to the Old Ones, the Trow who first came into this world. Discovered its magic. My ancestors were the ones who foolishly created the Humans. I suspect Faelen told you the Trow first created the various humanoids that populated this world. One Human group had a spirit that appealed to the Old Ones, so they kept them as pets and taught them useful skills, like how to catch food, sculpt, sing, make tools, meld various materials, and even cultivate pets themselves. We created the instrument of our own destruction.

"For many centuries they were simply amusing. Then through some Earth magic, they were able to procreate. They no longer needed us to sculpt them into existence. Their magic was different than ours, a product of the Earth like ours, but different. They were short-lived but prolific, and like an experiment run amok they spread everywhere." He stopped and stared at a point on the wall behind Aran for a moment.

"You did not come here, however, for Human history. This history is much on my mind, however, as the Trow seek to wipe out our mistake. You should not have come here at all, but you came hoping for answers about your own future."

How did he know?

Tegrat looked back toward the doorway. Aran remembered they told him the exit from the cave had read his thoughts, and the threshold into this room must do the same. He tried to remember what he'd been thinking as he arrived. He'd stood there for several moments.

"You wondered if you could find Trow who could continue to make Silth even if you won your war with Thest and Xafar. You also wondered if Trow who continued to hide in the world despite the withdrawal of the others might be willing to fight beside you when the Trow return. You were trying to figure out how we knew to take you to Faelen, and what you could do to help him. Finally, you wondered if we might instead simply kill you to keep our location secret."

He fell silent as if giving Aran an opportunity to contradict anything he had said, but when Aran didn't respond,

"Do you know anything about the Sohi?"

Aran shook his head. "I had only heard rumors of your existence."

"Ahhh, no, I meant the Human Sohi. They were Japanese warriors who became Zen monks. Like them, we have seen many battles and much death. We served our masters faithfully but chose a time when our departure would cause no harm and separated ourselves from the rest of the Trow so we might study life here on Earth more deeply. We renounced violence as aggression, so you need not fear for your life... unless we decide you are a threat. We still train, and perhaps train more deeply than any Trow warrior in the integration of magic and martial arts, but this is only for our defense. Any time the Trow have found any of us, we have had to defend ourselves, so we have become adept enough that they no longer seek us out. Over the centuries they seem to have forgotten us.

"Because we have renounced aggressive violence, we will not fight the Trow. Unless they attack us. And in our study of life and magic here on Earth, we have determined that while all magic comes at a price, the magic practiced by the Trow is the most foreign to the Earth and comes at the highest price. With Human electrical technology occurring in the world, a product of their magic, that price appears to be the Trow's mental stability.

"Consequently, in addition to aggressive violence we have also renounced most magic. We still practice battle magic to defend ourselves. We have learned some other Earth magics, some from Humans and some from the Silth. We have brought some of our biomorphic tools from the Land, like the thought-reading threshold and our lights, and with these tools we do well while avoiding Trow magic.

"We will not perform the magic it takes to create more Silth. We sympathize with your desire to continue your race, but we cannot be your answer." The corners of his mouth turned down. "We knew from reading Faelen's thoughts when he first arrived that he hoped you would find him, and we sensed you in your quest to find us, so we knew you would want to see him. We do not know what you can do for him."

He stood up, Lornix opened the door, her timing impeccable as usual, Aran thought. *Did she listen outside the doors?*

He stood as well and bowed, wings spread wide. "Thank you for your time and the answers you've given me, disappointing as they are. I will, of course, keep all information regarding this place secret, but I wonder if I could ask a favor." He didn't pause for permission. "Faelen is my friend and mentor. I'd like to come to see him. Perhaps there's something I can do for him to ease his pain. May I return?"

"No."

"When I met Faelen and he agreed to teach me Trow magic, he required me to ensure that I wouldn't be followed when meeting him. I was successful, even before he gave me the magic tools to avoid detection."

"If you are followed, you will be a threat to us, and you will die in an instant."

Aran said nothing. Tegrat glanced at Lornix, who showed no reaction, nodded his head, and left the room. Lornix led Aran back to the passage but stopped as they approached the doorway.

"Never come save by this door. Anything which appears suddenly in our midst is eliminated instantly since historically this could only be a Trow." She hesitated. "It would be good if you could help Faelen. He is in much pain, both physically and mentally."

For a brief moment, Aran saw a different pain flash in her eyes before they went flat again.

Aran walked through the glow-worm passage. He'd keep the secret of the Sohi. But explaining to Humans or even other Silth that not all Trow were their enemies, that some could be their friends, would be difficult. It was much simpler when you could just say they were all bad. He also realized that even if they won the war with the Trow, they'd still need to design a world where the Trow could live. And what of the war? How would these Trow fit into the war? Would they simply sit on the sidelines? Had he wasted precious time in searching for them?

He wondered what he was doing. The other Silth had clear roles in seeking answers or preparing for the war. He was simply … What had his mother called it? *Following his nose.*

Finally, he wondered what he could do for Faelen. He owed him so much.

Would it be a good thing or a bad thing to bring him liquor? Is there any more I can do?

CHAPTER 3

1

NADARA (SILTH)

Nadara had proclaimed the Brisbane Tiki scene weak when she and the Tiki Crew harvested a few paper umbrellas and knick-knacks from the couple of bars advertising themselves as tiki. The Jungle Bar was good, but the others, while they had wonderfully quirky personalities, were tiki only in name.

Now she sat in the chaos of the Crew's party, her head spinning from the fruit-flavored rum, listening to Tiki Joe's Ocean playing way too loud on a Bluetooth speaker hooked to the team's phone.

One of the compromises the WSC had made was to address the world-wide communication challenge by allowing shamans, warriors, diplomats, and a representative from each colony to utilize phones. Don carried theirs in a special backpack, bringing it out for directions, research, calls, and unsanctioned music.

The tree house in the Australian colony where they partied shook as they celebrated the completion of their role in uniting the Silth nations. At 3 a.m. it was down to the Crew; the other participants having wandered off to bed. Marina, Kirstn, Loana, and Nick danced with wobbly enthusiasm among the empty airline bottles of tequila, rum, and vodka littering the floor. Don and Vic were in deep and almost coherent conversation on the balcony.

While Nadara knew she should put on a better show of having fun for the sake of the others, she missed Aran and couldn't help worrying about the next phase of their jobs. Now that Humans knew of the Silth, there would be no more harvests. The WSC had decided it wouldn't help the Silth's image if Humans came to realize most of their stuff gone missing over the years had actually been stolen. Silth who had contact with Humans had been instructed to remove harvested items from their wardrobes, and all the harvest crews had been called back to their colonies. Because the Tiki Crew had supported the last several months' roll-out of the Plan, they would all be given good jobs but, as Nadara had been reminded by Storng in a call today, the likelihood of them staying together was low.

Her last conversation with Aran had been by phone as well. She still wasn't sure how she felt about phones. She appreciated the opportunity to talk to Aran, but not being able to see him or be seen was disconcerting. He said they could use a video connection as soon as either of them had time to learn how, but she was confident it would still feel like talking through a wall. Perhaps her unease came from his sounding somewhat evasive when she asked how his search for Trow was going. If she was with him face-to-face, she'd know if something was up. Or would she? She knew his reputation when they began but had been sure things would be different with her. She was aware of her effect on others and had been certain she would be in control. She always was. It wasn't a trap; she just was used to being in control of affairs of the heart. She depended on it.

Kristn interrupted Nadara's thoughts by dragging her to the bamboo dance floor, but just as they reached it, Vic shouted, "Hey. Hey, you! Shhhhhtop!"

He was pointing out the window, and they all rushed over. Nadara saw a group of Silth—it looked like ten or so—weaving among the colony buildings. They were dressed oddly, though in the moonlight it was hard to pin down exactly what was off. They were dashing into open windows or doors and coming out stuffing things in their pockets.

"Those sons of toucans are harvesting, right here in a Silth colony. They … they can't do that." The furtive zigzagging figures ignored Vic and Don's shouts.

The whole Tiki Crew piled out into the night, stumbling and bumping into things as the alcohol threw off their balance. Nadara flew off the balcony toward the last building where she'd seen one of the night invaders. No one was there. Then she heard a sound inside the building. Just as she reached a window, she was knocked aside by the Silth who came flying out, a female with white hather in wire-wrapped dreadlocks and a bright yellow crest. Weirdly, she was wearing a leather apron and some equipment on her back between her wings.

Nadara chased her toward the edge of the colony's buildings along the main street through its center. From the side paths and alleys other figures joined the one Nadara followed. The entire Tiki Crew had re-formed and were pursuing nine or ten Silth past the edge of the colony and through the Australian outback. Moonlight-infused grayness lit the way along a wide, heavily used game trail. The sounds of animals crashing off the path preceded them.

The strangers were fast, but the Tiki Crew was gaining on them. The forest disappeared, and they found themselves in a large open area filled with rusting equipment and old machinery of a sawmill. Nadara and the Crew had almost caught up with the slowest of the pursued when their quarry swooped through an open bay door into a large building. Nadara saw her target take a sudden left turn, but before she could adjust to follow, she hit the net. She was immediately flattened by Don, who couldn't slow down, and the rest of the Tiki Crew slammed into the net as well. Even though the adrenaline of the chase had flushed most of the drunk from their systems, the disorientation of hitting the net and the multiple collisions left them all stunned and hanging still for a moment. Then they began to struggle.

Nadara heard a sharp whoosh and felt a prick of pain on the back of her thigh. She contorted her body and spotted a dart sticking out of her leg. As she faded from consciousness, she saw a Silth lowering a blow gun and smiling. He had dark skin and hather with a shock of red at the temples below a top hat, and he wore a coat with tails hanging down to his boots. She heard odd tinkling music as the world went black.

When she awoke, she thought she heard the music again. She tried to focus. Bound and gagged, she was lying on her back on a stone floor, and the same face from earlier was smiling at her. The music seemed to be coming from the... from the figure's hat. Yes, the hat. She gasped as the hat's top abruptly opened and out sprang a small stuffed monkey. The smiling face laughed wickedly and moved out of sight.

She tested her ropes, but they were so tightly tied that working out of them was impossible. She turned her head to the left and could see an unmoving Loana, also bound and gagged. On the right was Kirstn, wiggling in her ropes. Across her friend she could see a number of figures moving around. Top Hat was talking with the female she'd seen come from the building. That one also had goggles. Her dreads and arms were wrapped in wires, and even bigger wires ran from the tank on her back to some device on her wrist. When she saw Nadara staring at her, she broke off her conversation and stomped over to her. Bending over, she glared at Nadara through black eyes with white irises.

"What are you staring at?" She gave Nadara a nearly rib-breaking kick and stalked away.

Nadara gasped in pain, and it took her several moments to focus again. She heard others talking, but she could see only one more. This one was considerably shorter than the usual Silth and certainly defied the conventional beauty most of the race projected. Standing alone and slightly hunched, she had a plump face, completely black eyes, and mostly green hather with yellow and brown highlights. She wore a tunic and dangling gold earrings.

Abruptly she began throwing out orders. "M-m-m-make sure the ropes are tight. Remember, they can still fire a Faerie bolt at you even when they are restrained, so don't walk at their feet. Get them ready to move in a few minutes."

She walked over to the row of bound Tiki Crew members. "Who's in charge of your group?" Nadara couldn't see who she was speaking to but whomever it was gave no answer. "Who's in charge?" When again no answer came, Nadara heard someone being kicked repeatedly and, "Who?" Vic cursed into his gag.

Nadara made as loud a noise as she could. The black eyes turned toward her, and the creature moved gracelessly over to Nadara's side.

"You're in charge?"

Nadara nodded and choked as the gag was ripped from her mouth.

"I am Rangi. Queen of the New Zealand Silth. Which of you has the power to transport yourself?"

"What? Transport?"

"The Faerie power to m-m-m-move from one place to another without flying."

"None of us. The WSC hasn't allowed anyone except the shamans like Aran and a few warriors to have that power."

"As I suspected. What I can catch can't give m-m-m-me what I want. If it could, I probably couldn't catch it. So, I will have to m-m-make someone give it to me voluntarily." Rangi eyed the prone figures around her. "We'll see if anyone cares about any of this lot. If not, we'll get rid of them and get m-more until we find someone they do care about." She spun around. "Jeeter, come here."

The reddish-skinned Silth had dark pink mutton chops, white around his eyes, and what Nadara had learned were Maori tattoos on his face and arms. He had a rounded light pink crest, a white shirt with puffy sleeves, a bow tie, and a bowler hat. Bands on each arm held multiple darts.

"I need information," she told him. "I want to know about Aran, the WSC, its plans. Get it for m-m-me, and fast. *Whatever it takes.*"

As Rangi walked away, Jeeter looked at Nadara sadly. "Well, this isn't going to be any fun for you luv."

2

Casius (Silth)

Reverend Jeremiah Tobias, tall and molasses-colored, sat ramrod straight on the ground in the public square. The white collar he wore with his mud-stained black suit was limp with sweat. Other than two large gold rings and gold bracelet on his left hand, he was dressed without ornamentation.

Casius watched him from the main council house. Two of Tobias's assistants flanked him, and the two other members of his entourage shifted nervously sixty feet away at the edge of the colony.

The old Silth colony in Costa Rica was now world headquarters for New Faerie, having been restored by the Newfies who'd followed Casius as he left into self-imposed exile. When Aran's powers were fully revealed and the Faeries confirmed as their source, he and everyone else had assumed that would be the end of New Faerie. But it hadn't worked out that way. New followers joined the movement every day, driven by distrust of the Silth leadership's plan to work with the Humans, or by fear of the Faeries, or simply by their longing for someone else to tell them how to make sense of all the changes happening around them. Casius sent those out to recruit others. They'd been particularly successful among the Silth who couldn't understand Human language and who had never learned to read. These Silth knew the world was changing, leaving them behind.

Casius spent several months deciding how to proceed. They could separate themselves from the other Silth and hope that when the Faeries came, they'd be able to recognize that the Newfies had kept their faith and hadn't opposed them. The Newfies could be more aggressive and help the Faeries by operating as a resistance group inside the Silth kingdom, hoping the Faeries would reward their service. But Casius had never been big on hope. Faith was one thing, hope another. He had faith that if he and his followers served the Faeries to their best ability, they'd be rewarded with true Faerie powers and join the Faerie host. But what was that service? Casius had decided it wasn't passive. It was up to New Faerie to disrupt the plan to oppose the Faeries. They'd do all in their power to undermine the WSC's preparations for the Faerie arrival and its cooperation with the Humans.

Finally, he'd decided to begin this undertaking by the contradictory act of conspiring with a Human. He saw Tobias eying the Faerie statue at the head of the square, an ornate carving in a wood hard to come by these days. Humans had harvested most of it and called it *iron wood*. The statue stood almost seven feet tall, which meant it towered over the Silth but was only life-sized for Tobias. The fruits and flowers surrounding it had been offered in homage. Tobias was making no attempt to hide his repulsion. Casius knew how the reverend would have reacted to last night's culmination of the week-long Festival of the Faerie. The bonfire had blazed tall in the middle of the square, firelight making the bodies of the surrounding dancers magical. The music, high flutes mimicking the calls of the birds, the drums—like the thunder of the jungle storms, and the other instruments making the sounds of the streams and the sounds of the forest, had worked the dancers into a fever pitch before they disappeared into the surrounding darkness. Casius knew better than to interfere with this aspect of Silth culture, but he was sure Tobias wouldn't approve.

Casius had picked out one of his finest Silth-made robes and wore no Human-produced materials. He knew he couldn't look much more foreign to the Human.

Tobias looked up at Casius as he emerged into the dappled gray light of the rain forest canopy embracing the colony's buildings. Casius wasn't sure whether Tobias was a brave man or simply as desperate as he was to change the direction of events. Whichever it was, he'd been willing to meet here in the rain forest with few others around. Casius suspected Tobias kept his delegation small for the same reason Casius had emptied out the colony. *If you're going to make a deal with the enemy, it's best done in secret, so others don't know you're someone who will deal with the enemy to get what you want.*

Casius hovered at eye-level. "Reverend Tobias, it's good of you to join me. Welcome to our home. You honor us with your presence." He flew to a nearby wooden balcony, beneath the roof made of reeds, cane, and a mix of mud, and slightly higher than eye-level to Tobias.

Casius had learned all he could about the man before his people had reached out to him by phone. He found the reverend was respected for all the good he and his congregation had done in their overseas and domestic missions, and in particular their post-disaster relief, but widely criticized for his insistence they'd provide benefits only to those who joined in their belief. This aggressive position was different than most of the Human missionary forces that attracted followers through their actions. They would insist only on the opportunity to share their beliefs as the price for help without requiring conversion. The New Faerie approach was similar to the latter groups. Access to food, tools and clothing from the public storehouses of the New Faerie required a commitment of three to five years of public service, and work on some construction or education projects During that time an individual would be exposed to New Faerie teachings almost constantly. Conversion was a common outcome but not required. Casius had also learned Tobias considered the Silth to be actual demons, the evilest of creatures in his religion.

Still, Tobias spoke politely. "It is you who honor us with your gracious invitation to your home. We were flattered and surprised to receive it. The caller gave us good instructions on how to find you. She spoke of the need to explore our mutual interests in the future and in the Faerie arrival." Tobias pointedly looked at the empty square and buildings. "She led me to believe New Faerie had a large congregation."

Casius chuckled. "There are, in fact, thousands of Silth in the New Faerie congregation. But I think today's discussion is one best kept to as few ears as possible."

Tobias leaned over and whispered to each of his assistants. Without a word, they stood and joined the others. "I was on my way down here to close our Costa Rica mission and escort our people back to our temple grounds in Detroit. Commercial planes won't fly much longer, so we're pulling our missionaries back home for end times. We have a world congregation far too large to house at the temple, but at least we can bring our missionaries back."

"Water? Or cocoa? We trade for the cocoa, from other Silth colonies." When Tobias declined with a wave of his hand, Casius continued. "If I understand correctly, your followers believe the arrival of the Faerie will be a good thing—the arrival of angels heralding the beginning of the ascension of the chosen into Heaven."

Tobias had cocked his head slightly, as though listening for derision in the summary. Finding none, he answered, "A simplified version. But essentially correct."

Casius went on. "Would it surprise you to learn I essentially agree with you, at least on the desired events? We too welcome the arrival of the Faeries and are distressed the Silth leadership has chosen to wage war on those who would save us. And I hope I won't offend you, but while I have nothing against Humans personally, I don't believe the social intermingling of our races is beneficial for either."

Tobias's eyes narrowed. "You do realize, and I, too, mean no disrespect, but in our belief the Paerries are demons."

"As are the Humans in ours. But I'm told there's a saying common to both our cultures—*the enemy of my enemy is my friend*. What if you could use the *demons* who agree with you, and we could use the *demons* who agree with us, to stop the foolish in both our races?"

As Tobias considered what he'd just heard, Casius watched the sweat trickling down into the reverend's collar. Casius appreciated that the man hadn't instantly responded—he had less faith in decisions quickly and easily made. What he was proposing, working with a demon to overcome worse demons and your own kind, would make his own people squirm if they knew. He had no doubt Tobias was thinking the same thing about his congregation.

Casius was struck by the difference between this meeting and the one with Aran and Storng a few days earlier. They'd also come to the old colony, though they referred to it by its ancient name, Anackma, not by the name used by New Faerie—Ianza—which meant "resolution" in Silth. Unlike Tobias, demon though he may be, there was little deference on their part. Instead, an ultimatum had been masked as an overture—join us and practice your beliefs quietly, or oppose us and we'll take away everything. Casius, corrected himself.

Only Storng gave him a choice. Aran made it clear he believed Casius had been Thest's informer and had set him up to die at the general's hand. While he denied knowing who Thest was, in fact Casius had often provided the Faeries with information about the shamans. His contact was, however, a one-eyed Faerie called Fod. He denied, truthfully, he'd been the source of the information given to Thest the night Aran was attacked.

The clouds were moving into the trees around them and a fine mist had begun to fall when Tobias finally spoke. Wiping moisture from his face, he said, "I can support an alliance where my people suffer no harm and their future is benefited. Since working together doesn't require either of us to agree to the beliefs of the other, I see no hypocrisy there. I'm not so certain the bulk of my congregation would understand the subtleties in such an alliance, however. I also wonder what it is you think we can do together that each of us cannot do alone."

"Yes, a small circle of true believers." Casius flew down from the balcony and hovered at eye-level. "We must stop Humans and Silth from working together to fight the Faeries. It shouldn't be hard to fan the flames of distrust between two such different races with such different goals. I will work to accomplish this among the Silth, and you could do so among the Humans."

"I'm already using all of my platforms—pulpit, radio, TV. and social media—to accomplish what you say."

"And there's no more you could do?"

"Sure, there is. Much more. I can hire PR firms, lobbyists, lawyers. Start political PACs and flood the media with advertising. It would only take more money. Right now, I'm spending most of our resources trying to keep my congregants alive and preparing for the end times."

Casius held up a finger and flew inside the dwelling attached to the balcony on which he'd stood. He returned, pulling a heavy bag along the floor, and motioned for Tobias to take it. With a surprised grunt at its weight, Tobias lifted it and returned to his seat. He looked in and then back at Casius, mouth agape.

"Diamonds, emeralds, and rubies still have significant value in your society?" Casius said softly. "Those are yours, provided you commit to using their proceeds entirely to undermine the Human-Silth alliance. I don't know what *PR firms* and *PACs* are. But if they can be bought, will this be enough to do so?"

"Of course." Tobias patted the bag. "But you don't know me well enough. Why would you take this risk?"

"If we are a few years away from the end time, that's just a bag of rocks. They'll have no value when the Faerie come. I give them to you because you'll use them to get others to do the things both of us need done. As to whether you'll do what you promise, I take that on faith." Casius added, "We also need to establish some way to communicate. I have followers among the leadership of the new Silth government and its military. They'll get me information I can share with you to help in the campaign."

"I can get you a cell phone that'll work from here." Tobias looked up at the gray sky. "Together with a crank charger that'll let you generate enough electricity for it. Solar chargers aren't much use right now."

"The leadership of the Silth are already using these accursed devices to talk to their Human counterparts. I've avoided using them myself." Casius landed next to Tobias but looked off into the mist.

"This is a hard choice today. I think there'll be many more in the coming days. Among our people these choices will pit brother against brother, and there'll be death. But there's too much at stake to proceed without risk."

Tobias stared grimly at the clouds filling the open spaces in the amphitheater and obscuring his view of his lieutenants, even though they stood nearby. "I am but a servant, tending the vineyard of my master, watering and feeding its crops.... There are days that bring me the joy of the harvest, and days in which my job is to deal with the pests and the creatures who would ravage it."

PENFIELD (HUMAN)

Penfield watched President Catherine Percrow step around her desk to shake hands with the Brazilian ambassador, Joao Luiz Sousa. Sousa's meaty paw engulfed her hand, and he went through the obligatory honorifics with pleasant gusto. He and the President had known each other for many years, and like many he'd openly admired her and her administration.

After providing an update on the status of his wife, several children, and grandchildren, Sousa asked about the President's cat, which in the absence of husband and children, the media had portrayed as the center of her domestic attention. In truth, Penfield knew, the cat, while loved, played second to the true center of the President's attention—her work.

She said, "Joao Luiz, I believe you know of Dr. Irvin Penfield from State."

"Dr. Penfield, my pleasure," he said as he shook Penfield's hand. "I've heard good things about you. You are Assistant Secretary for Conflict and Stabilization Operations?"

The President interjected, "He's also my new Ambassador-at-Large for Non-Human Affairs. Which is why I asked him to join us today, given the subject you told me you wanted to discuss."

"Ah, very well." The Ambassador cleared his throat. "Then I must embarrass myself and confirm your security clearance. The matter we must discuss today is extremely delicate...and I do not know your internal procedures all that well ...." He shrugged and looked at the floor. "In my country, it is unlikely anyone short of Secretary would have sufficient clearance. My apologies for my rudeness."

"No apologies are necessary, Mr. Ambassador," Penfield assured him. "Your concern is only prudent. The Secretary has her hands full right now with the refugee crisis and the destabilization of the food supply. I'm cleared for all matters relating to the Silth or the Trow, including military and security matters."

"Very well." The President motioned for them to sit as she took her seat in front of the desk. "Perhaps I'm simply delaying getting to the meat of the matter," the Ambassador said as he took his seat. "As you might imagine, our President does not find the current Silth occupation of our country acceptable. Not only is it a violation of our sovereign rights, at an enormous scale, but, also, we do not trust them. We don't know that they won't expand this violation as they consolidate their power. Consequently, we've determined we must drive them out this week. We'd like for the United States to join us in this effort."

The President and Penfield sat absorbing the Ambassador's words. Penfield was not surprised, and after a long silence began the line of questions the President had authorized.

"You call them *invaders,* but as we understand it, they've been in your country longer than you have. Isn't this really more of an *indigenous population* problem?"

Sousa scoffed. "They're not Human, so it is more of a *trans-boundary invasive species* problem. They have no rights in our country nor under any international treaty."

"Then as a trans-boundary problem, one replicated in multiple locations around the world, shouldn't you take this up with the U.N.

instead of taking unilateral action?"

"The U.S. would not tolerate such occupation, nor would you ask another's permission to defend your soil."

"These are unique circumstances, however," Penfield pointed out. "How do you expect to gain the Silth's assistance in quieting the volcanoes and defeating the Trow if we attack them now?"

"Our intention is to take them as captives and force them to provide assistance. Not only can we address the volcanoes and the Faeries, if there even really are such things, but we also can utilize their abilities to produce new types of products. This will lead to a new age for mankind. And that is why we offer this opportunity for you to join us."

Penfield looked down at the floor. After a few more moments of silence, the President spoke. "If I recall correctly, Brazil was the last nation in the Americas to abolish slavery, but it did abolish it. What I hear you proposing is to enslave the Silth for our benefit. You might imagine that, as my ancestors were among the last Humans defined as not being human enough to have rights, I'm a little skeptical of your approach."

The Ambassador stammered an apology and returned to the theme of violated sovereignty, but the President interrupted him. "We understand your country's position, and we appreciate your reaching out to us with this... opportunity. I'll give your suggestion all due consideration. But I would hope for the sake of a world that may depend on the assistance of the Silth, you will not take any rash action. It seems to me there's still plenty of room for diplomacy before there is any reason to spill blood—Human or Silth." The Ambassador's departure was frostier than his arrival.

President Percrow had ascended first through the ranks of litigators at the District of Columbia's office of the Public Defenders and then through the Justice department as one of their most aggressive tacticians. With a multicultural past, she'd been raised on a reservation and embraced her Santee Sioux heritage. Penfield had heard her complain about being first before, first Native American woman to head this, or be the deputy of that. She told him it was a heavy burden to stand for both your race and your gender and know anything you did wrong would likely hinder both. Now she was the first Native American President, woman or man, and perhaps the most powerful person in the world. She was one of the most unflappable, tactical individuals Penfield knew. Still, when she was angry, her voice gave it away by rising an octave, and her ever-present laugh would take on a cynical note.

She shook her head. "I expected something like this, but not so quickly, when we're all so exposed and there's so much at stake. We don't even know the full range of Silth powers, yet these people want to attack them and make them slaves? Never mind that if they are telling the truth about the Trow, and Homeland is indicating they are, we need them. And *gonnamake them slaves* ... does this man not have eyes?" She pointed to the chocolate hue of her arm, her heritage a rich cocktail of races.

"Not to defend him, but with the four million slaves Brazil ended up with at the end of slavery, the major indigenous peoples, and their multiple European populations, the Brazilians have done a very good job of moving past race as a social marker. They have perhaps created a better melting pot than the U.S.'s stew of backgrounds. He might not have even thought of how that would sound to you."

"Oh, he plainly didn't think about it, or he wouldn't have brought that shaggy dog in here. How are we going to play this? Obviously one reason Joao Luiz came here today was to give them cover if it goes wrong."

Penfield looked around her office as he considered her question. Two large paintings dominated the room, one by Georgia O'Keefe and the other by Jarrod Da. Personal photographs of the President with various politicians and celebrities filled the flat surfaces of the room interspersed with the many civic awards she'd received over decades of public service. An impressive bronze of three wolves caught his eye.

"We can't back the Silth into a corner this early," he finally said. "Before we really understand what's going on. They don't seem to be hurting anything on the ground—they're protecting the areas they've identified. Reports of how they're handling the people indicate they're serious but not severe. This is just Brazilian pride. Given everything else going on, there isn't time for this. We need to know more about the Trow and the Silth's powers. They may be our only hope."

Catherine Percrow had become President just a few months before the volcanoes had gone off. She'd arrived with a big agenda for social change while maintaining the robust economy she'd inherited. All her plans had changed in a single twenty-four-hour period as she learned the future of humanity was in doubt. The news made its way into the public, but few things played out the way dooms-dayers expected. As the skies clouded over and the scientists started calculating the effects of the volcanoes, the predicted rush of refugees from the cities into the countryside failed to occur. In fact, everyone quickly realized that the cities were the better places to be.

Cities rapidly turned every parking deck into a grow-light

driven agricultural operation. They might not have a wide variety of food, but major cities were able to feed their populations. As the crops withered in the countryside, those who had hunkered down for their dystopian survivalist future were surprised to find themselves packing up and heading to a nearby city with resources. Because of the storage of the last crops in the fields and early rationing, most of the developed world had not yet suffered starvation or the diseases that accompanied undernourishment. Their economies had been flattened. Air travel had been constrained for months, as had much truck, train, and automobile transportation. As filtering practices adapted to better protect engines, some transport returned, but moving stuff around was still difficult.

The biggest impact, however, had been at the borders of developed countries. Percrow had arrived in office an advocate of immigration as part of what made America great. After the volcanoes erupted, she had to oversee the largest deployment of troops the U.S. had ever seen to protect the borders along the southern boundary of the U.S. and throughout the Gulf of Mexico states. To everyone's surprise, the cities were working to help feed the countryside and the developed world to feed those at their borders. The problem was there was simply not enough food, and conditions in poor countries were rapidly deteriorating. Diseases were spreading. People were dying.

"I'll call Abriana," the President said, spinning a pen on her desk. "She's a reasonable person. She may not be able to keep her military from moving on this, though. This feels like a macho thing. Something her predecessor would have done. He'd have burned down the forest—what little he left behind. They've been insulted by these little people taking a big chunk of their country. If she can't stop this, what next?"

"I think we should let the Silth know through some back channel, so they can be ready. It'll be a prudent way to stay in their good graces while we see what kind of power they have. Needless to say, our fingerprints can't be on this, but someone better build some bridges to them."

"We need to think further than that. Let's assume they have the power they claim and all the Brazilians will do is piss them off. What next? Joao Luiz was right that we can't be sure of the Silth's intentions. We don't know what they really think about Humans. I got the impression we aren't universally liked. We don't know the extent of their real power or their actual relationship with the Trow. Just avoiding this crisis isn't going to get us where we need to be."

"I'll work on that part and get back to you." As he left, all he could think was, *the world isn't ready for this, and neither am I. But I'm glad Catherine's at the helm of this ship as it takes on water. We might survive.*

CHAPTER 4

1

Joss (Human)

Flying was scary these days. You didn't worry about fuel—you worried whether the engines could breathe.

Joss had watched a news program on the volcanoes' impact on airlines. Many had put special filters on their engines, but experts continued to debate their effectiveness. It had become commonplace for flights to be forced to land short of their destinations because of ash-clogged engines. She'd watched one video taken inside a plane as it fell from 37,000 feet to 13,000 after all four engines stopped. Today she was relying on the second of two airlines to have gotten it right.

The first leg of her trip took her from San Jose, Costa Rica to Miami, Florida, and the next on to Manus, Brazil. The trip logistics had been a challenge. Fewer planes flew these days, meaning fewer choices and more competition for seats. Night flights no longer existed and the daytime ones were subject to frequent rescheduling as the Volcanic Ash Advisory Center calculated the current disbursement of the ash plumes. Planes had to fly in the seams between plumes where the air-borne ash wouldn't choke the engines or slag the turbines with melted and re-solidified ash. In addition to those maintenance costs, there were increased maintenance costs from the ash erosion of the props, the need to replace cockpit glass every few flights, and the need to remove ash from air and water lines after every flight. Flying once again became a luxury, available only at a premium price. Seven months ago, this flight would have cost around $2,000, but now it cost $20,000. For once in her life, however, Joss didn't have to worry about money—Kate and Storng had quietly converted a large amount of gold and jewels into a gigantic pile of cash. They'd used multiple markets and had taken the money in cash, so it literally was in a big pile which they deposited as needed. Not only was Joss flying, she was in business class.

On the way to Miami, Joss had been trying to mentally keep the plane in the air, but she was distracted by something else. Distracted was too mild a word. Terrified? Angry? Determined? All the above. She'd been groggy as she made her way off the plane that morning and headed toward the next waiting area. As she stumbled into the bathroom, she hadn't noticed the woman following her. Joss assumed she'd followed her, maybe she'd waited there for her. Joss stepped up to the sink, and a woman in a plain gray pant suit walked to the sink next to her, choosing it instead of the ten empty sinks on the wall in front of them. Adrenaline wiped away Joss's sleepiness. In the last two weeks, she'd been approached by at least six government operatives for different agencies of different countries, all hoping to recruit her to spy on the Silth. She'd joked with Storng she was holding out for the right price.

The woman spoke to Joss's wary reflection in the mirror. "I'm not here to recruit you. I'm here to warn you."

Joss sighed and said nothing as she shook her wet hands over the sink and headed for the paper towel dispenser. Empty. She dried her hands on her jeans.

When the agent moved a little closer, Joss backed away an equal measure. "You're being followed by Brazilian Federal Police agents—their version of the FBI. They'll arrest you in Brazil after you're away from the airport and the press. In a week or so, Brazilian troops will attack the Brazilian Refuge. Their intent is to capture the Silth, force them to help Humans stop the volcanoes and the Trow, and return the area to Brazilian control. They also hope to make them create new manufactured products. The United States is not part of this plan. We hope you will convey to your friends that we opposed it as inappropriate. Whatever their response is, we encourage them to be as temperate as possible to leave open future negotiations."

Joss's mouth had fallen open. "Slaves? They want to make them slaves?"

"The U.S. government doesn't support this action. We've tried to talk them out of it, but the Brazilians see the Silth as an occupying force."

"More like an indigenous people asserting their sovereignty," Joss replied, remembering the many hours of discussion she and others had before the announcement had been made at the U.N. They'd even brought in lawyers to try out their arguments.

"Well, okay, but how's that worked out for *indigenous peoples?*" the woman said as she touched up her lipstick. When another woman came in, the agent tossed Joss a "Have a great day" and disappeared out the door. Moments later, Joss followed and spotted her hurrying down a long corridor.

She spent the flight from Miami reviewing their plans. The Brazilian position wasn't unanticipated, but she had hoped the Humans would be smarter, better able to accept what was best for all.

The *Caretakers,* what the mixed group of Humans and Silth managing the refuges called themselves, knew someone would test their resolve to protect these areas, and it was unlikely countries would simply cede them to Silth control. Selfishly, Joss had hoped one of the other areas would be tested, not hers. She had little doubt the Silth could defend the refuge. Her frustration came from knowing how much had to be done—she didn't need this thrown into the mix.

She ran through the scenarios and tried to still her mind as it leapt from problem to problem, drawing on the meditation exercises she'd begun in rehab and continued since. She thought through the steps of her arrival in Brazil. Today would be the last time she came in through the commercial airport because a private landing strip inside the Brazil Refuge would soon be complete so they could avoid the commercial airport. The strip had been the subject of extended debate as the Silth questioned why one of their first actions should be to bulldoze trees and build within their precious rain forest acres. In the end they'd agreed to put the strip on the already cleared land of one of the plantations operating within the refuge. Many Humans preferred to skip the planes and simply blip with one of the Silth shamans. The queasiness the blip caused made it Joss's least favorite means of transportation, but it might become her only option. Planes were in danger of becoming a thing of the past.

She tried to put the impromptu bathroom meeting out of her mind and distract herself by enjoying the last few moments of milky sunlight before they began the decent into cloud-covered Manaus. She wasn't worried about being arrested, first because she thought it was pretty unlikely to happen if she could make it to the refuge, and second … well, it wouldn't be the first time. *Still, a Brazilian jail might be pretty dangerous. No, put it out of your mind.*

Once on the ground, she grabbed her carry-on bags—a roll-aboard suitcase, and a big canvas backpack. She easily cleared customs. There were almost no tourists, so the lines were short. In fact, the big and modern airport was nearly empty, its shops and most food niches closed. She looked around, but airport personnel, several cab drivers, and a few reuniting families were all she saw. No one stood out as a Brazilian agent. She wondered if it could all be part of an elaborate recruitment effort—perhaps the Miami agent had lied and no confrontation was planned. But no, that didn't make any sense as the agent hadn't tried to recruit her.

Watching for her contact, she saw a young man and woman standing near the exit doors. Both wore green camp shirts and khaki shorts, the semi-official uniform of the Caretakers. The woman held a cardboard sign with Joss's name scrawled on it in big, black marker.

"That would be me," she said, immediately drawing relieved smiles and friendly handshakes from the pair.

Then the young man said, "Oh, but wait." He pulled out his phone and looked at the screen, then looked back at her. "Yes, it's you."

They introduced themselves as Maria Luis and Tonho, grabbed her bags, and hustled out the door, Joss trotting to keep up as they stepped out into the cool gray day. Tonho handed the bags to another man to be checked for bombs, bugs, and drug plants. She and the rest of the Caretakers had many enemies who thought they were traitors to Humans, as well as governments hoping to compromise them. Their legal status was uncertain. Technically they'd broken no laws. The Silth had negotiated state status with the U.N., but none of the countries where they'd established refuges were recognizing their status, and most, like Brazil, treated it as an illegal occupation. While it wasn't illegal to have contact with the Silth, it was against the law to aid them in their occupation. Because no one knew what the Caretakers did, no case had yet been made against them. They had been harassed but not arrested. They hadn't taken up arms against the state. All these things would change today, Joss thought.

"Is everything ok?" she asked, checking their worried expressions.

Maria Luis slanted a look at Tonho, who shrugged. "We don't know. Something feels off," she said. Her English was very good, which Joss appreciated since she had no Portuguese. "Some men seemed to be following us, but when we held up the sign with your name they disappeared. Probably nothing." As they climbed into a muddy Land Cruiser she continued, "Picked up some food for you. We have a long drive today, so if it's okay we'll eat in the car. We got banda detambaqui, the fish dish for which Brazil is famous, manioc cakes, and tacaca, a shrimp soup. Some sugar cane juice. They didn't have any pamonha, Tonho's favorite. Can't get any green corn."

Joss thought about what the agent said in the bathroom and the various spy movies she'd seen. Once Maria Luis and Tonho were identified, the agents could've come out and bugged their car. She considered pulling them aside before they got in the car, but then she remembered all the movies with guys wearing headphones and holding those high-tech-looking listening cones. She wondered about texting them, but her phone could be bugged. She had an app that would send an encrypted text, but it could only be read if the receiving party also had the app.

"Hang on a second," she said before they pulled out of the parking lot. She checked her phone and saw they were still within the internet range of the airport. Maria Luis was behind the wheel, so she handed her phone to Tonho.

"Can you download this app right now please?" She pointed to an app enabling encrypted texts and emails.

Without comment but with raised eyebrows, moments later he'd downloaded the program and set up his user name. Joss typed in a summary of the part of the bathroom conversation dealing with her arrest and the suggestion the car might be bugged. Tonho read it, gave a terse nod, and handed the phone to Maria Luis, who, reading it over the steering wheel, also nodded. Neither looked intimidated, only determined.

As Maria Luis navigated out of the airport, Tonho opened the food, giving some to Joss and eating some himself. He placed food in Maria Luis's open mouth, and she laughed when he claimed she'd bitten him.

They discussed the weather and how the Brazil Refuge was managing the Human populations within its boundaries. Maria Luis said all the poachers, illegal and legal logging and mining operations, and illegal homesteaders had been removed. The homesteaders had been given the option of operating edge farms. Clearing for cattle operations had been stopped, and the existing cattle were not being replaced as their owners drew down their numbers. The hardest interactions had been with the isolated tribes. Not the ones that still did subsistence hunting—those were little different in their impact than the cougars and jaguars. Some of the tribes had developed a *bush meat* trade through which they furnished surrounding villages with meat from jungle animals in trade for different commodities such as sugar and rice. They hunted with guns, not bows or darts. The Silth were used to them and treated them like any other jungle predators, but the biologists worried about their impact on the other species. The Silth gave them a choice, to return to ancestral practice—hunting with traditional weapons, not guns, and hunting for themselves, not others—or leave their ancient home. To the Silth's surprise, the tribes elected to fight. The fight was one-sided, and the Silth removed the guns and a few of the tribal leaders hoping the other members would not force their hand further. Where to put the members they removed was the Silth's challenge, one that would be exacerbated if they had to remove the entire tribe.

As they talked, every so often Joss checked over her shoulder, watching for a tail. They'd traveled about thirty miles from the airport and were on a stretch of road where she could see several miles behind them. No one was there. She relaxed some. *Maybe the agent had been wrong or maybe someone changed their mind.*

A helicopter swept in low, coming over the road from above the trees just as the car was going around a blind curve. Ahead, five cars, blue lights flashing, and a transport truck blocked the way, and armed officers held guns and rifles pointed at the Land Cruiser. Maria Luis stopped the car but kept it running. The helicopter landed on the road behind them, blocking escape, and an amplified voice told them in Portuguese to "turn the car off and step out with your hands in the air." The demand was repeated in English and Spanish.

As Joss angrily fumbled for the door handle, Tonho said, "No, no, wait."

Outside the amplified voice repeated its instructions. The three raised their hands so they could be seen through the window. Officers moved closer to the car, and the voice added a threat to the instructions.

Joss jumped as blue bolts flew from the tree line and dropped all the officers close to the car. Most of the remaining officers fired into the trees, approximately where the bolts had originated, but a couple reflexively fired their rifles toward the Cruiser. A blue shield appeared just in front of their bumper, and they flinched as the shots bounced off the shield. They heard shouts behind them and whipped around to see the helicopter's occupants fleeing as it was struck by blue bolts from the sky. The copter burst into flames a few seconds later.

Shouts came from the front as the vehicles suffered the same fate. When the officers ran from where the bolts originated toward the trees on the other side of the road, a series of stunning bolts from within these trees quickly dropped them. Maria Luis steered between two burning cars and tore down the road. It took a moment for Joss to realize she still had her hands raised. As she lowered them, she tried to speak, but Tonho put his finger to his lips. She leaned back in the seat and started her deep breathing techniques. Before long she was asleep.

2

Joss (Human)

Joss awoke with a start. She'd been dreaming of the attack and her hands were again in surrender position. The Cruiser swayed down a rutted dirt road and through dense jungle.

Tonho turned and grinned. "Almost there. Road's pretty bumpy the rest of the way in. You hungry? We've still got some not-very-warm-anymore food left. It'll be a while before dinner."

Nibbling on manioc cake and sipping juice, she watched the jungle slide by and reflected on how strange life had become. She felt safest when away from *civilization* and here in the jungle. The government of Brazil was trying to capture her. Her freedom, maybe her life, had just been saved by bird people who used magic they had learned from Faeries. She was responsible for the success of this refuge, and the rest of them as well. She led a team of scientists and wildlife experts working on how best to operate the sanctuaries. If their work didn't succeed, most of the world's wildlife would not survive the current crisis, either dying from starvation in the lands without sun or eaten by Humans for their own survival. If this effort to save the rest of the Earth's occupants failed, the Silth would not stop the volcanoes, and Humans would disappear as well.

She hunched lower in the backseat. When her sponsor worried the stress would cost Joss her sobriety, Joss laughingly dismissed her concern, thinking it unlikely that after almost a decade she would fall off the wagon. Now she wasn't so sure.

After another half hour of bouncing through the jungle, while the gray day was turning dark, they entered a clearing. This was the first time Joss had seen Silth homes, the small houses built in the branches and the balconies in front of tree holes. There were over a hundred of them in the big trees surrounding the clearing which contained around twenty Human structures.

"This is the main camp, with ten more spread out through the refuge," Maria Luis told her. "It's not too bad. Food's good. Mostly vegetables, some of the more plentiful local fish. Everyone has been too busy to socialize much, but there's been some time to get to know the Silth. They're great!" She winked at Tanho and they both laughed.

"This is your new base of *world-wide* operations," Maria Luis said as she pulled in front of a plank building with a thatch roof. "The Silth helped build it." Joss eyed the small building with the multiple antennas sticking out through the roof, wires running off to what she assumed was a generator. "It's one of the buildings with a composting toilet, so count yourself lucky you don't have to fight the tarantulas for a seat at the outhouse."

Tanho pointed to the largest of the Human buildings. "We eat and meet there. Dinner is in an hour. Best to be there at the beginning when the cooks put it out. It goes fast on the nights when it's good."

While Tanho moved Joss's bags from the administration building, where the other truck had dropped them off to her cabin, Maria Luis showed Joss around. She demonstrated how the composting toilet worked, telling her when there would be hot water and when the power went off, and explaining daily life in the camp. After they left, Joss leaned forward on the edge of her bed, head in hands. This was so similar to another rustic setting she had experienced as a youth

... rehab. The group meals. The interactions with people. Here too would be all the drama of interpersonal interactions, including those involving an entire new race of beings. And an impending attack. She couldn't even grasp the idea of an attack. People might die. People she was now responsible for.

She lay back on the bed and tried to chill, to meditate, but instead she spent most of the next hour reviewing the parade of worries. She'd be here for a while. She already missed Kate and her parrots in Costa Rica. Stress had always been her biggest trigger. But how could she refuse this job? She knew her most important qualification was that she was one of the few Humans the Silth trusted. If the world was about to end and all you loved was going to be destroyed, what risk wouldn't you take? She had what the psychologists had called an *addictive personality*. She combined that in her teen years with a yearning to explore. She'd been addicted to alcohol and cigarettes, explored every drug imaginable. It had almost killed her. She didn't understand how some people, particularly rock stars and celebrities, could spend years immersed in those addictions and come out unharmed. They were armed with great stories and deep wisdom and living to a ripe old age. It had taken her years to build a way to make it through the day, and she'd done a good job. She had a thousand responses to the thousand triggers every day held.

Alcohol would calm her nerves—she knew that from experience. And she could stop with just one ... tonight. Tomorrow it would be two and then the quick slide back into the old ways. No one would notice at first. She held her liquor well. And she was "the man" now. No one would tell her not to because she was in charge. That struck her as pretty funny. She could barely hold her life together, but there was no denying she was in charge. If nothing else, the clutch of communications equipment in the corner of her room reminded her she was supposed to learn what worked and didn't work for the refuges and share the best practices with all of them. She already had video and phone calls scheduled for the next week. Another wall had a map of the world with each of the refuges carefully drawn.

As she started across the compound toward the common room, she remembered how often in the past she had challenged whoever was in charge. Being in charge sounded like you could make things happen instead of being knocked this way and that by events. How long would it take everyone to figure out there was no way she could be a leader? Would someone ask her about her qualifications? How her degree in psychology qualified her to lead the world in managing this precious attempt at saving its wildlife? Could she answer "I knew a man?" *Well, actually it was more like, "I knew a birdman."*

She had already shared many meals with Silth groups, so when she walked into the cafeteria, she wasn't overly surprised by the scene. True, she'd never seen this scale of interaction before. There were easily fifty Humans in the room—Joss realized some buildings must be bunkhouses with many beds—and a good hundred Silth. She counted fourteen tables, each big enough for ten Humans, and a two-sided serving counter ran along one wall. Mostly the Silth occupied tables of their own, but a couple of the tables were mixed. Excited Human voices, some speaking Portuguese and others English, combined with Silth squeaks, whistles and laughter made the room loud.

Joss was a little late, but the buffet was still well-stocked, Humans going through one side of the serving area and Silth on the other. One side displayed nuts, cut-up fruits and raw vegetables, and some unidentifiable substances, while the other held cooked meats, potatoes, rice, vegetables, and a few unknown substances as well. The Silth clutched small trays as they flew to their tables.

Before Joss could pick up a Human-sized tray, she heard Maria Luis yell "Jocelyn!" The room hushed, and she walked toward the mixed table group, her cheeks burning with embarrassment. Three Silth ate cross-legged on the table top, and six Humans occupied chairs. A foil-covered plate of food was in front of her, along with a glass of water... and one of wine. The noise resumed when she sat.

Maria Luis introduced the others at the table. Most of the names and functions were a blur despite Joss's effort to pay attention. Her eyes kept cutting to the wine. The last introduction, however, drew her out of her distraction.

"This is Krackle, shaman for the Silth here. We're her guests."

Krackle's long green hather hung in dreadlocks filled with small feathers held in place by loops of copper wire. She wore a mix of traditionally made Silth clothing and Human artifacts. Her dark skin was highlighted by white tattooing. Solemnly she stood, spread her blue and yellow wings, and bowed, causing the Humans to either side of her to lean back to avoid being swiped in the face.

She broke into a wide grin. "I understand you survived meeting Storng."

Joss smiled, appreciating the lifeline of something familiar. "I first met him when I was young, and he saved my life. Then again when I helped Aran. Of course, we've spent a good bit of time together since ... since all of this began."

"To survive meeting my shaman brother once is amazing enough, but twice is unheard of. And then even more. Amazing."

Joss chuckled. "The second time he bound me to silence about Silth existence. A little bit without warning and certainly inconvenient as the rest of the world began to speak of you. Still, it was better than what he did to Kate. He took away her memory of finding out about the Silth. Later, when he gave it back, she was so pissed. She and her partner Sara head up the Costa Rican Refuge, and she named her chickens *Storng 1, Storng 2,* et cetera. The whole flock, named *Storng.* But I suspect he likes it. Thinks it's funny."

Krackle brayed her laugh, loud and raucous. "And you saved Aran, without whom we would have no hope. Your story is told by the fires almost nightly in the Silth world." As Joss blushed again, Krackle continued. "But now you join us in this nearly impossible task. A task I am told you helped dream up." Her elderly face grew grim. "What did we do that caused you to hate us so?"

As Joss tried to tell if Krackle was being serious, the shaman brayed again. Maria Luis touched Joss's arm and said in a stage whisper, "Krackle Shaman thinks she's funny, and the rest of us try to humor her."

Krackle frowned. "Turn you into a newt, I will."

"And we made the mistake of showing her both *The Empire Strikes Back* and *Monty Python's Holy Grail,*" Maria Luis went on. "So, we have no one to blame but ourselves."

As everyone resumed talking and eating, Joss slid her wine glass in front of Maria Luis and whispered, "Could you take this please? It was very kind, but I don't drink alcohol. Thanks."

Acutely aware of Krackle's sharp look, Joss said to her, "I know I've a lot to learn so I can help. I'm supposed to be the Human director here, but I won't be very useful at that for a while. And there is something urgent we must address before we worry about getting me up to speed." The table went quiet, all eyes upon her.

Tanho said, "Before you start, we already told them about the attack on the way from the airport."

One of the others spoke up. "Yeah, we get harassed constantly. That's why none of us can leave the refuge and why we sent the Silth to guard you on the way here. We have the necessary supplies shipped in, but mostly we're trying to be self-sufficient."

Joss filled them in on the airport bathroom encounter and the agent's warning of an imminent attack on the refuge. "She didn't know when. Not today or tomorrow, but sometime within a week or so."

Without warning, Krackle flew up toward the ceiling, giving a long shrill whistle followed by two short ones. All the Silth immediately joined her, leaving their dishes in place and following as she flew from the room. The Humans at Joss's table spread out through the room sharing the information at each table, leaving Tonho and Joss alone.

He asked her, "Is that what's called *burying the lead?*"

"Well, it was a little hard to convey all that while texting under threat of being whisked away to a cell somewhere and never seen again."

While she finished eating, he gave her more details on how refuge operations worked. Meanwhile the room decanted people, and she assumed they were rushing off to get ready for the attack. They agreed she'd rest tonight and join them for a planning meeting first thing in the morning. He said that many there would need to work through the night to inventory needs and make other preparations.

As Joss left the table, she noticed the half-empty wine bottle on the table, and an idea skittered across her mind like a roach—she could sneak back in and get the bottle later that night.

She stepped out into the humid evening air, Tonho beside her before he headed off to work. The buildings made a kind of courtyard, now lit with a mix of torches and hanging battery lanterns. Humans and Silth were clustered in the courtyard and on porches. She looked around, hoping to find a group that looked inviting. In some places, work was obviously being done and all the participants very focused. Joss had no desire to work that night. Others were laughing, and she felt drawn to them, just to relax for a few minutes. But as she passed one such group, she spotted wine bottles on the porch floor, so when they called out an invitation, she smiled, waved, and kept walking.

Suddenly something heavy hit her behind the knees, and she went sprawling face down into the grass. As she lay stunned, a wet tongue vigorously licked her ear. She rolled over into the full embrace of a big, black Labrador Retriever. She laughed as she tried to fend off the licking now focused on her face.

"Shadow! Shadow, sit! Shadow!"

With a little whine, the dog plopped her butt down, and a big man held out his hand. Joss took it, and he pulled her up as though she was weightless.

"All the slobber's her way of saying sorry. But it wasn't her fault." He picked up a luminescent orange ball from the grass, and when he threw it, Shadow chased after it at a full-out run. "It was mine. Sorry. Threw it further than I meant to."

"That's all right—no harm done." She brushed off her clothes, then, "I'm Joss. New arrival."

"I know. And I'm responsible for the new big cheese getting knocked on her grass. Way to make friends and influence people, huh? I'm Tiny. Your resident volcanologist. And this is Shadow," he said, taking the ball from the happy dog's mouth. He threw it again, and she bounded off. "I have no idea how she finds it in the dark. It's not that bright."

"Me either. I don't know what a volcanologist is or why one's here," she said as they stepped into the light of what she assumed was his porch. On it were a small swing and a couple of folding chairs in the circle of light from the lantern.

As Shadow, seemingly inexhaustible, kept chasing and returning the ball, Tiny explained that he was a volcano expert and at the refuge as part of a group of Humans and Silth planning how to stop the remaining volcanoes. They talked about their histories, where their families were now, and how it felt to be so far away. Joss told him her dog Macho, a Husky, was on his way across land from Brazil with friends who were transporting her belongings to Brazil. They'd arrive in a couple of weeks.

After a while, he offered her a drink. "I'm afraid all I have is tea, water, and papaya juice."

"That's all I can drink. I'd love some juice."

He left and came back with two glasses of juice. "Why is that all you can drink? If you don't mind me asking," he added.

She hesitated, not wanting to come off as too weird right away with a new potential friend. But there was no avoiding it. "Ten years sober. I'm an alcoholic."

"Excellent!" He said to her surprise. "Booze flows like water in this camp, and I don't drink either. We can form our own social club."

"You don't?"

"Nah. Mom said my people don't do well with alcohol so I wasn't allowed. And as I got older, she said only a fool would add alcohol to someone this big." He swept his arm up indicating his huge stature. "So, I just never have."

He checked his watch and then the sky, where gray clouds glowed with the moonlight behind them.

"It's time! You're in for a treat. Watch the sky."

She didn't see anything unusual about the sky, and she realized with a pang that she hadn't seen a star or the moon in almost a year.

"Keep looking. Wait for it. Wait for it."

Suddenly a hole opened in ash-filled clouds, and Joss could see stars through it. The hole rapidly expanded, pushing aside the clouds and revealing a bright, full moon. Around them was clapping, cheers and whistling.

"Wh—what just happened?"

"You got to witness the first refuge dome go into place. Each refuge will have a magical dome allowing the sun to shine down on the land beneath it. They're so big there's still rain and weather patterns inside of them, but sun! It's been so long since I saw the sun." His face beamed as he stared at the full moon. "Or the moon."

"How'd this happen?"

"The Silth aggregated the *eggs* that have always hidden their homes and somehow combined that with the Faerie shields they've learned to cast. Apparently, it requires a team in constant attendance, but it works. We decided to install it at night so it would be less shocking for the wildlife. Imagine, though, what tomorrow will be like when the sun rises in this place for the first time in ages."

They kept talking as the torches guttered out, the lanterns blinked out, and the voices drifted away in the night, finally saying good night when Joss could no longer hold her eyes open. As she left, she waved to man and dog, standing on the porch together. She was humming as she opened the door to her cabin.

3

STORNG (SILTH)

When Storng popped into the conference room in the U.N. before Penfield had put down the phone, he was slightly disappointed that Penfield showed no surprise at all. The novelty of such immediate arrivals apparently had worn off. But then Penfield was expecting him.

These days little of Storng's clothing reflected the extensive harvesting he'd done in Human settlements. Instead, he had a black traditional shaman's cloak with its many pockets over a simple white robe. Penfield wore a suit. He was one of those people who seemed natural in one, never uncomfortable, as though perhaps he'd been born in it. He had, however, taken off his jacket and was slightly portlier than Storng had realized.

Penfield was eating from an elegant, food-filled plate, and a glass of wine was on the table. Across from him a small plate piled high with chunks of fruit and nuts and steamed vegetables sat atop a stack of six books, a glass thimble of wine beside it. Storng settled on the shorter pile of books next to the makeshift table. Neither of them said anything for a few minutes as each ate and then they made small talk, asking about the other's health and families.

"The wine's good."

"It's Italian," Penfield told him. "Hard to imagine a world without it." Storng thought about the gray skies outside.

After white-jacketed waiters cleared their plates, Storng said, "When you called, I was meeting with the shamans from the other seven Silth nations. We've created a council specifically to work on the question of our future together."

"I've been engaged in similar discussions. Unfortunately, there are far more *nations* of Humans and none willing to allow anyone else to negotiate their future. So, the Human side of the discussions will be a little more complex. But before we go through that, can we talk about your phone?"

"My phone?" Storng looked down at the swag bag holding his smart phone.

"I know you read extensively, and you'd eventually find this out. And when you did it might undermine your trust. So, I'm not betraying any state secret when I tell you this. You can be tracked with the phone, and some agency may be able to activate it remotely to listen to your conversations. I suspect you already realize others may be able to listen to your conversations when you are on calls."

Storng tensed, trying to remember everything he had said on the phone. "What do you suggest?"

Penfield walked him through removing the phone battery and loading an app allowing both of them to hold secure conversations and send encrypted text messages. He explained that because the only way to avoid some of the consequences was to disable the phone, making it impossible to be contacted as well, his government had developed a device allowing the phone to be on but preventing it being tracked or hacked. Penfield slipped Storng's phone inside a shell he said also functioned as a backup battery.

"These batteries are fairly precious." He pointed to a box in the corner of the room. "But the thirty in that box are yours."

"A most generous gift. Both the knowledge and the devices."

Storng took two small packages from his cloak, each wrapped in a leaf and tied with a piece of vine. "I too have gifts." He unwrapped the larger parcel to reveal a diamond of considerable size. "I hope they are still valued by your people and can contribute to funding our work together." Penfield opened the second parcel, containing a small human figure delicately worked from stone. "And this is for you, personally. While without great commercial value, it is highly prized within our culture. Our artists made these as gifts for the Incas. We haven't given them to Humans in several hundred years, and most of the artists are gone now."

Penfield examined the small figurine with obvious pleasure. "Thank you, Storng. These are most appreciated." He bowed slightly.

They talked about history. Penfield told him Human historians were looking back at ancient figurines, drawings and tapestries with new eyes and seeing evidence of the Silth's prior contact with Humans. Storng said that contact had occurred all around the world in different cultures over different historic periods. Various events had ended contact, and then the Silth population and range plummeted. Contact with Humans was first reduced to limited ceremonial events and ultimately formally forbidden.

"Sometime your historians should come listen to our songs and stories. You might learn something new about Human history."

Penfield nodded. "That would be remarkable. Speaking of history, Homeland has finally authenticated and released the tape from Yellowstone. We have a lot of questions about it. Mind watching it with me and answering a few?"

When Storng agreed, Penfield pressed a button on the desk console, and a large screen lowered from the ceiling. He clicked the computer beside him, and the recording of the Yellowstone feed played on the screen. Penfield said he'd seen the video several times, so he asked questions and watched Storng as he reacted to the scene and Aran's desperate fight to stop Angel. Storng leaned forward as the roots came through the floor and wrapped themselves around the Trow while she was trying to restart the bomb. When they finished Storng asked to re-watch it, this time narrating what he knew of the events.

When the video finished the second time, Penfield said, "Aran was your student. I know you must be proud of him. He's a hero. People are, however, a little confused because the Faeries, the Trow, seem to be fighting among themselves."

"Faelen, the Trow who helped stop Yellowstone, is the only one we know of rebelling against their plans. They'd already killed him by the time the scene in Yellowstone occurred. His story is told among the Silth with great honor. We've never known one like him."

"Is it possible there are others who'd also oppose the Trow plans?"

"What we know is that Xafar, the Trow leader and Faelen's father, went insane while on Earth. He returned to his world to kill the Trow Queen and take control of what had been a peaceful land. The battles among their people went on for decades. We've never heard of any group actually being a threat to him. Also, be careful in your assumptions. We know Faelen only opposed the destruction of Earth's species. We don't know that any Trow opposes retaking control of the Earth."

"Is there some way to reach out to them to negotiate? To see if we can avoid the war?"

"We have legends of such negotiations. None end happily. That there appear to be no Trow in this world is certainly an impediment and if anyone can get to the Trow world, they don't return. As you learn more about the nature of the Trow, you will understand it would be similar to asking if one can negotiate with a bear. You might be able to persuade it for a moment, but when you turn your back the bear will behave according to its nature."

Penfield winced and said, "For us, yes, the challenge is we don't yet know the nature of the Trow. But we don't really know the nature of the Silth either. You can physically appear as you want, causing people to fear that perhaps you are not what you say you are. Humans don't want to share control in the first place but sharing with a partner they don't know frightens them. Some argue the Trow don't even exist, that the tape record is theater."

"Then deal with the volcanoes yourselves and those of you who still remain can fight the Trow when they come. We don't need anything from Humans." Storng sighed heavily. "We'll use the refuges to save ourselves and many of the other species from the volcanoes. We'll defeat Human efforts to take them away from us. It appears this will be tested soon in Brazil."

Penfield looked down at his hands. "Do you follow what's going on around the world right now? Large numbers of Humans are dying. Diseases that haven't been seen in a hundred years are sweeping through malnourished countries. Wars are being fought for food and for electricity. Governments are barely hanging on in the developed world. There's great suffering among Humans. They don't see the Silth suffering and think perhaps the Silth are taking advantage of the situation. The biggest territorial grab since the British Empire. They wonder if the story of the Trow is real. It is a classic ploy to make up an enemy so one can sell protection. I'm not saying this is how things are, I'm just saying there is increasing concern that we don't really know the truth. This tape helps, and for those of us who believe Homeland's confirmation means something, the tape means more. But a large part of humanity doesn't believe Homeland can be trusted."

Storng leaned forward and fixed his one black eye on Penfield. "We have no interest in Human politics nor any skill in dealing with them. We're having enough challenges reestablishing contact among the Silth of the world. Believe what you will. Do what you will. We can probably survive the volcanoes, you cannot. Have you seen the new 'domes' over the refugees? They let in sunlight, but they will also protect from Human attack. We will battle the Trow, whether Humans are still in the world or not. We fight for our brothers and sisters of the forest, sky, and sea. We will not fight for a future in which they are simply extinguished by Humans instead of the Trow. You say Humans are suffering. The Silth and every other creature on Earth have suffered at the hands of Humans for thousands of years.

"The Silth believe Humans, like other species, should continue to live and thrive, but no longer at the cost of Earth's other inhabitants. Humans must change their relationship with other species so they are equals, and the existence of none is threatened. Humans can no longer be the invasive species pushing aside everything else. And they must abandon electrically-based technology. You don't have very long to make a choice. We don't care about your politics. We have enough trouble with our own. For us to help save Humans, there must be a fundamental change in the world. Humans can no longer use all of the world and all of its species for their own ends."

Penfield laughed. "I'm sorry, but you can't seriously believe

Humans will accept what you're saying. Do you have any idea how Humans use technology? How many are alive because of a factory that makes medicine? How many can eat because of a factory that processes food. How many don't die because they can refrigerate their food or because a fire truck reaches their home in time. Just the value of light in Human psyche?"

Storng said nothing, just continued to look at him through the black eye.

"It doesn't even make sense. Technology is a problem for the Trow. But it doesn't seem to be as much of a problem for the Silth. Shouldn't we increase technology to ward off the Trow? Technology is how we make the medicines that save lives. The fertilizers that allow us to feed people." He nodded toward the computer. "Asking Humans to give up electricity is like asking the Silth or the Trow to give up their magic. They wouldn't do it."

Storng still said nothing.

"This is how you will begin negotiations with the U.N.?" Penfield's knuckles were white as he squeezed the edge of the table.

"No. There will be no negotiations. These are our only terms. We are happy to work on implementation and perhaps the continuation of essential services because there is much to be done. But these are our conditions. In return we'll stop the volcanoes and work with Humans to defend them as well as ourselves when the Trow come. Make no mistake, we would like Humans fighting by our side when the Trow arrive. Otherwise we wouldn't have come out of the rain forest. But for us, you are simply another animal in the world. We care for them all. But if the population of jaguars suddenly blossomed and began eating everyone else in the forest, we wouldn't allow that condition to continue. Why should we support the same thing by Humans?"

Storng stared at the scene on the video, frozen with Aran talking to the Human. He took advantage of Penfield's silence to breathe deeply and try to calm himself. He would accomplish nothing if he couldn't listen. He felt more settled when Penfield finally spoke.

"You can't hold all the animals of the world in your refuges. So, I know you'd like to reach an outcome where all the creatures of the world are safe. I also doubt you would have revealed yourselves to us if you didn't believe you needed help in dealing with the Trow. But be realistic. If we were bargaining about territory, I could imagine some agreed outcome. But you want all Humans to give up their electrically-based technology and fundamentally change their way of existing in relationship with the world's other creatures. Even if the U.N. agreed to this, there's little likelihood it could be accomplished. We know from centuries of Human interactions that they don't *redirect* well. If the Silth want a peaceful future with Humans, there must be another way."

Storng laughed ruefully as he stood. "The Silth do not want a peaceful future with Humans. It's likely the Trow will win no matter what. Both Humans and Silth will be wiped from the planet. But without Trow in the world, there will be no more Silth after a few hundred years. Thus, if we *win* with the Humans, we assure our disappearance as a race. We aren't bargaining for *our* future. We're bargaining for the future of all other species on the planet. If we cannot secure that future with Human cooperation, then we will do our best to secure it without that cooperation. There is no compromise to be had regarding this direction. There are many negotiations to be had on the path we will follow, but not the direction of that path."

He opened his wings and gave a little bow. "Thank you for your hospitality. Thank you for the gifts. For your honesty. Take our message to the U.N. We trust you to make them understand. The way things were is gone. There will be no going back. I look forward to moving forward quickly. One way or the other."

When Storng placed his hand on the box of batteries, both he and it flickered and disappeared.

CHAPTER 5

1

ARAN (SILTH)

Despite needing to be many other places, Aran was back in Australia, summoned when the Australian colony realized the Tiki Crew was missing.

No one could say how long the Crew had been gone. Because they worked with different groups daily, everyone thought the Tiki Crew was working with someone else that day. They'd last been seen eight days earlier. At first, Aran was angry, thinking they'd suddenly decided they needed a beach vacation. Before long he'd become concerned that something was wrong, and now he felt certain they had been abducted or killed. He was worried and frustrated because he had few leads and he had no clue who'd want to hurt or take them. When he finally suggested it might be the New Zealand Silth, who had once caused such turmoil in the Australian colonies, the Australians were skeptical, pointing out they'd heard nothing about them for decades. Why would they reappear now?

The flower fairy flitted around the porch happily. Aran had named her Kimper. When he left her behind as he slipped into some other part of the world, she followed other Silth. When he returned, she pouted for a short time but came back to follow him. She was, however, much more observant than he'd first realized. If she saw him making arrangements to travel, she stayed close to him and tried to touch him when he transported. After watching her frantically try to clutch for him and miss, Aran felt sorry for her and waited long enough for her to land on his shoulder before he transported.

Aran had acquired a taste for coffee. In the early morning darkness at the Silth camp, now the center of the Australian Refuge, he held a thimble of coffee with both hands and inhaled its aroma. It was still too early for the birds to be awake, and, Aran thought, it was too early for him to be awake as well. But today they'd head out to search for the New Zealand camp, if such a thing existed, of the Silth who may have taken the Tiki Crew. A few others, mostly Australian Silth warriors, sleepily moved around him preparing for the day. Was Nadara all right? What about the others? They were almost all his friends in the world ... disappeared. If they'd been taken, why? He slammed his empty thimble on the table, finding no productive line of thought.

An Australian warrior came onto the porch and spoke softly into his ear. All sleepiness evaporated as Aran jumped up and followed him outside to the square.

"Where?" The warrior pointed to a group of buildings along the edge of the rain forest.

In Australia, Silth buildings were mainly located along the ground, at the base of, and often inserted into the trees or small mounds of earth. Aran flew across the open space and slowed as he neared the buildings. He tried seeing through the morning gloom, suspecting it was just a dingo foraging for a breakfast snack. The Silth had persuaded most of the other animals to avoid the Silth enclave, but the dingoes were resisting. The issue was becoming more urgent as

Human workers would be arriving tomorrow, tasked with constructing buildings for the other Humans' involved in managing the Australian Refuge. Aran didn't think Humans would be as tolerant of the dingo incursions, though he had been told that on the coastal *Dingo Island*, Human tourists mingled freely with them.

He landed and slid up to the corner of a building, hugging the wall. He leaned forward to look around the corner. It was darker here in the edge of the forest, away from the torch-lit pathways of the central colony. As his eyes adjusted to the absence of light, he could see movement. No, whatever was moving in the alley wasn't a dingo—it wasn't big enough—and Aran thought he saw metal reflecting back a bit of the firelight from the main square. Before long he could make out a group of Silth moving among the buildings, darting in and out of windows and openings. A hushed giggle was the only sound he heard.

For an instant, he thought they might be the Tiki Crew, having returned drunk and harvesting in the colony, but as he watched he was sure it wasn't. The little bit of moonlight making its way into the alley reflected on all sorts of metal surfaces as the figures moved. When the warrior appeared beside him, Aran held up two fingers and made a slashing motion across them. The warrior nodded and left. The group coming toward Aran was almost to his end of the street. He couldn't tell what they were doing—their movements seemed almost random. He stepped out and shone a small penlight into the ten faces. They started at his sudden appearance.

"What are you doing?" he asked, his damaged voice even harsher in the quiet night.

"Whatever we want," was the instant reply from within the clump of low-flying Silth, but Aran couldn't tell who spoke. One moved to the front and landed before Aran, too close for the light to reach his face.

"Who wants to know?" the dark figure said, his voice smooth and sarcastic.

The figure was male, dark-skinned with a dark hather. Aran couldn't see his face, but he could make out a top hat and a coat with tails. The torchlight reflected off goggles on the hatband.

"I am Aran Shaman. What are you up to?"

The Silth stood completely still, devoid of expression, and growled, "Looking for you!"

Top Hat flew up and away, with the others right behind him. Aran launched after them, barely keeping them in sight as they wove through the trees. When they spread out, he stayed behind Top Hat. The Silth came back together and flew as a tight bunch, moving up above the canopy and flying faster. Still, Aran was gaining on them. They dropped back into the trees. Aran fired a bolt, aiming for a vine-covered tree in front of them, but they didn't hesitate.

Were they the ones who had taken the Tiki Crew? Were the Tikis led to a trap by just such a chase? This crew didn't seem to be moving in a random direction—there was purpose in their flight. Suddenly Aran found himself among the ruins of an old lumber operation. Rusting machinery seemed stopped in mid-operation in a clear-cut section of forest that had begun to regrow. Small trees at a uniform height had begun to obscure the trauma to the forest. All this was a blur to Aran as he, like the others, zoomed toward a wall of old growth trees rising among old, decayed structures. The group headed for a crumbling building then swooped below the remnant of an old bay door in one of its partially standing brick walls.

Aran stopped and hovered in front of the opening. Most likely they had just flown through and were long gone. Aran proceeded warily through the impressively thick doorway, staying in its deep shadows. As he looked out beyond the threshold, he sensed most of the roof and walls on the other side were gone, but the darkness was complete, and he could see nothing. Lighting his penlight would just announce his presence, so instead he lit his shield. Immediately a dozen darts bounced harmlessly off it. He lit the penlight and shone it into the partial building. Waiting for him were the Silth he had followed with probably a dozen more warriors, each clad in a uniform quite different than the Australian warriors.

Everyone froze in the sudden light, and the room full of Silth surged toward Aran. They shouted and struggled to stay in the air as nets dropped from above, tangling their wings and weighting them down. With a whoop Australian Silth warriors lit torches and flew down among the others. Aran moved to where Top Hat and his Silth companions lay, frantically cutting at the nets with small pocketknives.

"Don't move," he shouted, firing two quick blue bolts into the ground beside them.

They stopped cutting and watched Aran warily, waiting for him to be distracted so they could finish freeing themselves. But Aran ignored the fighting around him. When he did glance around quickly, he saw the Silth fighters who'd been waiting for him refusing to submit to the larger force of Australians and fighting on as they freed themselves from the nets. They were well trained with clever tactics, but were quickly overcome by the superior numbers and the Australians' use of the Faerie bolts and shields. Before long, only Aran, his captives, and the Australian warriors were still alive.

The squad put *wing-cuffs* on Top Hat and the others, which kept them from being able to fly. Aran studied them, unchastened, heads held high, in the strangest apparel he'd ever seen. Strange even by the eclectic standards of Silth. He took in the hats, goggles, corsets, and bits of machinery.

"I know some of your ... paraphernalia are weapons," he told them. "You've given the warriors the obvious ones. You'll now give them all of them. If I find you've held even one back, you will be stripped naked and every piece of machinery removed from your body, no matter what it's attached to."

One of the Silth warriors stepped forward holding a big bag already containing the blow guns, knives and bows they'd collected. The crew all turned to Top Hat, the tall Silth who'd first spoken to Aran. He glared at Aran, tested the tight hold of the wing-cuffs, frowned, and gave a slight nod. His crew lined up and started pulling bits and pieces of the mechanical objects off their bodies. As they stepped forward each was handed a smaller bag, which when filled was dropped into the big bag. Each bag was given a distinctive mark, and its twin was drawn on the forehead of the crew member who'd filled it. As this process went on, a group of warriors set up a tent with two chairs and a small table inside. Another group took the net that had been waiting to trap Aran and made it into a corral, escorting each member inside after his or her items had been placed in the bag.

After giving instructions to the squad leader, Aran sat inside the torch-lit tent for a few minutes thinking about how to approach the interrogation. He needed to know where they were holding Nadara—that was his first priority. But he was curious about who these Silth were and who directed them. What had they sought? Why were they looking for him? He thought about what he'd seen so far. Plenty of attitude, but unlike the warriors, no ferocious commitment to die for their cause.

The guard brought in Top Hat. Aran could now see that he had distinctive red stripes in the hather at his temples and along the top and under his wings, but otherwise his skin, feathers and hather were black. He was big and solid, with a large, slightly hooked nose and a long narrow neck that seemed out of place compared to the rest of him. The guard searched him, carefully checking the high boots and the tailed coat's pockets. After removing a small pocket watch and placing it on the table, he reached up and lifted the top hat. His expression immediately turned suspicious.

"Why is this so heavy?" He looked inside but found nothing.

Top Hat reached out for the hat, and Aran cleared his throat. The squad member and the prisoner both stopped and looked at him. When Aran pointed his hand at the ground, a blue beam shot into the leaves and soil, leaving a small fire burning and smoking. The prisoner took back the hat and touched some hidden mechanism, causing the front to spring open and expose a small turning mechanism that issued a slow tinkling melody. He looked at Aran, who nodded, and returned the hat to the guard.

The guard led Top Hat over to the chair in front of Aran. The other warrior standing behind Aran peered at Top Hat's forehead, pulled out the bag with the matching symbol, emptied it on the table in front of Aran, and slid the pocket watch and hat over to join the rest. Aran eyed the daggers, small gun, hypodermic needles, and other items. He looked over at the Silth seated across from him, glanced at his forehead, and slid a wet rag across the table.

As the prisoner cleaned his forehead, Aran asked, "Who are you?"

"Jules. I lead the Steamer Paerries."

"You took the Tiki Crew. Where are they?"

"In Rangi's colony in New Zealand."

"Is Rangi your leader?"

Jules looked thoughtful, but then said, "Yes."

"Why does Rangi want the Tiki crew?"

"She hoped to get information from them, but they didn't have what she needed."

"Are they still alive and well?"

"They're alive."

Aran's heart gave a little stutter. He eyed the torches stuck in cans on either side of the door and drummed his fingers. Jules was answering his questions, but something in the casual nature of his answers was irritating Aran. And why was he answering so readily?

"Why did you come looking for me?"

Jules looked at him like he was a schoolboy who wasn't following the lesson.

"To take you to Rangi so she could get the information from you."

"What information is she looking for?"

"I don't know."

But Aran already knew. Any rebel leader would want the Trow magic Aran had learned. The shield, the bolt, the transport.

"Where's she holding them?"

"The way is complex, but I'm happy to show you."

"Why?"

"My job is to get you to Rangi. Rangi wasn't specific about how, or whether I had to be in control—my job is simply to get you there. I see no reason for you to hurt my crew to get information I'll freely give you."

Aran decided to interview the rest of the Steamer Crew before he let Jules know that, apparently unlike Rangi, they didn't torture prisoners. He told the guard, "Get another chair."

Jules looked surprised but moved to the new chair when it arrived. The evening proceeded with a parade of Steamer Paerrie crew members. Each was searched and anything questionable removed. None of the items were obviously weapons and could possibly be benign, but Aran didn't trust these Silth. They were all too calm, too cocky. As each was brought to him, Aran had their paraphernalia spread in front of him, trying to understand the nature of the different members and the crew as a whole. He was familiar with crews being used to harvest, but this one was equipped for something else. They had no harvest bags, no tools for picking locks, no spray for a surprise dog.

After Jules came a small male with a red wispy crest on his red-hathered head. His skin and feathers were gray. A telescope emerged from his pith helmet, and his canvas pants and shirt were covered in loops and pockets holding many inexplicable wind-up gadgets. When Aran asked his name, he just smiled.

"Slatt doesn't talk," Jules said. "Never has. Don't think he can."

Then came Jeeter, reddish-skinned with dark pink mutton chops, white around his eyes, and a rounded pink crest over white hather. All the skin Aran could see was covered in tattoos the squad leader told him were based on the culture of the Maori, Humans who'd colonized New Zealand and displaced even earlier Humans. He wore a white shirt with puffed sleeves, a bow tie, suspenders, and a bowler hat. His arm band held what he admitted were poison-tipped darts before he surrendered them and the walking stick with its Maori axe head.

Arana asked each the same questions and got the same answers with no resistance. He added questions about the size of Rangi's army, the nature of their defenses, and the culture of the colony. Once in a while he received what seemed to be a genuine "I don't know," and for the most part his questions were consistently and quickly answered.

Vander, who followed Jeeter, was irritatingly arrogant. He wore a double-breasted wool jacket and an aviator's headgear, plainly custom-made for a Silth's smaller head. He'd begun the night with cargo pockets full of gadgets and still wore earrings of small gears and under-feathers. He had red skin and a black goatee, violet hather on the top and back of his head, and a yellow tattoo around one of the two most soulful brown eyes Aran had ever seen. His wings of greens, reds, and blues were more colorful than those of the others. Silth were often more identifiable by their wing patterns than their facial features because the wing patterns could be seen before the faces were recognizable. Of course, one might be looking at a glamoured pattern, not a real one.

The guard took an involuntary step back as the next of the Steamer Paerries came in, and Aran was tempted to do the same. She was huge, her hather, skin, and feathers all the same gray-black, with bright red tattoos on her face. Her head was massive, topped by a long wispy black crest, her eyes striking in their redness.

"You are …?" he asked.

He took in the gears woven into her crest with wire, her square goggles, a wide utility vest worn over striped pants, and the black vest over a silk shirt. Her size and ferocious appearance gave her a strange beauty. As Aran surveyed the brutal weaponry removed from her belt, he once again wondered about the purpose of this crew.

He raised his hathered eyebrows for an answer.

"Three of Five," she said sullenly. "But I'm also called Tara."

"What do you mean, Three of Five?"

She simply stared at him, the first time one of his questions had been refused.

Jules spoke up. "You'll understand better when you meet Four of Five and Five of Five. They won't tell us where the names come from either. Jeeter thinks it's from a Human television program, but all have their number tattooed on their arm."

"What happened to One and Two?"

Jules shrugged. "We don't know,"

Aran proceeded with his usual set of questions and got from Tara the same answers as the others. And then he posed a question he hadn't asked the others. "What is the purpose of the Steamer Paerries?"

Without hesitation, "We're mercenaries, sometimes assassins."

Jules frowned and shifted in his chair but said nothing.

"That's what you do for Rangi?"

"And for anyone else who pays us. We also steal and do whatever else our clients desire."

"You work for Silth merchants to compete with other Silth?"

"Yes, though not just merchants, also politicians. And not just against other Silth, sometimes against Humans."

"Explain."

"Well, if a Human was beginning to clear an area for farming, we might drive off his animals. Repeatedly. Until he decides the area is cursed or bad luck and leaves. This would be very expensive work for someone to hire us to do."

"And if he persists?"

Tara slanted her red eyes at Jules, who said, "The next level is too expensive for an individual, but sometimes we have been hired by a colony to ... remove nuisance Humans."

Four of Five, also called Abney, looked exactly the same in body appearance as Three of Five, only she wore a bashed-in derby, small safety pins for earrings, a corset, torn stockings, and high stiletto-heeled boots. Her gloves were fingerless, and she smirked when the guard tried to remove the long steel nails on one hand. "They don't come off."

Five of Five, a male named Blay, had a high collar, cravat, and high-top hat, and his monocle contained multiple lens of different colors. His walking stick with a spiked metal head had been surrendered and lay on the table. Aran obtained no additional useful information from him.

Ada was next to last. Her long white hather was in dreadlocks, each wrapped with copper wires, and more copper wire wrapped around her arms. She had a bright yellow crest and white eyes with black irises, and she wore a leather apron with pockets and denim pants.

Aran noticed her eyes kept flicking to the glove and backpack on the table. "What's special about these?"

A long silence, then, "When paired, flames shoot out the glove."

Aran had thought he could no longer be startled by the Steamers' answers but he was wrong. "What do you do with the Steamer Paerries?"

"Whatever I'm told."

Aran tried a different tack. "What's your specialty?"

"I make and repair the equipment. I'm the tinker."

Finally, Valente. Aran realized only now that none of the Steamer Crew was glamoured. While Valente was stockier than the Silth of Costa Rica ever glamoured, like the others she had a natural beauty, with brown skin and feathers bearing white hather, an orange-red under-wing, and red at the base of her tail. She wore a lab coat over frilly shirt and tights. Her small round glasses contained different lenses able to be rotated into place. Aran found her particularly interesting because she seemed to be one of those individuals who simply looked intelligent.

"What's special about these?" Aran repeated, gesturing to her backpack and glove.

But her answer was not the same as Ada's. She raised her hand, and her leather and gear bracelets jangled as she pointed to the glove. "When the pack is activated, that becomes a powerful magnet."

Aran had her remove the bracelets and asked a few other questions, but he'd saved the most important for last. "So, is this a trap? Will Rangi be expecting me?"

Valente smiled broadly. "Oh, most certainly."

2

ARAN (SILTH)

Beyond the dome of the Australian refuge, the next morning dawned its usual gray. Despite the fact they'd been trained in the use of the Faerie shield and bolt, most of the assembling Australian warriors still carried their traditional weapons. The weapons were different than those of Aran's home colony. Here were more cross-bows, some able to fire multiple arrows at once. The arrows were tipped in poisons extracted from the region's plentiful snakes. Aran had seen similar weapons in Indonesia among their Silth. These warriors also carried curved knives, and some had chosen lances instead of bows.

They'd practiced extensively over the last month and moved with all the proficiency Aran expected from Merit's training. He wished she was here leading this excursion, but she was in Brazil, preparing for an attack by Humans there. He should be angry about the Human response, but given that he was preparing to attack a Silth rebel, he couldn't pretend his species rose to speak with one voice. The Australian general walked among the warriors giving orders and words of encouragement. Aran was impressed by his confidence since they were attacking a force that decimated them years before leading to the Australian colony's disintegration.

Aran's only tasks were to help get them all to the rally point in New Zealand and to secure the Tiki Crew. He commanded a small squad of warriors who assisted him in finding and protecting the Crew. He was a little more concerned about the group that was supposed to help him with transport. To move the two hundred warriors, he needed twenty individuals with Faerie transport ability. When the Australian colony was destroyed by the Silth he now knew was called Rangi, it had more than twenty shamans. Unfortunately, time and mishaps had reduced this number to ten. Each shaman had fifteen students, trained not in schools but to the best of each teacher's abilities. Aran had taken the most proficient ten. To avoid the proliferation of the Faerie transport technology, in other colonies he'd carefully vetted each shaman or warrior who received instruction in the transport technique.

Right now, though, he was too concerned about the safety of the Tiki Crew to follow his usual procedures. He barely knew the shamans he taught, much less their students. Shamans and students were currently assembled discussing and practicing the technique. They would be responsible for moving the warriors to the *surprise* attack. Aran idly wondered if you could call it a surprise when the enemy had actually invited the attack. But if any of the transporters faltered or missed the location, the warriors who did appear in Rangi's camp would be slaughtered.

He was risking many for the rescue of a few. He told himself it wasn't about the Tiki Crew but about stopping Rangi, bold enough to direct agents—assassins—into the re-established Australian colony to kidnap the Tiki Crew. And yesterday to try to kidnap him. But he found himself thinking of Nadara instead. The Steamer Crew had hinted that their captives' conditions might not be good, which had his stomach twisted into knots. He checked his watch, a gift from Storng and a reminder of a time when he, Aran, wanted to kill Humans. Before joining the cluster of shamans and students, he made sure he had the bracelet and the locket that stored his unreliable magic reserves.

"Time to go, General," he called out.

He spread the transporters across the courtyard, and the warriors assembled around them in clusters of ten. There was no talking and no laughter. The evening was eerily quiet, and even the birds seemed subdued. The smells of breakfast lingered in the ashy air.

After insuring all was in order, Aran nodded to the general, who gave a quick hand signal to the warrior beside him. Three shrill whistles sounded, and the entire mass began flickering and disappearing from the clearing into the disorientation of transport.

The jump, or *blip*, as the Silth referred to the Trow transport technique, was not instantaneous. Aran had to concentrate on his destination the whole time, and if he let his mind wander for a fraction of a second, he would end up somewhere else. The magic supporting the blip came from air. As long as this element was present, the right focus words and mental moves would allow transport to the desired destination. There was a philosophical aspect of the transport, something to the effect of "all is one, the separation of distance and time is a measuring construct with no analog in the real world". But Aran knew you didn't really need to understand it to do it, you just needed to *hold your mouth just right,* as Storng had said when Aran taught him. Storng maintained the Trow, who had no shamans nor any study of magic, gained all their magic intuitively through trial and error. There was some passage of time in the transport when one was neither here nor there. Time enough to let your thoughts wander and end up far from where you intended, and perhaps in some dire circumstance—in a fire, beneath the ocean, or in a monkey troop.

So Aran gathered his concentration. He stopped thinking about the journey to New Zealand with the Steamer Crew. Let go of thoughts of the trap he was heading to. Released from his mind worries that Aerital, the Australian shaman student he just taught to use the bolt, the shield and the blip, had so little practice he might accidentally take the squad of Australian warriors he was transporting off to some unforeseen location. Aran concentrated on the destination, pushing from his mind the need to get there to rescue Nadara and the Tiki Crew. Only the destination.

He was half aware of the Steamer Crew beside him. He had agreed they would go, unarmed, and if he saw them pick up a weapon or take any action against his warriors, he would kill them himself. He also pushed this thought from his mind. Only the destination. As each connection to another Silth was made, each added to what he had to transport, and the blip became just slightly harder, with a little more resistance to its start.

Aran hoped the surprise of their appearing in the middle of the camp in force, rather than attacking from the edges, would give them some leverage to counter the fact Rangi was expecting them. He focused ... and the gray moonlight of the jungle blurred, as well as the faces of the warriors in the next cluster. Aran held his destination firmly in his mind, and the scene around him rapidly resolved into a new landscape, a large clearing lit by bonfires with several stick and mud-built structures on the ground near its center. Warriors filled the encampment, but, as he hoped, most seemed to be along the edges, prepared for an attack from the dark landscape around them, not from the center of their camp.

In a move they had practiced repeatedly, the Australian warriors turned in place and took several steps out from the center of their transport clusters. They quickly merged with their fellow warriors, blipping into the field so there were eight large circles. Those on the outside of the circle dropped to their stomachs, the ones behind them dropped to one knee, and the ones in the center arranged themselves standing shoulder to shoulder. They fired non-stop, blue bolts lighting the early morning gray in a withering storm of death. The bodies of Rangi's warriors littered the field.

But Rangi's warriors were not without skills and courage. Knots of her warriors regrouped, while others ducked behind buildings or into trenches around the edge of the field. A few arrows found their way back toward the Australians. An order from the Australian squad leader had blue shields dropping into place around the groups. The groups quickly reassembled themselves into eight phalanxes, each covered by a blue shield and they jogged out in different directions. Darts, arrows, and spears rained down on the blue-lit groups. Occasionally the sound of gunfire joined the wails of the wounded and the shouts of the fighting Silth. Nothing penetrated the shields as the Australian warriors at the front of the phalanx held long lances sticking out from behind the shield. They mowed through the knots of Silth opponents. Whenever they broke a group and it ran, the Australians dropped their front shields and fired after them. The effect of this tactic was devastating, with few Australian Silth lost but serious losses among Rangi's warriors.

Clustered together, Aran, the other shamans, and the students watched long enough to assure themselves the battle was going their way. He, five students, including Aerital, and six warriors moved toward the buildings in the middle of the clearing. Still wearing wingcuffs preventing them from flying, the Steamer Crew were left huddled low to the ground, trying to stay out of the line of fire. Aran's shadow was enormous in the light of the bonfires as the group advanced on the largest of the buildings. Rangi's forces appeared to be completely engaged in the fight around them, leaving no guards there.

An Australian warrior threw open the stick door, and the squad rushed in with raised shields. Aran and the students hurried in behind them, weapons raised, as Aran scanned the room. On his right, the Tiki Crew slowly twirled, suspended upside down from the ceiling's support beams. Their eyes were closed, and he couldn't tell if they were dead or alive. On his left was a low barrier with a group of ten or so warriors behind it. The Australians were chewing up the barrier with their bolts, and every so often one of Rangi's group would lob a spear or arrow at Aran's squad.

"Cease fire!" Aran shouted. He surrounded himself with a shield, and an arrow aimed at his head bounced off. "Rangi! I am Aran Shaman. I understand you wanted to see me. Which of you is Rangi?"

A Silth with olive-brown hather highlighted by overtones of blue stuck up her head. "I see many in the rags of shamans. How do I know you are Aran?"

"Surely, you have heard of my melodious voice." Aran looked hard at the speaker. "And you're not Rangi. You are Nestor."

Nestor giggled and ducked back down behind the barrier. Aran heard the sound of something being dragged across the ground, and another Silth stepped up on it so she could be seen above the rampart. This Silth was plump, her hather mostly green with yellow and brown around the edges of her face. She was short and slightly hunched. But what struck Aran was her solid black eyes, looking back at him without emotion.

"The Steamer Crew m-m-m-may have been too thorough in briefing you. I am Rangi. And you are Aran. Why have you committed this unprovoked attack?"

"Why did you kidnap the Tiki Crew?"

"I didn't kidnap them. They followed and attacked the Steamer Crew, who defended themselves, captured them, and brought them here for m-m-me to deal with. Which as you see I have done." Rangi's laugh sent a chill up Aran's spine.

"You monkey witch!" Aerital shouted. Wrapped in the blue shield, he rushed the barrier.

Rangi's eyes widened, and she made a noise like a donkey bray. "Sharrk! Sharrrk!" As Rangi and her warriors ducked down, Aerital easily jumped the barrier and disappeared behind it.

Everything was quiet. No sound of a scuffle. Two groups of his warriors advanced to the edge of the barrier, grabbed the corners, and pulled it down. Nothing behind it. They quickly searched for another door, but there was none.

While the search went on, Aran ran to the dangling Tiki Crew. He wondered why he hadn't realized it before—the only way they could be dead and their bodies still present was if Rangi had killed them with magic, and she had little magic. As squad members cut the crew members down, Aran counted them—all seven were here. He scanned the inert figures as they were laid on the ground.

He saw blue hather with blond tips. "Nadara!" He brushed a loose strand from her bruised face, put his arm beneath her shoulder, and gently pulled her toward him. She gasped, and her eyes fluttered open. To Aran's relief, her face, red from blood pooling as she hung upside down, was quickly returning to its natural color. He could hear the moans and mutterings of the other Tiki Crew members regaining consciousness.

"Did she ... did she ... get it?" Nadara asked.

"What? Who?"

"Rangi. Did Rangi ... get the Trow magic?"

Aran just stared at her, uncomprehending.

"This was all set up so ... you'd bring a shaman with you ... who'd been taught the shield, bolt and blip. That shaman was New Faerie. Rangi ... she made a deal with Casius. They're working together." Nadara stopped talking as one of the squad members gently pushed Aran away to give her medical aid.

Aran stood up, trying to comprehend what she'd said. Aerital was New Faerie. This was all a ruse to deliver Trow magic to Rangi, and he'd fallen for it. Handed her and Casius the magic they had worked so hard to control.

The general hurried over and reported, "Everything has gone well, with few casualties. We control the area. As we pushed toward the concentrations of the enemy on the edges of the camp, most retreated into the forest and slipped away. We've chased some, but they aren't really fighting, they're running."

Aran nodded. That made sense. They weren't on the edge of the clearing expecting an attack from outside, from the trees. They were on the edge to get away when Aran arrived in their center. Realizing he'd been out maneuvered at every turn, he slammed a fist into the mud wall creating a burst of dust.

He could barely get the words out. "Where's the Steamer Crew?"

"Nowhere in the clearing. They've slipped away."

"They can't get far in wingcuffs. Bring a squad."

Aran shoved aside the door and flew to the center of the clearing. Around him warriors were tending to the fallen enemies, giving aid to the wounded, and dragging the bodies of the dead into a pile. They worked in the grim flicker of the bonfires in the ashen morning light.

Aran stepped inside a ring of warriors and began a quiet chant, drawing the air deep into his lungs. Holding an image of Jules in his mind, one hand moved through a series of complex postures while the other clutched a fistful of dirt. His brow furrowed a moment before he nodded his head toward the northeast and told the squad leader, "That way, about one mile."

Instantly the warriors were in the sky. Teeth clenched, Aran flew as though rushing to a new battle. His mind kept scrolling back through the events of the last twenty-four hours, hoping to find some version in which he wasn't embarrassed, betrayed, and outsmarted. Each time the loop was interrupted as his pure fury toward the Steamer Crew eclipsed everything else. The sun was coming up over the trees, and he heard the welcoming chorus of the birds begin. He held onto the Steamer's location in his mind in case they decided to move, but they seemed to be holding still.

Why? They should be on the run. Was this another trap? He slowed and swung over to the squad leader, shouting a few quick directions. They hovered. The trees were too dense for them to see anything, but they heard raised voices. On the squad leader's signal, they descended as a ring into the canopy. Beneath the treetops it was still dark, but Aran could make out the Steamer Crew members standing in a circle in an open space beneath the trees and surrounded by a large group of Rangi's warriors. Aran squinted. Many of the warriors had their spears and arrows pointed at the Steamer Crew. Jules and one of the warriors—Aran assumed it was a squad leader—were shouting at each other.

"You should have killed them and delivered the shaman by himself," the warrior screamed. "They killed hundreds of us."

Jules' reply was almost too soft to hear. "We did what Rangi ordered, got them here. The rest was up to her. Get out of our way. We have to keep going."

"You were in on it with them. Somebody's got to pay. Those are my warriors lying out on that field."

"Take it up with Rangi," Jules said smoothly. "Don't forget who we are. You don't want to tangle with us ... last chance ... get out of our way."

The squad leader stepped back, and his arm shot up to signal the attack. Just as quickly, a bowler hat sailed through the air, slicing off his forearm and hand. As the squad leader shrieked, the warriors rushed forward against what Aran had assumed was an unarmed crew. But he was very wrong. The one called Jeeter, who must have been the source of the razor-edged hat, rushed forward using his suspenders as a garrote. Slatt was rapidly assembling tiny gadgets from his pockets as a warrior rushed toward him. Just as he was about to be run through with a spear, Slatt lifted a small gun and shot his attacker. Not only were the rest of the crew armed, sometimes with pieces Aran was sure he'd confiscated, they were also fast. They were among and behind the well-trained warriors before they could even react.

The first wave of thirty or so warriors died before their squad leader, staring in disbelief at the stump of his arm, dropped to his knees and onto his face. The crew was doubled over, panting from the intense energy expenditure and searching frantically among the dead for new weapons, as a second round of warriors encircled them. Aran and the Australian squad emerged from the surrounding trees and attacked Rangi's warriors, quickly dispatching them with bolts and shields. As Aran's squad surrounded the Steamer Crew, Valente took a step forward. Aran fired a bolt into the ground at her feet and she stopped.

Aran pointed his arm at Jules's head. "Strip them. Take everything off that can come off. Every wire, earring, anything you don't have to amputate to get it off." When Jules opened his mouth to object, the look in Aran's eyes closed it again.

"When you have them completely clean, give them tunics, chain their hands and feet, and chain them to one another with short lengths. You saw what they can do, so keep your eyes on them the whole time. If one of them flinches, kill them all immediately."

He looked Jules hard in the eyes, put two fingers together, and moved his fingers so they were almost touching Jules's forehead. The air pulsed blue around them. Jules just smiled, shrugged, and started undressing. When Aran was sure the crew was under squad control, he flew back to the clearing.

The bodies of Rangi's warriors were laid in respectful rows. They'd leave them here, assuming the survivors would come back and give them the proper ceremonies. Aran saw a warrior chase a pig away from the rows. Or perhaps the pigs would eat them. A field hospital had been set up between the buildings, the outside light, gray as it was, being preferable to the inside torches. Aran worked his way among the wounded of both sides as they waited for the healers to attend to them. He found the area where the Tiki Crew lay on blankets, slightly apart from the warriors and more subdued than he'd ever seen them. No talking, no laughter. Those without their eyes closed were simply staring at the sky.

When he found Nadara, he squatted beside her. Her eyes were closed, and there were salves on her face and bandages on her arms and legs. He leaned forward, slid his arm under her shoulders, and lifted her into a light embrace, taking care not to hurt her. She lifted her arms to a weak response before dropping them again in exhaustion. He lowered her back to the blanket.

"Hey, where's mine?" a tired voice asked. Loana was smiling at him through bruises and black eyes, and he moved over to her, putting his hand gently on her shoulder.

"Are you ok?"

"I'm fine. Just a little beat up. She reserved her worst for Nadara and the boys." She looked over at Nadara. "She tried to escape. Got away several times. To get help. Each time Rangi caught her and punished her."

"What was she after?"

"You … and anything we know about Faerie magic. Details of the politics of the Silth tribes. Interactions with Humans. Lots and lots of details."

"Could you tell why?"

"No," Loana said sadly. "We couldn't figure out what she wanted. Or how to get away. We knew you'd come, but we were afraid that was just what she wanted."

Aran was about to answer when his head was filled with a voice—the shaman call.

"Storng has been poisoned. Come quickly to New York."

3

Aran (Silth)

Aran instantly arrived in New York City, but it took him some time to locate Storng in New York's Presbyterian Hospital. They'd placed him in the ward for premature babies, where the equipment was sized to deal with smaller, more fragile creatures.

Storng was guarded by an army of shamans, and a similar army of Human doctors and nurses shuttled in and out of the room. Most of the shamans hovered in the air or sat on the shelves of the room, but some stood in groups out of the way of the much larger Humans. Storng's body was small in the baby bassinet, and tubes and monitor leads wrapped him like a nightmare octopus competing for space on his body to pull data out or push fluids in. Three shamans had taken over the table next to his bed, leaving the other side clear for the Humans to work. Penfield occupied a recliner in one corner of the enormous room, out of the way of the others but monitoring everything happening.

Jabtar, the head of the shaman council, left Storng to greet Aran. Both moved to the side of the room out of the flow of traffic.

"He's in a coma. It isn't clear whether he'll recover. Whatever it was, it was in his food. He was eating lunch with him," he tipped his head toward Penfield, "and collapsed."

"Poison?"

"Yes, but not like anything we or the Humans have seen. They've taken blood for analysis and tried general antidotes to no avail. But we haven't told them what the shamans believe. This poison actively resists the efforts of the shamans to magically heal him. It's not of Human origin—it's magically based."

"Tell the doctors so they will stop trying things that may have side effects. What else can we do?"

"We're analyzing his food as are the Humans, trying to determine what the poison is. If we could do that, we might be able to respond. Otherwise it's out of our hands." He lifted his shoulders in a shrug. "He's mostly stable, but he'll die within a few more trips around the sun."

"This is the work of New Faerie. They're the only ones who'd gain by it. This morning we were betrayed by an Australian shaman who took the Faerie magic to an enemy in New Zealand. The shaman was New Faerie, and Casius had brokered the deal."

"That can't be. New Faerie rejects the fundamental beliefs of the shamans."

Aran looked around at the room's shamans. "Nonetheless, it is. Two shamans with Storng at all times, both battle-magic trained, and at least one of them known personally to you to be loyal."

Aran suddenly realized that while he was on the World Silth Council, he was actually a low-ranking shaman, not really in a position to order Jabtar to do anything. But Jabtar only nodded and began sorting through the shamans in the room and halls outside to make assignments. When Aran noticed a grim-faced Penfield watching him, he flew to the window sill beside him. Penfield stood so they could be at eye level.

"You're Aran. I recognize you from the video. Thank you. The world owes you a great debt. I'm Dr. Irvin Penfield, U.S. Ambassador for Non-Human Affairs. I'm so sorry we meet like this."

"Ambassador Penfield, Storng's spoken highly of you."

"Do you have a moment for us to talk?"

"Of course," Aran said in an undertone. "Somewhere a little less crowded, perhaps?"

"There's a conference room at the end of the hall. Would you like to wash up first?" Penfield raised his eyebrows.

Aran looked down at his robes. The hem was caked in mud, and splashes of blood dotted his sleeves. His hands were filthy and he suspected his face was similar.

Penfield led him down the hall to a restroom. When Aran had cleaned up as best he could, he flew beside Penfield to the four-person conference room. The room felt heavy, steeped in the terrible news of loved ones' impending or actual deaths delivered within its walls. Aran considered asking for some food, but he remembered what happened to Storng and decided it best that he get it for himself later. Penfield held up his finger for Aran to wait, left the room, and returned with his arms full of books. He created the same makeshift desk for Aran he had for Storng.

Without further ceremony Penfield updated Aran. "We followed all of the normal protocols for foreign representatives. The cooks were screened. There were guards in the kitchen supervising preparation. We've interviewed the servers. We don't know how someone pulled this off."

"This poison didn't come from Humans, and the Silth are experts at moving among Humans undetected."

Penfield visibly relaxed. "You're sure?"

"Absolutely. The poison is magical, so it couldn't have originated with Humans. This morning we learned that a group of Silth called

New Faerie who oppose our work with Humans to stop the Trow, have begun an active campaign against us. I've just come from a battle connected to this betrayal. All Silth know Storng was in charge of our efforts to work with Humans. He was an obvious target. We should've anticipated something like this."

"Apparently Storng did. He told me if anything happened to him, you would be the one to step in and work on our negotiations."

Aran was stunned. "I'm not sure I'm the right one for this job. In fact, I'm pretty sure I'm not."

"You are the second most recognized Silth after Storng. And you have the advantage of having been taped being a hero and saving Humans."

"I wasn't saving Humans," Aran said, almost as reflex. "I was working to save all creatures on Earth. Humans just happened to be among those."

"Nevertheless, you are the only Silth hero around. And Humans need some heroes. Things are getting really bad. Some countries are just gone, others on the edge. Anyone with resources is struggling to keep them and feed their own people, and those without have become desperate enough to try to take from anyone weaker. The cities have become the sanctuaries as people slowly figure out that the ability to make electricity equals the ability to grow food and make water in this long darkness. But about twenty percent of the Human population is gone."

"That much?"

"Some say more," Penfield said grimly.

"How can that be? I was just at Machu Picchu, and there were plenty of tourists."

"All of the ancient power centers are mobbed as people spend their last resources to go, hoping for some answers. But because there isn't enough food and clean water, diseases are spreading quickly. While the cities are better at creating resources, they are also more susceptible to the rapid spread of disease. Some are closing their borders, building walls to try to keep out the sick. And ..." Penfield lowered his eyes, "there is rising anger against the Silth."

"Why us? We're victims as well."

"They believe the Silth care more about the creatures of the jungles than people."

"Not more ...."

"I understand. I've had long discussions with Storng, but most people don't get the distinction."

"And the fact we can put aside the years of harm we've suffered at Human hands to care about them at all ... Storng, who never knew anything he didn't share, told you of my history with Humans?" Aran's voice, normally low with every word dragging across glass shards, became lower still as he fought to stay seated. To stay in the room.

"Yes."

"Then you know what an unlikely candidate for this job I am."

"He also told me how you saved Humans after a hurricane. And that you *represent the complexity of the Silth situation*. That's how he put it."

"Sounds like some of the coati scat he'd say. I'll talk to the Council, see if we can't find you someone better to work with."

"You should know the challenges go deeper still. One reason I think it needs to be you is because you have personally battled the Trow. Around the world an increasing number have advanced the theme the Trow don't exist. In the United States, a very popular televangelist is saying the story is just cover for the Silth taking over the world. That what you call Trow are angels coming to benefit Humans. Reverend Tobias's story is gaining traction around the world. I know from experience this could be trouble. Room to work together could become very limited."

"That sounds like a Human problem to me. Unless you simply want us to kill him."

Penfield stared at him. "No, that's not what we want."

"Good. That's good." Aran ran a hand down his face wearily. "We don't do that sort of thing. I'm dealing with the possibility of an internal revolt led by our own New Faerie priests that would prevent us from helping ourselves as well as you. Our people are dealing with constant assaults by Humans on the refuges. We still have to conclude our arrangements with you on the post-volcano world, stop the volcanoes, and prepare for a war with the Trow. You have to deal with your Humans. I'll talk with some others and have an answer for you by tomorrow."

Aran stood and bowed slightly. The Silth had adopted the practice in lieu of shaking hands because the act of shaking the enormous Human hands made them feel small. Aran had been told their bow was a *western bow*, with none of the nuances of the bows of eastern Humans. Aran hadn't met a Human from the east yet, much less seen one bow, but Storng had told him it was a polite way to signal the end of a conversation.

After checking on Strong and finding nothing had changed, he blipped from the room.

He appeared in the *safe zone* in Merit's colony, an area

specifically designated for these sorts of sudden arrivals. Because the warriors of Merit's colony had found it disconcerting to have Silth suddenly appearing among them, they'd quickly established a heavily guarded zone of tolerance. They put out the word anyone outside that zone would be killed immediately upon their appearance, questions asked afterward. So far as Aran knew, no one had tested their resolve. He, like everyone else, appeared in the designated area and asked to see Merit. As he waited, he thought about how similar the Sohi defense to blipping was—if it blips in, kill it.

A guard escorted him to a large building, high in a huge tree forming the center of the colony's operations. Apparently, Merit had left some standing instructions regarding his arrival, because previously he'd endured the slow bureaucratic pace of a normal visit. They flew up to the building's balcony and went inside.

Merit had maps and drawings spread on the table beside her, and she was surrounded by warriors, each waiting their turn to speak with her. As soon as one would disappear another stepped forward. More kept appearing and stepping into the queue, and she moved smoothly from one to the next. Periodically someone would appear at her elbow, and at her nod, whoever had been reporting would step back. The interloper would report, receive a few quick words from Merit, and leave.

Aran watched her calm efficiency before finally stepping forward into her line of sight. She cut her eyes toward him but continued to answer the warrior standing in front of her. As soon as she cleared the chair, another officer slid in and continued the process without interruption.

"Aran Shaman. It's good to see you."

They grasped forearms in the formal Silth greeting. She directed him toward a small, windowless side room and closed the door behind her. There her demeanor was that of a stern, but indulgent sister with a wayward brother. Aran filled her in on Storng, the morning's battle, and his loss of control of the shield, bolt, and blip magic.

"It's a bad loss. My warriors will pay the price," she said immediately, shaking her head in dismay. She looked down at the table and swept away some dust that Aran couldn't see. "But honestly, I wouldn't have seen it coming either. A trap well laid and sprung with a betrayal. I don't see what you would have done differently. Not trust the shaman student? Have we ever known one to betray their cause? The Shaman Council will end him. This technology would have escaped eventually anyway. And the day yielded many other moves by New Faerie. Every colony is reporting some effort to recruit, some move to undermine the work with Humans or the work to prepare for the Trow attack. New Faerie spies are everywhere." She slammed her wooden hand on the table in an unusual display of emotion. "Even my warriors are not immune."

Aran's eyes widened in alarm. "What?"

"We don't discuss our colony's discipline with others," she said, wiping at the same non-existent spot on the table. "But there are two fewer warriors in our colony than when the day began."

"Son of a monkey! This is all we need now. A fight on three fronts. The Trow, the Humans, and our own."

He told her Penfield wanted him to replace Storng as the ambassador to the Humans and what Penfield had said about the Humans turning against them.

"Do you trust him?" she asked.

Aran thought as he looked around the room. Nothing was out of place. Nothing was there but the necessary. "I know Storng does."

"He does. He told me so. He also told me he wanted you to deal with the Humans if anything happened to him."

"Did the two of you forget I don't like Humans?" Unbidden, an image of Shra wrapped in the mist net in the jungle surfaced, and he pushed it away.

"You don't *like* peccaries. But you still deal with them, and you didn't argue to lock them out of the refuges."

"True, but I don't have to sit in the room with peccaries or negotiate with them. And the better analogy would be monkeys. I think we should exclude monkeys and toucans from the refuges."

Merit laughed, holding her hand in front of her mouth. As the corner of her eye crinkled, he felt his mood lift.

"Discussing this is a waste of time," she insisted. "There's no one else to do the job. The Humans know you from the recording and that gives them some trust. Storng says you've dealt with Humans before to help them, and I know you've dealt with them to punish them. You crossed the line before all of this began. No other Silth leader has this experience. Yet another consequence of your refusal to follow the rules. Perhaps it will not be for long. Perhaps Storng will be well soon."

Aran sighed heavily. "Unlikely. He looked awful and the shamans are stumped. We need to identify the poison. I should be going after Rangi and dealing with Casius. As well as getting an antidote for Storng and ending the Silth internal fight. I don't need to be dealing with the games of diplomats. I don't know how to play."

"Ha! Rangi's mine to deal with. I'm the hunter. You're a storyteller. Tell the Humans our story. The story of a shared future.

Then one of a different future, where we are not working together."

"So, this is your advice? The art of diplomacy reduced to tolerance and story-telling?"

She gave a small smile with the half of her face that moved. "I'm no diplomat so what do I know? Besides, stranger things have happened."

•

CHAPTER 6

1

RANGI (SILTH)

In the early evening, Rangi and Nestor appeared in the old colony. Casius had renamed it *Tae Kirtum*, which meant *Bright Future* in Silth. They had both changed from their morning's battle clothes into their ceremonial best, all Silth-made goods. Rangi envied how good Nestor looked in her clothing, but she felt awkward and foolish in hers.

When guards immediately surrounded them holding spears close to their faces, Rangi gave their names and said haughtily, "Casius is expecting us."

They were escorted to the center of the colony. Some of the structures were old, showing careful repairs, but many were new and finely built. The tallest tree had layers of structures built into it and on branches. Nestor flew up to a porch with their escort, and after a brief discussion with the guard, they lowered a rope to Rangi. She looked at it disgustedly and wondered if she could use the Trow transport technology for this short distance. She was sure it could be used that way, but the transport to the colony was only the second time she had tried that magic and it still felt strange to her. Slowly Rangi was hauled up to the porch. As she dangled and twisted, Silth stopped to stare at her, adding to her humiliation. Once she'd been pulled to the porch and untied, the door to the structure opened. Their escort led them to a small reception area where another guard stood outside the door connecting to the rest of the structure. They took two of the four stools and waited.

Rangi became angrier as time passed, while Nestor created a small blue bolt and used it to carve figures on the floor. When the door finally opened and a robed priestess came out, Rangi thought about killing her, just to emphasize her irritation. It must have shown, because the priestess paused in mid-step, stared hard at them, and then came over. The priestess looked them over and without a word gently lowered Nestor's arm. The floor smoked with the black burn marks of an intricate pattern. Nestor frowned as she looked up at the priestess.

"Casius sends his apologies for the delay. He was expecting Aerital Shaman to be with you, so he was waiting for him to join. But now he wonders if something has delayed the shaman."

Rangi shook her head sadly. "Aerital won't be coming. He was m-m-mortally wounded during our escape and did not survive the morning."

"Yet, he taught you the bolt." The priestess's eyes narrowed. "And you transported here with Faerie magic."

"Well, yes ... he taught us with his dying words."

Nestor snorted. Rangi had seen no reason to keep the shaman alive after she tortured him into showing her all the Faerie magic he possessed. He had believed her when she said she had an antidote to the poison she'd administered to keep him from simply transporting. Now she would be the only source of the information for Casius. Rangi straightened on the stool defiantly.

"I see."

The priestess left, exiting through the same door through which she'd entered. Nestor shrugged and resumed carving the floor, while Rangi fumed and paced as the delay stretched on yet again.

Finally, the priestess held the door open wide for them to enter. Nestor on her heels, Rangi walked into the room. She heard a thump behind her and spun to see Nestor crumpled on the ground in front of the priestess's raised arm. She turned back in alarm toward the figure already in the room, Casius she assumed. He lifted his arm, pointed his finger at her, and fired a blue bolt.

Rangi heard Nestor screaming before she opened her eyes again. She held her breath as she felt the ropes tight around her, the hand on her shoulder and the knife blade at her throat.

"If you blip away, you will take Tarren with you, and she will slit your throat as soon as you rematerialize. You'll also take your ropes with you, so there'll be nothing you can do to stop it."

Rangi opened her eyes, realizing that Casius had the same blue, green and yellow coloring as Aran, though he was slightly bigger. He was unnaturally gaunt, resulting in sharp angles in his face, and wore a black robe with a red sash.

"Not that I'm sure you care, but if you blip away, I'll instantly kill this one." He tipped his head toward Nestor, who was tied in a chair with another priestess standing behind it. Nestor had a long needle inserted in the edge of her eye socket, sticking out about three inches beyond. "One tap and that goes into her brain."

Nestor was no longer screaming but whimpered while remaining very still. Rangi tested the ropes. Very tight. *Well, scat burgers.*

"Aerital was a gift, a rare one as shamans are not easy to come by. I could have had him simply come here when he learned the transport magic." Casius slowly walked back and forth, head bowed and hands clasped behind his back. "But your idea about getting Aran to disclose the technique was a good one, and I saw no reason not to honor our deal."

He moved over to the window and closed his eyes. The cacophony of bird calls welcoming even the muted morning light of the new day had swelled into a raucous ensemble easily heard inside. "There's no coordination among the birds as they sing to the morning. They each have their separate aim. But they don't work against one another. One does not benefit at another's expense." He spun back to Rangi, who was tracking his every movement. "But you thought you would gain some negotiating advantage by eliminating my shaman. While I was perfectly happy to share his knowledge with you, you hoped to come here and use it to bargain with me. Perhaps you thought I didn't have the bolt and shield magic, giving you the upper hand."

Rangi shrugged, as best she could inside the ropes.

"There is no New Faerie in New Zealand, is there?" Casius didn't bother to wait for an answer. "We welcome the arrival of the Trow, the Faeries who will help us turn this Earth into the magical place it should be. We're saddened by the use of this stolen magic and believe it's polluted by its theft. We will, however, use any means—polluted magic, alliances with creatures like you—any means—to ensure the victory of the Faeries as they return to Earth. In return, they'll treat us as equals and raise us to be the magical creatures we were born to be. We live by the words and the code of the Enlightened One, who taught us there would be a time when the success of the Faeries would depend on us, and we mustn't fail them." Casius stooped down, unblinking eyes boring into Rangi's. "What is it you want?"

Rangi had to look away. She looked around the opulent room before her eyes settled on a painting of three Trow descending from the air to a group of prostrate Silth. "New Zealand ... and Australia. I want every Paerrie in both places to bow down before m-m-me. I want to eliminate the Humans there." She hesitated, considering how much to reveal. "And ... I want to fly."

Heavy drops pattered on the thatch roof as Casius paced behind her. Unable to swivel to watch him, she found herself looking instead at Nestor, still frozen in place with the needle obscenely jutting from her face.

"Ahhh. Good! This is how this conversation could have gone. With a civil discussion of our goals and how we might work together. But, of course, it would have opened with you giving me what I had already bargained for."

The knife came away from Rangi's throat, and her chair was suddenly jerked backwards, sending her crashing to the floor. Tarren dropped to her knees and held the stiletto to Rangi's temple.

"Tell me the magic of transport or die now."

Thinking hard, Rangi decided Casius still needed something else from her. "I will tell you," she said calmly. "But first take the needle from Nestor's eye and let her go."

"I could simply order the needle in a fraction more. She would not die, but she would live the rest of her life unable to speak. You're in no position to negotiate."

Rangi said nothing. Casius nodded to the priestess holding Nestor, and Nestor tensed as the needle was extracted. The priestess used Nestor's hather to pull her back hard so that her throat was taut and put a knife to it.

"Watch what happens if you make another demand of me before you give me what I want."

Rangi slowly nodded her head, and Tarren shifted to right her chair.

As thunder rolled behind the patter of rain and the air filled with the odor of ozone, Rangi spelled out the steps to the blip. It was more difficult to do without her hands free to show certain motions, but she managed. The first time Casius tried it nothing happened. Rangi described the necessary adjustments, and when he tried again, he suddenly disappeared. In seconds he reappeared, grinning wildly, and then disappeared again. A short while later he returned, staggering slightly.

"I think this m-m-magic uses lots of energy," Rangi said. "You m-m-might not want to do that again, because you m-m-m-may get stuck and have to wait until you recharge to come back ... of course it's up to you."

Casius nodded to the priestess holding Nestor again, and Nestor tensed, gasping, but all the priestess did was release her hather and move the knife away from her neck. Then she removed the ropes holding Nestor to the chair while Tarren retied Nestor's hands in front of her and connected them to a belt around her waist to keep her from raising them. She repeated the process with Rangi. She pushed both to their feet.

"Leave if you want. Or stay and talk. The ropes stay on your hands for now, until the sting of our discussion has left you."

Casius positioned himself on a stool at a nearby table, his wings and tail hanging down behind it, and gestured to two stools opposite him. Rangi could feel Nestor watching her for direction. She had figured there would be negotiation, so she joined Casius and Nestor followed. Five acolytes came in, each carrying an enormous tray of food. Roasted corn, each kernel the size of a Silth hand. Nuts and fruit and flowers covering the trays. Small cups with nectar-infused water. The last tray was beneath a wooden cover, which the acolyte removed as soon as he set it upon the table, revealing a pile of raw lamb.

"Eat, guests," Casius said, with a grand sweep of his arm.

They sat, and the acolytes stepped forward to feed them. As they ate, Casius described what he and New Faerie wanted. In many ways, their desires were similar to Rangi's—an end to Humans and a means of obtaining the powers of the Trow, or Faeries as Casius called them, which included the power to fly without wings. Casius desired all Silth to bow before the Faeries ultimately, but he didn't care who they served among the Silth as long as that service ultimately belonged to the Faeries. Casius wanted Rangi to wage war on the Humans and on Aran. She found it odd the way he worded it—not "wage war on the Silth trying to stop the Trow," but "wage war on Aran." In return, he would support her with the New Faerie forces and spies in New Zealand and Australia, which he claimed were numerous and expanding rapidly. She would destroy the Humans and any Silth that didn't join New Faerie. Then, so long as she bound herself to an allegiance with the Faeries, Australia and New Zealand were hers. She'd participate in the powers the Faeries bestowed upon them and answer to no one but the Faeries.

"One more thing," Casius said. "I understand you have Nadara, one of the Tiki Crew. I want her."

Rangi looked at Nestor, who seemed puzzled and then brightened, telling Rangi, "You know, the one with all the tattoos and the blond hather."

Rangi told Casius, "I had her. I got the information I needed from her, and I left her behind when Aran attacked."

Casius frowned. He played with a piece of avocado for a moment. "Well, no matter. If you ever come upon her again, I would greatly appreciate it if you would bring her to me." He spoke with the avocado in his mouth, "Now, let's talk war."

2

Aran (Silth)

In the week since their rescue, the Tiki Crew's bruises and cuts had mostly healed. Aran was surprised to learn most didn't hold the Steamer Crew responsible for their capture or their torture. He had listened as Don explained over his rum and French fries, booming voice slightly slurred, "A good crew does what they are told to do. That's what we do. We don't ask, *why'd you want this or that*." He smoothed back his spikey yellow hather and looked earnestly at Nick, who was matching him drink for drink.

"Monkey scat!" Nick said. "They liked doing it. Maybe not all of them, but Three of Five smiled the whole time they were beating the monkey juice out of me."

Don seemed like he was going to disagree, but instead, "Alright, I'll give you that the *Fives* are psychos, but the rest are okay."

Now that the dome held back the ash clouds over the Australian Refuge, including this section of beach, it was one of the few places in the world with a *beach day* experience. Aran lay in the sun, surrounded by hand towels laid out on the sand, and Tiki Crew members sprawled on them or sitting up and talking. Down the beach, under canvas canopies, sat the Steamer Crew. For all his charity, Don had still given them only aloha shirts, shorts, and sarongs to wear. Still in wingcuffs and handcuffs, the crew members looked miserable.

Aran watched Loana and Nadara playing a game something like Human volleyball, hitting a Bunya nut back and forth over a rope strung between two posts. Nadara was radiant in the sunlight. She wore her hather longer than she did when Aran first met her, blue, still tipped in blond. Her shorts showed long, strong legs and the halter top the impressive muscles in her shoulders and arms. They moved smoothly under the covering tattoos. The sun caught her silver piercings and made her sparkle. She laughed as she dove for the ball, and Aran marveled at the Tiki Crew's resilience. Today was a holiday, the last day of recuperation before they all began to work again. But even on this day, he had decisions to make.

He forced himself to overcome the sun-induced torpor and pulled himself to his feet. He trudged through the sand to the clutch of Steamer Crew. Marina was sitting in front of Jules with an open space of towel between them. On the towel were some of the Steamer's various gizmos and gadgets. She was holding up Jules's small pocket watch, asking about its true function. After watching them in action, Aran had determined the Steamers had nothing, no gadget, no clothing, no body augmentation that was not a weapon.

"Careful," Jules said gently, "Don't open it. Unless you push the buttons in the right sequence, you get a face full of sleeping dust."

Jules looked confused as Marina laughed, apparently delighted at the ingenuity, put it back down on the towel, and picked up another piece of gadgetry. He and most of the rest of the Steamer Crew had been subdued since Aran rescued and captured them. Surprised by their abandonment by Rangi, hurt by her warriors' betrayal, and embarrassed by their rescue and capture, they seemed without energy or direction. Except Three of Five. The guards had learned they could not relax their watch when she was around. None of the Silth other than the Steamers could tell Three of Five or Four of Five apart without their costumes. Each had their number tattooed on their arm, but Aran and the others were still learning which personality went with which number. She continued to test the guards and several times came close to escaping until Aran threatened to clip the wings of the whole crew. Jules ordered her to stop and she did so immediately, with none of the backsquawk such a command would produce from the Tiki Crew.

"Marina, could I have a moment with Jules, please?"

Marina gathered up the blanket and the devices laid out on it. When she finished, she noticed Jules's quizzical expression. She counted the items and then looked back at him, mouth open in mock dismay, and he moved his foot to reveal the wind-up device he'd slid from the blanket without her notice. She grabbed it and stuck her tongue out before trotting away across the sand.

Aran untied the twine binding Jules's hands. He suspected the Steamer Crew could get out of constraints whenever they wanted anyway. Seeking shade, they sat on a pair of coconuts lying under a palm tree.

"You've thought about what we discussed?" Aran asked.

He and Jules had had several conversations over the last two weeks. Given all the other things he had to focus on, he'd spent a disproportionate amount of time working on Jules. Jules and Aran had discussed the two crews and their purposes. Aran explained the Tiki Crew were good-hearted thieves conscripted into more important work as the Silth tried to deal with Humans, volcanoes, and the coming Trow war. He also told Jules that they were very important to him and he'd do anything to protect them. He then did something he hadn't done with any other Silth. He showed Jules some of the powers he'd gained from Faelen that had not yet been revealed to anyone, mostly because he didn't trust that these, like the ability to transport, would not be spread among the Silth and misused by some. Jules had shown no sign he was intimidated, but Aran could tell he was impressed.

For his part, Jules had confirmed that the Steamer Crew members were assassins, intended to kill or intimidate whomever Rangi indicated. Although very good at it, they had no love for this purpose. Except perhaps Three of Five, who seemed to have an unnatural level of hostility toward all living things. They also had no love of Rangi. Many of the physical implants worn by the Steamer Crew were involuntary—Rangi thought them up and forced them upon the crew members. Jules believed One and Two of Five died as a result of Rangi's more extreme ideas.

The Steamer Crew were, however, united in their hatred of Humans. Jeter's feelings were especially deep because of the Human war on the Galahs, the parrots who had fledged him. Humans considered them pests and culled them. Similarly, Vander had been born into a red-cheeked parrot colony routinely trapped because they ate Human crops. Three of Five's colony had been hunted by Humans who used arrows smeared with sticky resin to capture the parrots. The depth of these feelings persuaded the entire crew to despise Humans. Jules said any of them would easily give their lives for the others, but beyond these comrades, they had no loyalties.

"I spoke with all of them, and we agree we will work for the Council. Our conditions are that we are freed from the wingcuffs, our clothes and devices are returned, and we are never dressed in these ridiculous clothes again. We are not to be separated, no one is involuntarily augmented, we are not asked to interface with Humans nor directly benefit them, our service ends when the Trow are defeated, and we are allowed to retire to the location of our choice with wealth beyond our imagination."

Aran looked out at the waves, trying not to smile in the face of Jules's very serious pronouncement. "We may need to explore just how grand your imagination is, but these terms are acceptable." Jules agreed each of them would be magically bound to their agreement.

Aran could see Don and Nick down the beach and gave a shrill whistle. He made a complicated serious of hand motions ending by pointing back to his wings. One of the benefits of belonging to the same crew was sharing the sign language often used in their stealth explorations of buildings. Don nodded, and he and Nick started walking toward the tarp where the Steamer Crew was.

"You go confirm the arrangement to the rest of your crew. Make sure all have agreed, because if one of you goes sideways, the deal is off for all." He waited for Jules to nod his acknowledgment. "Then Don and Nick will remove everyone's wingcuffs. We'll give it a few days with you and the Tiki Crew. If Three of Five doesn't kill anyone in that period, we'll teach you the bolt and shield."

As Jules left to deal with his crew, Aran dropped on the towel next to a napping Nadara. Exhausted, he promptly fell asleep. When Shra appeared, he knew it was a dream, but unlike any he'd previously experienced. She was standing in front of him, smiling. He reached for her, but without moving she was suddenly beyond his arms. She pointed her index finger at the sky, using a repetitive motion as if to emphasize that was where she wanted him to go. Then she lowered her arm and with both hands made a shooing motion, flicked her fingers forward, and said, "Jalutra."

Aran awoke slowly, and as he sat up, Nadara stirred next to

him.

"There's a story about Jalutra, the jaguar prince. Do you remember it?"

"Ummmm," Nadara mumbled into the towel and then turned her face toward him. "Tell me."

"Jalutra was a jaguar prince, and he fell in love with a Human princess. He came upon her in the jungle. Her name was …." Aran struggled to remember, and then it came to him. "Her name was Sofanja."

"At first Jalutra planned to eat her, but then as he watched, he was taken by her kindness and grace. He decided instead to marry her. So, he went to his father and asked him to petition the Human king for her hand." Aran grinned. "This was back when these things were largely arranged by the males. A much more enlightened time, if you ask me." That earned him a sharp whack.

"Now the jaguar king believed this marriage was a bad idea, but he knew Jalutra would not relent. He loved his son and wanted him to be a strong king when it was his time, so the jaguar king visited the Human king. He laid out the proposed marriage and why it would be good for both the Humans and the jaguars of the region. The Human king also thought it was a bad idea, but he didn't want to insult the jaguars and have them as enemies. Mostly they kept to themselves and hunted the forest animals, not Humans.

"The Human king said he'd let his daughter decide. Her response was, 'That sounds like a really bad idea. Why would I want to be the wife of a jaguar?' But she too didn't want to insult the jaguars. She was a very bright young woman, however, and said, 'I don't know that this jaguar is worthy to be my husband. Let him prove his worth by performing three tasks. First, he must stop the flow of the mighty river that runs through our shared kingdom without any Human help. Second, he must build a tall pyramid, with only Human hands. Third, he must complete something, with the help of both Humans and animals, that causes them all to agree this is the greatest thing ever accomplished.' The Human king was pleased, because he, like his daughter, was confident no one could complete these three tasks. When the jaguar king was told Sofanja's answer, he too was pleased by its wisdom. But when he shared it with his son, to his surprise Jalutra simply nodded and set out to accomplish the tasks.

"Jalutra began with the first task—stopping the flow of the mighty river. He sat by its banks for several weeks just thinking about how such a thing could be done. Spies told Sofanja that all he did was sit there, staring at the water. Sofanja smiled to herself and went about her life, sure she'd never be wed to the prince.

"One day the prince sprang up and ran toward the river, waving his arms. In the river was Boto, the pink river dolphin, said to be the smartest animal alive.

"'Boto, I have a problem'. And Jalutra told the dolphin what he was trying to do.

"'Well, it can be done. It would be easier in Africa where you have many big animals, and it would only take a few to work together to do this. But here in the Amazon are only smaller animals, and all would be needed. And why would they do this for you?'

"Jalutra thanked Boto, sat under a tree by the river's edge, and watched the water yet again. He stayed there through the rainy season, only moving when he needed to eat or when the water rose so high that he needed to climb the tree.

"His father worried about him. 'Find yourself a nice jaguar girl. One with no tattoos.'" Aran got another whack. "'Forget this silly Human girl and her trials.'

"Jalutra reached out to the other animals. At first, they were nervous, but when they realized he wanted to understand what they wanted in the world, they talked to him. Finally, Jalutra's plan came together, and he promised each of the animals that if they helped him, he would work to get them what they wanted. He waited for the rainy season waters to recede and for the draught to set in. When the river was at its weakest, reduced by months of draught, he called the other animals. The many capybaras entered the river and stood on the backs of caimans and crocodiles. Green anacondas, helped by electric eels and red-bellied piranha, started filling the holes in the living wall. When the water was reduced to a trickle, poison dart frogs plugged the last small holes. The mighty river was stopped. The kings were summoned, and they were astonished but agreed the first task had been completed.

"Jalutra moved on to the next task. Sofanja wasn't worried and neither were the kings, for they believed it impossible for Jalutra to persuade the Humans to build anything on his behalf. But they had no way of knowing this task was far easier than the first. Jalutra went and sat with the Human priests, and they talked of the world and its mysteries. Jalutra had spent much of the time he sat on the banks of the river thinking about his tasks—why he wanted to accomplish them and what was important in the world. He learned much from the priests, but he also taught them. Because he was enjoying himself so much, he'd almost forgotten he needed something from the Humans. He wasn't even sure he cared that much about completing these tasks. But the priests were so impressed by his wisdom, they asked if they could talk to him when problems beset the Human kingdom. Jalutra thought about the help he'd received from Boto and the animals and readily agreed. Ecstatic, the priests told him they'd build a tall pyramid at the edge of the jungle allowing them to call him when needed. And so they did. When it was completed, the kings were again summoned and confirmed the completion of the second task.

"Sofanja and the kings were a little worried. Jalutra had completed two of the three tasks. Sofanja had to admit, however, she was a bit impressed by this jaguar prince and was a little disappointed she'd made the final task impossible. She remembered her words, 'Third, he must complete something, with the help of both Humans and animals, that causes them all to agree this is the greatest thing ever accomplished.' Jalutra was also concerned about this third task. He had no idea what the greatest thing would be and Humans and animals working together? Why would they do that? He went back to his tree. After much reflection, he realized he no longer felt compelled to complete this task. If Sofanja didn't want to marry him, then he didn't want to force her. But had he decided this only because the task was so difficult? As he sat, the normal, seasonal draught that had caused the river to drop continued far past its usual time. Sofanja's city ran out of water, and all its people were faced with leaving it to survive. Sofanja's father was afraid they'd never return and the city would die. He called his priests, but they said they'd been praying for weeks with no change. 'Do something!' he ordered. So, they went to their new pyramid and called Jalutra.

"When they told him the problem, he shook his head sadly. 'I can only think of one way to solve this problem, but it's unlikely to work.' He told them the Humans could dig a ditch leading from the river to the city's quarry, a great hole created when they dug out the stone for the pyramid. The animals again could dam the remaining river and divert enough water into the quarry to last until the rainy season finally came.

"The priests were very excited about this idea and asked, 'Why won't it work?'

"'The animals will only do this if they gain something to make their lives better,' was Jalutra's answer. 'What would it do for them?' The priests conferred and concluded that they could make several of the animals sacred, so that they could not be hunted. They could also share their cities with all the animals, finding ways for them to live together, whether in the jungle, the fields or the streets. Jalutra presented this proposal to the animals. They debated it. The monkeys opposed it, no great surprise, but the tapiro supported it. Finally, the animals agreed. All went according to the plan, and as the reservoir filled, the king pronounced this the greatest thing ever accomplished.

"Jalutra, having not even considered this one of the tasks, was skeptical.   'Filling a bucket is the greatest thing?' The king said, 'No. Finding a way for Humans and animals to work together is.'

"As Sofanja waited for the jaguar prince to come for her, she realized she no longer dreaded marrying him. He had completed all her tasks. He'd always been handsome and powerful, but now he had become wise as well, respected by Humans and animals. He'd make a good king and perhaps a good husband. But as the days passed, he didn't come. Finally, she tired of waiting and went to the tree beside the river where her spies told her he did his thinking. When she found him, she was angry. 'Why have you put me through all this worry,' she said, 'and then you don't even come to marry me?'

"He looked at her with an open heart and asked her to sit beside him. He nodded toward the river, now full of water, but not yet rising over its banks. 'I thought I should thank this river, because it was the key to my performing your tasks.' They talked about the river and life. Both learned from the other, and time passed easily. Eventually they wed, because it was what they both wanted. The kings pronounced them both very wise in their choices and over the years, under their leadership, the kingdoms of both men and animals prospered."

Aran rolled onto his back and absorbed the sun.

"I've never heard that story before," Nadara told him.

"It isn't very popular anymore, because no Silth can imagine wanting to work with the Humans, much less actually accomplishing it. And Silth females aren't fond of the way the princess is cast in it, though it always seemed to me she was the wisest of any of them."

"Why did you think of it?"

"A dream. It was suggested to me in a dream." He stood and brushed sand off his legs. "I think it means I'm supposed to work with the Humans in Storng's place for now, but I've got to think about it some. Perhaps it means more. I'm going to walk for a little while, want to come?"

"No, I'll let you contemplate your river."

3

Aran (Silth)

Aran sat next to Faelen's bed as Faelen drank the rum he'd brought. He'd walked in by the mind-reading gate, and just to make sure, he'd been thinking about the rum as he entered. The Trow made no move to stop him.

Lornix frowned at him as he came through the infirmary door, looked at the emaciated figure propped up on the bed, sighed heavily, and left. Aran went through the motions of asking Faelen if he really wanted to drink again when he'd managed to complete the painful process of alcohol withdrawal. The conclusion was foregone. Faelen happily guzzled the rum. Aran tried his hand at cheerful conversation, but his heart wasn't in it.

Between long pulls on the bottle's contents, Faelen insisted that Faeries did not become addicted to alcohol the way Humans or Silth did. Their bodies adapted to crave the liquor, but their minds didn't bend to tell them lies about their circumstances. Consequently, a Trow who drank excessively did so by choice, not compulsion. They knew full well their destructive path and embraced it. Aran had no idea whether this was true or monkey scat. It didn't make him feel any better.

"I haven't told the Silth you're alive or that this place exists. I know if I did, they'd have hope that perhaps our race will not end with the coming Trow war. But if the Sohi won't perform magic, it would be a false hope."

"As best I can tell they will not," said the now cooperative Faelen. His face darkened. "And if you are suggesting I can be the brood hen for the Paerries, the answer is no."

Aran had seen a parrot *brood hen* once, while in Florida. She lived her whole life in darkness with little contact with her own kind except as necessary for her to lay the eggs sought by the pet stores and without any love from Humans. When he saw her, she was about to be shipped to a Virginia refuge that took in parrots unable to be placed in Human homes. She bit anyone who came near. He didn't recall ever having seen such an unhappy being.

"I think the better analogy would be a prize stud bull," Aran said. "In Florida I saw a bull so huge he couldn't breed normally. They had him mounted on this metal contraption and wheeled him from cow to cow."

Faelen scowled and took another long drink.

"I'm more concerned that if you're healed, you'd return to fight, and this time they really *would* kill you. I've lived through that once and would rather not do it again."

"Do you have the magic to heal me or not?" Faelen didn't meet Aran's eyes. "I will not beg for your help or bargain for my future. Not with you. Not with my father. Not with the Paerries. Not with the Sohi."

Aran broke the long silence that followed. "I don't know about any of the others, but you've done so much for me and for the world, you certainly have the right to make your own choices. As to whether I can heal you ... I don't know." He held up the edge of a large rowling bag. "I brought the things I'd need in order to try. This is Silth magic, not Faerie magic. But it will take lots of magic, lots of potions, lots of pain on your part whether it works or not. There's a reasonable chance you will die. There are other Silth shamans who would have a much better chance of accomplishing this ...."

"Sounds great. You will do."

"I don't think I ever told you the Silth magic didn't work quite right when I tried to sober you up after your crocodile encounter."

Faelen said nothing and stared at Aran.

Aran began to build the sweat lodge in a park next to the infirmary. Having observed his intentions when he arrived through the gate, the Sohi had already gathered most of the necessary materials and placed them next to a stream. Aran assumed this was also their tacit permission to perform magic within their retreat.

For the next two days Aran filled Faelen with potions and drugs. He sweated him and then cooled him with the stream water. He chanted and used his strong emotional ties to draw on all the energy he could access. He tried to reach the energy stored in the bracelet and necklace he wore, what Storng called the *Butcher Energy,* but as usual it remained beyond him.

Faelen's heart stopped at the end of the second day. Not since Shra's death had Aran been as frantic as those few moments when he was working to restart the Trow's heart. When it began beating again, Aran was ecstatic. It stopped again later that night, but since Aran was staying awake through the entire treatment, he was able to start it again. Lornix brought him food and water. He drank the water but left the food.

At the end of the third day, as a nearly exhausted Aran chanted over the colored sand painting made with moonlight infused sand, Faelen sat up. Aran watched him gingerly stand, testing his legs. His face broke into a wide grin, and he disappeared.

Aran flung himself back against the interwoven sticks of the lodge and closed his eyes. He'd almost fallen asleep when the telephone's ring jolted him awake. His first thought was amazement that the phone, one of the ones supplied by Penfield, received calls in this location. He struggled to get the phone from his cloak. A voice he didn't recognize said, "Rangi and New Faerie are attacking the Australian refuge. From the questions they're asking prisoners, they're after Nadara." The phone went dead.

He tried to transport to Australia. Nothing happened. He tried to stand, but he couldn't. Outside he heard the sound of dishes being collected, and in a voice so thready it worried even him, he called out to Lornix for help.

4

MERIT (SILTH)

Like many Silth who now *carried* phones, Merit didn't actually carry hers—instead, one of the warriors wore a backpack designed just for the phone. Merit used a small Bluetooth headset enabling her to answer it.

She was in Brazil mopping up after repelling the Brazilian attack on the refuge. The attack had been half-hearted at best, more for the politics of having made the effort, she assumed.

The Brazilian army had made their intentions clear in advance, as though warning the Silth to be prepared for where they would probe. When the probe came, the Silth were careful to avoid killing any of the soldiers, limiting themselves to stunning bolts and the destruction of equipment.

Merit and her warriors were resting in Joss's encampment, full from feasting and happy in the bonhomie of the grateful refuge workers. When the phone chirped, she tapped the *Bluetooth* earpiece. "Merit … what? … I can barely hear you."

She struggled to hear through wind noise as Aran told her he was on a Peruvian mountain and needed help getting to Australia, and that Rangi was attacking its refuge, trying to recapture Nadara.

"Why Nadara?"

"I have no idea. Rangi already had her captive and could have taken her when Rangi left before."

After getting more details about his location, Merit quickly gathered nine warriors. The group disappeared from the Brazilian rain forest and reappeared on the side of a snow-covered Peruvian mountain. She spotted Aran lying in the snow about a hundred yards away.

She shook him awake and helped him to his feet. "Why are you here?" She studied him closely. "What's happened to you?"

"I'm paying the price of using a great deal of magic. And as for what I'm doing here ..." he paused and looked around at the array of warriors, "that'll have to wait until later. Let's go."

As soon as they blinked to the Australian bush, sizzling blue bolts struck their shields. Before her warriors could fire back, Merit yelled, "Hold, hold." She realized the bolts were coming from the Australian warriors reacting to a new threat suddenly appearing in their midst.

"Stand down," she shouted.

As warriors' arms dropped to their sides and the blue shields lowered around them, Merit looked around for a squad leader insignia and finally found one.

"What's going on? Are you still under attack?"

"No. Rangi and her forces withdrew just before you arrived. We're regrouping and preparing in case they try a second time. We're also attending to the wounded. There're several dead as well."

Merit saw Aran flinch as she rounded on him, her face twisted in anger. "This is what I was afraid of. We're not prepared to fight an enemy that can simply appear among us at will."

"Yet this is the tactic we used to attack Rangi," Aran said gently. "And it'll be the tactic the Trow use when they come. If we aren't prepared ..." then, almost as if to himself, "it is the new way of war. Rangi is no longer a factor."

With a growl, Merit spun back to the squad leader. "What were they after?"

"The sole purpose of the attack seemed to be to capture one of the Tiki Crew, Nadara."

"Why do we believe that?"

"As soon as the attack began, they questioned anyone they captured about where she was. When they finally learned her location, the entire force was directed there."

Merit thought about the implications. First, she was concerned someone had told them where Nadara was. But second, she was confused—why Nadara? "Where is she? Did they take her?"

"No, the assassins, the Steamer Paerries, were unassailable. They and the Tiki Crew defended a building against a far greater force. Rangi's force was shredded and finally withdrew as our warriors increased the pressure on their flank. She's in there." He pointed to a cabin on the edge of the jungle.

As Aran and Merit hurried to the building, the number of bodies around them increased. Most were Rangi's warriors. A few were without armor, and Merit assumed they were New Faerie followers who'd joined Rangi.

As they neared the cabin, Aran called out, "Helloooo, it's Aran. We're coming in."

They stepped over the pile of bodies at the front door and went inside. The room was a makeshift infirmary. Around them bandages were being applied and wounds cauterized. Two shamans moved among the crews applying magical potions and healings. Merit watched Aran take in the scene and locate Nadara. When the two embraced, Merit tried to remain clinical in her analysis, but she thought she saw more than just Aran's relief that Nadara was safe.

Merit joined them, greeted Nadara, and asked, "Why were they after you?"

"The Australians told me I was their target, but I don't know why. They just had me and tortured me.   What more could they want?" Nadara slammed her palm on the foot of a bed. "What is wrong with this Rangi creature?"

Merit was impressed someone who'd been tortured and was the object of an attack would be angry, not scared. "There has to be a reason." Brows arched, she looked back and forward between them until she could see Aran understood.

"You mean could it be about getting to me? Perhaps." He held Nadara closer. "But why now? She already had her. Used her and the Tiki Crew to bait her trap before. Why would she spend so much to get her back?"

Merit shook her head. "You're right. It doesn't make sense. We're missing something." Around her, the Steamer Paerries had been sufficiently patched and were busy rearming themselves. "Nadara, you're lucky the assassins were on your side. I think they made the difference. Now I need to rethink the strategy for defending these places since the transport magic is out."

But as she left the room, she wasn't thinking about defense tactics. How did she feel about Aran's relationship with Nadara? Why was she even thinking about it? Was she jealous? She laughed to herself as she recalled an old Silth saying, "Silth don't get jealous, they just compete." Did she want to compete? She had plenty of potential romantic partners. She attracted males and females to her power like flies to honey. Mostly she ignored them or engaged in quick utilitarian couplings. It was simply too stressful—she found herself watching them all the time, trying to detect some reaction to her scars. To her missing hand. She was disciplined, and they weren't. Even the soldiers were sloppy in the wash of emotion. *Ha, and they were all far more disciplined than Aran, the paragon of chaos.*

In the compound warriors were removing the dead and repairing buildings. The Australians had taken heavy losses in the initial surprise of the attack. Rangi had left her fallen troops behind. Historically when Silth battled, there were no dead bodies to deal with, because when they died the Silth disappeared. Consequently, the Silth had evolved a funeral practice of hanging small figures in the surrounding trees to honor the dead. That would be done today, for both the Australians and Rangi's New Zealanders. But in this new day of magical battles using Faerie bolts, the bodies of the magically dead didn't disappear. The Silth had a traditional ceremony to deal with the passage of spirits into the energy of the world, but these days they were dealing with the unfamiliar task of returning the elements of the bodies to Earth to use again. They piled up friend and foe alike and burned them. The dismal undertaking was already underway, the smoke adding extra weight and noxious odor to the morning air.

How would they prepare for future attacks, not just here but around the world? No place was safe now. But her mind kept coming back to Aran. What was Aran doing on a mountainside in Peru that had left him exhausted? Did his use of magic have to do with his search for the Trow? She would need to get him alone to ask.

With great effort, she forced her thoughts back to her specialty—tactics.

CHAPTER 7

1

Joss (Human)

Joss tried to work herself into a good anger, but it was useless.

Having heard Shadow whining at the door before the knock came, she knew it was Tiny. It was 10:00 at night, so he'd just be arriving back in camp. She'd said *come in* without removing the unopened wine bottle from the table, where she'd been staring at it for the last half hour. Tiny entered, jovial as ever, and without breaking stride, picked up the bottle and unscrewed it. While telling her about his trip to study one of the still-erupting volcanoes, he poured the contents down the drain. He'd paused one moment before tipping it, giving her a chance to tell him to stop, but she'd said nothing.

The wine had been the center of her world for the last twenty-four hours. She'd swiped it from the dining hall and repeatedly talked herself out of opening it. She meditated and exercised like a banshee. She went on-line to her support group, but when she told them she was in trouble, she didn't mention the bottle was in her room. Now, just like that, it was gone. He poured a couple of glasses of juice and sat down opposite her at the table, talked as though nothing unusual had happened and tried to draw her into conversation. After their mandatory ear scratching, Shadow and Macho flopped down at their feet.

Joss gave up on the mad, admitting to herself he'd done what she hadn't found the strength to do. What she had hoped he would do. It didn't resolve anything, but it bridged the current crisis.

She answered his question about Kate. "Talked to her this morning. Everything is going well at their refuge. Costa Rica has no army so they've never been a big threat to them. Mostly they're dealing with desperate folks trying to sneak in to hunt. It's heartbreaking for her. The first time, they use part of the refuge's share of the neighboring farming production to feed the folks they catch and send them on their way with food. They've had to be harsher if the same people come back and it tears her up. She said Brophy came by—you remember he was the one the Faeries tried to get to set off the Yellowstone bomb."

"If I remember correctly, he's the one who'd like to be your boyfriend."

Joss rolled her eyes. "I might share too much with you." She leaned her elbows on the table. "It was a one-way deal," she said, wondering why she felt compelled to explain. "Anyway, it doesn't appear that anyone's trying to find him anymore. They have bigger fish to fry. He asked her for a job at the refuge, but she said no, that if people found out about him it would just raise questions about Silth involvement with him and his group. Really, she never liked him anyway, so I think that was an excuse."

"Probably a pretty good one."

They talked on about anything and everything. He told her the volcanoes showed no signs of stopping. All sorts of ideas were being explored to try to shut them down, but few seemed feasible. He worried that they were settling into a state of permanent eruption, which might continue for years. Temperatures around the world were already stabilizing far below their norms as the long winter set in. He noted there have been several previous long winters, each caused by a single volcanic eruption. They had caused famine, contagion, revolts and widespread death. Joss saw his happy armor crack for a brief moment before he poured optimism into the chinks and smiled again.

He'd been away when the Brazilian army finally made their move against the refuge, so she filled him in. "Merit had the Silth warriors ready and had been reading the army's moves carefully. She said because they didn't use air support and made their approach obvious, with no initial effort to send in any sort of stealth troops, she didn't think they were serious about the attack. She read it as something they needed to do to show they tried, more of a political move than a strategic one. She had her warriors hold back. They stunned soldiers instead of killing them and gave them time to clear out of vehicles before they blew them up. It made for dramatic footage on the evening news, but in reality, no Humans were killed.

"Because the soldiers didn't try to surprise the Silth, the Silth warriors were always protected by the Faerie shields and they had no losses. Since then the Army has sent in several reconnaissance patrols. The Silth don't try to stop them, since they're careful not to violate any of the rules of the refuge. But they make their own presence known by obviously following them through the jungle. The patrols have set up a temporary camp in an open meadow beside a stream. They strip and lie out in the meadow, enjoying the sunshine only available there in the refuge. When the third patrol made a beeline for the meadow, the Silth were amused, and some of their warriors were permitted to take a cooler of soft drinks and beers into the meadow to build rapport."

Joss wondered if they should talk about the wine. Was he

disappointed in her? Was she making her problem his responsibility? But she just wanted to forget it had happened.

Joss told Tiny how strange it was to have a deadly army that would strike at her direction. Even though she didn't command the Silth—that was Krackle's job—they respected her judgment. When she suggested they act, they discussed it as a council, allowing Joss to participate. Her responsibility struck her as ironic given she'd shunned violence in pursuit of her cause. She and Tiny agreed it seemed like a time for heroes, and neither felt qualified. Neither desired hero status. They just hoped for a better world. But she was concerned about the Silth. There were several signs of dissent among them. Krackle assured her that it was nothing she couldn't handle, but there was a tension there that was new.

It was late, and they both were tired. But Joss was still wound up and feeling overwhelmed by her job. They talked about Joss's work leading a group outlining the Silth position on future Human, wildlife, and Silth relations. If they won a war against the Faeries, what kind of world would they build on the other side? Aran wanted a Human commitment to this new world before the Silth fixed the volcanoes, but they all agreed that the details would have to be negotiated at length afterward. In the next couple of weeks, however, they wanted to put the broad outline before the United Nations. The group discussions were intense. The Human participants were having difficulty breaking free of what they themselves referred to as *Human exceptionalism* suggesting the Humans deserved some priority. The Silth were gentle but insistent they didn't recognize their priority, but neither did they advance an exception for themselves. They insisted on the rights of all things to life and an opportunity to thrive. Joss went to bed each night with a stress headache which only got worse as the deadline approached.

The conversation began to wind down. Shadow and Macho were happily twitching in deep doggy dreams. Joss had somehow ended up in Tiny's lap, feeling very safe in his arms.

"Aran told me a story when he was explaining the different kinds of magic. He said the tortoises living on the Galapagos islands today are unique to the islands, meaning they evolved on the islands away from the mainland. But the tortoises are older than the islands on which they live. This showed they evolved on islands now gone and managed to get to new islands and continue to live on them. He said this was an example of the slowness of Earth magic." She stroked Tiny's chest. "But maybe in these times, it isn't as slow as he thinks."

She turned off the light and took his hand, leading him to the bed. *Sometimes the best way to break a bad habit is to replace it with a good one.*

2

JOSS (HUMAN)

The next morning Joss left her cabin early. The grass of the compound shimmered with dew, the air lighter than it would be when the sun warmed it and filled it with moisture. As a sloth ambled through the opening toward a new tree, Joss carefully stepped over a line of leaf-cutter ants carting small bits of plants back to their mound. She heard a pair of macaws talking to the morning but was unable to locate them in the dense canopy.

At the edge of the clearing she found the enclave of Silth buildings. Other than her official tour of the refuge, she'd never come over to these buildings. She hadn't been sure she'd recognize which one belonged to Krackle, but standing here it was obvious. All the dwellings blended into the jungle, mirroring its browns, grays and greens, except for one. That building, about eye level for Joss, stood out in a riot of bright colors like someone's paint ball practice target. Chimes hung from the porch rafters. Metal sculptures whirled and clanked in the morning breeze. The Silth enclave was noisy anyway, with squawks, clucks and hoots coming from all the buildings, mixed with soft morning conversations and the sounds of water tumbling from showers.

Joss started to turn away from the intimacy of the setting when Krackle stepped through her doorway, stretched her arms overhead, and spread her wings wide behind her.

"What can I do for you this fine morning, Ms. Joss?"

"Do you have a moment to walk with me?"

"These old legs will never keep up with your big ole long ones. But I'll keep up another way." Krackle launched off her porch and flew beside Joss as she walked down the path into the jungle.

"So, something's on your mind you don't want to discuss in that nest of Silth ears. What would that be? Is everything all right?"

Joss picked up a stick, carefully examining it for ants and biting bugs before using it as a walking stick. "Everything's fine. I have a personal problem, and I wondered if there was anything you could do."

Krackle clapped her hands together. "Ohhhh, honey, I specialize in solving personal problems. On a typical day I've solved ten or twelve before breakfast! What can I do for you?"

Joss laughed. "I'm a *recovering alcoholic.*" She paused, deciding what came next. "Which means at any point I'm one drink from being an alcoholic again. I've been sober for a decade, but all the pressure, the expectations, the decisions are getting to me." She poked the stick into a fungus mound on the ground, releasing a cloud of spores. "It's taking too much of my energy and focus to keep on my path. I need to free up attention for my job."

"And for that young man who's sweet on you."

Joss felt herself blush. "Yeah, maybe for that, too. Is there a potion or some magic that would help?"

Krackle landed on a stump next to the path. "That's a hard one, baby. There's no cure for addiction. The Silth have tried for ages. We have the same sorts of problems with drugs, alcohol, and such that Humans do. Addiction is mental as well as physical. I can't do anything about the mental. If you decide to drink, you will. I'm always here to talk to you if you want. Share the load." She smiled. "We do have a root we chew that lessens the physical cravings to let you focus on other things. Sort of like how Chuck Corley is chewing nicotine gum as he stops smoking. The root is beneficial. Gives you more energy, isn't addictive. I'll have some for you later today. Don't know how well it works on Humans. Never tried, but I bet it'll help."

"I'd appreciate it." Joss lowered her voice, "Quietly though. I have enough trouble earning my authority without everyone knowing my weaknesses."

Krackle's donkey bray of a laugh sounded particularly loud in the jungle morning. "You're so funny. Everyone has seen you dancing with liquor. You stare at the bottle. You hug it. You push it away. Everyone knows your weakness. What you're hiding is your strength."

"Oh, just great."

Krackle flew over, lifted Joss's arm, and hugged it close. "It'll be all right, child. We all believe in you." She let go. "Now if this little thing is all, I've got to go solve another nine personal problems before breakfast. Come back by my place later, and I'll have some of the *vexin*—that's the name of the root." Krackle flew off down the path and around a bend, back toward the Silth enclave.

As Joss kept walking, she heard a quick, muffled noise. She spun around and rushed back after Krackle, afraid that a cougar had jumped her. As she rounded the bend, she saw Krackle on the ground with a Silth sitting on her chest, wings flapping to create downward pressure and an arm raised holding a penknife. Krackle had both hands on the arm's elbow trying to stop its downward thrust. Joss didn't break stride but rushed toward them and threw herself at the Silth. She knocked it off and both tumbled onto the path. She scrambled to her feet, in time to see a snarling female Silth flying toward her, knife pointed forward.

Still holding her walking stick, Joss swung it like a baseball bat. She connected fully with the body of the Silth and drove her into a large jabuticaba tree, where she crumbled to the bottom. Joss waited; stick poised to swing again. When the Silth didn't move, she dropped it. Whether from adrenaline or just the sight of the broken beauty, she found herself sitting on the ground and sobbing.

After a few moments she felt Krackle leaning against her. Warmth seeped in like sunshine as it spread through her. The tears stopped, her arms encircled the old Silth shaman, and they stayed that way without speaking until the actual sun's rays reached the path. Then they slowly made their way back to the enclave.

3

ARAN (SILTH)

"The whackadoodles of my enemy are my friends?" Jabtar repeated with no hint he understood it.

Aran should have known better than to repeat a joke Storng told him, particularly here in a World Silth Council meeting. He was forced to spend the next ten minutes explaining it was a play on a famous Human quotation that the enemy of my enemy is my friend, and that *whackadoodles* was a humorous Human word for individuals or groups you considered crazy. Furthermore, the joke was an acknowledgment that the Silth had groups led by crazy individuals like Casius and Rangi, and the Humans had crazy groups too. Sooner or later they would reach out to one another for support and assistance, even though they had very different, even conflicting motives for their actions. Thus, the alliance of Rangi and Casius. Storng had expected there would be alliances of Silth fringe groups and, eventually, Humans.

After Jabtar finally nodded his head in understanding, Aran ended up reflecting yet again just how much he hated meetings. He hated discussions. He simply wanted action. But he had to admit he wasn't completely sure what the right answers were to so many challenges.

The morning got underway with a discussion of how they'd handle the volcanoes. Aran was continuing to work on his idea but still not ready to share, so he listened to the others' suggestions, none of which survived the discussions. They moved on to how they'd handle the Trow when they arrived. Again suggestions, discussion, and no resolution. Merit had been quick and efficient in eviscerating all the ideas, not out of hostility but just to move forward. They then brainstormed about Casius and Rangi. In some ways this should have been the simplest of the tasks, but because of the extent of the Newfie spy and sympathizer network, it wasn't. Again, there seemed little hope of a resolution.

In addition to Aran, Merit, and Jabtar, who was filling in for Storng on the council, there were two representatives from each of the seven colonies. Most were personable, long-time leaders and wise advisors to this council. As one of its two representatives, Costa Rica had sent Aran's nemesis, Tellick, the council chair who'd exiled him. She made a big show of asking his forgiveness and claimed the loss of her niece Qwert affected her judgment on the day she exiled him, but he didn't trust her. Possibly because he simply didn't like her. She became the chair of this council as well, filling the void when no one else volunteered.

When Tellick suggested that they send yet another delegation to negotiate with Casius, it was more than Aran could take.

"Casius has to be stopped. He's gone beyond merely entertaining other perspectives. He is waging war on us."

"Aran Shaman, I know that you have a long history with Casius." She glanced at Nadara sitting in a chair against the wall among those who were supporting the meeting, "And I know that you have personal reasons for your anger with Rangi. But we can't let these cloud a clearheaded approach to resolution. I know Casius from our time together on the council, and while he has deep convictions, he is reasonable. We can't let him and the Newfies be a distraction."

"And I think that it's you who *cloud* the approach. The longer we wait, the deeper Casius embeds his spies and saboteurs. The more alliances he creates. The stronger he becomes, and the weaker we are." Tellick said nothing as she and Aran glared at one another.

Jabtar began describing the steps the shamans were taking to identify any more Newfie spies, and the council slid past the confrontation.

Aran went outside when they broke for lunch. The sun shone inside the Costa Rican refuge, though it would no doubt rain by afternoon. Even with the Silth umbrella over it, this was still a rain forest.

Flying up into the canopy and settling on a big limb allowed him to see across most of the treetops. As he stretched his wings and tried to loosen the stiffness caused by sitting all morning, he breathed in the rich, humid compost of the rain forest. For a few moments he lost himself in the birds' clicks, caws, and bickering. He heard the grumpy grunt of a bull crocodile and relaxed into the rhythm of the bug noises and the day frogs.

His reverie was broken when Merit landed next to him. It must have showed on his face.

"Sorry. But I have known you to slip away during these breaks and not return, so I wanted a moment with you."

Aran wished the moment was really for him, but Merit was all business at the council meetings. She was condensed leadership. He admired her ability to focus and sustain the role. He didn't bother to deny he was considering going someplace else.

"Well, in a perfect world, we need you to stay for the next discussion. It's on how we interact with the Humans—the area where you're in charge."

"Reluctantly. I don't know anything the rest of you don't." He hesitated, then, "But I do have one idea. I think we should ask Penfield to work closer with us in managing the world coordination of Human-Silth affairs. We've involved Humans in every aspect of our planning for a future world except the part on planning how we interact with them."

"But we're negotiating with them."

"We are negotiating with their entire race. He's only one person, and not the one in charge of any of it."

"Do you trust him?"

"I only trust one Human so far." He shifted his weight on the branch and twisted so he could see her better. "But Storng trusts him. I have little doubt he'd spy on us, and I don't think we could share everything with him, but we need some counsel. We don't know Humans well enough to know how best to achieve some agreement with them. I think if we can't work with them, we won't defeat the Trow, and even if we do, the Humans will return to their old ways when we're gone. I also think that if I advance this idea, I will have to listen to a bunch of backsquawk from Tellick, and I'm not in the mood."

"You know that you provoke her, don't you? There is value in a chain of command. How will it work if all the council just does whatever crosses their mind?"

"Is that what you think I do? Whatever crosses my mind?"

"Yes."

He took some nuts from his pocket and handed half to her. "Well, I can't say you're wrong. But it usually works out alright." He chewed for a moment and then moved so he could see the horizon. "Talking to her is like talking to a powerful, but slightly dim animal. You know, perhaps like when you talk to Stalbon."

"I don't talk to Stalbon. I can't talk to animals. Or Humans."

"Oh … yeah." He looked down, angry with himself for forgetting.

"I know. You assume no one could reach my position unless they could. All I have is discipline." She paused. "You know that."

They gazed out across the canopy. The dark rain clouds were moving toward them, and they could see sheets of rain coming down on the treetops. Thunder rolled in the distance.

"What if the Humans won't accept our proposal for the new world?" Merit asked.

"We go on without them the best we can. We won't stop the volcanoes. We'll save all our resources to fight the Trow. The Trow are not hostile to non-Human life on the Earth. Even if we lose, the animals we save will be fine." Aran hesitated before continuing. "But I'm also exploring another possible path, a plan b, I think is what Storng calls it."

He felt fortunate to have someone with whom he could talk. Someone on whom he could rely. With Merit, there was none of the distracting deference to a hero he encountered with others, but at the same time there was trust—a trust that understood his weaknesses.

"Thank you for not pushing, by the way."

"About …?"

"About why I found myself powerless on a snow-covered mountainside." He tossed the shells of the nuts he'd been snacking on, and they bounced down through the leaves. "I know you've wondered."

"It's crossed my mind. I finally decided that, like your first meetings with Faelen, you had your reasons. And that you'd tell me in good time."

Not long now and the rain would be upon them, Aran saw. "This is different. Well, maybe not completely. I didn't tell you about Faelen in part because I knew you'd try to stop me, but also because he indicated that if anyone followed me, he'd leave. I didn't trust you to not follow me. I trust you now, and I'd tell you anything I could. I just want you to know that. It's the second part that's kind of the same—I've given my word not to disclose certain conversations. That's what left me on a mountainside."

"Doesn't sound safe."

Aran looked at her again with arched eyebrows, and she smiled. As the rain began, Merit dropped off the treetop and glided to the ground. Aran watched her through the branches and stayed where he was, pelted by raindrops and reveling in the storm's power. He understood Storng's joy in riding storms.

After a few more moments, he transported away. The afternoon's meeting didn't really need him.

4

PENFIELD (HUMAN)

Penfield had always liked meeting at the Greenbriar. Even in these harsh times the food was great, the service left nothing to be desired, and the setting was far more relaxed than DC. He and President Percrow were there to meet with the disaster response teams and discuss the state of the nation.

Although rationing had impacted even the Greenbriar, the resort still accessed a number of unregulated sources. On the menu were several venison dishes, reflecting the region's large white-tailed deer population. Also, quail, wild boar and wild turkey. Hunting restrictions had been removed by the West Virginia legislature. While these menu items drew appreciative comments from the other attendees, Penfield saw them as proof of the Silth prediction regarding how Humans would respond to scarcity. Soon these animals would be gone from the region.

He also felt guilty enjoying any of these surroundings. The news from around the country was dire. Rationing was stretching the reserves. The cities were using their resources, electricity and scrubbed wastewater from the sewers, to grow food at an enormous scale. Every parking deck had been converted to production, mostly hydroponic. Every open space was filled with cargo containers converted for food production. The cannabis industry had been stripped of its grow lights and they were being used for strawberries, tomatoes and root vegetables. While micro-greens were easy to grow, there were gaps in the production of other fruits and vegetables. Grains were mostly absent. Some successes had occurred in the rural areas in experiments with larger hoop houses strung with grow lights, but nowhere near the scale they needed to feed themselves, much less the refugees at the southern border. Every home had converted as much of their interior space to food production as possible. Most restaurants were closed, unable to obtain supplies of rice, sugar, milk or a broad number of now rationed commodities. Soon there would be none.

Goats, chickens, and pigs were being raised in every town. Cows were gone. Dogs and cats were disappearing. Eventually, there wouldn't be enough vegetation to support the goats, and as the insect population declined other options would become limited as well. Transportation was a nightmare. Commerce was at a standstill, so people were without work in many parts of the country. They had no money for food. A moratorium had been placed on foreclosures and rent evictions, but that meant real estate companies and financial institutions were failing, so there was no maintenance and, increasingly, no banks. As disease swept through a starving world, the U.S. had closed its borders and was about to ban most international travel to postpone the inevitable epidemics. There would be no distribution of flu vaccine this year, so the world was facing potential flu deaths on a scale not seen in generations. Winter, far colder than North America had experienced since the ice age, would kill many as well.

Even though little of this showed inside the walls of this perpetual celebration of wealth, enough of it was on Penfield's mind that he was ready to leave. If his feelings of guilt weren't enough, the weight of his conversations was sufficient to remove any enjoyment.

Penfield and the President agreed that even if they had some hope of fighting the Trow, Humans weren't going to survive the volcanoes. They must find a solution. So far, the best scientists in the world working round the clock in unprecedented cooperation had none. Many believed the volcanoes would eventually stop on their own, but no one could answer when, and it would take years after that for the Earth's systems to right themselves again. Worryingly, there was a small, but growing group that believed that several of the volcanoes would settle into constant eruption and could continue that way for years. Arenal, in Costa Rica, had erupted for almost five decades.

And then there was the issue of fighting the Trow. There was only one encounter with the Trow available to study—the Yellowstone tape. In it a Human and a Silth were fighting the Trow called Angel. She essentially won the encounter with superior tactics, though Aran was still learning to use the Trow magic and the Human was unarmed. According to the Silth, the Trow would be armed with biologically-based weapons, magic powers, years of fighting experience, and little regard for battle ethics. They could pop in and steal any Human weapons they wanted. They'd be highly motivated. The Silth were plainly intimidated by them and, so far, the Silth had been an easily superior force when matched with the Humans. The Generals argued there'd been no serious engagements yet, but with the ability to transport in and out of the battlefield at will, the entire notion of engagement had changed. Yes, maybe they could nuke the refuges—it wasn't even clear that would work with the domes over them—but the Silth who were left could assassinate every world leader until Humans descended into chaos.

Penfield thought about the number of times in Human warfare when a change in technology had changed the course of history, whether it was an atomic bomb, a repeating rifle, or a catapult. When technologies were equal, tactics won. When technologies were unequal, unless there was a tactic taking advantage of a moral constraint such as guerrillas hiding in civilian populations, the superior technology won. Hollywood loved the notion that an upstart band of furry little warriors could best overwhelming technology, but history had repeatedly denied the premise. He thought of a *quotation—if the enemy is in range, so are you.* Here Humans would be in range, but the Trow weren't.

"You off somewhere?"

"Sorry, Madam President. Lost in the maze of our challenges." Penfield and the President were dining alone during a break in the presentations from the disaster response teams. "Can we talk about the request from Aran? That I work with the Silth to address Human concerns about the shared future. It's apparently his hope we'll see a future with the Silth is preferable to one with the Trow, or taking on the Trow separately."

"Is it dangerous?"

"Depends on what you mean by *dangerous*. Do I think there is physical danger? Yes, but not necessarily from Aran and his group. They already have many mixed teams with Humans around the globe. All indications are these teams have integrated well, are working on solving various problems and are preparing for a shared future. But they've been attacked by both Humans and by other Silth. As things get more desperate, these attacks will likely increase. Aran says I would spend some time in each of the refuges, but mostly I'd work with them in New York, with the U.N., and with the elected officials in Washington. I don't think I'd be in much physical danger.

"Do I think there's political danger? Yes. There'll certainly be efforts to use this as evidence your administration is too close to the Silth. Tobias is rabid now, and his message that good things are coming with the Trow is everywhere. The news networks who don't like you echo him and will continue that if the Trow are hostile, a well-funded Human military is the way to respond to them. *Faeries, not Paerries* is Tobias's slogan. He's spending millions on getting his message out. His political action committee is funding your opponents. The only good news is everyone is working so hard on trying to grow or find food no one is listening to the TV. On the internet there are so many voices no one view is dominating. But I don't think it would be in your interest to advertise the arrangement if you did agree to it. It needs to be classified."

"I'm stunned Tobias is making any headway with his 'Faeries are angels' crap. How gullible are we?"

"Desperate times …."

"What do you want to do, Irvin?"

Penfield hesitated and picked at his plate before answering. "I know I sound like an academic, but I'd love to see inside the Silth leadership. I've studied organizations and leadership all my life, and there's never been an opportunity like this, though there is some precedent for Aran's request that might be useful. The Romans and the Huns exchanged hostages—the children of important figures. Attila the Hun was sent to the Romans at the age of twelve in exchange for Flavius Aetius."

"How'd that work out?"

Penfield laughed. "The Romans hoped to civilize Attila, so they taught him Roman manners and all sorts of civil graces. For their part the Huns hoped Attila would spy on the Romans. In the end,

Attila still helped bring the Romans to their knees as leader of the Horde. But one of the few generals who could defeat the Huns in battle was Flavious, who learned battle tactics in his time with the Huns. Unfortunately, he also brought back their political approaches and became one of the most ruthless political operators ever seen in Rome."

The President's smile made her whole face crinkle. "And this is what you want to propose? With a better outcome?"

"Yes. I want to propose an exchange. Aran would send us someone important to him, and I'll go help the Silth. Just as with the Romans and the Huns, everyone expects these emissaries to spy, but we may be able to help formulate Silth policy and, at the very least, understand and assess their intentions. I feel a little awkward because I'm frankly excited about the prospect. In these terrible times, it feels unseemly to be excited about anything."

"I don't know. This seems like a risk. I can see what's in it for them, but I'm having trouble finding much upside for us. My inclination is to say no. We can create some committee in the U.N. to formally discuss questions with them."

They said nothing as the waiters cleared the plates and dusted crumbs from the tablecloth. Percrow ordered dessert, strawberries grown in the on-site hydroponic farm, sprinkled with some of the vanishing store of confectioner's sugar.

When they were alone again, Penfield said, "Another reason I'd like to do it is because it may make a difference. I think that they're right, it may help them work out an arrangement with Humans. But I think that I may be able to change their view of Humans for the better. In either event, in this desperate time it would feel like more engagement than just sitting in an office or committee rooms. I would like to make a difference."

The strawberries arrived and Percrow ate them without saying anything. After a few minutes, she said, "I marched in civil rights parades. We were dealing with serious subjects, but I was young to be there at all. I was tagging along with my sister, who was in high school. I remember being slightly abashed about being excited, but feeling like I was doing something important, even though we were up against institutions and very angry people."

She sat as though some movie reel of images played in her head. "We're at the end of an era. The future will be different, no matter what. Maybe we're at the end of Humankind. It feels like we are groping in the dark for answers. Let's see if we can inject some light. We'll send you to the Huns."

5

Aran (Silth)

"I think this is the first well-told story I've heard from a Human," Aran said after Penfield told him of Attila. "And I like the fact you told the postscript even though it isn't the perfect outcome. They both go on to use their knowledge to the other's detriment, but there's balance."

Aran listened to the beeping of the machines attached to Storng. Doctors and nurses came and went, and the two young shamans sitting outside the door checked in periodically, but mostly he and Penfield had the room to themselves. The old Silth looked so small on the big hospital bed where they'd moved him. Aran looked at Storng's face, his real face and not the secondary projected glamour. He wished he could see Storng's eyes. He had always wondered if they, so much a part of his character, were real or part of his glamour.

Giving Aran time to process what they had discussed, Penfield was scrolling through information on his phone.

Aran finally said, "So, the Silth I send to be hostage to the Humans should be someone who can display our customs but would be sensitive enough to learn Human ways. Able to spy but be open about it. Someone important enough to me that your safety is ensured."

"All true. Though I wouldn't get too hung up on the *hostage* idea, since he or she will be free to come and go just like me. More *student exchange* than hostage. This Silth will be included in meetings and briefings to understand the challenges facing the United States and the Human world. We don't have many social events right now, since travel is limited and there isn't food for parties. But to the extent there are gatherings, the Silth representative will be invited and will gain a network of contacts among the Humans."

"All right let me think about this. The problem is I only have a few Silth I care about, and all are working hard on preparations. We have many Silth in official positions, who like yourself would carry the assumption that someone cares about them ...." Penfield snorted. "But, almost by definition they have no experience dealing with Humans. No one in high office among the Silth has because it was taboo. And in return for us sending this Silth representative, you'll work with us and assist us in preparing to talk to Humans about the future? And you will be an *open spy?*"

"The death toll among Humans, particularly in what were called *developing nations,* is mounting fast. Refugees are at every border of every country with any resources. They're increasingly desperate. Even the populations of those countries with resources are nihilistic as their economies crash and they see no future beyond struggle, followed by a war they are not likely to win. They want an easy answer. Just as you have your internal struggles, we have those who are trying to take advantage of this situation. We have Reverend Tobias who seems to be everywhere. Even though to most Humans you're a hero, he has suggested you caused this crisis by angering the Trow. His followers believe the Trow are angels who offer technological advance and a bright future for Humans followed by a divine beyond. We have countries like North Korea who have kept their people in poverty for decades. They see this as an opportunity to expand their boundaries, consolidate Humanity under one authoritarian rule to fight the Trow, or to at least negotiate by threatening to destroy the Earth themselves.

And then there is the Silth position—a new world order in which the bees and bunnies sit at the table with the Humans and the Silth to set up a world free of technology, and full of happiness … once we get rid of those pesky volcanoes. Oh yes and defeat an enemy we promise you is out there even though you pretty much have to take our word for it. This is what you want me to help you with?"

Aran understood why Storng liked Penfield. "Yes. Exactly. But you need to understand a few more challenges. The Silth are essentially a friendly race. They used to fight wars for territory and power, just like Humans, but other than one struggle in Australia, that hasn't happened in centuries. Still, while the Silth make friends with individual Humans, they don't especially like humanity. They have no reason to—Humans destroyed their homes and the homes of the animals they care about. They also aren't especially fond of jaguars. Or monkeys. But they accept that these animals have a right to exist and are part of Earth's balance. If, however, the jaguars came to the Silth and said, *save us from the volcanoes, but we plan to eat every animal and destroy the forest,* the Silth would decline. We'd save ourselves and the other animals in the refuges, but we would leave the jaguars to fend for themselves. We wouldn't hurt them—we just wouldn't expend the energy to save them. The Silth are very serious about this. They have no reason to stop the volcanoes unless Humans change their approach to the world. Perhaps the Humans can figure out a way to stop the volcanoes, and we won't interfere. But we won't do it unless there is a different world to be achieved on the other side. And I don't know how to make Humans understand there will be no negotiating with the Trow. Does a lion negotiate with its victims? That is why we need your help."

They both sat quietly, letting the emotions bleed away. Then Aran said, "I'll be right back," blipped from the room, and appeared next to Nadara.

"I need you to come with me for a few minutes to talk about something important."

"Right now?" She looked around at the several Silth and Humans sitting around the table, papers in front of them, multiple coffee cups, thimbles and plates piled in the center.

Aran recognized some of the faces. "What you're doing is important, Nadara, and I apologize. But I need you. Now."

She stood, and he took her arm transporting them into the hospital room. Quickly taking in her surroundings, she moved to the head of the bed and sat cross-legged next to Storng. She stroked the hather on the side of his face.

"Any improvement?"

Aran frowned. "No change. It is taking everything the shamans have just to keep him alive."

"Meaning I'm not here because he's dying. Why was it so urgent I come?" She finally made eye contact with Penfield.

Aran introduced them and explained the arrangement they'd discussed.

"Ok. I understand, but why are you suggesting me? I'm not a trained anything, unlike the ambassador. I'm a harvester."

"Many reasons. It's true you have a harvester background. That means you're comfortable being around Humans. From working with you, I know you have empathy for the Humans. You're a leader." He told Penfield that Storng had trained her. "Nadara, you can take what you learn and help lead the Silth in dealing with Humans. And you're much more than a harvester—you and the Tiki Crew have been the ambassadors to all the Silth tribes, helping them accept the new world and learning their different personalities. This is your opportunity to do the same with the Humans."

"What else? There's always more with you."

"What?"

"You think if I'm not in Australia, I'll be less of a target for Rangi." Her voice rose. "And as a bonus, maybe this is Heartless's way of getting out of a relationship."

Penfield cleared his throat. "I'm going to the cafeteria for coffee. Anyone want anything?" He didn't wait for an answer and hurried out the door.

Aran couldn't blame him. He'd like to disappear himself—almost any other place would be better than there. He spent the next thirty minutes in an unexpectedly personal argument. But by the time Penfield returned, Nadara had agreed to the task, somewhat mollified by Aran's insistence he'd selected her because the chief requirement was it be someone he cared about.

"What am I supposed to be doing?" she demanded of Penfield. "I get that you'll help the Silth understand Humans and prepare the presentation of their position for the U.N. But all I hear so far is I'm supposed to be a hostage, so maybe the Silth don't kill you or attack Washington, neither a real threat. What exactly will I be doing?"

"You'll have an insider's place at the table for the operation of the government. Be briefed on what's going on around the world and how we're trying to cope with it. I hope you'll get a full sense of the challenges we face and how we're trying to address them. I hope you will also get to know the President and others well enough to trust them. Your opportunity to personally advise the President of the United States is one no other Silth has ever had."

Aran thought Nadara looked satisfied, though when she faced him again there was still fire in her gaze.

CHAPTER 8

1

ARAN (SILTH)

According to Penfield, U.N. security was high because of threats against Aran. The meeting was taking place in the U.N.'s Geneva offices. Penfield stood with Aran hovering next to him beside the podium where Aran was about to speak to the security council and answer their questions.

Penfield had prepared a position paper outlining the Silth willingness to proceed and what they wanted in return. He outlined the preliminary responses for Aran. The U.S. supported exploration of the Silth proposal. Unfortunately, prior administrations of the U.S. had sacrificed much of the country's leadership position in the U.N., and while U.S. support was important, it was not determinative. China opposed even discussing the proposition until proof of the Trow's existence was provided. The Chinese didn't believe the Faerie story was real—they asserted it was U.S. trickery intended to gain access to natural resources. The Faerie concept and the Homeland tape, they said, were manufactured by Hollywood. They claimed their own scientists were working on ways to shut down the volcanoes. Finally, they called for the Silth to withdraw from all occupied lands. Aran, hands fisted, was poised to leave after hearing this, but Penfield explained it was normal and didn't mean he was wasting his time.

Aran flew to the top of the podium and spoke into the microphone. He outlined the Silth position for the thirty or so attendees. First, there would be no rescue of Humans without a commitment to a different world when the volcanoes were no longer erupting. Second, there would be no cooperation in a fight against the Trow without such a commitment. He waited for the muttering of "blackmail" and "Faeries are a fantasy" to die down so he could continue.

Suddenly there were shouts of fear from the audience, and when fingers pointed to Aran's left, he turned. His mouth fell open.

Faelen was standing on the stage, glaring at the room's occupants and the camera facing him. He wore full Trow battle attire, leather with strategic placement of metal inlays to stop a sword or dissipate a bolt. His hair hung in dreadlocks halfway down his chest. His scarred face was cleaner than usual, though there was still dirt pushed deep into the creases. He carried a sword in a belt at his waist and knives and some organic-looking bulbs dangled from his armor. He flew to the podium and staggered just slightly as he landed. As he shooed Aran away, Aran could smell the liquor on him.

With a crackling sound, the barbs of a taser shot into Faelen's chest. Faelen looked down at them, stuck ineffectually in his armor, and then up at the guard at the end of the wires. That guard was standing next to another with his gun drawn. Faelen threw forward both hands. A blue shield materialized, smashing into the guards and hurling them into a wall, pieces of which crashed down on their unconscious bodies. He scanned the suddenly still room.

"Do you still think I am a fantasy?" No one moved. "I am *General* Faelen. I am Trow. You think I saved you. You thought I was dead." He grinned maliciously. "I am here to clarify a few things. I did not save you. I saved the Paerries. I saved parrots and the beauty of this Earth. You are merely the accidental beneficiaries of this action. If I could have done it without sparing you, I would have. Like all Trow, I despise what you have done to this magical place. You talk about making peace with Xafar, the Trow King. Some of you idiots believe the Trow are *angels* and their arrival will be beneficial, just as some of the Paerries believe they will be smiled upon and rewarded by the Trow. My father Xafar ordered me, his son, killed for interfering with his plans for the destruction of the Paerries. He wants every last Human killed and every last Paerrie eliminated." Faelen slammed his fist on the podium, causing it to squeak as if in protest. "There will be no bargaining with the Trow. There will be no peace with Xafar. Only fools believe there will be anything other than death."

He paced on the podium. "Some of you think Humans can stop the Trow. If I wanted to, I could kill all of you right now." He raised his arm menacingly. The council members and their staff shrank back in their chairs. "And you could do nothing to stop me. How will you battle the Trow?" He glared around the room and then shook his head.

He flew back down to the stage and shouted, "But you will never get to fight the Trow. You will be long dead before then. Killed by the volcanoes as Xafar planned. You sit here debating terms. You are dead people. Instead of negotiating for life, you are negotiating the circumstances of your death. I have traveled to every part of the world. Outside of the Paerrie refuges all are dying. You may be the last to go, but you will go."

He walked close to the Chinese delegates as though daring them to deny his existence.

"You wonder if the Paerries can save you from the volcanoes. I wonder about this too. Of course, if not, then you have lost nothing." He stopped and said, "I know something about death. Xafar left me for dead. His warriors did not completely finish the job, but they left me crippled, unable to move. A few days ago, that one …." He pointed to Aran, standing on a table next to Penfield. "That single Paerrie restored me. I did not think it could be done, but he did it. I do not know why they are interested in saving you. I certainly do not want to. But if they think they can stop the volcanoes, you better hope they are right, because no Human action is going to do that. If they believe Paerries and Humans together can fight and beat the Trow, you better hope they are right, because you have no hope against them otherwise. To the Trow, you and the Paerries are vermin, and they believe the world will be better off without you."

He held up his hand, and with a blue bolt he blew every bit of glass out of the huge window behind him. They were high up in the building and the wind roared into the room. Faelen floated slowly out of the room, snarling down at them, until he cleared the window and then he flew up out of their sight.

Back at the microphone, Aran asked the stunned crowd, "Any questions?"

2

ARAN (SILTH)

As the next day began, Merit appeared and dressed Aran down for not telling her about Faelen. Through the night he had fielded calls from the other council members, similarly angry about his withholding the information and concerned about the impact of the U.N. meeting. Most had now seen the internet feed of the interaction.

The Silth were rapidly becoming as addicted to the information stream their phones provided as Humans were.

Aran told Merit, as he had told them all, he'd given his word to keep Faelen's existence a secret. He didn't specify to whom he'd given it, so they assumed it was to Faelen. Merit speculated aloud that helping Faelen was why she had to rescue Aran in Peru, but he refused to confirm or deny it.

"And why was it so secret if he was going to announce to the world that he was still alive?"

"I don't know. He's a coati-crazy Faerie, Merit. I had no idea he was going to be there. But Penfield thinks it's a good thing. Now the Chinese are having a hard time insisting the Trow aren't real, and it appears Faelen's words shook up quite a few people."

"And Silth," she added.

"The Humans weren't going to take us seriously without something like this, and Faelen knew it. He jolted them. He didn't kill anyone, and his insults, while colorful, were less personal than usual."

"You set high standards for your friend."

"He's saved both of our lives," he reminded her. "We should forgive him a little roughness. His intentions are good."

***

A few hours later, Aran stood outside the Sohi enclave waiting for his escort. The guard had already confirmed that Faelen still lived there. His escort turned out to be Lornix.

"Thank you for healing him," she said, walking along the path as he flew beside her.

"Sorry about the liquor, though."

"Why?"

"I assumed it was against your rules."

"There are few rules here. Mostly we know liquor does not contribute to the strength of mind we seek. But it is up to the individual to choose their way. Faelen was broken physically and you fixed him. He is still broken, but perhaps he will allow us to fix what remains to be healed."

They arrived at a small round hut made of a carved rock foundation, with sticks and mud for walls and bundles of reeds and grasses for a roof. Lornix knocked and opened the door without waiting for a response. After Aran flew in, she closed the door and retreated. Faelen stood at the window, bottle in hand, looking out at the serene beauty of the enclave.

He turned to Aran. "Even in the grayness it is beautiful." Aran could hear a stream moving across rocks though he had not seen it as he arrived.

"Thank you for yesterday."

"I hope it helps." Faelen sounded sober and less hungover than Aran expected. "A little theatrical, I am afraid, but they really do irritate me."

"You didn't sound very hopeful we can end the volcanoes and stop the Trow."

"I have no idea how you end the volcanoes, and you are running out of time."

"I'm working on one. Inspired by this place actually, and the Sohi quest for alignment with Earth magic. But I haven't finished it. We haven't told the Humans how hard it was to calm the one volcano, much less that we don't actually know how to stop active volcanoes."

Faelen snorted. "Do Paerries play cards? No? Too bad. You might be good at a game Humans call poker. It involves what is called *bluffing*. I assume you also have no idea how you will stop a Trow invasion."

"We really haven't had time to think about that yet."

"You should assume they will know you are all armed with Trow powers. And that they will have sent spies to know what defenses you have prepared."

"I don't see how you fight an enemy who simply appears in your midst and then disappears at will."

Faelen stared at him with a puzzled expression. "I take it I did not teach you how to keep someone from transporting away?'

Aran's eyes narrowed. "No. There's a way?"

"Yes. It is not easy, but it can be done."

"And you could have taught this to me before?"

"Why do you assume someone has taught you everything they know?"

After they spent some time practicing the complex technique, Aran asked, "Do you know anything about magic poisons and their antidotes?"

"Some, not much. Growing up in a hated royal family you had to learn about them, learn antidotes because you could never avoid all the opportunities someone had to poison you."

After Aran described Storng's symptoms, Faelen said, "Definitely magical. Probably Trow in source, though they wouldn't bother to give it to a Paerrie. Someone else, Human or Paerrie, would have done that. But I don't know which poison."

Aran's shoulders slumped. He'd allowed himself to feel hopeful.

"Of course, one general antidote exists that heals all magical poisons. It is an herb that grows on the side of a volcano in what the Humans call Indonesia, but is extremely difficult to obtain. The field is guarded by Javan hawk-eagles bred by the Trow to have poisonous talons. They attack Paerrie or Trow that come there."

"Wait, you mean like the legends of the Harpies?"

"Those were not legends. Most of the Harpies are gone. Too stupid to survive. The hawk-eagles are smart."

"What is the volcano?"

"Tambura."

"Of course it's there. That's one of the volcanoes the Trow ignited."

"The area where the herb grows is very old and has survived previous eruptions. Perhaps it is still there."

They talked on through the afternoon, and then as Faelen was nodding off, Aran slipped away.

Full of thoughts and plans he felt ... what? It was hard to

define. Potential? That was it. He felt as though there was potential for success. Not a likelihood nor even a real possibility yet. Just potential. It made him realize just how much he had been ... what did Faelen call it? ... *bluffing.*

3

NESTOR (SILTH)

Nestor didn't like it at all. She'd grown up hating any animal that attacked the young of another. Humans were such an animal, and she hated them for it. But now she, Rangi, and Rangi's dwindling forces were about to do the very thing she despised.

She'd never felt any conflict over what she did for Rangi. A simple Paerrie with simple desires, she liked having a strong leader she didn't question. But she was questioning today as she studied the large Sydney playground full of small Humans. Despite the cold and the gray skies, the children were running around in mobs like little lambs in the spring fields. Rangi wanted to turn the Humans against the Silth, so she'd chosen this target. They were going to attack and kill children. Nestor tried to steel herself by thinking about how many times the Humans had done the same thing with the wild parrot populations across the Australian farmlands, but it wasn't working. Not because she couldn't work up a hatred for Humans. If they'd been attacking adults, she wouldn't have flinched. But this act made them as bad as Humans.

Nestor looked around for Rangi, hoping for maybe one more chance to try to talk her out of it, but she couldn't find her. She caught glimpses of warriors to her left and right, hiding among the trees and buildings surrounding the school. When a bell rang and some of the older children filed into the building, a new group of younger ones marched out in snaking lines until released to run and shriek in the delight of a moment's freedom.

After the failed effort to kidnap Nadara, Rangi only had fifty or so warriors left, but all were trained with the Faerie bolt and shield and could transport themselves to wherever they needed to be. They were all here and their intention was slaughter. Not just of the small ones outside, but to wipe out all six hundred or so children and adults. Rangi believed this would drive a wedge so deep in the relationship of Silth and Humans there would be no recovery and no joint opposition to the Faeries. Nestor wasn't sure Casius would approve of this tactic, but Rangi wasn't asking him. Rangi was also stinging from her recent defeats. She wasn't used to losing, and she didn't do it well.

Nestor heard a shrill whistle far to her left, and she dreaded it as it moved toward her. When the warrior nearest her whistled, Rangi repeated it to the warrior she could see on her right. She eyed the small Humans and chose a group of six as her prey.

Suddenly, two Australian Silth warriors materialized in front of her. Simultaneously a band of blue shields appeared in a large circle around the children and tightened backwards, forcing the children toward the doors of the school. Blue bolts were striking the shields with no effect. Nestor caught a quick glimpse of Jules hovering over the children and directing the Steamer and Tiki crews. But before she could completely decipher the scene, the warriors attacked her, and she transported toward the children. She reappeared in the middle of the group she'd been watching and activated her shield, instantly struck by repeated bolts. The children were escaping, but she couldn't fire and defend herself at once. When she disappeared and reappeared closer to the building, right in the middle of the running mass of children, again her shield lit up with the impact of bolts. The two Australian warriors were still advancing toward her, flying over the children's heads. Around her was chaos, with Rangi's warriors appearing among the children, but immediately drawing so much fire they accomplished nothing. The line of shields had now formed compact circles around the children still in the open.

Nestor pulled out a long thin knife. If she could get in the middle of one cluster, she could maintain her shield but attack with her knife. She disappeared but reappeared with a thud, flat on the ground in front of one shielded group. She shook her head. Apparently transporting through a shield wasn't possible. She dodged the spear thrust from behind the shield and disappeared again, this time ending up inside the school. As screaming children darted down the hall, adults held open classroom doors and shooed them inside. Nestor dropped her shield and raised her arm to fire at the little girl about to run past her. But before she could, a bolt struck and threw her into the lockers. She blacked out as she blinked away.

4

MERIT (SILTH)

Merit moved down the halls, head swiveling like an owl's. She popped into each classroom—children screamed as soon as she appeared—and transported to a new location after confirming there was no threat. When she sensed the presence of a new warrior from Rangi's group, she transported there and retaliated. All the Silth were able to use the Trow magic of the bolt, shield and blip, but the ability to do Silth magic was uneven and Merit's competence was minimal. But this ability to sense the presence of others was a useful Trow tool.

She had a hundred other warriors flying randomly through the halls watching for attackers, but she was the only one taught to identify the attackers' presence and follow them. She wished there were more with this ability but Aran had been adamant—no more technologies would slip into the world without controls. Still, she thought as she flashed to a new threat, everything was at risk here. She appeared beside the Rangi warrior as the warrior raised her arm toward the small dark-haired girl. Merit fired the bolt instantly, angling it slightly so it would knock the warrior into the metal shelves instead of into one of the running children. Consequently, it was not a killing shot. She watched the Silth slide down the metal wall and disappear as she was losing consciousness.

Suddenly she sensed another. As Merit appeared in another hall, Three of Five was lowering the body of the dispatched warrior to the floor, loosening the garrote from his throat. Smiling triumphantly, she ignored Merit and flew down the hall in search of more prey. The pace seemed to be slowing as fewer of Rangi's warriors were left to attack from within the building. After several minutes in which nothing happened and no new intruders arrived, one of Merit's squad leaders approached her.

"There's no more activity outside. We believe several dozen died there, but the ones killed with blades have disappeared so it's hard to tell. We're removing the remaining bodies now. We've only lost one of ours, but twenty were wounded. Most of the damage seems to have come from Rangi herself."

"And what of her?"

"We think she's wounded. But she is no longer on the field, so we don't know what's happened to her."

"Any children hurt?"

"Only the ones who ran into things or fell or were stepped on. None seriously."

"Good. Finish the mop-up and gently help the children. We want them to remember there were good Paerries here. But watch out. There may still be snipers around." Merit sent her newly found sense out beyond the school walls. "I don't sense anyone, but send patrols out, nonetheless. And move quickly to gather the bodies of Rangi's warriors. We don't want the Human media using them to emphasize this was a Silth attack."

She flew down the hall to what appeared to be a central office and tried the locked door. She looked down the hall and saw Marina shooing a group of children into a classroom. "Marina, come here!" Marina hurried down the hall to her side. Merit tilted her head toward the closed door. They both disappeared and rematerialized on the other side to the sound of gasps from the group huddled inside.

"Everything is okay. The ones who were attacking are gone. They won't be back. Who's in charge?" Puzzled eyes looked back at her. She nodded to Marina who repeated the statement but used the voice that Humans could understand.

A woman stepped forward. "I'm Mrs. Montego, Head of School. What's going on?"

"All of the children are fine. Just some scrapes and bruises."

Merit, Aran, and Penfield had discussed beforehand what her next words and actions should be. When the spies they had among Rangi's New Faerie supporters reported plans for this attack, it had been too late to avoid it. All their efforts were concentrated on containing it and then dealing with Rangi.

"Do you have a loudspeaker so I can talk to everyone?" Each time Merit spoke, Marina repeated her words exactly.

"Yes," Mrs. Montego said hesitantly. She hurried to a microphone and switched it on.

"Can you video what I say?" She pointed to the phone Mrs. Montego held. The Head of School touched her phone and held it up.

Merit flew over to the table and said into the microphone, "I'm Merit, leader of the Silth World Council's warriors. Everyone is all right here. You will all be okay. Some bad people wanted to scare you, but the World Council stopped them. They will not come again, ever. You were very brave, and I know you are scared. Please stay in your rooms until your Human authorities get here. Everything will be fine." She handed the mike to Marina and continued speaking to the phone camera.

"This school was attacked by a renegade Silth general who

opposes our cooperating with Humans to stop the Trow. She hoped to drive a wedge between the Humans and the Silth. We've repelled the attack without loss of Human lives. Most of the attacking force was..." She looked at the small children clustered behind the adults and chose her words carefully. "dispatched, but there were many wounded and one of the defending Silth will see no more mornings. The leader of the attackers got away, but we're seeking her now and will deal with her so she's no longer a threat to anyone."

She disappeared, leaving Marina to finish translating and reappeared outside to gather her squad leaders, listening to their reports and confirming completion of the mop-up. Moving quickly, they finished just as cars with flashing lights surrounded the school grounds. Small trucks with various emblems and rooftop equipment began to gather further back. Merit's warriors assembled out of view of the new arrivals who proceeded cautiously toward the school buildings.

Merit stood on the grass, chanting the simple finding spell Aran had taught her. Unlike the Trow, and even an experienced shaman like Aran, she could not do the spell without speaking it and using a focusing talisman. She held a small handful of dirt and muttered the spell a second time. Ah, there it was—a clear vision of Rangi, back in New Zealand.

5

Rangi (Silth)

Rangi's physical wounds were few. She squatted next to the badly wounded Nestor and held her hand.

They'd taken refuge on the southern end of Rangatira, on the Chatham Islands several hundred miles south of New Zealand. They and the five remaining warriors were in the woods near the shore. Because the cries of the gulls, petrels, shearwaters, and terns were so loud, she could barely hear in the distance the bark of fur seals making their way through the thick kelp. Black robins and red-crowned parakeets flitted through the bushes around them.

Silth had been on these islands a very long time. They'd been friends of Moriori people before that tribe was enslaved by the Maori. They'd stayed until the Europeans came, not long after the Maori, and cleared the island for their sheep.

"It would have been fun to live here … after," Nestor said weakly, looking wistfully toward a small inlet.

"They don't have sheep anymore. They removed all of them from this island."

"But if you ruled … you'd let me bring them back, wouldn't you?"

"Of course."

Nestor closed her eyes. "Do you think if you die from magical wounds … but it's sometime after you were wounded … you don't go to the joining?"

Rangi sat quietly for a while before saying, "You've asked the wrong Silth. I don't think m-m-much about what happens after death. But it seems whether it's all at once or in a couple of steps, like after your body is burned or there's a sky burial, you end up in the same place." She could tell Nestor was listening to the cacophony of sea birds. "This would be a good place to be a part of."

Nestor nodded slightly and went still. Rangi carefully laid Nestor's hand on her chest, stood up, and walked through the surrounding brush to the rocky shoreline. She swiped at her eyes and didn't flinch or move to help when she heard the shouts of her warriors a few minutes later, quickly begun, quickly ended.

"I am quite old," she said as the female warrior stepped from the nearby bushes.

"Is this a request for mercy, in light of your advanced years?"

Rangi smiled thinly, "No, it is a request for an honorable death." She made no move and kept gazing at the sea.

"I am Merit, leader of the Silth World Council's warriors. I have the authority to bring you back to the seven nations with me. You don't have to die."

Rangi held her short, plump frame taller and said without rancor, "I am Rangi, leader of the Seventh Nation. Having defeated the Australians years ago and scattered them into the bush—I am the seventh, and I've never joined your *seven nations*. I have not surrendered, and never will." She turned toward Merit and slowly pulled a stiletto knife from the sheath at her side, pointing it in the air. "It's about the *how*, not the *whether*. I do not wish to leave a body to linger here."

Merit stood still for a moment, as though assessing the situation, looking for a trap. She nodded and removed the Silth sword from the scabbard hanging at her waist. Rangi crouched slightly and tipped the long knife toward her. Merit gave a shout, rushed forward, and with a quick tap knocked the knife aside, plunging the sword into Rangi's throat above her leather armor. She caught Rangi and lowered her to the sand, turning her on her side facing the water.

As her sight dimmed, Rangi watched the shorebirds wheel and twist in the coastal drafts, and she thought about how it would feel when she joined them in their wind dance. *I will finally fly.*

CHAPTER 9

1

ARAN (SILTH)

Aran watched Merit as she readied her warriors—she was liquid motion, inspecting a squad one moment and receiving bits of information the next. She flew to a table to check a map of the old colony. When she caught him staring, it was too late for him to look away, so he just shrugged. She scowled at him before turning back to talk to one of her squad.

On the wall hung a big Google Earth picture Kate had made of the forest around the old colony. Even though they were marshaling in the Costa Rican Refuge, other than Kate, the Refuge manager, none of the Humans knew what was going on. Aran didn't want them thinking about the Silth using the refuges to strike from. The Silth had no choice—both the old colony and the capital were inside the Costa Rican Refuge.

Aran's calculations were only slightly less complicated with Rangi's death. Mostly he ignored the factors on the Human side. Penfield told him they were countering Reverend Tobias's media campaign and slowly public sentiment was turning toward the Silth, but it was difficult because of Tobias's massive financial resources. Penfield said the intelligence community had decided the reverend's resources were not coming from his operations, and they could find no outside source of funds. They knew he'd been selling massive amounts of jewels and gold, but they didn't know where it came from. Aran knew, though it surprised him. Spies sent among the New Faerie ranks had confirmed what he suspected—Casius was funding Tobias, though most of his followers didn't know it. Similarly, Merit had learned from the last of Rangi's warriors that Casius had a deal with Rangi to support her efforts with regional New Faerie forces. Because Australia and New Zealand had been cut off from the rest of the Silth world for so long, Newfies had only begun recruiting there recently, but their success rate had been high. In the end, Rangi had not made much use of them, although a few joined the school attack. The warriors speculated Rangi didn't trust them because it was too easy to slip spies among them. Unfortunately, that meant the Newfies were likely still in hiding among the Australian Silth as spies.

Penfield had helped manage the public perception of the school attack. He told them few things unnerved Humans as much as an assault on their children. At the same time, few things excited the public as much as the heroic defense of those children. With Rangi's forces wiped out, it made for a clear story of good winning over evil. Merit was the new face of Silth heroism. Penfield told Aran it actually helped that Merit's face was damaged, and she was missing part of her arm. For Humans, this *humanized* her, giving them someone with whom they could identify other than the perfect glamours of other Silth. Aran hadn't shared this with Merit. In fact, she had no idea she was now a hero among Humans. She would hate it.

Aran had listened to some of the news accounts as they described the attack, the loss of Silth lives, the complete destruction of the attackers and their leader, and perhaps most importantly, the news that no children were seriously injured. Media had a rich trove of images from the security cameras showing how the Silth had defended the school. Three of Five had her own fan club of young men drawn to her violent and showman-like dispatch of multiple targets. Several members of the Steamers and Tiki Crews had developed media followers, but none as big as Merit, who's exotic, reassuring voice, first comforted the children and then provided the quick explanation of events. They played repetitively over the televisions, computers, and phones of Humans around the world.

Penfield said Humans had started to imagine the Silth would be good allies in a war with the Trow.

But the Humans weren't aware of today's operation, except for Penfield. He'd gotten used to being transported around the world by Aran and various Silth so he could participate in discussions and planning sessions. He'd proven his value repeatedly. While aware they hadn't yet admitted him to the inner circle, he knew he was only one ring away from it. Making him a part of their thinking had been a good plan. But at what cost? Nadara was so angry and hurt when Aran left her in Washington. What was she learning? What was her experience? He hadn't had time yet to talk to her about it. Was his absence really about lack of time, though? Had there been time and he simply didn't take it? As he looked around at the group preparing for battle, he thought he was on safe ground saying he hadn't had the opportunity to go to Nadara. But if he was honest with himself, he wasn't sure whether he would have gone.

He had his hands full, though, in arranging this attack on Casius. He didn't trust the WSC anymore and believed that if he got its approval to move against Casius, someone would warn the Newfies.

Even if she wasn't a Newfie herself, Tellick was far too close to Casius. Consequently, Aran had to persuade Merit to attack without explicit WSC approval. Fortunately for him, she was also wary of Newfie spies and had enough direct information on Casius's involvement that she had little question the attack was the right approach. Still, she was troubled by the breach of the chain of command, and it had taken him most of the night to convince her that the WSC had already given her authority to strike where she believed it was necessary to unite the Silth.

Twenty shamans entered the room; Aran recognized many but not all. Unlike the warriors, they had no armor and wore their traditional robes and cloaks. Aran knew every pocket was stuffed with potions, weapons, and talismans they thought might be useful in today's confrontation. They weren't here to help in the initial attack on Casius. They were here because Aran didn't know yet what the consequences of that attack would be. He knew Casius was confident the possibility of revolt among the warriors or the shamans allowed him to hide in plain sight. Spies reported he was sure Aran would be afraid to attack New Faerie directly and risk such a revolt. Aran wondered if Casius was as confident today, however, since word would have reached him Rangi had been removed from the game.

Merit said she was assuming they'd encounter a prepared force, largely made up of deserters from the warriors of the different nations. Few of her own had deserted, but a substantial number had quietly disappeared from the warrior groups managed by the different Silth nations. They could be collected anywhere in the world, but whether they were in the old colony already or standing by to respond to an attack, she assumed her forces would engage them today. The shamans were a contingency against shaman interference at the old colony or more likely in the refuges and colonies around the world. Most of the shamans would stay here as a strike team that would go after other shamans, wherever in the world they were needed. This group had been carefully vetted by the Shaman Council to eliminate any chance of betrayal and all were bound to the action they were undertaking. Five of them were joining the group attacking the old colony today. Aran knew each personally. They were teachers at the shaman school, and their job was critical to today's undertaking.

He closed his eyes and took a few deep breaths to find his calm place as Merit began to order the warriors into their squads. He was traveling alone. The Tiki and Steamer Crews were scattered among the colonies, prepared to respond to any attempt by New Faerie to strike or take hostages. His job was to find Casius and try to end the rebellion within their ranks so they could focus on the volcanoes and prepare for the Trow arrival.

When Merit gave the signal, he transported to the main building of the old colony. As soon as he materialized in the big room that was Casius's office, he cast a shield, but the bolts he'd expected did not come. The room looked much the same as when he and Storng had visited Casius, but so different from when he and Shra had been there. Opulent by Silth standards, it contained rugs and paintings of Faeries as well as beautiful gold statues, also of Faeries. No one was there.

Aran heard shouts outside as Merit's forces fought with whatever they were finding there. She had pretty good information from the spies. He was confident she could handle it, but all this would be useless if they didn't neutralize Casius. Just as Aran started for the door, it flew open, and Casius rushed in with three of his priestesses. He and one priestess, wide-eyed, stopped a few feet in front of Aran as the other two were closing and bolting the door. Aran threw a handful of dirt at them and shouted an activating word. Casius and the priestess stared in horror at the dirt sprinkled across their chests. When nothing happened, Casius grinned and said, "Depart." The two priestesses by the door, untouched by the dirt, immediately disappeared. Casius and the last priestess remained standing in front of Aran, and Casius's grin faded. Aran held up his arm and hit the priestess with a bolt, knocking her unconscious and slamming her back against the wall. He raised his own shield in time to block the bolt coming from Casius.

"Brother, it is time to stop."

Casius circled him, his own shield up, fury in his eyes. "I'm not your brother, blasphemer. I despise you and all who pretend to the Faerie powers without their blessing."

"That appears to be Faerie magic you're using, brother. Did you get it from the Faeries or a turncoat shaman?" As Aran spoke, a hard rainfall began, and the noise on the thatched roof was deafening.

They both rushed forward, but as the shields made contact, they were thrown back. Casius pulled out a dagger and swooped into the air. Aran pulled out his own and did the same. When Casius dropped his shield, Aran did as well. Casius flew forward and tried to stab Aran, who easily dodged the attempts. They grappled and fell to the floor, struggling and parrying each other's knife thrusts. Casius was bigger than Aran and physically stronger, but Aran's shaman schooling better trained him. Each flapped his wings for leverage when on top of the other, trying to pin him down to strike with the knife.

Casius ended up on top, but he had trouble stopping Aran's knife hand as the weapon moved slowly toward his throat. When it was an inch away, Casius suddenly smiled and looked down. Aran followed his eyes almost involuntarily and saw a plastic flower pinned to his brother's robe. Casius released Aran's hand he had pinned against the floor and struck his own chest. A stream of liquid shot into Aran's eyes, and he pushed Casius away, swinging the knife wildly around him as he tried to wipe away the burning liquid. He opened his eyes— through one there was only blackness, while the other could see shapes but no detail. He made out the shape of Casius standing over him and heard him laugh.

"Little Brother. It is sometimes the simple things that win. Goodbye."

As he lifted the blade to strike, two figures appeared on his left and right, but Aran couldn't make them out. They grabbed Casius, and the three vanished. Aran struggled to his feet as the last of his sight faded and he could no longer see even shapes. Surrounded by darkness, he heard a door crash open, and a warrior ask breathlessly, "Aran Shaman, are you all right?"

No. I'm far from all right.

2

MERIT (SILTH)

The shout from the watch went out as soon as Merit and her warriors began appearing inside the old colony. The New Faerie warriors appeared quickly with shields raised. Merit recognized some of her own defensive tactics, which meant some of the deserters had arrived recently after her training.

The New Faerie warriors vanished and materialized in more tactical locations. Merit's five shamans spread out, each with several guards, and tossed handfuls of dirt whenever they neared a group of New Faerie warriors. The shamans and their guards randomly winked in and out of sight as they tried to get close to groups of warriors. Though the fight was still noisy, with the warning shouts of different groups as an enemy group appeared nearby, as the New Faerie warriors lost their ability to transport Merit's warriors were rapidly reducing their number.

Merit was wary, though. Something was wrong. The spies' reports gave her the impression that more New Faerie forces would be here. She decided this was a delaying tactic.

"Regroup," she shouted to her signal assistant, who quickly blew a horn communicating the order.

The blinking groups of shamans and warriors coalesced into five defensive groups surrounded by shields. They stood in the center of the old colony's commons area. After a few tense seconds, each of the four entryways into the commons filled with New Faerie warriors and their shields. The already gray day darkened, and Merit looked up to see the sky filled with civilian New Faerie Silth, carrying anything they could to drop on her troops. Sometimes three of them would be carrying a log or rock big enough to crush someone when dropped.

One of the four entering columns advanced into the square with two shamans and a rogue commander at its head. Merit recognized her as Tai'mon from the Indonesian Refuge. She first rechecked the array of forces to make sure she understood the enemy's tactics and then said to one signal assistant, "Jaguar, 4." He quickly repeated the word into the phone he was carrying. At the signal, the one with the horn blew a long note, followed by four short bursts. When four of her five squads disappeared simultaneously, she knew they were reappearing on the other side of the New Faerie columns facing her.

Overhead the screaming began. Merit's harpy eagle Stalbon swooped among the civilians, her strong beak severing arms and legs even as her talons drove into unarmored torsos. Debris, limbs, and bodies rained down on the commons, mostly missing both armies, but a few pieces struck a New Faerie squad as the latter advanced. The eagle was joined by more of Merit's warriors as her first reserve filled the air above the commons displacing the civilians. Horns sounded from the New Faerie ranks and were answered from the WSC side. All the warriors stopped advancing and held.

Tai'mon and the two shamans walked forward from the New Faerie column. Merit flew to her own force, landed, and joined by the shaman standing in the center of the group and one other warrior, she advanced toward the three. Silth custom was that such meetings, if convened, were under truce. But so much military custom had already been abandoned, Merit warned her companions to be on their guard.

Tai'mon spoke first. "Honored general. Will you surrender? We have you outnumbered by far." It was largely a ceremonial greeting under the circumstances, as she was well aware Merit wouldn't surrender.

"Commander Tai'mon, I call upon you to honor your oath to your people and withdraw from this field. You bring dishonor on your troops and yourself in your breach of your duties."

The three shamans stood peacefully, one on either side of Tai'mon and the other next to Merit. They neither spoke nor met anyone else's eyes.

"I serve higher masters now. I serve the great way of New Faerie, as we prepare for the glorious future."

As Tai'mon uttered her last word, the shamans flanking her suddenly moved. Each hurled a dagger, one at Merit and the other at her shaman. Merit tried to block the weapon but wasn't fast enough.

"Stop, stop!" Tai'mon batted at her shamans' arms. "This is not our way!"

Merit's shaman raised his arm, and the folds of his robe caught the dagger without harm. In one fluid motion that arm continued forward, and a throwing star, cut down to Silth size, flew from his hand. Immediately, a second star whipped out from his other hand. Each found its target, the bridge of a shaman nose and smashed through the light Silth cartilage and bone. Both shamans fell dead on the commons. Tai'mon reached toward Merit, on her knees clutching the dagger sticking from her throat, but the blue shield Merit's warrior had thrown around her prevented it. A feral growl arose from Merit's columns, but their training held them in place.

Tai'mon glared at the dead shamans and raised her own shield. "*This* is dishonor. I am ashamed of this violation. It was no plan of mine.

We will give you a space of time to treat her before we proceed." She reached into her armor and removed a small hourglass. "Unless you engage first, we will not attack before the sands have fallen in this."

She looked disgustedly at the shamans' bodies as they began to disappear. "No one will remember you," she said to the remaining mists.

Merit faintly heard Tai'mon's words, having collapsed with the dagger still in her throat. Struggling to breathe, she lay motionless on her back and watched as black leaked in from the sides of her vision.

***

Merit gradually became aware of the tent in which she awoke. The rough feel of the blanket. The tightness of bandages on her throat. The smell of blood mixed with that of the shaman's ointments. She tried to speak but couldn't. She tried to stand, but something held her legs in place and she didn't have the strength to sit up.

An aide had run from the room as soon as Merit began to move and returned with her second-in-command. He responded to her questioning look with an update, though she lost consciousness twice while he reported.

He told her it had been all her commanders could do to hold the warriors in check as the sand dropped through the hourglass. Like any good leader, Merit had trained her ranks so they could function without her if necessary. If there had been some surprise or additional tactical change, perhaps it would have been a problem but, as it was, the strength of her leadership structure, the tactical advantage of controlling the air, and the unbridled fury of her warriors meant this battle was over before it began. When the last grain of sand fell, squads on both sides began rapidly disappearing and reappearing. Merit's shamans frantically cast spells immobilizing the New Faerie squads, leaving them easy prey. Her squads had recently added a new tactic which they called *stutter transport*. They would transport, appear in one place, drawing in the enemy, but almost immediately they would flicker and reappear on the enemy's flank. When half her warriors were gone, Tai'mon tried to surrender, but none of Merit's commanders would acknowledge her. Finally, when they were down to the last quarter of her forces, and Tai'mon was badly wounded, her warriors dropped their weapons, kneeling wherever they were, hands behind their heads. Merit's forces were too professional to strike someone in this pose, and the battle ended.

Merit made a hand gesture to signal her approval. She lay thinking about having survived another day. *I had to get special permission from the WSC because some think I'm too young to lead, but I'm already old for a fighting general.*

After the prisoners were secured and Merit's forces had gone door-to-door rounding up remaining Newfies, a shaman led Aran, his eyes heavily bandaged, to where Merit had been moved, a bed in a dwelling about twenty feet up a tree. Awkwardly, Aran flew into the room with the shaman holding his arm. His hands were out in front of him, and he could only move where directed in the strange environment. He was led to Merit's bed and assisted in being seated.

"How is she?" he said, his sandpaper voice breaking with emotion.

The shaman attending to her said, "She's awake and looking at you. She'll live, though recuperation will take some time and treatment.

Although she cannot speak right now because of the damage the knife did, I believe her voice eventually will be restored."

"Wait. You mean I have this opportunity to say things to her, and she can't say anything back?" Aran's face split in a wide grin.

"General Merit is making a motion of poking you in your eyes, Aran Shaman."

Aran laughed. "Then all I'll do is congratulate her and her warriors. Merit, yet again you've done brilliantly. You've broken the back of the Newfie forces. It appears the bulk of them were here, expecting our attack. They had groups in the refuges, but those showed themselves when the fighting began and were dealt with. I'm sure there are still others hidden, but I think we've cut off the primary source of their funding and organization. Unfortunately, Casius and two of his priestesses escaped. My fault. He was trickier than I expected. He can't transport himself anymore, and only I know the antidote. But still, he's out there."

"General Merit is asking about your eyes."

Merit put her hand on Aran's arm. He shrugged.

"Casius shot acid into them. They're gone. There's nothing for the shamans to fix. They can't grow new eyes. I will be blind."

His bravado seemed to crumple with the admission. He leaned forward with his head on Merit's chest and rested there. She wasn't sure who was comforting whom, but she returned his embrace nonetheless.

3

Jules (Silth)

Jules led the fifteen members of the combined crews, only six members of the Tiki Crew since Nadara was still in Washington and the nine Steamer Paerries. They appeared over the ocean off the island of Sumbawa where Tambora smoked and sputtered lava.

The groups were very different. The Tikis tended to work in bonded pairs, staying with the same partner and almost always male with female. The Steamers, other than the Fives, tended to work alone. When they paired up sexually it was utilitarian, and none except Blay and Valente were particularly picky about their partners' gender. The Tikis were primarily thieves, who because of the nature of their work over the last year had become good at fighting, whereas the Steamers were assassins, good at stealth. The Steamers had been raised by Rangi and had known little love or praise, so they shed no tears when told she was dead. The love and respect the Tikis had for Storng, their mentor, was obvious, and Jules envied them for it. While there had been a lot of backsquawk from the Steamers about this mission, at the same time they were proud Aran and the others trusted them with something so obviously important.

Before the crews left, Tiny and Aran had briefed them. Jules studied the stark landscape around the volcano. They were searching for the remains of the village of Doro Mboho, which was south of the volcano and where they would begin walking. For a Human it was one hour from there to the caldera under normal circumstances. But the

Silth were not Humans, and these were not normal circumstances.

Kirstn had resumed a leadership role in the Tikis, and Jeeter, who was always Jules's lieutenant, flew beside him. Kirstn wore a sarong with enormous multicolored flowers, but Jules had learned not to be fooled by her appearance—she was one of the best strategic thinkers among them. Jeeter was no less misleading in his attire. The bowler hat, white, puff-sleeved shirt, bow-tie, and pink mutton chops hid the deadliest personality among them, except perhaps Three of Five, and she was insane. Jeeter was just angry.

Jules gathered them around. "We go to the village and walk from there. We'll be in constant smoke, sometimes poisonous sulfur and radioactive surroundings. We have to maintain our own personal version of the refuges to survive. We're looking for a meadow on the side of the volcano that has survived each prior eruption, and we're hoping it survived this one. In that meadow, something will alert the Javan eagles to our presence. They will most likely attack. We have to fend them off while we collect leaves from the type of akeake or sticky hopbush that grows only here."

"This old Paerrie better be worth all this," Jeeter said, staring without emotion at Kirstn.

As the storm gathered on Kirstn's face, Jules inserted, "It's a volunteer mission. If you ain't all here, don't be here."

Jeeter just shrugged.

"Okay, Kirstn, approach?"

"We don't know what else is here. Or what alerts the eagles or when that happens. I think we should break into three groups of five, stay in sight of one another but spread out some. One member of each group watches the sky at all times."

"Jeeter?"

Jeeter shrugged again.

"Ok, let's go."

They broke into groups with Jules, Slatt and Valente from the Steamers and Don and Loana from the Tikis in the first. As the group advanced, Don and Loana talked about how Nadara was faring living among the Humans. Loana was concerned about her, imagining what it would be like to be without any of her friends and how lonely Nadara must be.

Don, whose voice boomed even now when he was trying to whisper, wore shorts and a Hawaiian shirt, manufactured as doll clothes for Human toys. With his yellow spiky hather and the constant presence of junk food in his hand, he appeared childish to Jules, as someone who would have no serious thoughts. But Don talked of Nadara, musing about what it would be like to really understand Humans and how, even after invading their homes for years, he had no idea what they were like.

Slatt appeared to be listening with interest, his wispy red crest tucked back under the small red head beneath his pith helmet. His dark gray wings were folded behind his canvas shirt with all its loops filled with contraptions, and the pockets of his canvas pants bulged with the wind-up gadgets, brass knuckles, knives, and other devices that made him so deadly. As Jules had told Aran, Slatt never talked. Someone or thing had crushed his larynx when he was small, so he communicated through expressive growls and creaks.

Valente, who also rarely spoke except at night just before lights out when she became exceptionally chatty, also listened intently to Don and Loana, asking a few questions about Nadara but saying little. Mostly brown with white hather on the top of her head and an orange-red spot under each wing and at the base of her tail, Valente was beautiful without a surface glamour. She wore her round, green-tinted glasses, a lab coat over a tight frilly shirt, and leather and gear bracelets above her *magic* gloves. She was complex, afraid of wasps, but their best bomb maker. Jules had always been attracted to her, but she was only interested in other females.

Even though the Tikis and Steamers could not be more different, they had fought beside one another in multiple settings and begun bonding as only those who share such intense experiences can. Normally, there was also humor. They shared a broad range of humor dialects. Today, however, little of that was on display.

As Jules listened to the discussion of Nadara's secondment in the Human management structure, he tried to imagine such a fate. He couldn't believe any Silth could survive there for long. For him, the urge to kill them all, especially those who led, would be too strong. What would Humans have to teach? But even as he thought that, he remembered how useful Penfield had been to the Silth. He believed Aran's arrangement had been beneficial to the Silth, but he was still perplexed because he was under the impression Aran had feelings for Nadara. Sending her into this sort of torture didn't seem like the act of someone who cared, particularly if the rumors were true that Aran had lost someone close to him to Human poachers.

Don mused, "I wish somebody would send me to live with the Humans."

"Why?" Loana asked, wincing as though she was afraid of the answer.

"I want to go to Hollywood and make movies." Loana made a

face. "What? I'd be good at it. I'd make horror movies like *Squirrelnado* and *Monkeys on a Plane.*

They'd been on the path for more than an hour and nothing unusual had happened, but the smoke darkened around them and a hot air current reminded Jules of where they were.

"Enough chatter. Death is near."

Don mimicked him in a low whisper. "Death is near." He chuckled. "Did you get your leadership dialog from the first Star Wars movie? Or maybe …."

Jules silenced him with a scowl.

The group trudged on in silence, heads swiveling and Valente watching the sky. Every so often the air currents would blow aside enough of the smoke that they could see the group a few feet behind them. They came upon a bus parked on the rough road. Jules hadn't even contemplated vehicles might be able to make it here, but this one was designed for rugged terrain. He did a quick calculation. The vehicle had twenty double seats, so it could hold forty plus the driver and more in the aisles. But they would need equipment allowing them to move around in the smoke, heat, poisonous gases, and radiation, and that would probably take up half the space. Thus, there could be between ten and twenty Humans on the mountainside. The Steamers could dispatch twenty without breaking a sweat.

But their orders were to not engage with or harm Humans and not to use the Faerie bolts and shields. Aran had emphasized this because of the school attack. The agreement with Humans hung in the balance. Humans were especially sensitive to Silth motives, and an attack would play into the narrative being advanced by Tobias and others.

As Jules got closer to the bus, he could see that temporary signs had been placed on its sides. They were pictures of a dark-skinned Human, Reverend Tobias, Jules assumed—but Jules could not read what it said beneath his smiling face. As the other groups coalesced, Kirstn read aloud, "Reverend Tobias's Campaign to Protect the Angels."

Jules tensed as a roar rumbled through the smoke.

"Here's some more over here," a muffled Human voice shouted through the smoke eddies.

The smoke not far from them suddenly glowed orange as there was another whoosh of noise. They could see flames licking the grayness as the noise ended.

"They're burning the bushes we need," Loana said with urgency. "How would they know?"

An eddy of hot air blew away some of the smoke, and briefly they saw a dozen Humans in reflective suits with hoods and tanks on their backs. Two had flame throwers pointed at the ground. Jules, at the front of the group, stepped off the road into the edge of what had been a mountain meadow before the volcano blew and Tobias's people began burning it. In the distance they heard an eagle scream.

Vander checked the sky. "The meadow itself is the alarm. As soon as a Silth foot touched it the eagles were alerted. They'll be coming now."

Jules looked at his feet ruefully. "Suggestions?"

Vic was the youngest of the Tiki Crew. Jules mostly dismissed him because he was small and seemed foolish with his various hats and talk of tiki. He said enthusiastically, "Smoke. We can be smoke."

"What?" Jules didn't have a clue about what he meant.

But Marina seemed to. "That's very hard. You have to maintain a moving secondary glamour. It's harder than matching moving parts to a glamour because it has to shift randomly."

"You can drop your primary, and it only has to be good enough to let us get close," Vic shot back.

"True, but you'd have to be so close the eagles couldn't tell you from the Humans. I don't think they'll attack the Humans otherwise."

"Koala nads," Jules said quietly. "If one of you doesn't tell me what you're talking about in two seconds, I'm going to hurt you both."

Marina joined him and Kirstn, and she outlined a plan.

"Okay," Jules said. "It's not very sturdy but it's the best we've got. Do it."

Kirstn called the others over and began the cloaking spell Aran had shown them before they left. It wasn't Faerie magic, but old Silth shaman magic for hiding from predators. Jules remembered Aran had said it worked the opposite of an egg. A Silth egg hid the colony, or wherever it was used, but this spell worked like a skunk's spray, obscuring and muddling sight and sound for anything looking into its field. Aran called it a *Confusion Field*. Humans would still react to the anomaly, but the hope was it would sufficiently confuse the birds.

They all watched Vic and Marina change their glamour to resemble smoke. It wasn't perfect—they were the right color, but the movement was awkward and jerky. To the Silth, the smoke had a blue aura, but the Humans wouldn't detect that. As they stepped a short distance into the smoke, they disappeared. There was another whoosh as a plume of flame blasted into the hillside. Suddenly they were surrounded by the high-pitched whistles of the Javan hawk-eagles. They could see dozens of the brown shapes swooping down through the smoke.

"Let's move. But stay together. If you step outside the Confusion Field, they'll know you're here."

They clustered together tightly and walked into the smoke. Ahead they saw four eagles harrying one of the two Humans carrying a flame thrower. A blurry, blue-gray blob clung to the Human's back. Vic gave up maintaining the glamour, and they could see him desperately hanging on and dodging the eagles' talons as they lunged for him. The Human was trying to use the flame thrower to bat away the eagles as they swooped and dodged, while three other Humans rushed forward to help him. A sharp eagle talon pierced a line coming from one of the tanks on the Human's back. Liquid sprayed out over Vic and the Human, and when it reached the burning tip in the Human's hand, fire raced back along the liquid toward the tank. The tank exploded, and the four Humans, several eagles, and Vic were simply no longer there.

"No!" Loana screamed.

She had flown about four feet beyond the group when Jeeter tackled her. A dozen eagles surrounded them, and several more landed next to the cluster of Silth nearby. Their crested heads moved up and down suspiciously, but their yellow eyes were unable to see through the Confusion. The ones surrounding Loana and Jeeter had no such distraction. She jabbed at the birds with her sword, an unfolded stiletto knife, and he swung his walking stick with its Maori axe head when any bird got close. With his other hand he rapidly threw the darts sheathed on his sleeve. Several eagles staggered as the poison from the darts reached their systems.

"Get back in here!" Jules could not move the group toward the fight without touching the birds eyeing them.

"I can't understand you," Jeeter shouted back, still swinging the axe. "If we both suddenly disappear back into the Confusion, the eagles will figure out it's something to attack, and they'll come after you all. One of us will need to keep fighting. Move toward the others, he yelled to Loana, just as she successfully stabbed one of the eagles at the cost of a deep gash down her arm.

In the swirling smoke, Jules saw more eagles approaching, attracted by the sound of fighting.

Jeeter shoved Loana back into the Confusion field just as he threw his last poison dart at the eagle closest to him. He looked at the knot of Silth and mouthed the words Jules knew were intended for him—"He better be worth it."

Then Jeeter threw his razor-edged bowler hat at the eagle closest to the Confusion, slicing away its head. The remaining eagles turned their attention to him. He swung his axe fiercely as he led them away from the others. The eagles harried him from all directions, and as his arm tired and his swings slowed, the slashes and punctures increased until he was awash in his own blood. The others watched helplessly when a large eagle swooped from behind and snatched him up, crushing his wings in its grip. Jeeter dangled below the bird, unable to reach it with his axe. The eagle disappeared up into the waning smoke, and a few moments later Jeeter's torn and broken body dropped to the ground in front of the group. In spite of their horror, all held their places as the remaining eagles swooped and searched the field.

The smoke cleared enough that Jules could look across the field. Nothing but eagles moved. Finally, the eagles wheeled as if on some shared command and flew to the west. An engine sound made Jules turn—the bus was tearing down the road, leaving dust in its wake.

Jeeter's body vanished in the grass, and Loana let out a sob.

"Marina! Marina!" Don shouted as the group raced across the field.

The Humans had left their colleagues where they lay. The group found the body of the Human who had held the other flame-thrower. Her suit leaked blood from dozens of holes, as well as from the broken face mask. Around her were the charred bodies of other Humans. In her desperate last efforts, she had apparently sprayed the flames everywhere, igniting at least four other people. But they did not find Marina's body.

"She's already moved on," Kirstn said, holding Loana. Nick wrapped his arms around them both.

Jules let them have a little time before giving instructions. One group he sent to search for any remaining hopbushes, since it seemed the Humans were interrupted before they could clear the whole hillside. Another group he set to gathering the dead eagles to burn them. The Humans would question why a bunch of eagles would attack them, so all the creatures would have to be removed. Tobias would try to blame the Silth. The less evidence there was, the better. The last group he instructed to retrieve Jeeter's hat and all his darts, warning them to avoid the poison tips. He told them to erase any Silth footprints.

He flew over, picked up Jeeter's cane, pulled out his shirttail, and rubbed the blood off the axe as best he could. As he watched the crews completing their tasks as though walking underwater, he agreed with Jeeter's last sentiment. *Storng better be worth this.*

CHAPTER 10

1

ARAN (SILTH)

"There's a reason there're no blind Silth."

Aran had made a more dramatic entrance than he had hoped as he came down hard in his landing despite the Silth warrior who held his arm and coached him. The building housed their main conference room, and he'd landed on its porch where Joss and Tiny occupied rocking chairs. He let himself be guided to a small table on which were Silth-sized benches, and draped his wings and tail off the back of one.

"They're quickly eaten in the jungle where we live," he went on. "It's much more difficult to fly blind than to walk, so most end up walking. Not a good way to survive out here." His bandages had been replaced with a black cloth hiding his disfigured eyes. "When I transport somewhere now it's disconcerting because, when I arrive, I have no idea if I'm in the right place. Trandan," he pointed toward where he thought the warrior who accompanied him stood, "has gotten good at immediately describing my surroundings."

He listened to the sounds of the jungle. It was probably his imagination but there seemed to be more than he remembered. He heard the deep booms of a distant bird and the soft trills of another nearby. But it sounded like thousands more in the trees around them. In the distance he heard the scolding growls of a troop of howler monkeys.

"How's Merit?" Joss asked.

"She's recovering nicely. Already has her voice back, and it's better than mine. She is directing operations from her bed, fighting more with the shamans and doctors than anything else."

"What does she think of the recent change?"

"She doesn't know what to make of it. UN troops have surrounded each of the refuges. Human Caretakers have tried to talk to them, but they simply say they're following orders. They have made no hostile moves, but it is worrisome. Merit's preparing for the worst. She's sent instructions to the warriors here, and they'll defend this place if need be. You'll need to make a decision as to whether you want to be inside or outside if it comes to that."

As he took a deep breath of jungle air, its moisture soothed his lungs. "I can't see your faces, but I promise you none of us will think less of you if you want to leave. You signed up to help build a new world, not to fight a war with your own people."

"Joss and I talked about this." Tiny hesitated, slid a look at Joss.

"Go ahead. You tell it," she said.

"We got all the Humans together and walked through scenarios. There're almost two hundred of us working inside this refuge now. No one wants to leave, since this is too important to them. Most have no desire to fight, nor any idea how to do so. And most wouldn't really be staying to help the Silth, but to help the animals and the idea of a different world. No offense intended."

Aran laughed ruefully. "Most of the Silth would say the same thing. If it was just about us, we'd probably fade back into the jungle and just wait things out. The stress of dealing with Humans, fighting among ourselves, and trying to deal with volcanoes is different than we've experienced in generations."

"What does Penfield say about all this?" Joss asked.

Aran shook his head. "We can't reach him. We've tried every way. He isn't talking to us. Which may be the most worrying thing of all."

"Do you think he's turned against us?"

"That's hard to imagine. Could be. I'll be very disappointed if so. But it's more likely he's been told not to communicate with us if the Humans don't trust him not to reveal their plans. Again, worrisome."

Joss continued. "Otherwise, things are going well here. The weather balance is right. The Refuge is full of wildlife. Silth and Humans are working well together, both on the daily tasks and on the work of fleshing out proposals for how Humans and Silth and the wildlife would work together in the future. The farmers on the edge of the protected zone are happy as they raise significant crops in the Refuge's sun, two-thirds of which they can sell to others. We've had to extend the protection zone to them because their fields were being robbed as they neared harvest In return, they've become a great alarm system for anything unusual at the borders. Since the attack on Krackle, there have been a few more incidents, but most of the Newfies seemed to have been flushed out."

Aran heard her tone soften, and he imagined she was reaching out to hold Tiny's hand. "Things are coming together very well." He heard the sound of claws clicking on the boards of the porch and tensed.

"That's Shadow and Macho. They like Silth as friends, not food."

Reassured, Aran felt the breeze of a nose thrust in his direction and smelled the decidedly wet canine odor.

"Shadow!"

Aran felt for the soft muzzle and stroked it. He reached and found a big floppy ear and leaned forward to whisper in it. Shadow suddenly sat down. "Woof!" Then he rolled over and smiled a doggy smile.

They all laughed.

"What did you say to him?" asked Joss.

"I just told him he was a good dog."

"So, you spoke to him in dog talk?"

Aran smiled. "Each dog makes up his own set of sounds. Their language is mostly visual, accented with growls and whines. I spoke to him in English."

They talked on about the current thinking about how Humans and Silth could rebuild the world and the wildlife populations and natural systems. Aran was amazed at the competence of the team of Humans and Silth working here. They had accomplished so much. He was also surprised at how comfortable he was sitting here and talking to these two Humans. And that he really did care what happened to them.

Tiny was telling him that he was concerned that the volcanoes would soon be past the point where it was likely Humans could do anything about any of them.

"Maybe it has something to do with the high level of radioactivity, but there's something different about what's going on. They seem to be settling into a state of constant, self-sustaining eruption. It's no longer driven from below."

Aran heard the buzz of his phone in Trandan's backpack and listened as the warrior answered. When Trandan stopped talking, Aran held his hands out for the Blue-tooth ear-piece.

"We need you to come to the UN right away," he heard Penfield say.

"Hello, good to hear your voice. Yes, I'm fine, thank you. Blind now, but otherwise not much new."

"Sorry. Nadara told me. And sorry for being out of touch. Things are getting bad all around the world. The President has had to impose martial law along the border and in some of the territories in order to preserve order. We need you here."

"There are UN troops around all of the refuges, Penfield. What does that mean?"

"Come to our usual conference room. I'll explain." Penfield hung up.

"Well, that's weird. He wants me to come to the UN. Wouldn't give me details."

"Maybe it's a trap."

"Perhaps, but what good would it do them to have one blind Paerrie?" Trandan cleared his throat. "Ok, and his escort. More likely they want to deliver some ultimatum. He said things are getting desperate." Aran stood up and held out his arm for Trandan. "We shall see." Tiny coughed and Joss guffawed. Aran shrugged.

2

ARAN (SILTH)

Was it a trap? Aran doubted it but couldn't rule out the possibility. Was it the prelude to a war with the Humans? Given the troops massing around the Refuges, this seemed the most likely reason he was summoned.

As soon as they materialized, Trandan told him only Penfield and Nadara were in the room. Aran relaxed, unclenching his fists.

"Nadara!" Aran let out a *whoosh* of air as she smashed into him.

When he could breathe again, he asked, "How are you? What's going on?"

"I'm fine. Miss you and the Tiki Crew. Desperate for news. Good news is I've learned a lot about Humans. Irvin and I were comparing experiences on being embedded in another culture when you arrived." She broke off, and Aran could tell she was assessing the blindfold and his condition. "And you? How are you?"

"I'm fine. Not much new," he said as Trandan helped him into a seat. He waited for her punch he knew was coming. Sure enough it came, though softer than he anticipated. "Later. I need to know what Penfield has in store for us today. Ambassador Penfield? I hope you are well. We've missed you."

"Yes. I'm sorry to have just dropped out. But events have been unfolding quickly here." Aran thought Penfield sounded excited, maybe even happy. He heard heavy footsteps followed by the door opening and felt the room air pressure change.

"Mr. Secretary-General," Penfield said.

Hearing Penfield's chair scrape the floor as he arose, Aran, who'd been seated in the Silth-sized chair present these days in most of the U.N. settings, stood.

"Please be seated all. I'll get to the matter at hand in just one moment." The Secretary-General spoke in English, but with the accent of his Nigerian roots. "First, how are you, Ambassador Aran?" The Humans had struggled over a proper way to address Aran given the vagueness of his portfolio and the lack of surnames among the Silth. "I was saddened to hear about your eyesight and the circumstances of your loss. I hope the steps proposed today will be beneficial."

"Thank you, sir. I'm fine. My wounds have healed, as best they will." Aran had no idea what steps he was talking about, and he wanted to get on to the business of the meeting.

"Eiyaah! I am told this was the act of your brother, in some kind of civil war. But you have prevailed. Chei!"

"*Civil war* is probably too strong a term." Aran stretched out the words as he remembered his rehearsed answer to the implied question. "Ambassador Penfield has told us Humans go through similar struggles at times when a minority takes up arms to oppose the direction of the majority on philosophical grounds. Particularly when these struggles over direction take place during wartime and there isn't time to work out a shared solution. We have a group that believes the Trow will bestow magical powers on them if they support their effort to retake this world. They were supporting a rebel army in New Zealand, the one that attacked the school, and were providing economic support to a Human group, led by … Reverend Tobias, I believe."

"Ahhh. That explains some things," Penfield interjected. He

hesitated, but at the Secretary-General's urging, he went on. "Tobias's campaign for the *angels* has suddenly stopped its worldwide influence push. They were spending millions daily."

Nadara said to Penfield, "It's my understanding you thought this to be both good news and bad news."

"Yes. It means Tobias's efforts to recruit new followers are at an end. But he still has many followers, and they grow more desperate to achieve their goal of preparing for the arrival of the Trow."

"A *civil war?*" Aran asked innocently. "I would have thought the speech Faelen gave would have ended the idea the Trow could be angels."

"Ha. Imagine!" the Secretary-General said, a smile in his voice. "A group who disagrees with the direction of the majority! Your friend Faelen made a lasting impression. Unfortunately, the devil was also an angel. Tobias's people are not our biggest problem, only *one* of our problems. Faelen persuaded the Chinese they should work with the rest of the world, but still several groups disagree. That is why we decided to deploy U.N. troops to help protect the refuges. We have also taken up the task of working with the countries where the refuges are located and working through the steps for satisfying their claims and concerns. Though, in truth, these have greatly diminished now that so much food has begun flowing out of the protected areas."

"These troops are there for our protection? This is not the precursor to war?"

"At all. At all. No, it is my fault you should even pause to think this. We received intelligence suggesting some Human groups plan to move against some of the refuges, and we had little time to coordinate with you before taking action."

Aran listened without reply. What was the likelihood that Penfield or someone else could not have given them some warning or information about the deployment?

"I will be blunt. I sense you are skeptical about our lack of communication. As the troops deployed, an internal fight was still going on as to whether the deployment would be for the protection of the refuges or for their control. This fight was only resolved this morning, and the results communicated to the Honorable Ambassador Penfield as the liaison to the Silth. We have worked day and night for several days. And have agreed to accept the terms proposed by the Silth for the management of the volcanoes."

It took Aran a moment to realize that in the Secretary-General's eyes, he was meeting with a Silth delegation, which included Penfield. He was still absorbing the answer as the Secretary-General continued.

"Many details are yet to be worked out. I hope you will agree some can be completed after the Silth have stopped the volcanoes. Thousands of Humans and other life forms on the planet are dying daily."

Aran sat quietly as thoughts bubbled through him. At a nudge from Nadara, he realized that without seeing the body language of the room's occupants, he'd forgotten that they would expect some response from him.

Never had he been more aware of the coarseness of his voice than at this moment. He wanted to make a memorable speech about their shared future. He wanted to inspire them, perhaps tell a story highlighting a shared response to a challenge, but unable to see body language and reactions, he felt blind in a completely different way than his physical blindness.

He cleared his throat, but when his voice came out, it was no better. "Thank you for your explanation, Secretary-General. It is greatly appreciated. Events eclipse us and strain our abilities to communicate. One of the first steps we'll take is to try to remedy this. We have been preparing plans and discussion points with groups of Humans— *committees,* I think you call them. These committees are ready to begin meetings with larger groups of Humans. In the meantime, we'll sign a treaty outlining our way forward. This will be the legal words on a paper your people use to bind one another. The Silth have no written word and little confidence in such papers. We will risk much in stopping the volcanoes, and we want to know that even though it will be hard, Humans will stay the course of their commitment after there is no longer a threat. That's why we'll expect the representatives of every Human nation, as well as yourself, to *bind* yourselves to our agreement. This is a magical promise, that if broken will bring death. With this in place, we can immediately proceed in our efforts on the volcanoes, even if we haven't worked out all of the details of the future."

The room fell silent until the Secretary-General finally spoke. "And thus begins a new world for Humans, where our promises are truly binding. As you can imagine, this will take a little adjusting to for the delegates."

"Your Excellency, I'm sorry but I wasn't clear enough. We're not certain that in the future Human countries won't sacrifice their delegates to avoid the consequences of their commitment. We want the leaders of each country to sign and be bound. This binding will bind the entire country. If the country goes back on its commitment not only that leader, but any leader who replaced him or her will die. We'll assign a team to work with you on this. I think Nadara can lead this group. She's got the most experience with your ways and customs. But it's up to her."

"Well, we all have much to think about and plan for. Let us begin our journey!" the Secretary-General said, and Aran heard him push back his chair. Aran stood and bowed toward the sound.

He remained standing after he heard the door close. He admitted to himself he was stunned by the rapid acceptance. Things must be getting worse quickly.

Penfield said, "Please stay a moment longer, Aran. We have something else to discuss."

More footsteps outside the door indicated to Aran several more visitors had arrived.

"Aran, this is Dr. Stein. He's one of our tech miniaturization experts. He and his team make things small. When we heard about your mishap, the President asked Dr. Stein if he could miniaturize an existing technology for seeing. I'll let him explain."

"Good morning, Ambassador," said a bright voice with the slightest trace of accent. "We took the *fly eye* technology developed some years ago and ran it through an AI-managed VR program that rebroadcasts the view directly into the optic nerve."

The technician paused, as though expecting some reaction, and Aran wondered if everyone else thought the man talked gibberish. He felt increased pressure from Trandan's hand on his shoulder, and he took what felt like a small headset with two semicircular pieces of glass.

After a moment of silence, he said, "You do know the Silth live without any technology except these phones we've had to use." He shook his head. "I have no idea what the coati scat you just said."

Penfield laughed. "I don't really either. I made them explain it multiple times. Let me try to translate, and Dr. Stein, check me if I'm wrong. *Fly eye* is like a pair of glasses that have a hundred cameras, each pointing a slightly different way. It's the way a fly sees. Very efficient, since it allows him to see above, below, behind, and in front simultaneously. But not as useful to binocular creatures used to seeing only two views, one from each eye. Humans can't process multiple views, and I suspect Silth couldn't either. The Artificial Intelligence, essentially a really smart computer, quickly stitches together all of the views into a binocular version and, instead of trying to use the real pictures, the computer projects a virtual reality depiction of the surroundings onto the nerve going from your eye to your brain. With this apparatus, which Dr. Stein has made small enough for you to wear, you should be able to see again. Kind of. Is it okay to try it on you?"

"Sure. And thank you for this effort, whether it works or not. This is very thoughtful."

"Aran?"

"It's okay, Nadara. Sort of like wearing the boom-box. Let's see how it works."

Aran sat back down, and the technical team fitted the device on him. It was heavy but manageable. He felt a switch get flipped, and the whole apparatus tightened around his head, exerting pressure on his eye sockets. As he watched a series of lights and random geometric shapes, he wondered whether this technology would render him a literal *tech head*.

"Ready?" Stein flipped another switch. "Tell me what you see."

Aran realized he was sitting with his mouth hanging open, and he closed it. The world around him had resolved into a picture of the room. It was vivid, though when he moved his head things looked slightly more sketched before resolving again into a realistic picture. Disconcerting at first, because he was observing so much more than he usually saw. Without moving his head, he could see pretty much all the room simultaneously, including Nadara behind him frowning, the technician and Penfield in front of him smiling.

"You look like a bug," Nadara said.

He ignored her. "Amazing. I can see." Penfield held a mirror in front of him. He looked like a bug.

Well, I'm probably not going to live long enough for this to make me crazy. He remembered a quotation by the Human Hunter S. Thompson he had read a few days before losing his sight. *Faster, faster, until the thrill of speed overcomes the fear of death.*

3

ARAN (SILTH)

Wearing his new eye apparatus, Aran transported into Storng's room, the first time he had shifted without Trandan since his fight with Casius. Nadara brought Penfield with her. One of the concessions Aran had made when he sent her to live with the Humans was to teach her the transport technology.

As usual the room was filled with shamans and doctors; Penfield immediately started conferring with the latter. Jules and Kirstn were sitting glumly on a window ledge. Kirstn hugged Nadara and began to sob. Aran held out his hand and took Jules's forearm in the welcoming grasp of the Silth.

"If that's you, Aran Shaman, you look like one of us now," Jules said without mirth. "We retrieved the antidote and," he nodded toward the doctors, "they'll administer it within the hour. But the price was high.   Too high.   I take full responsibility." He hung his head.

Aran turned his head toward Kirstn. Knowing the others couldn't see his eyes in the reflective lens, he made his attention obvious. She understood and responded. "There wasn't anything Jules could do. Tobias's people were burning the fields. They plainly knew to destroy the antidote. And the eagles came … Marina and Vic … and Jeeter were so brave."

Aran turned back toward Jules. "How did you leave it with Tobias's people?"

"They never saw us. But eagles attacking Humans in that

fashion is not normal, so they will certainly blame magic. Of course, they would need to explain why they were on the edge of the volcano." Jules paused. "We could have just killed them all. There would have been no issues then. No one to report. Cleaner."

Aran understood how Jules chaffed under the restriction on killing Humans except in battle. After a long pause, he responded. "Rangi was not right. Normal Silth do not use death to advance their policies or desires. We may kill a jaguar or a dingo threatening our colony, but we don't seek out the dingoes and kill them just because they are dingoes. We live with the jaguar and we live with the dingo."

Jules looked like he'd expected this answer. "I don't know that I'm cut out to lead the Steam Tiki Crew." As Nadara's eyebrows went up, he said, "Yes, that's what they are calling themselves now. I'm an assassin. I know how to do that very well. I screwed up being something else and got three Silth killed."

"Don't you do that!" Kristn said angrily. "Don't you take away the bravery of those three like that. Marina and Vic were brave and they solved a problem. They didn't die because of a mistake. If anyone is to blame for Jeeter's death, it's me for stepping out of the Confusion, but he didn't die because of me or because of a mistake." Her voice shook and her fists clinched. "He died to save all of us so we could complete an important mission."

Jules lowered his eyes. "I can't even take responsibility for screwing up without screwing up."

"I set the quest and its parameters," Aran said. "I couldn't be prouder to be a part of Steam Tiki. None of you did anything except complete one of the hardest tasks we've ever attempted. There will be stories about this for the rest of Silth days. Maybe I screwed up in taking the risk for one Silth. And I keep running the reasoning over and over to make sure I didn't do it because he means a lot to me." He looked at Nadara and Kristn. "And to them."

He tipped his head toward the other Silth in the room. "He symbolizes the *outreach* to many Silth. He's the most experienced among us with Humans. He is the one who's read the books the rest of us have not. I think he's very important to the next stages. Who's going to speak for us with the Humans? Me? I couldn't sound or appear much scarier."

Nadara joked, "You could glamour over the *bug-look* and do the rest of us a favor. It's very distracting. I think Jules is the only one who likes it." Everyone laughed, including Aran, as he took her suggestion.

One of the doctors announced, "We've distilled the antidote, and our shaman colleagues have taken the additional steps they believe will activate its magical powers." He shook his head, "You cannot comprehend how much I never expected to utter a sentence like that in my lifetime."

Jabtar, the senior shaman, said, "We're ready for it to be administered. If it works, we'll know pretty quickly."

The Silth crowded together on the bed with Penfield and all but one doctor standing beside it. That doctor loaded a bag on the IV pole and started the slow drip of the antidote into the liquids being fed into Storng. Almost immediately, everyone in the room jumped as a dark shadow in the rough shape of a Silth rose up from Storng's body. It gave an angry howl as it dissipated in wisps of smoke that the Silth had to dodge. As soon as the dark thing was gone, Storng moved his head slightly, and his eyelashes fluttered. Suddenly his eyes popped open.

"What in the coati scat happened to me?"

Later, after all the good wishes had been expressed and Storng had eaten, bathed, and slept some, Aran, Penfield, and Nadara convened with him. Jules and Kirstn returned to the Steam Tiki Crew for much-needed rest and to give them the good news about Storng. As the Silth settled cross-legged on the bed, Penfield pulled a chair up beside it. Storng was dressed, sitting up, and seemed almost wholly recovered. Nadara sat beside him and leaned on his arm.

Aran said, "Ambassador Penfield, we have much to tell you and to seek your council on. But some of it cannot be shared with other Silth or the Humans yet. I'm loath to disclose all unless you bind yourself not to share the information from this conversation. You've always been honest with us about your spy role. We need your counselor role here, without the spy role."

Seeing Penfield's hesitation, Storng told him, "For an individual binding simply holds you to a commitment you voluntarily make. You will retain the knowledge of what is discussed, but you won't be able to share it with anyone else. Having that knowledge will allow you to better counsel us as well as your President. I think it's a reasonable request and a good alternative to having the conversation without you."

Storng's words persuaded Penfield to say, "I agree. And I consent to be bound."

After Storng completed the binding process, Aran proceeded to update him, quickly working through Rangi's defeat, the breaking of New Faerie, and his fight with Casius. Storng gasped when Aran dropped his glamour and showed him the technology he wore.

"Are you sure about this?"

"No, but being blind was worse than lying on a monkey's bed. I can't afford it for now. Maybe I'll stop using it after we've dealt with the Trow."

Aran told Storng about the meeting with the Secretary-General and the U.N.'s acceptance of the Silth terms.

"That's fantastic!"

"We'll see. I told them their world leaders had to agree to be bound to the outcome. I'm sure many of them agreed to the terms intending to renege as soon as we repaired the volcanoes. Let's see if they can hold the agreement together when they have to take it seriously." Penfield nodded his agreement.

"Storng, you must step back into dealing with the Humans," Aran insisted. "I don't have a diplomatic bone in me. This isn't like negotiating with the Silth villages over swag and services. This is the future of our race and all the creatures of Earth. I'm unqualified."

"It seems to me you've done fine. But I look forward to discussions with my Human friends again."

Aran told Storng the teams had been working on post-volcano plans which were almost ready. Then he looked at Nadara and his tone changed. He softened his voice as much as possible and talked to her because he could not bear to address Storng directly. He told Storng the high price paid for his antidote. No one spoke as they allowed him a few minutes to grieve.

"Storng, I take full responsibility for this. I know if you'd been conscious you wouldn't have allowed them to go into danger for you, but the Silth, the Humans, and the rest of Earth's creatures need you right now. You have no blame in this."

Storng sat with his eyes closed, rocking back and forth. "You take too much on yourself. The blame is on the poisoner. Do we know who did it?"

"No. We're confident it wasn't a Human because the poison is a Trow one. It could've been administered by Silth or Trow. There are still New Faerie sympathizers, and we don't know how high up their spies may be."

"Trow? But they've all withdrawn."

Aran glanced at Penfield and told Storng of Faelen's appearance at the U.N.

"Ha! That must have disrupted things. Angel said Faelen had been killed. How is Faelen still alive? And if he is alive, he certainly wouldn't poison me, would he?"

"Faelen was nursed back to health by other Trow who are still in the world. I can't disclose where or tell you anything about them other than the fact they don't use magic, and they're not hostile to Silth or Human. I don't think they poisoned you. It was either a Silth who was taught by a Trow, or another Trow who has chosen to stay in the world as a spy. Whether Silth or Trow, somehow a spy got close enough to poison you."

"There are Trow in the world?" This from Nadara. "So perhaps our time isn't over?"

"They don't do magic, which means they won't create more Silth."

Aran stood and paced on the bed. "We have a more urgent problem. The volcanoes. When the Humans finally accept our terms, they'll expect us to quiet the volcanoes." He cut his eyes toward Penfield again. "Even though we've had many shamans working on this, we're still not sure of how to accomplish it. I've developed a plan I think might work, and I want to share it with you to begin testing and questioning it. I'm not ready to share it with the other Humans yet, for reasons I will explain."

He stood at the end of the bed, facing them. "You know how much magic it took to quiet one volcano, and it was only barely active. The Silth alone might be able to end all the volcanoes one by one. But it would take a long time, and it would be difficult to maintain and protect the refuges in the meantime. I believe if we harness *all* the Silth magic, *all* the Human magic and if we can, the magic from the Trow in the world, we can stop the volcanoes all at once. But if this action is something that goes *against* the magic of the Earth, it will kill every participating Silth. And may kill the Humans and Trow as well. Even if the Earth accepts the action as one of balancing, the Silth will be weak after the event and completely vulnerable. We'll have only the Human military to protect us. Everything will depend on our ability to trust the Humans. And … I do not trust the Humans."

They all spoke at once and argued long into the night. Storng periodically fell asleep and then awoke to rejoin the discussion. Penfield participated as readily as the others. Trandan had food brought to them and then, except for checks on Storng by the medical staff, kept everyone out of the room.

When they finally reached consensus, they were all bleary-eyed, sure of what they should do, but unsure of how it would end.

CHAPTER 11

1

ARAN (SILTH)

From the window Aran watched Kimper play with Merit's harpy eagle Stalbon. The flower fairy had been around the creature enough to know it wouldn't eat her.

What surprised Aran was the little fairy's willingness to risk a bad result in the interest of amusement. Kimper was using bushes and trees to obscure its flight toward Stalbon's back. The very serious harpy eagle stood looking toward the building, awaiting its mistress's commands. Aran would have been afraid to reach out and touch the bird, with its enormous talons and sharp beak, and he was six or eight times Kimper's size. Yet when she was close enough, Kimper leaped on the bird's back. Aran heard the tinkle of her gleeful giggle through the window. The eagle bucked and shook, but the mirthful flower fairy held tight. Finally, the eagle rolled over and knocked Kimper from her perch. As the flower fairy lay on the ground immobilized by laughter, Stalbon cocked her head and looked down at the little creature. She reached over with one great claw, and Aran was afraid this would be the end of the flower fairy. But the eagle gently grasped Kimper, hopped on one foot to a deep puddle about a foot away, and dropped her into it. Kimper disappeared below the surface before coming up sputtering and laughing even harder.

Aran turned from the window to listen to Merit, Storng, and the rest of the Council argue. He had already spoken at length. He had updated the Council on the plan that was in motion and the members had already approved it, though you wouldn't know it from listening to the way they continued to second-guess it. Some argued the Silth were taking the greatest risks in Aran's plan, so perhaps they should hold back some forces. Would they be able to hide their weakness from the Humans? Was there a risk to the Humans? Should they be told? And then all the old discussion had to be recycled. Why should Silth, with no hope for a future, help Humans who'd never helped them? Could they trust the Humans to build a new world? Shouldn't they just let them die out and focus on saving the animals? Then even if the Trow wiped out the Silth, they wouldn't go out of their way to harm the animals. Aran really got them going when he told them there were still Trow in the world, though he wouldn't tell them where. He didn't share with them his increased concern about a spy, if not in the Council itself then someplace near, in trusted staff or in the warriors.

When it was his turn to speak again, he began by updating them on what the Humans had done to date to implement the plan. "It depends on them utilizing their magic. But it has to be done their way. Most Humans do not believe they do magic because, over the years, they have cloaked it in their rituals and philosophies. Consequently, marshaling them is difficult. After working with Penfield and our Human advisers in the refuges, we laid out a plan to the Humans. Kate, in charge of the Costa Rica Refuge, has taught us about New Agers and their beliefs. There are countless subgroups such as Zen Druids, Wicca, Crystal Mavens, and various old religions that have been revived. Each of these has its own way of trying to influence the world, and they have all begun to practice focusing their energy on the volcanoes. There are major religions around the world, each of which believes it can influence the world through prayer and the intervention of its god. They'll be gathering their practitioners for a *day of prayer* to focus on the volcanoes. The Humans who believe in the power of positive thinking have been similarly mobilized. There is something called an *x-prize* that will be awarded before the target day for the scientific lab coming up with the best solution to the volcanoes. Similarly, militaries and government agencies around the world are engaged, all with the intent of implementing their best ideas on at least one volcano on the target day. The Humans manifest their magic in many ways. We haven't told them there is a risk, to them or to us. We aren't sure their hearts would be in the undertaking if they had more fear. They have plenty already. As for telling them about the risk to us, we see no tactical advantage since we don't think they care much about us to begin with. All it does is disclose an opportunity to take advantage of us."

Aran paused as a ruckus of eagle screams and flower fairy hoots came from outside. Merit looked seriously cross, but Aran couldn't tell if it was because of the interruption or because her companion was being teased.

"Even under our best-case scenarios, we'll be exposed throughout the world for a while after stopping the volcanoes. We'll be reliant on the Humans to protect the refuges. We're not sure they can, or even that they will."

As soon as Aran finished, the Council erupted into argument again. He went outside and flew into the steamy Costa Rican rain forest, landing at a small waterfall nearby. He checked the area carefully for dangers before stripping down to bathe in the cool water. He felt reassured by the steady rain forest noises around him. The last thing he did was take off his augmented glasses. While they were water resistant, he had been warned not to immerse them in water. He felt very vulnerable in the waterfall—the sound prevented him from hearing anything around him and without the glasses he was once again blind. The water refreshed and invigorated him, though, and was well worth his nervousness.

As he stepped out of the water and reached for his clothes, he heard the loud sound of a throat being cleared. He scrambled for his glasses and quickly put them on. On a rock a few feet away, facing discretely away from him, sat Storng, watching the parade of birds glide among the branches lit by the sun that Silth protections allowed into this area. Aran didn't say anything but continued dressing before joining Storng.

Storng's deep voice was quiet in the openness of the place. "If you think about it, what we've done so far is amazing. We've helped stop two of the volcanoes the Trow tried to activate. Protected these refuges, greatly increasing the likelihood some of the wildlife of this world will survive. Defended ourselves against the Trow for the first time in our existence and re-engaged with Humans after years of hiding away. Our engagement allowed us to negotiate the beginning of a new world order. We've reunited the Silth of the world and defeated internal enemies."

"You came out here because you thought I needed this recital? And the old stories tell of the Paerries fighting the Faeries before. Granted the Paerries always lose and the entire rebel nation is wiped out …."

Storng chuckled. "No, I came out here because you're not the only one who has trouble sitting in a room that argues so much to accomplish so little. It's a necessary process. An important process. But also, a painful one. When I left, they were getting to the right results." He pulled out a small bag of nuts and offered some to Aran. "And I came to tell you a story. An ancient Human story said to be the source of both a military tactic and a business tactic—*The Emperor of the Empty City.*"

Aran shifted, settling himself more comfortably on the rock to listen.

"It's a story of ancient China, retold many times as it is the thirty-second of the thirty-six stratagems told over centuries as an essay on war, politics, and business. In the essay it's called the empty fort strategy. I've heard many different versions of this story, so I'll tell you the one I like the most.

"Liang, a Han regent, found himself the senior official in the city of Xichengas. The Wei general Yi approached with his army of 150,000. Xicheng's army was out gathering supplies and the city was exposed. Liang dressed scarecrows like soldiers and put them on the walls. They were obviously not real. Liang dressed the few men he had as civilians, and after throwing open the gates, he stood at the front of the small group sweeping the entrance to the city as though preparing for Yi's arrival. Yi stood outside the city and recognized Liang, who had a reputation as a wily tactician. Yi told his men it was a trap and led them away. After a day's march and deep thought, he decided he'd been tricked and turned around. Again, the doors stood wide open, and this time no one was in sight. Yi's men marched into the city to be wiped out by Xicheng's army, which had returned in the two days' time."

Aran reflected upon the story before saying, "You believe this is a strategy we might employ after we stop the volcanoes. Of course, it will only matter if we survive them."

"Of course."

"And you told me out here because you too have concerns about the Council and who we can trust."

"One would be foolish not to. Shall we return to their discussions?"

2

ARAN (SILTH)

As the meeting ended Nadara cornered him. She led him outside and over to the side of the creek. Kimper landed on his shoulder. Gray mist filed the trees, and the babble of the water obscured the other rain forest sounds.

"You were going to blip away from here without saying good-bye, weren't you?" She looked hard at Aran, and so did Kimper. She stamped her foot, and so did Kimper, causing Aran to wince.

"Well, weren't you?" Then addressing Kimper, clearly mimicking her, "Stop doing that! Shoo, shoo." She waved the flower fairy away from Aran's shoulder.

"You've been avoiding me. First you send me to live with the Humans. Then you give me this job organizing their acceptance of the treaty."

"You said you wanted to do that," he protested.

"All very convenient. Do you have any idea how lonely it's been living with the Humans? At least now I have a few Silth working with me on the treaty binding. But still you don't come to see me. You could be here any time you wanted. I don't hear from you. And don't tell me you've been busy. I know you could have used the phone and it would just take a little time."

"You're right, but wearing this—this thing, I don't feel right. I don't feel like someone who should seek out their lover. I feel like an abomination."

"You're no abomination." Her tone softened slightly. "At least not because of that apparatus." She turned her back to him. "I think you are simply being *Heartless,* and I've been foolish for thinking you were someone else."

Even through the strangeness of his artificial sight, he was struck by her beauty and strength. He wrapped his arms around her and said quietly into her ear, "I am not that person, but I am not sure I'm the Silth you want me to be either. It all feels like a fraud. I was a Silth. Now I'm something else. I was a storyteller. A shaman. One moment I'm a general. The next an ambassador. I had a brother, bad as he was. I had a home. I was blind. Now I'm not. I thought I could trust all Silth, now I know I can't. I thought I could hate all Humans, all Trow. Now I can't."

He released her and went on. "You're right, I may have pushed you away. But it's not because I'm bored or there's someone else or for any of the old reasons. I'm simply not someone who is good to be around right now. And I know you'll say that's up to you, but it's not. Every time I realize how distracted I am, and how fantastic you are, and how you deserve better, I'm even sadder. I can't do that right now. So perhaps you're right. I'm protecting myself, but I didn't mean to hurt you."

She turned and held him, leaning on his shoulder. Kimper came and hugged her as well, causing Nadara to chuckle and then sniffle. She wiped her eyes. "Well, that's a load of coati scat, but too much to unpack right now." And she disappeared.

Aran flew to the top of a tree a few hundred feet into the jungle. There he was above the mist. As the sun sank down into the volcanic clouds parted by the Silth protective barrier, he could watch the odd sunset that characterized the refuges. He stretched on the big branch, and Kimper lay down on his stomach as they watched the stars come out. He thought about his physical inability to cry now as the sadness leeched into him.

3

ARAN (SILTH)

Penfield sounded furious on the phone. Aran appeared in the White House conference room and Storng arrived seconds later. Penfield's face was pale.

He said nothing as he motioned them to take the prepared seats on the table, pointed toward the screen at one end of the room, and pressed a computer key. Casius's face filled the screen. Dressed in his New Faerie robes, he spoke calmly and earnestly as he described the Council meeting of the previous day. He said the Silth had been lying to Humans about what they could do and the nature of the Trow. He insisted the Silth didn't know what they were doing with the volcanoes and that they knew Humans would be endangered by the effort to stop the volcanoes. He said the Silth themselves would probably be destroyed by this effort. He told the internet audience that Aran was working with the Trow, who had not left the world as he'd told everyone. Finally, he urged them all to hold on and negotiate with the Trow.

When the clip finished, Penfield said disgustedly, "I've just spent the last hour trying to explain to the President what was actually going on, but I can't since every time I try to talk nothing comes out! She thinks I'm an idiot at best, perhaps complicit in deceiving her and the rest of humanity. This is really bad. The trust and credibility that has been built is damaged, and world efforts will be set back."

Storng looked at Aran and at his nod said, "Ambassador, please be discrete with the information you have. I hereby release you from your bind to not discuss our meetings."

Penfield looked relieved. "Wait here. I must speak with the President."

"Monkey spit," Aran said once Penfield left the room. "Casius's knowledge could only have come from a Council member. And they're not trying to hide it."

"But how do we flush them out?"

After almost an hour, Penfield walked in with the President. Aran and Storng stood.

"Madam President," Storng said, as he and Aran both dipped their heads.

Percrow said nothing as she stalked to the head of the table and sat down. She stared at them for a long time before saying, "Penfield explained to me what was going on. Finally." Penfield wilted slightly under her glare as she took a deep breath. "I think I understand, and I get why you didn't share all of this as it was developing. I've been in politics and dealt with other nations long enough to know that none of us share everything."

She poured herself some water and drank it. "I want you to walk me through everything he says and tell me what's really going on. Then I want you to tell me anything else that you've withheld. I know you were waiting for us to make it clear what side we were on. Well, we've done so. Now it's time for us to act like partners. If I'm satisfied with your answers, we're going to get some of my speech writers in here. They're going to work with Irvin and Aran to prepare Aran to go out to the world with a response to Casius. It must be delivered in a few hours at most before this has a chance to dominate the news without answer.

In the meantime, Storng and I will visit the Secretary-General, update him, and seek his assistance. Any questions?"

She didn't really look like she wanted any.

4

JOSS (HUMAN)

In the Brazil Refuge, Joss and Tiny sat at the head of the common room filled with Silth and Humans. Between them was a computer attached to a projector facing a screen. For the past two hours, television and internet news sources had been announcing that at 6 p.m. EST a major announcement on next steps in the world response to the volcanoes would be live-streamed.

There was little conversation in the room as they waited. Ignoring the talking heads currently occupying the screen, most of the Humans had their heads down over their phones searching the news, and many of the Silth were gathered in clusters, some around phones as well. Joss hoped it was her imagination, but she thought there was a little more distance between the two groups than usual. Though all of them discounted Casius's video as propaganda, it was an ear-worm—a song even Joss couldn't get out of her head.

Suddenly, the screen changed to show the Secretary-General, flanked by the U.S. President and the Chairman of the People's Republic of China. Their expressions could not have been more serious. To one side, Storng and Aran were sitting on top of a table, each with a small desktop in front of him. Having been told about Aran's augmented glasses, Joss realized he must be glamoured so they were not visible.

"Turn it up!" someone shouted.

The Secretary-General began with, "Many of you have heard the assertions made recently by the Silth, Casius, high priest of the group called *New Faerie*. These claims were troubling enough that we immediately requested a response from The Seven Nations of Silth. We've reviewed their response, and the support they have provided for it in detail. After intense scrutiny, we find no reason to change the course of our actions and our work with the Silth to stop the volcanoes and establish a new approach to all life on Earth. We will also continue to prepare for the Trows' return. Our report will be released tomorrow morning. But now Ambassador Aran, representing the Silth Council, wishes to address you."

The camera zoomed in on Aran, who sat still at his desk for several moments, before leaning forward and looking straight into it.

"I am Aran Shaman, a member of the Silth World Council. Some of you may recognize me as the Silth who fought the Trow when they tried to blow up the Yellowstone volcano." He paused, then, "Well, you might not recognize me if you saw how I actually look now. You see, we Silth can project how we want to appear. And while I used to have the face you see before you, I don't any longer." He dropped his glamour so that his bug-eyed apparatus was visible. "I must wear this now in order to see. Without it, I am blind. I wear this even though the proximity to this kind of technology is probably killing me."

Again, he stopped, and Joss reminded herself he was a story-teller. He reached behind his head and undid the clasp holding the apparatus. He stared back toward the camera with two black empty sockets surrounded by deeply scarred skin. "I wear my glamour like you would wear makeup, or perhaps have plastic surgery to hide my disfigurement. This was done to me by my own brother ... Casius, the Silth who spoke on the video and leads the remaining New Faerie splinter group." He took a sip of water and continued. "I'll admit that when I decided not to show others how I really looked, it was in part because I feared their reaction. But mostly it was because I was still dealing with the scars myself and sorting out how I wanted to be seen.

"I'm told Human nations behave in a similar way. They do not lie to one another. At least the good ones don't. But none volunteer their weaknesses or, for the most part, their fears, particularly when they are still developing information. Have we suffered such fears? Yes. Are we still developing information? Yes. But because this impacts all of us, it's fair that you know our concerns and what we know.

"Casius said we don't know how to stop the volcanoes. Well, you've already seen us stop one. Had we ever done such a thing before? No. Did we know for sure it would work? No, but we had a pretty good idea. The results are not in doubt, however. If we had not stopped that volcano, a whole chain of them would have erupted, and none of us would be here any longer. Similarly, have we ever stopped seven volcanoes? No, of course not. We never said we had. Do we have a pretty good idea how to do so? Yes. Implementation of our approach has begun, and we are confident we can succeed.

"But stopping seven volcanoes requires an enormous amount of energy from Humans and Silth alike. There are risks. The Silth will be applying magic directly to the Earth. This is very different from our usual practices. For the Silth, if our plan goes awry, we could die … instantly. Humans will be doing what they always do, utilizing their science, technology, intentions, and prayers to impact the outcome. While there is some remote risk Humans could be harmed, it's extremely unlikely. Moreover, it's no different than what you are already doing, just more concentrated and coordinated.

"Casius also said we've hidden the fact that there are still Trow on Earth. When we first told you the Trow had gone, we were reporting what the Trow warriors had done. They left with the intention of returning in a few years. As far as we knew, that was all the Trow in the world. After that, as many of you saw, we found out Faelen, the Trow who helped save the world, was still alive. So, you already knew there was one Trow in the world. I discovered Faelen was nursed back to health by a small group of Trow who have been living peacefully on Earth, hidden away for years. They've cut all ties with the Trow world and are as much at risk as you or me. They also refuse to practice magic, and all they desire is to be left alone. I have honored their request, but the result has been I didn't share their existence with you or the Silth until this week. We will seek their help in stilling the volcanoes, but we're not certain they will, since this would violate their core belief that the use of magic is the root of all their people's problems.

"Why would Casius tell you these things and try to turn you against the Silth? He heads New Faerie, a group of Silth who believe that the Trow are benevolent, despite all evidence to the contrary. His organization, once powerful, is reduced to a few followers. He funded the Human movement led by your Human Reverend Tobias. That movement believes that the Trow are angels. Their funding from Casius has been cut off. He also aided what you would call a *war lord*, a Silth named Rangi, who killed many Silth and attacked the Human school in New Zealand. That attack was thwarted by the warriors of the Seven Silth Nations.

"Some of you don't know that the reason I replaced Ambassador Storng in negotiations was because he was poisoned. He nearly died, and it took the combined efforts of Silth and Humans to save him. We believe this was the work of my brother as well.

"He'll do and say anything to try to bring the Trow into this world, and he believes they'll reward him. We've removed almost all his power but unfortunately haven't been able to catch him. He has no power now unless we give it to him."

While everyone watched, Aran took his time putting the apparatus back on. He stared bug-eyed at the camera a moment and then restored his glamour to his normal self.

"We will proceed with the plan to shut down the volcanoes. I know some of you are skeptical about this plan, in part because it relies on Human magic as well as Silth." Aran reached into his pocket and pulled out a lighter. He flicked the flame and said a few phrases before waving his arm in a circle above his head. A ring of fire appeared there, out of which arose a flaming image of a Silth with wings spread.

"There is no doubt about the Silth magic. You have many names for yours—faith, technology, intention, science. All we are asking is that you concentrate all these endeavors to one end, our mutual goal. We can end the volcanic eruptions. If we do, Humans will live. Then we will begin rebuilding this shattered world. We will rebuild it as a world for all its creatures, where Humans and animals alike can thrive.

"Finally, we'll prepare for the arrival of the Trow. We know there's no negotiating with Xafar, the king of the Trow, except from strength. We're doubtful that even then he'll negotiate. But if he arrives and finds the volcanoes did not wipe out Humans and Silth, that they have found their strength and are prepared to resist him, that is our best opportunity to explore peace. Or fight and win a war, if we must.

"I'm sorry I haven't told you all these things before. I commit to you that as long as you, Humans, are open and honest with us, we will be with you as well. It is a long road ahead, and I hope we can travel it together as allies."

The ring of fire went out. All the figures on the stage stood. The Humans shook hands, and they and the Silth bowed to one another. The feed ended and the talking heads returned. The room in Brazil was silent.

Joss walked to the front of the room, standing before the screen. She looked over at Krackle, who looked deep in thought. After Joss caught Krackle's eye and waved her over, the shaman flew up and landed on the lectern to Joss's left. Krackle's always eccentric wardrobe was bright tonight with mismatched colors and patterns. The copper wire in her dreadlocks reflected the room's harsh overhead lights.

"Krackle Shaman, I thought that it might be good if we talked some about what Casius said and what was said tonight. Could I ask you to start us off?"

"Hooo, you know I hate to talk, now don't you?" Laughter broke the room's tension. "First let me tell you, I know this Casius fellow. If you will excuse me, I'll use an expression I learned from Tanho—*I wouldn't cross the street to piss on him if he was on fire.*" The room exploded in more laughter as Tanho just grinned.

"What?" Krackle said innocently. "Didn't I say it right?"

"No, I think you got your point across very well."

Krackle turned back to the room. "We can ignore what Casius said, but Aran Shaman said several important things. It's a good thing they didn't let that Storng fellow talk. We'd still be here in the morning and would have gotten more information from Storng 137, my chicken. But Aran was a storyteller before he was a shaman, and his story tonight was packed with information. Of course, a really good story also implies a lot of things without directly saying them. He told a good story.

"You Humans should know this was the first time most Silth heard there was any threat to their survival in addressing the volcanoes. You might have noticed that while he said there was probably little risk to Humans, he put no sweet coating on the risk to the Silth."

Krackle paused at the excited Silth chatter. When it died down, she asked, "Cinda, had you ever heard there were still Trow in the world?" When Cinda, a Silth with orange hather and blue wings, shook her head no, Krackle went on, "Neither had I. Aran Shaman was not just speaking to Humans tonight, nor was he apologizing just to them. He was apologizing to the Silth, as well."

She closed her eyes and swayed from side to side for a moment. When she opened them again, she spoke louder. "I cannot speak for all the Silth here tonight, I'm sure they will share their thoughts, but I stand with Aran Shaman. I trust him, and even the old goat, Storng. I think we're on the right path. And that's all I have to say."

Joss studied her feet. She hated to stand in front of people, so why had she impulsively started this discussion? She spoke, but to the floor. "Some of you know I met Storng when I was very young, and he saved my life. I didn't know then that to do so he violated some very important Silth rules, but I'm glad he did. I think many of you know the Yellowstone story by heart and Aran's role in it. But some of you may not know I met Aran when he was severely wounded by the Trow." She looked up to see expressions of surprise. "You Humans may not know he didn't always have that horrible voice of his. It happened as a side-effect of his saving a Human life, again in violation of his people's rules. In the battle we've taken on, he's lost his eyesight, been betrayed by his brother, and seen those around him be hurt and some killed. He has already given a lot, and we've only just begun. It doesn't surprise me his first instinct is not to trust others. But I trust him."

"Hey," someone shouted from the back of the room. "Turn the video feed back on. Aran's being interviewed by Oprah."

Joss and Krackle moved from the front of the room as Humans and Silth scrambled to turn off lights and get back to their seats. Someone else added, "Storng is being interviewed on a Chinese feed. Wow. The U.S. President, China's Chairman, Ambassador Penfield, and the Secretary General are all on different feeds. It's an all-out blitz."

The screen came back to life with Aran sitting, looking relaxed in front of the TV personality. She had apparently just asked him whether he hated his brother, and he was answering earnestly, "No, I don't. We've never been ... close. It is more like he's simply become a stranger to me. He's no longer my brother. He is someone who believes his path, however misguided, is the right one, so I don't think of him as evil, just wrong. And you know, the Silth don't really hold a grudge very long." He leaned forward. "We can get really pissed off, but we're not very good at saving that feeling.

"But just because I say I don't hate him doesn't mean I'm not angry with him and the Newfies."

Oprah shook her head. "If my brother blinded me with acid, I would have a hard time believing he wasn't evil. I think I'd hold a grudge." Aran just shrugged without comment.

Joss and the rest of the Brazilian refuge stayed awake until almost morning watching the media discussions and talking among themselves. As light came and they staggered to bed to catch a little sleep, she believed the team was strong and united in their commitment to move forward. She knew, however, that she had a self-selected, already deeply committed group, so she could only hope the rest of the world had a similar response.

CHAPTER 12

1

ARAN (SILTH)

"One of you has betrayed this Council, betrayed the Silth, betrayed our efforts on behalf of all living things."

"Aran Shaman, that is not the tone to take with this Council," Council chair Tellick admonished.

"There's a traitor here, and there isn't time for games. We must determine who it is and banish them." Aran stared back at her, hoping his brashness hid the fact that he was well aware he was not only one of the youngest in the room, but he was the only one there that didn't have some official title or designation. Even the ambassador title was now honorific, as he had returned the role to Storng.

Aran studied the twenty or so Silth gathered in the whitewashed, humid room at the Costa Rica Refuge. They were all here—delegates from each Silth nation, representatives of various Silth institutions, Storng, and Merit, who was boldly displaying another scar without bothering to glamour. They occupied chairs pulled up to a Silth scale table, placed on top of the Human conference table that took up much of the room. There were no Humans here today, though. Other than Storng and Merit, any of them could be the traitor. Coati scat, it could be several of them. The only thing he knew for certain was the Council could no longer function with a spy.

"Why does it matter?" Tellick said. "You've promised the world transparency. What would a spy have to tell? In fact, this Council really is of little use, isn't it? You and Storng and Merit Warrior do what you want anyway. We're simply here to put the seal of authority on your actions."

Aran eyed her more closely. Was she trying to bring suspicion on herself or just being her usual cantankerous self? Something wasn't right. Something was different. He glanced at the door. He flew over to the window and looked out. He quickly flew to the door leading to the hall and opened it. The hall was empty.

"Have you lost your mind?" Tellick said.

"Merit, where are your guards?"

Merit jumped up. "They should be where they always are, Aran."

"They aren't."

As other Council members started to rise from their seats, Tellick shouted, "Stay seated!"

Two Silth in New Faerie robes appeared beside her, holding a device of wires and clay-like lumps. They put it on the table and stood behind Tellick, arms raised, ready to fire Faerie bolts at anyone who moved.

"You two, back at your seats. Everyone stay where you are. Some of you would be able to transport away, but the majority of you haven't bothered to learn, so you will die when this goes off."

Aran knew Tellick herself couldn't transport, but the priestess at her shoulder was ready to take her.

"Sit back down," she said through clinched teeth.

Slowly, Aran obeyed. Beneath the table he reached into his

robe and began pulling things out of pockets.

Storng said, "Tellick, what are you—"

"Shut up, Storng! On this one day, I don't have to listen to your toucan song."

Behind her, two more figures appeared. A New Faerie priest held Casius's arm—because of Aran's spell, he could no longer transport himself. Casius stepped up to the edge of the table, looked around, and stared at Aran as though trying to see through his glamour.

"This will be quick," he said.

He raised a small, red button-topped device, plainly of Human design since he had to hold it in both hands. He flicked a switch on the side and pushed down on the button on top. "This is called a kill switch. This device will detonate three seconds after I remove my finger from the button. You fire on me or anyone with me and I'll set it off. You kill me and it will go off. In three seconds, some of you will escape, but not most of you. Understand?" He didn't wait for a response.

"I'm here to give you one last chance. Join New Faerie and help us welcome the Faerie host." He looked around the room, but no one moved. "I didn't think so." His gaze stopped on Aran again and he squinted, apparently detecting Aran's lips moving slightly. "Then die!"

He took his finger from the trigger.

Kimper swooped down into the face of one of the two priestesses who was prepared to fire on the group. She shouted, batting at the furious flower fairy and drawing the attention of the other priestess. Storng and Aran both leapt to their feet and bellowed as they each thrust a hand toward the bomb and the five Silth assembled at the head of the table. Immediately, all five and the bomb disappeared. Kimper hovered in the empty air, tinkling furiously.

After a few seconds of stunned silence, everyone began talking. Merit rushed from the room to determine why her warriors were no longer at their posts.

"The Land?" Storng asked Aran under his breath.

"I thought perhaps deep beneath the sea, but I wasn't sure that magic would work," Aran reached up to his shoulder and stroked Kimper affectionately.

Storng said, "I'm still not ready to share that ability with others. So, do you mind if we simply say they were sent somewhere from which it's unlikely they'll return?"

Merit came back into the room fuming. "Ordered away by another New Faerie spy who has now disappeared. Storng, do you shamans have a truth-telling spell we can use to review our warriors?"

Storng thought a moment before answering, "We could adapt a binding spell."

"I want to start at once. Where did you send them?"

Aran slid a look at Storng and said, "Someplace from which it's unlikely they'll return, especially since the bomb probably went off as they arrived."

"I've never seen a shaman make things disappear. Plainly you two have magic you haven't shown before."

Aran chuckled to himself as he heard Storng's familiar reply, "Why would you assume someone has taught everything they know?"

"Okay," called out the council member from Malaysia, named vice-chair many months earlier. "There's much to do. We must finish the planning for *Operation Fairy Ring,* as our friend Storng calls it. And I suppose we need a new council chair."

Joss (Human)

Joss and Tiny were tense. Even their dogs were tense. As Joss listened, there was no rain forest sound, as though all life knew it was at the edge of the precipice. Today was the day.

Tiny spent the morning setting up a command center, filling it with computers to monitor world events. Multiple cameras had been mounted along the edges of the refuge. Additionally, they had televisions and radios and a bank of cell phones. Finally, they had radios connecting them to the surrounding U.N. troops. Several staff, some with military training, were managing the center and in charge of any necessary defense.

It would have been better if they had more time. Time to coordinate more. Practice even. But Tiny and a team of volcanologists had released a paper two days ago that said they were out of time. They didn't speculate as to whether magic could fix the volcanoes— they simply explained that by the end of the week all of them would have reached a tipping point where no imaginable force had any hope of stopping them. This report was leaked at the same time the U.S. began rationing food and sixteen former nations were declared *nongovernmental zones* essentially without government leadership or services.

Everyone in the refuges knew the critical time would be immediately following the quieting of the volcanoes, if it worked … and probably even if it didn't. The WSC had made peace with the

Brazilian government, which had come to depend on the flow of fresh vegetables and fruits from the edge of the Refuge. They'd stopped doing things like trying to cut off cell coverage in the Refuge. But the government's control of the countryside was breaking down, and no one could assure some group wouldn't try to take it.

Joss went through one last check-in with each of the refuges. She was proud of the way they had stepped up to their challenges. She was a little proud of herself as well. Supported by Krackle's elixir, she'd overcome her crisis. She didn't care whether it was a placebo or not. She didn't care that she had gotten some on-line criticism that she'd substituted one addiction for another. She only cared that she was doing her job leading the Human side of the refuges.

Well, that and she had a real relationship. She looked over at Tiny. He smiled at her but continued his work.

But Joss felt particularly exposed right now because most of the Silth were gone. Like the Silth around the world, they were gathered around the various volcanoes and would immediately return after the conclusion of the operation.

They called it *Operation Fairy Ring.* Storng had an elaborate explanation of the name, but in its essence, the name reflected the fact that Humans had multiple explanations for *fairy rings*—those circles of bright green grass or mushrooms that sometimes appeared in fields. There was a scientific explanation—they were the result of a fungus's spread; there was a religious explanation—they, like all things, were the work of God; and there was a magical explanation—they were the mark of fairies dancing in the moonlight. Joss thought that the name did a good job of capturing everything they were throwing at the volcanoes.

Today, at 12:00 noon EST, almost every Human would be focused on stopping the volcanoes. They would be praying or meditating or merely imagining a world without erupting volcanoes. They would be applying scientific or technical solutions. The winner of the X-prize was supervising implementation of her idea and the Scandinavian scientists were working with Japanese engineers on a solution. Humans around the world were coordinating their timing with Twitter. Aran had talked the Trow Sohi into participating, or at least he'd secured their promise that they would. While they wouldn't explain what they'd be doing to help, they assured Aran that they'd join the effort from their hideaway. He said that they didn't appear to lie about anything, so there was no reason to doubt their commitment. Finally, there were the Silth themselves. Every active volcano was ringed by Silth. Every Silth who could fly was up in the skies around the world. A few stayed back with those who were too young or too old to participate, but the rest were hovering nervously, waiting for noon.

Tiny said it felt like deja vue for him. On a computer screen, he'd watched the first Silth effort to address a volcano. But this time, instead of his single struggling drone, there were several different angles of filming, from drones, satellites, and telescopic lenses. At each volcano Silth wore small body cameras that provided continuous feeds.

Joss was slightly nauseous as she watched one of the feeds, and the Silth who was wearing it, bob in the hot air currents coming off the volcano. She wondered whether she would be alive in a few minutes. From talking to the Silth at the Brazilian Refuge, she found out they were more afraid of failing than dying. They knew the future and standing of their race and the future of wildlife hung on their success today. They'd been quiet the last few days. Even Krackle had spent all her time chanting in her sweat lodge and purifying herself for today's confrontation.

In a close-up shot, one of the Silth started to chant. It was time. As Tiny bowed his head, Joss took his hand and closed her eyes to begin praying. After a few moments she realized that she couldn't stand not seeing what was going on, so she opened her eyes and watched the screen while she recited prayers she knew by heart. Nothing had changed on the screens. One showed a close-up of a Silth face, eyes clinched shut in concentration. Another screen showed an engineering team setting off a charge in one of the volcanoes.

***

Like all the other shamans, Aran was holding a handful of earth as he chanted. The shaman chant was different than that of the rest of the Silth. The others were simply channeling their energy into the shamans spread among them. The shamans were focusing that energy and the energy from every talisman they had, as well as every bit of magic they had inside themselves into the Earth and closing the volcanoes' access to the lava and gases below. They only retained sufficient energy to maintain their lives.

This was the magic that Aran knew well. It had almost killed him before. He and Storng had reviewed it with every single shaman around the world. Many objected, having been taught this was an unnatural kind of magic. They would have to use the Earth side of the Silth heritage to draw on an Earth magic, augment it with the Silth magic drawn from an astral plain that surrounded the Earth, and apply it to force the Earth to their will. In his fight with Angel, Aran had forced a root to take a life, an act that violated the Earth's essential forces, and it had poisoned him. This time none of them knew what the result would be, because these volcanoes had not begun as a natural act. They existed because of interference by the Trow, creatures from another world. If Aran was right, the Earth would respond to the will of Humans and Silth and end the volcanoes without resistance. If he was wrong, every shaman in the Silth nations would be poisoned at once, with none to save them as Storng had saved him. If he was wrong, the Earth's response would most likely kill not only the shamans, but the Silth channeling the energy as well.

When noon arrived, he pushed these thoughts out of his head and concentrated on the volcano in front of him. He felt his consciousness slip beneath the Earth. He was aware of every heartbeat, every breath, and all the tension of the Silth in the air around him. As he moved beneath the Earth, he could feel the flow of Human will prodding and shaping the earth. It was not powerful enough by itself. He felt the power of the other shamans as they, like him, began pushing harder on the Earth, shutting off the flow of magma and gases. But each time they would shut down an area, a new one would open up because of the pressure pushing up from below. The Earth didn't seem to be resisting them—they were simply not quite powerful enough.

Aran concentrated harder, aching from the tension in his muscles. It wasn't enough ... it wasn't going to work. And then a burst of new power joined them. Not foreign, not Trow, but a new surge of enormous energy from the Humans and the Silth. Aran knew what this was. The Sohi had not tried to apply magic to Earth and bend it to their will. They sent their energy into their children, the Humans and Silth, to allow them to change the Earth. Aran felt the volcano become still, the channels allowing the magma to travel upward collapse, the ground cease to shake. All was quiet.

Aran opened his eyes and saw the shamans dropping from the sky, with other Silth rushing in to catch them. He saw other groups of Silth gathering and transporting away. He saw ... nothing else as his world went dark.

3

ARAN (SILTH)

"It really was a stupid plan."

Aran heard the voice near his face and peered into black-centered, brown eyes too close for him to tell who they belonged to. But his brain processed the voice.

"Hello, Dawn Defender."

Merit's familiar yellow tattoos below her eyes and the red hather around her face became visible as she leaned away from him. One side of the face smiled. "It's alive!"

"You think all my plans are stupid. Why do you keep agreeing to them?"

"Sadly, because they're better than anyone else's." Her smile slid away. "We'll see if the next part works. I think it may be the most toucan-stupid plan I've ever participated in." She opened the window curtain so he could see rain pouring down in the jungle. "*Operation Fairy Ring*. And, by the way, the foolishness of your plans is exceeded only by the silliness of Storng's names for things. Operation Fairy Ring was a success. The volcanoes have all stopped. And before you ask, you've been unconscious for one hour. More good news, the Silth and the Humans are still alive. Unfortunately, so are all the shamans."

"Well, you can't have all your wishes come true at once. Where am I?"

"I've done briefings all my life. If you will not interrupt me, I'll tell you all you need to know." She distractedly smoothed the hather around his face and shooed away Kimper, hovering near her shoulder and eying Aran with concern. "You're at the Sumatra Refuge as we agreed. Penfield and the American generals appear to have been correct in predicting this would be the refuge attacked after the repair of the volcanoes. North Korean planes have been landing at the island's airports for the last hour. Several North Korean ships are off the coast. They must have left before Fairy Ring even started. Tanks and troop carriers are already moving on the roads toward us. General Cogbill, who's in charge of the U.N. troops, says he expects the Koreans to use field nukes and chemical agents on anything outside of the protected zone, but not within it since they want to keep it intact. Consequently, he's pulled the U.N. troops within the farming zone at the edge.

"All civilians are evacuating to the other side of the island. The troops are concentrated along the roads into the Refuge, because the edge is too big. This Refuge runs the length of the Bukit Barisan Mountain range from the Genung Leuser National Park to the Kerinci Seblat Park." She started pointing to a nearby map, propped on a stand. "Koreans are advancing here and here. U.N. troops are here, here, and here. But the Koreans are flying helicopters off the ships, so they can insert troops anywhere along the edges of the Refuge. Cogbill says to expect Special Forces insertions in multiple locations. The U.N. has their own counter strike forces spread out around the Refuge. He seems ... pessimistic about our chances."

"Have you told him about *Operation Big Monkey Scat?*"

"No. I hoped to retain some shred of credibility with him. Not *Shadow Puppet* or *Kabuki Theater* or any of the names Penfield suggested, except *Big Monkey Scat.*"

Aran smiled. "How are the Silth doing?"

"The shamans have all experienced magical exhaustion before, though perhaps not to this extent. They seem happy that the Earth didn't push back on the effort and that they're alive. They, like you, are weak but recovering. The rest of the Silth aren't used to the effect of extreme magical use, so, like someone who uses a muscle they've never stretched before, there is a lot of whining and moaning. Doesn't appear that there is any real harm. They're recovering faster."

Aran tried to stand but ended up falling back on the bed, frowning.

"Most Silth are walking around, a little dazed, but walking. You shamans aren't there yet."

"Everything depends on the U.N. holding off the North Koreans for a while. Will they fight?"

"Cogbill says they will. They believe that this is for the future of their families, and the troops trust us more than the North Koreans with that future."

"What about the other refuges?"

"A few local groups explored the defenses right away, but no major threats. According to the monitors, the Humans are debating how long we'll be debilitated and how they'll tell whether we're dead. They seem to have agreed that one obvious sign is if the refuge protections are still in place, we must not have died. As you can imagine, there is a mixture of concern, fear, and opportunism in play. There are also huge celebrations going on. Parties to express gratitude that the volcanoes are quiet."

They heard a far-off rumble, and Merit explained. "Cogbill said that they would begin shelling the edges of the Refuge from the ships. He thinks the shells will contain poisons. The barrier will block the poisons along with the volcanic gases."

"We need about eleven more hours to recover enough to fight. Nine more before we can implement Big Monkey Scat with a few of the shamans."

"Let's move you to the command center. I need to be there now as well."

One of the Indonesian team's Humans carried Aran into the center. He barely had time to register the array of monitors and communications devices before he lost consciousness again. When he awoke, he felt like little time had passed, but as he looked around at all the Humans and Silth in the room he wasn't sure. He recognized Trandan, the warrior who had accompanied him when he was blind. Trandan flew over to him.

"General Merit asked that I watch for when you regained consciousness so I could update you. She's occupied with the defenses."

"Tell me."

"The Koreans shelled the western edge of the Refuge from the sea. They've engaged with the U.N. troops along the roads. They've used field nuclear devices and poison gases, but because of the shield, most action has been in conventional fighting just within the edge of the Refuge. As soon as any Silth civilians recovered enough to fly, General Merit deployed them with phones throughout the forest. Our warriors are still not ready to engage. But the Silth have been able to spot and call in the location of Special Forces teams. The U.N. troops are holding against the frontal attack, and they've been able to kill or capture the ones moving behind the lines that we've seen. There are likely others we have not. The U.N. troops fight bravely, but they're taking heavy loses. General Cogbill doesn't think they'll be effective at stopping the North Koreans much longer. New Korean forces are arriving from the ships to the west. Those ships are now fighting other U.N. allied ships, but they've been able to send their troops toward the shore under cover of night. The North Koreans sent us a message that if we surrendered, the Silth would be spared to work for them in a glorious future that they would lead. No mention of what would happen to our Human team members. After that they tried to jam our phones and other communications, but the U.N. eventually shut that down. We were able to pass their threat along to the outside world. We are told that China has attacked North Korea, but it's made no difference here."

"How long have I been out?" Aran pushed himself up and tested his wings. He was still weak, but strong enough to move around. He remembered how long it took for him to be fully functioning again after he tried to save Shra, but that was before he had renewed his shaman conditioning. He knew that he'd be able to fight in a few more hours. But would they have a few more hours?

"It's been nine hours since Operation Fairy Ring."

Aran slowly stood up. He swung his arms and rotated his shoulders to work out the knotted muscles. "Is the Big Monkey Scat team ready? Do we know where the Korean command center is? Is there any food around?"

✶✶

Aran hovered at the entrance to the Refuge beyond the edge of the field protecting the lush rain forest and surrounding farms. The vegetation was sun-starved and struggling. Kirstn, Loana, Don, and Nick were with him, and all had their shields raised. The Tiki members of the Steam Tiki crew were dressed in their finest aloha apparel. Aran wore his shaman robes and had lowered his glamour so that his unmistakable seeing apparatus was visible.

Before their arrival, a drone tested the air and deemed it clear, the wind had blown away the noxious gases. The five flew about a foot off the ground with Don and Nick pulling a red wagon that held the radio patched into the speakers in... everything. The U.N. troops had placed speakers facing the North Korean troops along the edge of the jungle in each of the areas where fighting was focused.

Just as Aran and the crew exited the jungle, the U.N. hackers had commandeered the airwaves and every phone, radio, computer speaker, everything that listened, now reflected what was said into the microphone Aran was carrying.

Aran was talked casually to the crew as if unaware the microphone was on, even though his voice boomed out from all around.

"We'll invite them in as guests, feed them, and then perhaps they'll leave. Maybe they're just hungry."

After a pause, and fainter but still audible all around them, Kirstn's voice reminded Aran, "They said they intended to enslave the Silth."

"Well yeah, I know that's what they said, but don't you think that's just tough talk? Lots of Humans get pretty grumpy when they get hungry. I mean, so do Silth if you think about it. Son of a toucan, look at all of these bodies."

Aran and the crew stood in the middle of the first contact battle zone, and Humans lay all around them. They had to weave between them to pass down the road. Ahead they could see the field bunker the North Koreans had assembled as their forward command center. They stopped in the road and continued to hold their shields in front of them—the shields would stop a sniper's bullet, but a tank round would crush them against the trees. Aran couldn't see any evidence of life. Other than their voices, he heard nothing. The birds had left the area and the animals had moved into the mountains. There was no sound or movement from the Korean line.

"Hello, Honorable North Korean invaders," Aran said through the mike. His voice boomed out from behind him as well as in front. "Are you hungry? Would you like to take a break and join us for lunch?" He turned to Loana with the mike still on. "What do you think they eat?"

"Silth?" was Loana's answer, and Don's booming laughter echoed around them. Aran shook his head in mock disgust.

"We have some nice soup for you," Aran called out. "Full of nutritious vitamins and vegetables." He waited for a response.

After a few moments, he said to the others, "I don't think they care about our soup." The crew expressed their certainty that the soup was great and the North Koreans were really missing out.

Again, Aran addressed the Koreans. "We don't have much of anything else. There really isn't any need for all of this fighting."

Suddenly, Aran's voice on the speakers was replaced by a great roar. Aran and the rest of the crew turned. Appearing over the treetops was Jules, only he was several hundred feet tall. He sneered down at the command center. Another roar over the speakers and Merit stood next to him, also his size. She angrily pointed down at the center, nudged Jules, and gestured toward the mountain range to the south. He nodded and they strode off in that direction as though checking out the situation.

Aran turned back to face the North Korean line. "Oh, don't mind them. That's just a little experiment to see if we could change our size. Looks like it works! You want to come meet them? That's Jules and Merit. You'll like them. Jules has killed lots of creatures, and Merit has never met someone she didn't want to kill."

For the next hour Aran kept up the patter, talking with the crew and periodically calling to the Koreans to come into the Refuge. Twice the colossal Jules and Merit returned to look down on them.

The second time a Korean tank rolled up next to the forward command center, raised its barrel, and fired. Towering above them, Jules's face twisted with anger. An enormous blue bolt shot from his arm, obliterating the tank and the forward center and leaving a great crater where they'd been.

"Son of a coati!" Aran said.

Jules looked at his hand and over at Merit as if confused, then shrugged his shoulders.

Aran clicked off the mike and said, as much to himself as those around him, "That wasn't supposed to happen." He shook his head and looked back toward the Korean lines. With no forward command post left, he wasn't sure who he was talking to.

"Okay guys. We're hungry and we're going to go on back and eat. You are welcome to come on in. We won't try to stop you." He looked up at Merit and Jules. "I suggest that you don't shoot at the big guys, though."

Don and Nick turned the wagon around and began flying back toward the jungle. The others faced outward as they slowly flew backward, protecting Don's and Nick's backs. For an hour and a half, they'd maintained the shields and their bravado. Aran continued to converse with the Tiki Crew on the open mike, wondering aloud why the Koreans had not taken him up on his offer. Once they reached the trees, he switched off the mike. Trandan handed him a Bluetooth earpiece for the phone he was carrying.

"How's it going?" He listened as a voice on the phone updated him. "Thanks!"

He turned to the rest of them. "The North Koreans haven't advanced for the last two hours. Jules and Merit continue to ham it up all along the lines, but the shamans can't keep the projected glamour going much longer. The five are very young shamans in training, and it's hard to project someone else's glamour. Though apparently there's more power in this spell than we were led to believe. One of the novices lost consciousness when Jules fired." In the distance he could see the colossal Merit beginning to flicker, and suddenly both she and Jules disappeared. "We need to move back into the trees some since there's no telling how much longer the Koreans will take to decide what's going on. They're fully mobilized on both sides of the Refuge now, and the U.N. troops don't have much left to give."

Silth showed up in the trees all around them. Slatt and Vander appeared next to Aran, followed by all three of the five, Ada, and Valente. A moment later Jules appeared and told Aran, who still had his glamour down, "Yes, you definitely look like one of us now." Aran smiled but raised his glamour back in place.

Jules reported, "We exhausted the young shamans. One is unconscious and the others seem concerned he might die. Merit went back to the center." He looked at Slatt. "How'd we do?"

Slatt frowned and growled.

"What'd he say?" Kirstn asked.

"I think it's a Human saying—*don't quit your day job,*" was Vander's response.

Aran cocked a brow at Jules.

"I have no idea," Jules said to the unasked question. "I was just trying to point menacingly and next thing I knew that bolt fired."

They spread out into the trees now full of Silth. With the other refuges secure and the Silth recovered, all seven Silth nations sent warriors to defend the Indonesian Refuge. It was two more hours before the Koreans decided that it had all been a bluff and began their attack. The Silth were ready. They devastated the attacking forces and followed them on their retreat, appearing suddenly in the centers of operations and destroying everything. They were angry and, Aran had to admit, savage in a way he'd never witnessed. They moved fast, as though hoping that no one would have time to surrender. Merit told him over the phone that the reserves the Koreans had been moving forward had been intercepted by Human forces. They'd made no effort to surrender and simply fought until destroyed.

She told him that China had invaded North Korea but reported that almost no one was left there. Apparently, most of the population had starved, already resource-strained before the volcanoes had started erupting, and the Korean government had sent all its remaining population to try to take the Refuge.

CHAPTER 13

1

ARAN (SILTH)

"Penfield," Aran said gently. "I'm not angry at Humans, so you don't need to explain the Koreans to me. I understand they were starving, and I don't hold others responsible for them." He was sitting on the table in the U.N. conference room along with Storng and Penfield. "I'm awed by the bravery of the Humans in the U.N. forces. These were men and women from all around the world. They're the ones who paid the price for the Korean attack. Very few Silth died."

Storng leaned forward. "We want to honor them and their families. We've created a special memorial area in the Sumatra Refuge with all their names. I think perhaps you've seen a video of the place."

"Yes, it's gorgeous. The sound of the chimes, the beautiful tiny figures hanging from the trees."

"A small thing for what they gave, and what Humans did to honor their bargain with us."

Nadara appeared and took the third seat on the table. "Storm Rider, Ambassador Penfield," she said. For a moment Aran thought that she was going to ignore him, but then she gave a curt nod to him. "Aran Shaman."

At least she hadn't called him *Heartless.* She was poised and erect. Aran thought about how much she'd grown in the last year, how much of a leader she'd become. If anything, she looked more beautiful as well. Yet again he told himself he was a fool.

Penfield said, "As you may remember, all the world leaders had been bound to the commitment before the Silth began the transformation of the volcanoes. The Koreans shouldn't have been able to attack, but we have learned that they had one of the leader's body-doubles take the binding. Now we begin work on the transition. It'll be complex because we must simultaneously prepare for the arrival of the Trow and Human technology may be necessary to repel them."

Storng picked up the discussion. "Nadara and I will be the primary contacts for the Silth in creating various teams to work out the details of the new world. The reduction of technologies, the change in the relationship with the rest of the living creatures, the changes in land use. The ways in which our societies will work together."

"Well, this may be easier than you think," Penfield told them. "Working with the Silth to stop the volcanoes has awakened in many a great curiosity about the power of Humans. Each group feels confident that such power flows through their particular approach—religion, science, spiritualism, technology or whatever. But they all felt the power and want to understand it more. Turn it to a less destructive use."

"So, everyone will work together?" Aran said skeptically.

"For about twenty minutes," was Penfield's response. "But enough will do so that we can move forward. What about you, Aran? What's your role?"

Storng answered for him. "He's requested that Nadara replace him on the Council." Nadara's jaw dropped. "They agreed but made him a *provisional member,* meaning he can officially do what he was doing anyway, come and go as he pleases."

Aran carefully avoided looking at Nadara as he spoke. "They've also done the Humans a favor and relieved me of any ambassador duties. I'll work with a team to prepare for the Trow. It's still being formed, but I know it will include Merit, Jules, and General Cogbill. The Council recognizes that I'm better at destruction than I am at building things."

"I think that you made a fine ambassador," Penfield said. "You're welcome at any table where I sit, at any time."

Storng asked, "And what table will that be, Ambassador?"

"I've been asked to end my seconding to the Silth and utilize my understanding of Silth ways to help the Humans in negotiations. So Nadara and I are free of our reciprocal hostage bonds." He leaned back in his chair. "I'll be on the U.N. committee to manage the various committees interacting with the Silth in creating *Earth 4.0.*"

"I'm familiar with Human numbering systems, but how did you get to 4.0?" Storng asked.

"Earth 1.0 is before the Trow. 2.0 is with Trow but no Humans or Silth. 3.0 is after the Humans and Silth arrive, the era we are now finishing. Thus 4.0 is the era we are creating, one of Humans and Silth, without the Trow."

"Maybe not *without* the Trow." The others looked puzzled, and Aran explained. "The Sohi helped stop the volcanoes, despite it being a serious breach of their commitment to avoid magic." He paused, then, "And they tell me that there are more Trow communities still on Earth. At least two under the Earth's waters and maybe one more on land. I intend to seek them out and ask for their help in preparing for the Trow forces."

Storng fixed him with his black eye. "The first that I've heard of this."

"Why would you assume that someone has taught you everything they know?"

2

ARAN (SILTH)

"That went better than I expected," Aran admitted.

A grim-faced Joss sat across from him, clutching Tiny's hand. She held the face for a fraction of a second more before bursting out laughing, and Tiny visibly relaxed. Aran caught Merit's eye roll and wondered for a moment how such a gesture had developed independently in both Silth and Humans. Shadow and Macho stood by the low window intently watching a coati wandering through the yard of the Brazilian Refuge.

It had been a rollicking morning. The only goal for this first meeting of the two hundred-member U.N./WSC Committee on Species Relations was to get to know one another, while the afternoon was reserved for working through the agenda of issues to be covered, priorities, and timelines. Similar meetings were going on all around the world to address different aspects of the new world order. The committees had the lead, but each was set up to allow anyone with access to a smart phone to participate in the deliberations. The meetings were being streamed and the comments and feedback analyzed and processed. This was also the first meeting where Silth interpreters would translate the Human statements into Silth, so that all Silth, not just those with the gift of language, could understand what was being said.

The committee met in a large tent erected in the Refuge compound and was currently the most popular entertainment on the planet. Consequently, millions of Humans and Silth witnessed the committee's shocked reaction when Merit and Aran led four tall, red-robed Sohi into the tent. Their shaved heads, androgynous features, and loose robes made it difficult to distinguish males from females, but there was little mistaking their alien nature. When the shouting stopped and all committee members coaxed back to their seats, the initial acting chair signaled for Aran to address the group.

On the podium, he spread his wings wide and slowly lowered them as the murmuring died down. Many Silth had stopped projecting glamours as they experimented with appearing as they really looked. To Humans they were so wonderfully exotic and interesting that they seemed magical and beautiful in different ways. But Aran still projected his glamour, feeling self-conscious about his bug-eyed equipment. Recently, a Human told him he sounded like Tony Robins "and he's made a lot of money and helped a lot of people despite his voice." After Aran watched a video clip of Robins, he decided the Human was simply being kind, that Robins' voice was far less challenging than his own.

"These are the Sohi I've talked about. They aren't allied with the Trow who set off the volcanoes, and they were of critical assistance in shutting them down. I don't think we could've done it without them. The fact that the Earth didn't reject our three-way effort to manipulate its system caused me to form a new theory. I began to think about the fact that neither Silth nor Humans are completely of this Earth. We were both created by the Trow from the Earth's own creatures. I have this kind of complex theory about how it all works, and like Operation Fairy Ring itself, the theory does not deny the basic validity of Human or Silth religion, belief, or science. Remember that the Trow have occupied the Earth far longer than Humans or Silth.

It wasn't Earth that drove them out, but they were expelled by the poisonous consequences of their own creation—Humans. In the end, I've concluded that the Earth must be as open to the acts of the Trow as it is to our acts, so long as they're in alignment with its principles.

"One of the principles of the Earth appears to be it welcomes new versions of creatures. In its own fashion, Earth loves all creatures and gives them a chance, with no assurance of success. Some survive and continue to adapt and others pass away. Earth favors the resilient. The Sohi have been seeking to understand the balance with the Earth for thousands of years. The four you have joining you today represent more than ten thousand years of learning among them. They are excited about your undertaking. They've come today as a resource for you, but I hope you will include them in your committee. In the end, as we figure out how to make room on this small orb for all the creatures that would like to be here, and how we help one another thrive, I believe that we must have room for the Trow as well. Just not the way that Xafar would have it happen."

The Sohi had sat unmoving through Aran's speech. As Aran turned away from the mike and the still-stunned audience, a solitary clap came from the back of the room and quickly rallied into full applause. The Sohi gave the audience slight bows, accepting this as their welcome.

In the room with Joss, Tiny, Merit and her interpreter, Aran relaxed. "I think that I'll take a week off." He and Merit had transported the Sohi here and stayed to make sure they were accepted, but he had no intention of being stuck in another committee.

"Oh, come on," Joss said. "This afternoon we'll try to decide what to tackle first, feeding the world through the next couple of years as the seasons are restored, assessing the impacts of the radiation zones, cleaning the plastics out of the oceans or the chemicals out of the lands, restoring migration routes, integrating predators ...." She took a big breath. "The list goes on for several pages."

"And yet you seem excited and happy." Aran grinned at Tiny as he said this, and Tiny blushed.

Joss hugged him Tiny. "I couldn't be happier! I like building things much more than fighting. We have a lot to build."

Lunch was brought in for them, and they talked on through the break. When it was time for the meeting to start again, Joss stood next to Aran, who was standing on the edge of the table. She leaned down and held him close to her face in a gentle hug. "It seems so long ago when you first showed up in my clinic." She waved to him as she took Tiny's hand, calling "come on, puppies" as they left.

"Take care, brother," Tiny said as he nodded to Aran.

Merit told Aran, "I have news for you. It came while you were torturing that poor crowd in there."

"Mind if we went somewhere else to talk? I'd like to go to the old colony."

"All right. Meet you in the main building."

As Aran reappeared in the central square of the old colony, he was overwhelmed with memories. He could still see the outline of the place, now in ruins where he and Shra had played and made love. In his mind he could see the Newfies filling the streets and bringing it back to life. He reached up and felt the apparatus over his eyes. He could see Casius as well. He thought about him more now than he did when he was alive. He doubted he could forgive him but would settle for simply forgetting him, getting his multiple betrayals out of his head. What he'd said to the Human interviewer Oprah was true. He understood why Casius did what he did, but it didn't really explain why he had never cared more for Aran, why he was willing to harm him so. Aran shook his head to clear away the thoughts.

He flew down toward the main building, reminding himself he had chosen this place in part to awake and exorcise the ghosts. He had learned this concept—*exorcism*—recently. He thought it was pretty useful, even if he didn't understand all of the religious elements. To be able to move on, he needed the ghosts out of his head. He'd been thinking a lot about Nadara and why, yet again, he seemed to have destroyed a potential relationship. He decided it was ghost problems. Mostly.

He landed on the porch entry to the big central room, thirty feet from the forest floor. Once inside, he knew instantly the monkeys had again taken the buildings as their own. The room was filled with the smell of monkeys and filled with the debris of what had been coherent contents. Merit wasn't here yet. He stood at the window above the colony that was rapidly returning to ruins. He dropped his glamour and thought about the emptiness of the place.

Upon her arrival not long after, Merit said, "Sorry, I got held up making some arrangements. You'd think that as I get more really good Silth and Humans managing different parts of the process it would get easier, but it just means that only the harder problems make it to me. I miss having my hardest problem be whether I can trust a warrior to not fall asleep on guard duty."

"I doubt that was ever actually one of your problems." He watched her carefully as she took in the bug-eyed spheres of his apparatus and came closer than he would have normally. He looked into her eyes but realized that she would only see the reflection of her own face in his. She didn't step back.

"I have other news. The clutches in the parrot colonies around all of the refuges are full of Silth babies."

Aran's mouth fell open. "How? Who? Faelen?"

"No one knows. But that isn't the biggest news. There are at least three confirmed Silth pregnancies. No one knows whether the fetuses will be viable, but in all the days of Silth there's never been a pregnancy."

"Earth has done it again."

"What?"

"The Trow complain that they didn't make Humans with the capacity to have children. This trait developed spontaneously, a gift of Earth magic. That's amazing. And troubling."

"Why troubling?"

"It will alarm the Humans. One of the reasons they trust us is we have no stake in the future other than the well-being of other creatures. If we have power and a stake, they'll be worried that our intentions will change."

"Then don't tell them."

"That didn't work too well the last time, and I promised we'd follow a different path. We'll need to seek the Council's input on this, but I want to think about how to share this with them."

"Well, you better work fast, because pregnant Silth are kind of obvious, and the news is already moving like a wildfire through the colonies."

Aran stepped even closer and took Merit's good hand in his. "Merit—"

"Aran, before you say anything, please let me say something to you." She left her hand in his. "I want to remind you that you are talking to someone who once cared for you deeply. And … whom you hurt terribly." She pulled her hand from his and backed away a few steps. "I never believed that we would be anything like friends again, much less anything more than that. I was really pissed off."

He made no response and tried to breathe normally.

"When I realized you and Nadara had become a pair, I'll confess that I felt some envy. To my surprise. But then we were both busy saving the world and all that stuff so there wasn't much time to think about it. When I heard that you and Nadara had parted, I wondered if there might be a moment like this. A moment in which you acknowledged that you have feelings for me." She paused as though searching for words. "But how do I tell if these feelings are something to rely on? Am I just a rebound? You've never liked to be alone. Or worse, am I someone to settle for, because," she held up her wooden hand, "I too am damaged?"

"No, that's not …."

She stopped him with a finger to her lips. "I might be persuaded that none of these concerns have weight. But in the end, there's this. How can I tell that you're any different than the Aran I've always known? *Heartless* is his name. Not because he has no love. I have seen repeatedly that he has love and honor. But because when it is time to do more than simply spend time together, time to exchange a piece of heart to share the next steps, he shows up empty-handed. He can't do it. He can't commit to tomorrow because he doesn't know himself— who is it that is committing? He doesn't know what he'll be doing tomorrow or what he wants to be doing."

She said softly, "He doesn't know which way the wind will blow, and he knows that he will likely follow the wind. So, I offer you this, and only this. I'll give you until we've defeated the Trow. I know you are going searching. Searching for the Trow. Searching for a plan to deal with Xafar. An offense. In that period, I'll be working on building a defense against the coming invasion. We'll be too busy for a normal life. In this time, search also for yourself. If, at the end of this time, you still have feelings for me and I've not yet come to my senses, then we'll talk." For the first time since they had seen each other again in the clearing in Costa Rica, she held him. Head on his chest, arms tight around him. And then she flickered and disappeared.

Aran's first thought was that arguments in the future were going to be a lot harder if one party could give their side and just disappear without hearing the other. He thought of all the answers he had for Merit's questions. Good answers. But were they good enough? Should he chase her and make his case? He didn't know where she'd gone. And when he stopped to consider it, could he answer her last challenge? Did he know for sure he had a heart to give?

The heart to give wasn't really a standard for most Silth relationships. The only questions were whether you were enjoyable and sought enjoyment. Or at least that was what Aran thought until he met Shra. He'd wanted to give his heart to her. Or so he told himself. In the end that desire was untested. Was Merit right, that he really couldn't do it? Apparently, he'd have some time to find out. He shifted his focus. He would have some time. Merit, the impossible fortress who had once sheltered him but seemed forever lost to him, said there was a chance. In the last year he wouldn't have taken a bet that this was even remotely possible. That was, in and of itself, a cause for celebration.

He knew there was a celebration at Joss's compound and tonight he was in the mood for company.

3

ARAN (SILTH)

"What will you do now?" Faelen asked Aran, sitting in the sun that now shown down on the mountain retreat of the Sohi. When Aran appeared with the egg he had taken from the old colony, there was little discussion and no objection as he placed it in the Sohi's hidden valley. He activated it and created the protective spells that would render the place unfindable. Now that the Trow were known to be in the world, there would, no doubt, be efforts to locate them.

He also used the spells that the Silth performed to create the refuges, producing an area of sunshine and normal weather patterns until the volcanic ash settled from the atmosphere. It was a small thank you for the Sohi participation in turning the volcanoes. Although the world's weather patterns should begin returning in a year or so, the relief from the still clouded skies would allow the Sohi to grow their own food and enjoy the light once again. The Silth had created as many similar openings as they could for Humans to help the Human and wildlife populations around the world survive the long winter ahead.

Faelen, Lornix, and Aran sat on the ground in the sunshine when Faelen asked his question.

"I'll be searching for more Trow around the world, with the Steam Tiki Crew's help. Krackle, a Brazilian shaman, and Temkaa, an African leader, will each join me for part of the search. Based on what you and the Sohi have told me, and the legends that I've gathered from the various Silth nations, there are perhaps three or four more colonies of Trow that could be on the Earth. I've a general idea of where each is, and I'll look for them in the same way I searched for this place."

"You should be careful, fledgling. You were lucky here. Before you arrived, I was able to convince the Sohi that you wouldn't be a threat to them. That you could be trusted. You will not have anyone to vouch for you with the others."

Faelen looked at Lornix beside him, a silent answer to Aran's unasked question. Faelen would not accompany him. He was cleaner than Aran had ever seen him, and the gauntness was gone from his face. He was wearing a Sohi robe and had cut his hair short—not yet shaved like the Sohi, but close. Aran almost didn't recognize him when he arrived at the tunnel entrance. He recognized Lornix, who had helped Faelen through his alcohol withdrawal once Aran restored his body.

Faelen wordlessly poured out the bottle Aran had brought and watched the liquid trickle down the hill.

"No more drinking?"

"I will try. It is not the first time I have tried. A Human saying … *I know I can quit—I have done it many times.*"

"Another Human saying that has a parallel in Silth sayings is *Fall down six times, stand up six times.*"

"Do you think Humans have more aphorisms than the rest of us?" Faelen mused. "Why do we end up quoting them?"

"Storng says it's because of writing. Humans have a written language, and the Silth don't."

"Trow have a written language, but it is not used to record anything other than facts. There are historical facts, technological facts, medical facts. But no literature nor *sayings.*"

Aran was happy for Faelen. His friend wore his own happiness, his obvious fondness for Lornix, and his acceptance among the Sohi like an ill-fitting piece of clothing. He grumped and blustered but made no sign that he wanted to give it up.

They talked about the new Silth babies in the parrot nests.

Faelen denied that he had anything to do with their appearance. He doubted the Sohi were responsible. Other than their involvement in the adjustment of the volcanoes, an action they justified as correcting an imbalance created by the Trow, he had seen them perform almost no magic. He had no explanation for the babies. Aran didn't tell him about the pregnant Silth. It seemed too soon, almost as though discussing it would jinx the outcome.

"I am busy trying to make babies here," Faelen said. Lornix did not smile, but nudged him gently, the playful motion the closest thing to humor Aran had seen from a Sohi.

Aran changed the subject before Faelen could share any baby-making details. "Merit is preparing the Silth and the Humans for the Trow arrival. But when I imagine them fully prepared, I still can't imagine them besting a Trow army."

"Nor can I," Faelen agreed, at once looking dispirited. "I have thought a lot about it. If planning does not go deeper than confrontation, you will lose. The Trow will send spies back into the world first, so they will know what is going on. Then they will not come in any way that you might expect. The only advantage you will have is you know the only two portals that still work between their world and this one."

Aran was quiet for a moment. "But we don't know the only two portals."

"Patience, you will when I tell you. It is a miracle that I taught you anything as impatient as you are."

"Could we simply blow up the portals? Then the Trow couldn't come."

"There used to be more portals and Xafar destroyed all but two. It was how he learned the Earth can be a harsh host when angered. Half the Trow living in this world, and there were many, died when the portals were destroyed. And half the ones who did not die went mad then and there. It is why Xafar has so many of his advisers working on understanding what events will create *psychic disruption* in this world. Apparently, Earth is connected with the Land in a way none of us understand."

The three of them went in the cottage, and Faelen led them to a rough oak table where he rummaged through some papers. He found what he was looking for and bent over it for a moment with pen in hand. He held up a hand-drawn map and pointed to one of the two stars on it. "This is *Angkor Wat*. It is in what the Humans call *South East Asia*." He pointed to the other. "This is what the Humans call *Newgrange* in Ireland. These are where the portals are." He lowered the paper. "I would prefer not to die or go mad so please do not disturb them."

Aran chuckled and stood, preparing to go. Lornix nudged Faelen again, and he looked at her frowning. She widened her eyes, which would have lifted her eyebrows if she had them, and Faelen said, "Oh, yes. The Sohi want to give you a gift, but they are afraid that you will take it wrong."

"They don't owe me any gifts. The whole world is in their debt."

"If they owed it to you, it would not be a gift." Faelen led Aran to the table, on which lay a large, organic-looking lump. "Besides, it is really for their benefit. You see, they think that your bug-eyed glasses make you look like the uglier end of a tapir. And they worry that the technology will make you crazy. They believe the world does not need another crazy Silth."

Lornix shook her head slightly at Aran.

"Ok, maybe I augmented their reasons. They do not exactly explain a lot of what they do." Faelen held up the lump. "But they made this for you."

"Wow. Thanks." Aran looked dubiously at the lump. "What is it?"

"She. She is called a Quitquot. She is a living creature. When you place her over your head in place of your bug-eyes, she will provide you sight. Like the bug-eyes it will be 360 degrees. Because she is organic, you will not be exposed to technology. She was grown and trained by the Sohi for this function. They tell me that she is symbiotic and enjoys the melding, so you are not enslaving some creature."

"Do they just grow them to replace sight?"

"No. Because of the Trow's long lifespan, accidents happen. The Quitquots can be utilized for many different replacement parts, but each is special to a part."

"Can they replace a Silth hand?"

Faelen looked the question at Lornix, and she nodded once. "Yes, but they take some time to produce. Are you planning on losing a hand in your travels?"

"No, I was thinking of a friend."

Faelen thought for a moment. "Ah yes, the warrioress Merit. Great conversationalist, I recall."

"She grows on you."

"So does the Quitquot."

"Could you discuss price and see if I could do this for her?"

Again, Faelen looked at Lornix, who gave a single nod. Faelen turned back to Aran. "I will work on it, oh tiny master. Now you need to be ready when you put this on your head, as it will hurt a little." Faelen looked up at the ceiling, "Actually, *hurt a little* may be understating how it will feel as it stabs its tentacles into your eye sockets and melds with the optic nerves."

"Great. And does it do that every time you remove it?"

"Taking it off would be akin to ripping out your own eyes. It would hurt much worse. There is no taking it off."

"What will I look like?"

"What do you care? It cannot be worse than looking like an over-sized bug."

Lornix spoke up with, "It will form a band around your head and over your eyes. It will try to contour closely to your head. It will be masked by your glamour just as your current apparatus is."

Aran considered the creature for a moment and said to Lornix, "This is a truly magnificent gift. Thank you."

He lay on the table, taking off his glasses to reveal his damaged eyes. As Faelen placed the creature on his face, he asked, "Your brother did this?"

"We weren't close."

A few seconds later Aran was screaming and writhing. After an hour or so, the pain had eased to the point that he could sit up. Barely.

"I think you look better than when we first met."

Aran was shrouded in darkness. "I don't see anything."

"You need to practice opening your eyes," Lornix said. "Just imagine that you have eyelids and are directing them open."

Aran did as instructed. "Everything is purple."

"That is one of the spectra that the Trow see in. The Quitquot sees in Trow spectra. If you blink, it will change the spectra. There are twenty different ways of seeing the world."

Aran realized that with no eyes to lubricate, the only reason to blink would be to change the spectra. He had no eye lids, so *blinking* was simply tightening the muscles around his eyes. He blinked several times and moved from infrared to a view of magnetic forces to a view of evapotranspiration. "Wow." In a couple of blinks, he came to a conventional spectrum for a Silth. As with his glasses, he could see all around him.

"Oh, yuck. X-ray vision," he said, looking at Faelen.

"What?"

Aran laughed.

Later as they stood at the mouth of the tunnel, he flew to Lornix and bowed. "Thank you for this extraordinary gift!" To Faelen, "Guard your happiness well, and thank you for all you've done. Farewell, Crocodile Bait."

Chapter 14

1

THEST (TROW)

Thest was in his *war room* when the summons from the palace came. Most of his home had become a war room. Except for the cook and a valet, he had gotten rid of all the servants. He never received visitors anymore. He went nowhere. He slept little and worked until late at night on the plans for retaking the Earth.

As the messenger was escorted into the room, Thest glanced up from his work and went right back to it. "Go away. I am tired of the invitations to galas and dinners. I never go, and the royal court knows that."

"This summons comes from Xafar, not the court," the messenger said. "Sorry to disturb you, my Lord. But the honorable Xafar, Master of the Land, requests your presence immediately."

"Why?"

"He did not share his reasons, sir. But it may have something to do with the arrival of a scout party from the Faraway. His request followed their report."

Thest hated to leave his work even for a moment. He took his meals among the many stacks of materials spread through the rooms of the house. But if he did not respond to Xafar, he would probably not lead the forces into battle. He would probably not stay alive. When he stood up and saw the messenger's eyebrows arch up, he looked down at the stained tunic he wore to work and to sleep. He called for his valet and instructed him to prepare his bath and clothes, and he sent the messenger to wait in the courtyard.

The acts of bathing and dressing helped him focus and prepare for his meeting. Any meeting with Xafar had always been dangerous, but even more so now. The King's mind continued to deteriorate from years immersed in Human technology. These days he was barely coherent, but still with a quick trigger to rage. What used to be theater had now become deadly reality. No Human servants were left in the palace, and the court feared every event because some Trow courtier usually died.

Thest retrieved the messenger from the courtyard, and they hurried to the palace. Xafar had become enraged at the ugliness of the Land's native vegetation and destroyed all within sight of the palace. Soon they were walking through a blackened landscape where a few Earth crops had been planted and struggled to survive. The irony was that even Earth vegetation became ugly in the foreign soil and light spectrum of the Land. It took a large amount of labor to make it resemble the same crops back on Earth.

Thest carefully composed his thoughts at the doorway into the King's chambers. The room was occupied when he arrived, but Xafar was not there. He recognized two of Xafar's advisors, rarely allowed out of their chamber-prisons and never beyond this room. Two soldiers and a captain Thest recognized as one of the leaders of the patrols in the Faraway were also present. All had gathered around something on the table that Thest could not see.

"General Thest," the captain said, "I am Zenon." He bowed.

"What turmoil have you caused Zenon?"

"I have brought a prisoner from the Faraway."

Thest's first thought was that this seemed unlikely. The Faraway was a portion of the Land where nothing much grew except a type of flower that provided sustenance for no living thing except the gulaps, an irritating pest that sometimes escaped onto Earth as *flower fairies*. Gulaps were poisonous to the Trow, so no Trow inhabited the Faraway, at least not very deep into the immense land. Humans could eat gulaps without ill effect, but since there was no standing water in the Faraway, escaped slaves rarely survived there long. Mostly being sent on patrol into the Faraway was punishment for incompetence.

Thest looked over at the table. He still couldn't see what was on it, but if it was up on the table it was neither Trow nor Human.

"You have captured a marauding gulap?"

Zenon's face colored. The others parted so Thest could see the table surface. "I have captured a Paerrie who is unmarked, so it has never been enslaved."

"Not possible." Thest approached the table.

One of the advisors addressed him. "It is possible, General. Humans and Paerries have entered the Land through the portals before. It was one of the reasons the portals were reduced to two. But those two portals are heavily guarded. These days nothing could come through we do not know about. We do not think this came through the portal."

"And that is possible?"

"There are stories from a very long time ago of a Paerrie spell that could do this. That spell was made illegal and every Paerrie who knew it exterminated."

Storng! This is Storng's work. "Meaning this is a spy?" Thest looked closer at the Paerrie, bound, gagged and laid upon the table. "Why is it gagged? Is it not our desire that it talk?"

The captain looked over his shoulder toward the King's chamber before whispering, "What it was saying sent Xafar into a rage. We decided you would want to hear it, and to allow it to survive that long we had to gag it."

Thest scanned the room, which had grown more gruesome since he had returned from his campaign on Earth. Spattered blood was dried on the walls and floors. Although bodies were eventually removed, the rate of their creation was so high they frequently lay for several days. Currently a pile of once well-dressed Trow bodies occupied one corner. Bowls of half-rotten food covered the table, shoved aside so there was room for a meal. Heads had been mounted on the wall, still alive despite the absence of their bodies, kept from dying by yet another of Thest's biological monstrosities. Their lips were sown shut but their moans were a constant background. The smell was the worst part. Most Trow burned their clothes when they left the chamber, if they were lucky enough to leave the chamber.

"Ungag and untie it. Let us hear what it has to say." He could not tell whether the Paerrie was male or female, young or old. One of the soldiers pulled a knife from the sleeve of his tunic and stepped forward to cut the binding. The others stepped back in horror. The penalty for bringing a weapon into the room was instant death.

Thest grabbed the knife, a small but sharp dagger. "How did you even get in here with this?" he asked, thinking about the guard's search and the portal's ability to read minds.

"I-I did not even consider it a weapon," replied the soldier, who would usually be heavily armed. "In the confusion of getting the Paerrie in here quickly, the guards missed it."

"Go now." Thest tilted his head toward the door. "You will be dealt with later. Move fast if you value your life."

As the soldier ran from the room, the heads moaned enthusiastically. The other soldier stepped over to the table and began untying the gag and the ropes. It took a few moments, but at last the Paerrie stood. He wore a robe blackened on one side, and Thest noticed the hather on that side of the Paerrie's body was charred as well.

"Before you die, spy, you will tell us everything you know."

The Paerrie looked back at Thest, obviously unafraid. "I am no spy, Thest. At least not for the Silth. You know me. I am Casius, high priest of New Faerie."

Thest leaned down to look closer at the Paerrie. He really could not tell one from the next, but he recognized the voice, and nothing in his appearance seemed to deny the truth of the assertion. "I remember you. You were one of those who gave Fod information on the Paerrie Aran. That service buys you a few more breaths to explain why you are here."

"I'm honored to be here, but it is not by choice. I was setting off a bomb to destroy Aran, Storng, Merit, and the rest of the World Silth Council when I was transported here together with those assisting me. For some reason, I was slightly further away from the bomb when it went off upon our arrival here. Only I survived." His voice faltered slightly. "Could I have some water? It's been several days since I had any."

Thest shoved some food aside on the table and found a half-consumed goblet of Earth wine. He poured some into a plate and set it next to Casius, who got down on his hands and knees and greedily sucked up the stale wine. He stood again and wiped his face with the sleeve of his robe.

"I have been a loyal and faithful servant of the Faerie. I hope to claim the reward promised to us long ago for such service."

Thest grimaced. Somewhere back in Earth's past, some Trow had thought it great fun to contrive a religion. Rumor was it started as a bet—no one individual could found an entire religion. He or she had filled the religion with preposterous gods and demons and created ridiculous rituals. There could be no doubt substantial amounts of alcohol were involved. Over the several thousand years since, most of the absurdities had been dropped from the quite successful theology, and what was left was the belief that service to the Trow would result in the delivery of great magical powers on Earth. On occasion Thest used these believers to track the progress of errant shamans. He was about to say something dismissive when he reconsidered. Perhaps there was a use for this Paerrie.

"All due rewards will be yours, Paerrie priest, should you prove yourself worthy. In a moment, you will go with these distinguished scholars," Thest gestured to the advisors, "and they will help you recover from your ordeal. They will get you food, clothing, and a warm place to sleep. You will tell them in detail everything about the current state of matters on Earth. Every detail. They will reward you with teachings about the magic of … Faeries. This will not benefit you here, for no magic occurs in the Land. But when you return to Earth as our emissary, you will be more powerful than any Paerrie alive."

Casius nodded somberly as though his words had been an incantation eliciting the right response.

"But first, one question." He glanced at the doorway to Xafar's inner chamber and lowered his voice. He believed Xafar was likely listening to everything occurring in the throne chamber, but the show might elicit more cooperation. "What was it you said that so enraged our noble king?"

"He too asked about the status of the Earth. I told him the Silth have united themselves around the world and banded with the Humans to repel your arrival. They have successfully stopped the volcanoes with the help of Faeries who are still on Earth."

"That cannot be. No one but Faelen remained on Earth, and I … he died."

"Faelen lives. He has joined with the other Faeries who remain there."

Thest struggled to hold his anger. "I see why Xafar was so upset with this news. But it is not your fault. From what you said earlier you were trying to stop this."

"Yes, one moment I was in the Council room about to detonate the bomb and transport away, and the next I was here with the bomb exploding close to me."

"Transport?"

"Yes, the magic Aran learned, that of the bolt, the shield, and transport, is now widely distributed among the Silth."

Thest gritted his teeth. "Very well, enough for now as I am sure you are tired." He told the closest adviser, "Take Casius as our guest to the advisors' chambers. I am confident Xafar will want him to remain in the august position of adviser to the King. Keep him safe or you will likely suffer Xafar's wrath." He walked over to stand by the door. "Away, all of you. I will wait for Xafar's return. Good work, Zenon.

Perhaps it is time for a duty other than patrolling the Faraway."

The advisors signaled for Casius to follow them into the doorway to the advisors' chambers, and the captain and his soldier left through the main entrance. After they had all left, Thest waited patiently by the doorway.

Moments later, Xafar entered and walked directly to the throne, but the severed head occupying the seat prevented him from sitting. He picked it up, used the hem of his robe to dab at the blood in the seat, and sat down. Holding the head up, he addressed it as the little blood left in it trickled down his arm.

"Yeafonz, you were a wise one. Perhaps you can advise me. What am I to do with a general who fails so dismally at his duties? Not one thing done successfully."

Thest said nothing. As he searched within himself for how to respond, he realized he really did not care. Life, death, it did not matter to him. He simply did not want to be one of the ones kept half-alive, suffering for eternity, and he hoped to avoid his punishment extending to his son, whom Xafar had threatened previously.

"True, I have had generals fail before, and I have found fitting punishments for them. But never have I had such a spectacular failure."

Xafar paused as though listening to the head. Its eyes were open, and it bore the look of horror Yeafonz must have felt as he understood his last moment. Yeafonz had never been an ally of Thest's, although he had been one of Demist's confidants. Not that any of that really mattered right now.

"Your point is well taken, Yeafonz. He did warn me the Paerries should be eradicated before we left. He was right. But there is the matter of not killing Faelen, which he promised had been successful."

He paused to *hear*. "True, again. Faelen is of a wise and wily lineage. It is not really a surprise he is difficult to get rid of. I suppose I should be complimented and unsurprised he outsmarted Thest. As always, Yeafonz, your counsel is excellent. I have decided what to do." He tossed the head into the pile of bodies.

"Thest, you are, sadly, the best of my generals. And I need you. I have decided I will personally lead the next attack on the Earth. We will make peace with the Paerries. It is only Human technology that must be eliminated. The Paerries are a distraction."

He did not look at Thest but instead was staring at the heads. He walked over to them. "You know these things are usually so noisy, but they are quiet right now. What is wrong with them?"

He reached up and slapped the face of a girl, who stared back at him with hatred. He whirled in a complete circle. "And I cannot have my subjects think I tolerate incompetence. So, I need to punish you but also incentivize you to win back the Earth." A few quick steps brought him in front of Thest, who saw that the King's macabre necklace of fingers had grown heavy with trophies. "And then, according to the door's read of your mind, there is this problem of you not caring if you live or die. What kind of attitude is that for a general? You have three children, correct?"

"No," Thest said, suppressing his emotions. "Leave them out of this."

"Your oldest, Hepler, I think, has been our guest before. A charming young soldier himself now as I understand it. I think you know I will kill him if you do not succeed on Earth. But your daughter, proud like her mother. Looks like her too. I think it is time she takes up residence here at the castle as a pleasure for the guard. It is a hard life, and most take their own lives if given a chance. And … I think the head of your youngest son will look good on this wall." He gestured to the row of heads, still staring quietly. "Perhaps you will be more incentivized to free them from their fate than you have been to protect them from death."

Thest dropped to his knees. "No, my King. They are all I have of Demist." He shuffled forward to Xafar's feet. "Please, your mercy is all the incentive I need."

"I am being merciful. I have left you one child." Xafar arched back, laughing. "*Children are innocent and love justice, while most of us are wicked and naturally prefer mercy.* A Human quotation, but a good one."

Thest knelt, his arms crossed over his chest, sobbing with head bowed. Xafar reached down to give him his hand.

"Get up, you fool. This is no posture for a general."

Thest pulled the dagger the soldier had surrendered from the sleeve of his tunic and drove it up through Xafar's throat and into his brain. He twisted it quickly to do maximum damage. Xafar staggered back clutching his throat, unable to call out for help. Thest got to his feet and walked over to Xafar, whose eyes were open wide.

Thest took hold of Xafar's dreadlocks and pulled his head down to one side. He leaned in close. "I do not know if I will survive the day. I do not care. But there will be no peace for the Paerries, and you shall not harm my children. Thest drove the dagger into Xafar's chest, pulled it out, and shoved it in again. "And I know you will certainly not survive the day, you mad abomination."

He let go and Xafar dropped heavily to the floor. Thest looked up as the row of heads resumed their efforts to communicate. He bent to check for a pulse, looked at the body a moment, and drove the knife through Xafar's eye, once again deep into his brain. Given the news that Faelen still lived, Thest was taking no chances. He withdrew the dagger and wiped it off on the king's robes before approaching the row of heads. He used the knife to carefully cut the sutures on the lips of the young Trow female Xafar had struck.

"Kill us. Kill us now, please," she whispered hoarsely. "Be merciful."

That was what he expected her to say. When he put the knife to her throat, she smiled. He quickly cut her throat and those of the other heads. Blood flowed down the wall in a sheet.

Thest looked around the room unbelievingly. He sat on the bloody throne, elbows on knees and deep in thought. Much later, an adviser tentatively looked around the corner and entered the room. He bent down over Xafar's body and assessed its condition. Seemingly assured Xafar was dead, the adviser knelt before Thest.

"What now, my king?" he asked. "What comes next?"

Thest stared at him before shaking his head and saying almost to himself, "That is the question. What comes next?"

Continue the adventure in
Book 3 of The World of Paerries Series:
Stepping into the Faerie Ring

Thanks for reading!
If you liked the book and have a moment to spare,
I'd really appreciate a short review as this helps
new readers find my books. Reviews can be left on Amazon.
You can check out the timing for the next book on the
Facebook site @worldofpaerries and subscribe for information
on the series as well as bonus material and news on the
author at www.worldofpaerries.com.

AKNOWLEDGEMENTS

THANKS TO:

Phyllis Bleiweis and Martha Slone for their copyediting. Sparkfire Branding for its book design. My beta readers for their encouragement and support, as well as their willingness to handle a story before it is polished. The family of my friend and mentor Irvin Penfield for allowing me to cast him in his role here.

A PORTION OF THE PROFIT FROM ANY SALES OF THIS BOOK IS DONATED TO A SANCTUARY FOR PARROTS WHO HAVE BEEN CAST OFF OR OUTLIVED THEIR OWNERS.